# Someone To Run With

# Someone To Run With

# DAVID GROSSMAN

Translated by Vered Almog and Maya Gurantz

BLOOMSBURY

First published in Israel as
*Meeshehu Larutz Ito* in 2000
First published in Great Britain 2003

This paperback edition published 2004

Copyright © 2000 by David Grossman
Translation copyright © 2003 by Vered Almog and Maya Gurantz

The moral rights of the author and translators have been asserted

Bloomsbury Publishing Plc, 38 Soho Square, London W1D 3HB

A CIP catalogue record for this book is
available from the British Library

ISBN 0 7475 6812 X

10 9 8 7 6 5 4 3 2

All paper used by Bloomsbury Publishing, including that in this
book, is a natural, recyclable product made from wood grown
in sustainable, well-managed forests. The manufacturing processes
conform to the environmental regulations of the country of origin.

Typeset by Palimpsest Book Production Limited,
Polmont, Stirlingshire
Printed in Great Britain by Clays Ltd, St Ives plc

www.bloomsbury.com/davidgrossman

For my children –
Yonatan, Uri, and Ruti

I

A DOG RUNS THROUGH the streets, a boy runs after it. A long rope connects the two and gets tangled in the legs of the passers-by, who grumble and gripe, and the boy mutters 'Sorry, sorry' again and again. In between mumbled sorries he yells 'Stop! Halt!' – and to his shame a 'Whoa-ah!' escapes from his lips. And the dog keeps running.

It flies on, crossing busy streets, running red lights. Its golden coat disappears before the boy's very eyes and reappears between people's legs, like a secret code. 'Slower!' the boy yells, and thinks that if only he knew the dog's name, he could call it and perhaps the dog would stop, or at least slow down. But deep in his heart he knows the dog would keep running, even then. Even if the rope chokes its neck, it'll run until it gets where it's galloping to – and don't I wish we were already there and I was rid of him!

All this is happening at a bad time. Assaf, the boy, continues to run ahead while his thoughts remain tangled far behind him. He doesn't want to think them, he needs to concentrate completely on his race after the dog, but he feels them clanging behind him like tin cans. His parents' trip – that's one can. They're flying over the ocean right now, flying for the first time in their lives – why, why did they have to leave so suddenly, anyway? His older sister – there's another can – and he's simply afraid to think about that one, only trouble can come of it. More cans, little ones and big ones, are clanging, they bang against each other in his mind – and at the end of the string drags one that's been following him for two weeks now, and the tinny noise is driving him out of his mind, insisting, shrilly, that he has to fall madly in love with

Dafi now – because how long are you going to try to put it off? And Assaf knows he has to stop for a minute, has to call these maddening tin followers to order, but the dog has other plans.

Assaf sighs – *Hell* – because only a minute before the door opened and he was called in to see the dog, he was so close to identifying the part of himself in which he could fall in love with her, with Dafi. He could actually, finally, feel that spot in himself; he could feel himself suppressing it, refusing it in the depths of his stomach, where a slow, silent voice kept whispering, She's not for you, Dafi, she spends all her time looking for ways to sting and mock everyone, especially you: why do you need to keep up this stupid show, night after night? Then, when he had almost succeeded in silencing that quarrelsome voice, the door of the room in which he had been sitting every day for the last week, from eight to four, opened. There stood Avraham Danokh, skinny and dark and bitter, the assistant manager of the City Sanitation Department. (He was sort of a friend of his father's and got Assaf the job for August.) Danokh told him to get off his ass and come down to the kennels with him, now, because there was finally work for him to do.

Danokh paced the room and started explaining something about a dog. Assaf didn't listen. It usually took him a few seconds to transfer his attention from one situation to another. Now he was dragging after Danokh along the corridors of City Hall, past people who came to pay their bills or their taxes or snitch on the neighbors who built a porch without a license. Following Danokh down the fire stairs, then into the courtyard in back, he tried to decide whether he had already managed to defeat his own last stand against Dafi, whether he knew yet how he would respond today when Roi told him to quit stalling and start acting like a man. Already, in the distance, Assaf heard one strong, persistent bark and wondered why it sounded like that: usually the dogs all barked together – sometimes their chorus would disturb his daydreams on the third floor – and now only one was barking. Danokh opened a chain-link gate and, turning to tell Assaf something he couldn't make out over the barks, opened the other gate, and, with a flick of his hand, motioned Assaf down the narrow walkway between the cages.

The sound was unmistakable. It was impossible to think that Danokh had brought Assaf down here for just one dog; eight or nine were penned in separate cages. But only one dog was animated; it was as if it had absorbed the others into its own body, leaving them silent and a bit stunned. The dog wasn't very big, but it was full of strength and savagery and, mainly, despair. Assaf had never seen such despair in a dog; it threw itself against the chain links of its cage again and again, making the entire row shake and rattle – then it would produce a horrifying high wail, a strange cross between a whine and a roar. The other dogs stood, or lay down, watching in silence, in amazement, even respect. Assaf had the strange feeling that if he ever saw a human being behave that way, he would feel compelled to rush up and offer his help – or else leave, so the person could be alone with his sorrow.

In the pauses between barks and slams against the cage, Danokh spoke quietly and quickly: one of the inspectors had found the dog the day before yesterday, running through the center of town near Tziyyon Square. At first the vet thought it was in the early stage of rabies, but there were no further signs of disease: apart from the dirt and a few minor injuries, the dog was in perfect health. Assaf noticed that Danokh spoke out of the corner of his mouth, as if he were trying to keep the dog from knowing it was being talked about. 'He's been like that for forty-eight hours now,' Danokh whispered, 'and still not out of batteries. Some animal, huh?' he added, stretching nervously as the dog stared at him. 'It's not just a street dog.' 'But whose is it?' Assaf asked, stepping back as the dog threw itself against the metal mesh, rocking the cage. 'That's it, exactly,' Danokh responded nasally, scratching his head, 'that's what *you* have to find out.' 'Me? How me?' Assaf quavered. 'Where will I find him?' Danokh said that as soon as this *kalb* – he called it a *kalb*, using Arabic – calms down a little, we'll ask him. Assaf looked at him, puzzled, and Danokh said, 'We'll simply do what we always do in such cases: we tie a rope to the dog and let it walk for a while, an hour or two, and it will lead you itself, straight and steady, to its owner.'

Assaf thought he was joking – who had ever heard of such a thing? But Danokh took a folded piece of paper out of his shirt pocket and said it was very important, before he gave the dog back, for the owners to sign the form. Form 76. Put it in your pocket – and don't lose it (because, to tell the truth, you seem a little out to lunch). And most important, you have to explain to the esteemed master of this dog that a fine is included. A settlement of one hundred and fifty shekels or a trial – and he'd better pay up. First of all, he neglected to watch his dog, and maybe that will teach him a lesson to be more careful next time, and second, as a *mi*nimal compensation (Danokh enjoyed sucking, mockingly, on every syllable) for the headache and hassle he had caused City Hall, not to mention the waste of time of such s*uperb* human resources! With that, he tapped Assaf on the shoulder a little too hard and said that after he found the dog's owners, he could return to his room in the water department and continue to scratch his head at the taxpayers' expense until the end of his summer vacation.

'But how am I . . .' Assaf objected. 'Look at it . . . It's like, crazy . . .'

But then it happened: the dog heard Assaf's voice and stood still. It stopped running back and forth in the cage, approached the wire mesh, and looked at Assaf. Its ribs were still heaving, but it moved more slowly. Its eyes were dark and seemed to focus intensely on him. It cocked its head to the side, as if to get a better look at him, and Assaf thought that the dog was about to open its mouth right then and say in a completely human voice, Oh yeah? You're not exactly a model of sanity yourself.

It lay on its stomach, the dog; it lowered its head, and its front legs slipped under the metal grid, begging with a digging motion, and out of its throat a new voice emerged, thin and delicate like the cry of a puppy, or a little boy.

Assaf bent in front of it, from the other side of the cage. He didn't notice what he was doing – even Danokh, a hard man, who had arranged the job for Assaf without much enthusiasm, smiled a thin smile when he saw the way Assaf got down on his knees at the blink of an eye. Assaf looked at the dog and spoke quietly to it. 'Who do you belong to?' he asked. 'What happened to you? Why are you going so crazy?' He spoke slowly, leaving room for answers, not embarrassing the dog by looking into its eyes for too long. He knew – his sister Reli's boyfriend had taught him – the difference between talking at a dog and talking with a dog. The dog was breathing fast, lying down. Now, for the first time, it seemed tired, exhausted, and it looked a lot smaller than before. The kennels finally fell silent, and the other dogs began moving again, as if coming back to life. Assaf put his finger through one of the holes and touched the dog's head. It didn't move. Assaf scratched its head, the matted, dirty fur. The dog began to whine, frightened, persistent, as if it had to unburden itself to someone right away, as if it could no longer keep silent. Its red tongue trembled. Its eyes grew large and expressive.

Assaf didn't argue with Danokh after that. Danokh took advantage of the dog's momentary calm: he entered the cage and tied a long rope to the orange collar hidden in its thick fur.

'Go on, take it,' Danokh ordered. 'Now it'll go with you like a doll.' Danokh jumped back when the dog leaped up and out of the cage, instantly shaking off its fatigue and silent surrender. It looked right and left with fresh nervousness and sniffed the air as if it were listening for a distant voice. 'See? You guys already get along great,' Danokh said, trying to convince Assaf and himself. 'You just watch out for yourself in the city – I promised your dad.' The last words were thick in his throat.

The dog was now focused and tense. Its face sharpened; for a moment it was almost wolflike. 'Listen,' Danokh mumbled with misgiving, 'is it okay to send you out like this?' Assaf didn't answer, only stared in astonishment at the change in the dog once it was free. Danokh tapped his shoulder again. 'You're a strong kid. Look at you. You're taller than me and your father. You can control it, right?' Assaf wanted to ask what he should do if the dog refused to lead him to its owners, how long he should walk after it (the three lunchtime sandwiches were waiting for him in his desk drawer). What if, for instance, the dog had a fight with the owners and had no intention of going back to its home –

Assaf did not ask those questions at the time, or at any other time. He did not return to meet Danokh that day, nor would he return over the next few days. Sometimes it is so easy to determine the exact moment when something – Assaf's life, for instance – starts to change, irreversibly, forever.

The moment Assaf's hand clutched the rope, the dog uprooted itself with an amplified leap and pulled Assaf with it. Danokh raised his hand in fright, managed to take a step or two after his hijacked employee, even started running after him. It was useless. Assaf was already being tugged outside City Hall, forced to stumble down the stairs. He broke into the streets, later smashed into a parked car, a garbage can, the people passing by. He ran . . .


The big hairy tail wags energetically before his eyes, sweeping aside people and cars, and Assaf follows after it, hypnotized. Sometimes the dog stops for a minute, raises its head, sniffing, then turns down a side street, sweeping along its way, running. It looks as if it knows exactly where it's going, in which case this race will end very soon. The dog will find its home and Assaf will turn it over to its owners, and good riddance. But while it runs, Assaf starts to think about what he will do if the dog's owner doesn't agree to pay the fine. Assaf will say, 'Mister, my job doesn't allow me any flexibility in this matter. Either you pay or you go to court!' The man will start to argue, and Assaf is already answering him with convincing responses, running and mumbling in his heart, pursing his lips decisively, and knowing all too well it will never work. Arguing has never been his strong suit. Eventually, it always becomes more convenient for him to give in and not make a fuss. This is exactly why he gives in to Roi, night after night, in the matter of Dafi Kaplan – just to keep from making a fuss. He thinks about it and sees Dafi in front of him, long and lean, and hates himself for his weakness, and notices that a tall man with bushy eyebrows and a white chef's hat is asking him a question.

Assaf appears confused – Dafi's face, very pale, with a permanent mocking gaze and transparent lizard eyelids, is morphing into a different face, fat and grumpy. Assaf quickly focuses his eyes and sees a narrow room in front of him, dug into the wall, a searing oven in its depths. Apparently the dog has decided, for some reason, to make a stop at a small pizzeria, and the pizza man bends over the counter and asks Assaf again, for the second, or perhaps the third, time, about a young lady. 'Where is she?' he asks. 'She disappeared on us – we haven't seen her for a month now.' Assaf glances around: perhaps the pizza man is talking to someone standing behind him – but no, the pizza man is talking to him, inquiring as to whether she is his sister or his girlfriend, and Assaf nods in embarrassment. From his first week of working at City Hall, he's already learned that people who work in the center of town sometimes have their own habits and manners of speaking – and a weird sense of humor, too. Perhaps it was because they worked for odd customers and tourists from faraway countries; they got used to speaking as if they were in a sort of theater – as if there were always an invisible crowd watching the dialogue. He wants to get away and keep racing after the dog, but the dog decides to sit and looks at the pizza man hopefully, wagging its tail. The man gives it a friendly whistle, as if they're old acquaintances, and with one quick flick, like a basketball player – his hand behind his back and around his waist – throws a thick slice of cheese, and the dog catches it in the air and swallows it.

And the slice that follows it. And another one. And more.

The pizza man has pearly white eyebrows that look like two wild bushes, and they make Assaf feel scolded and uneasy. The man says he never saw her so hungry. 'Her?' Assaf asks silently, baffled. It never occurred to him until now that the dog was a bitch. He only thought of it as a dog with a dog's speed and strength and decisiveness of motion. Why, in the midst of all this crazy running, in his anger and confusion, there were moments when Assaf liked to imagine that they were a team, him and his dog, sharing between them a silent, manly oath. It all seems even stranger to him to know he was running like this after a bitch.

The pizza man knits the bushes of his eyebrows and stares at Assaf intently, even suspiciously, and asks, 'So what, then? She decided to send you instead?' And he begins to spin a flying saucer of dough in the air, throwing and catching expertly, and Assaf nods diagonally, on the border between yes and no. He doesn't want to lie, and the pizza man continues by spreading tomato sauce over the dough, although Assaf doesn't see any other customers there but him. Every once in a while, without looking, the man throws a small piece of cheese over his shoulder, and the bitch who was, until a moment ago, a dog, catches it in the air, as if she had anticipated his movement.

Assaf stands, looking at these two in wonder, at their synchronized dance, trying to understand what, exactly, he is doing there, and what, exactly, he is waiting for. Some question he has to ask the pizza man is floating through his head . . . probably something about the young lady who apparently comes here with this dog. But every question that comes to mind seems ridiculous and inextricably tangled with complicated explanations about methods for finding lost dogs, about summer jobs in City Halls. Assaf finally starts to grasp the immense complications of this mission he has been assigned. Because, what – you can't start asking every person in the street if he knows the owner of the dog. Was that even part of his job? How had he allowed Danokh to send him on such an errand without even trying to object? Quickly Assaf's mind runs through everything he should have told Danokh back in the kennels. Like a cunning, seasoned lawyer, and even with a certain arrogance, he unfolds brilliant arguments against this impossible operation, and simultaneously, as always in such situations, his body shrinks a little – he plants his head between his wide shoulders and waits.

Inwardly, he feels all mixed up – feels all the irritations, large and small, that had been bottled up inside him explode like tiny sparks of lava. He feels them transformed – on his chin – into one little burning pimple of anger at Roi, who had succeeded in convincing him to go out tonight, just the four of them, again, for the umpteenth time; who had even taken pains to explain that Assaf would soon realize Dafi was his type exactly, if you consider the inner being and all that. This is what he said, Roi did, giving Assaf a long, concentrated look, a conquering look. Assaf looked at the halo in his eyes, the thin golden halo of mockery that surrounded his pupils, and thought, sadly, that over the years their friendship had become something else. But what would you call it now? Seized by a sudden fear, Assaf had promised he would come, again, tonight, and Roi had patted him on his shoulder again and said, 'That's my man.' Assaf wished he had the guts to turn around and throw that 'inner being' crap back in Roi's face, because all Roi really needs is for Assaf and Dafi to be there as a mirror opposite, to make his and his Maytal's glamour and ease even more apparent as they walk together, kissing every two steps, while Assaf and Dafi drag after them in silent, mutual contempt.

'What's the matter with you?' The pizza man was getting angry. 'Somebody's talking to you!'

Assaf sees that the pizza had been packed up in a white cardboard box, cut into eight slices, and the pizza man says, with special emphasis, as if he is sick of repeating his words, 'Look, you got the usual in here: two mushroom-and-onion, one anchovy, one corn, two plain, and two olive. Ride fast so it will get there hot. Forty shekels.'

'Ride where?' Assaf asks, in a whisper.

'Don't you have a bike?' The pizza man is surprised. 'Your sister, she puts it on her basket. How will you carry it like that? Give me the money first.' He reaches a long, hairy arm out to Assaf. Assaf is dumbfounded. He puts his hand in his pocket, and anger rises out of him, boiling through him: his parents left him enough money before they went, but he had planned his expenses to the last detail. Every day he skipped lunch in the City Hall cafeteria so there would be enough money left to buy another lens for the Canon his parents had promised to bring from America. This unlooked-for expense he was now mixed up in really makes him boil, but he has no choice: the man quite clearly prepared the pizza for him especially, that is, for whoever came here with this dog. If Assaf hadn't been so angry, he probably would have just asked who this dog's girl was; but, probably because of this anger, absorbed by the feeling that someone always determines his actions for him, he pays the man and turns away sharply, in a manner that's supposed to express his indifference toward the money that had been taken from him unjustly. And the dog – she doesn't even wait for the exact emotion to bloom on his face. She starts running again, immediately stretching the rope to its full length, and Assaf sails after her with a silent shout, his face twitching from the effort to balance the large cardboard box in one hand and hang on to the rope with the other. Only a miracle keeps him from getting hurt as he passes through the people on the street. With the box waving high in his outstretched hand, he knows – and has no illusions about it – that right now he looks exactly like a caricature of a waiter. On top of everything, the smell of the pizza is starting to leak out of the box; Assaf has eaten only one sandwich since the morning. Of course, he has the complete and legal right to eat the pizza he is now holding above his head – he paid for every olive and mushroom on it. And yet he feels as if it's not completely his, that, in some way, someone else bought it, and it's for yet another person as well – and he doesn't know either of them.

And so that morning, pizza in hand, Assaf crossed through more alleys and streets and ran more red lights. He had never run like this, never broken so many rules at once – people honked at him from every direction, stumbled into him, cursed and screamed; but after a few moments this ceased to bother him, and step by step his anger at himself washed away. Because, in some unexpected way, he became completely free out there, out of that stuffy, boring office: free from all the small and large troubles that had burdened him in the past few days, wild like a star that had broken free of its orbit, crossing the sky and leaving a trail of sparks behind. After that, he stopped thinking, stopped hearing the roar of the world around him; he was only his feet pounding on the pavement, his heart beating, his rhythmic breath. And even though he wasn't an adventurer by nature – the opposite, if anything – he was filled with a new, mysterious feeling. The pleasure of running toward the unknown. And deep inside him, a thought started bouncing like a good ball, supple and full of air, the happy thought – *I hope it doesn't ever end.*


A month before Assaf and the dog met — thirty-one days before, to be precise – on a curving side road above one of the valleys surrounding Jerusalem, a girl stepped off a bus, a small, delicate girl. Her face could hardly be seen under the mane of her curly black hair. She went down the steps, stumbling under the weight of a huge backpack hanging from her shoulders. The driver asked, hesitantly, if she needed help, and she, recoiling at his voice, shrank a little, bit her lips, and shook her head: no.

Afterward, she waited in the empty station until the bus was far away. She continued to wait, even after it had already disappeared behind the bend in the road. She stood, almost without moving, glanced left, glanced right, looking again and again, a ring of light flashing every time the afternoon sun hit the blue earring in her ear.

Next to the station sat a rusty gasoline drum, pierced with holes; an old cardboard sign was attached to an electric pole: TO SIGI AND MOTI'S WEDDING, with an arrow pointing to the sky. The girl looked both ways one last time and saw that she was alone. There weren't even any cars passing along the narrow road. She turned around slowly, passing the shade of the bus stop, now watching the valley at her feet. She made sure her head didn't move, but her eyes swept back and forth, scanning the view.

At a glance, anyone would have thought she was a girl going

on a little hike. This is exactly what she wanted to look like. But if a car had passed by, the driver might have wondered, for just a second, why a girl was going into this valley by herself; or perhaps another disturbing thought might have occurred to him – why it was that a girl going for a little afternoon outing in a valley so close to the city was carrying such a heavy backpack, as if she were ready to sail away on a long journey. But no driver passed by, and there was no one else in the valley. She went down through the yellow mustard flowers, between rocks warm to the touch, and disappeared into terebinth and great burnet bushes. She walked quickly, on the verge of falling at every moment because of the weight of the bag, which tipped and made her teeter back and forth. Her wild hair waved around her face, her mouth still tight with the same tight, decisive, hard tension she had used in saying no to the bus driver. She was panting hard after a little while, her heart pounding quickly. The bad thoughts were spinning out of control; this was the last time she'd be coming here by herself, she thought. The next time, the next time –

If there was a next time.

Now she had reached the creek bed at the bottom of the valley, glancing at the slopes as if enjoying the view. She followed the flight of a jay, bewitched, scanning, with its help, the whole arc of the horizon. Here, for example, was a part of the path where she was completely exposed – somebody standing up on the road by the station would now be able to see her.

Perhaps he had noticed that she had come down here yesterday, and the day before as well.

At least ten times in the past month.

And could trap her here the next time she came back –

There will be, there will be a next time, she repeated with effort, and tried not to think about what would happen to her between now and then.

When, for the last time, she squatted down, as if to fasten the buckle of her sandals, she didn't move for two whole minutes. She checked every rock, every tree and bush.

And then she was no more, she simply vanished, like magic.

Even if somebody had been following her, he wouldn't have understood what happened: a moment ago, she was sitting there, had finally taken the bag off her shoulders, leaned back on it, inhaled – and now the wind moved through the bushes and the valley was empty.

She ran through the lower basin, the hidden one, trying to get the rolling bag in front of her, moving like a soft rock, smashing oats and thorn bushes. It was stopped only by the trunk of the terebinth tree; the tree moved and dry gallnuts dropped from it, crumbling into fragments of reddish brown.

Out of the side pocket of the bag she took a flashlight and, with a practiced motion, pushed a few dry, uprooted bushes aside, exposing a low opening like the door to a dwarf's house. Two or three steps in a crouch, ears pricked and eyes wide to hear and to see every motion and shadow. She sniffed like an animal. Every cell in her skin wide open so she could read the darkness: Had anyone visited here since yesterday? Will one of the shadows suddenly detach itself and attack her?

The cave unexpectedly widened, became tall and roomy. You could stand, even walk a few steps from wall to wall. A faint light was leaking in from an opening somewhere in the ceiling of the cave, covered by thick bushes.

Quickly she poured the contents of the bag out onto a rag. Cans, a pack of candles, plastic cups, plates, matches, batteries, another pair of pants and another shirt she decided to add at the last minute, a foam water cooler, rolls of toilet paper, crossword puzzle booklets, bars of chocolate, Winston cigarettes ... the bag was growing emptier and emptier. She had bought the cans of food this afternoon. She went all the way to Ramat Eshkol so she wouldn't see anyone she knew. Still, she ran into a woman who used to work with her mother in the jewelry store at the King David Hotel; the woman spoke kindly to her, and when she asked why Tamar was buying so many cans of food, Tamar said, without blushing, that she was going on a trip tomorrow.

Moving quickly, she arranged and organized what she had brought, counted the bottles of mineral water – the most important thing was water. She had over fifty liters there already. That would do. It had to be enough for the whole time, the days and nights. The nights would be the hardest, and she would need a lot of water. She swept the place again, for the last time swept the sand from the stone floor, tried to imagine herself at home here. Once, a million years ago – until about a month ago, at least – this was her most beloved hiding place. Now the thought of what was waiting for her here was twisting her guts.

She laid the thicker mattress by the wall and lay down on it to see whether it was comfortable. Even when she was lying down, she didn't allow herself to relax – her brain buzzed constantly – what would it be like when she brought him here, to her 600-square-foot forest, to the Restaurant at the End of the Universe? What would become of her in this place, with him, alone?

On the wall above her the players of Manchester United shone with happiness after winning the Cup. A little surprise she'd prepared to make him happy, if he noticed at all. She smiled to herself unconsciously, and with the smile the bad thoughts returned, and fear again shrank into a fist, clenched in her stomach.

What if I'm making a terrible mistake? she thought.

She got up and paced from wall to wall, clutching her hands forcibly against her chest. He will lie here, on this mattress, and here, on the folding plastic chair, she will sit. She prepared a thin mattress for herself as well, but she had no illusions: she wouldn't be able to shut her eyes for even a moment during all those days. Three, four, five days like that – that's what the toothless man in Ha'atzmaut Park had warned her. 'Take your eyes off him for one minute and he'll run on you.' She had stared, depressed, into the empty mouth that sniggered at her, into the eyes that ogled her body and especially the twenty-shekel bill she held in front of him. 'Explain,' she demanded, trying to hide the trembling in her voice, 'just what you mean by "run on me." Why should he run?' And he, in his filthy striped gown, cradling himself in a matted fur blanket in spite of the heat, laughed at her innocence.

'You ever hear about that magician, sister? The one who could escape, no matter how they locked him up? That's exactly how it's going to be with him. Put him in a box with a hundred locks, in a bank safe, in his mother's belly, and he has to run. Guaranteed. Can't control it. Even the law can't help.'

She had no clue how she would be able to stand that. Maybe, when she was here with him, strange new powers would awaken in her. She could count only on that now, on such faint hopes. It didn't matter, everything was faint and hopeless anyway; if she started thinking about her chances, she'd collapse in despair. The fear swept over her, shook her in the little cave – don't think, just don't think logically, she was going to have to be a little crazy now, like a soldier on a suicide mission who doesn't think about what might happen to him. She checked the food supplies again, for the tenth time maybe, calculated once more whether the food would do for all the days and nights. Sat on the folding chair in front of the mattress and tried to imagine what it would be like, what he would tell her, how he would hate her more and more from hour to hour, what he would try to do to her. The thought made her jumpy again. She ran to the hole in the back of the cave and checked over the bandages, the iodine, the dressings. She couldn't calm down, moved a big stone aside, exposing a flat wooden board. Under it, in a little hole, dug in the ground, were placed, side by side, a little electric cattle prod and handcuffs she'd bought in a camping equipment store.

I'm completely insane, she thought.

Before she left, she stopped and cast another glance over the place she had been preparing and equipping for a whole month. At one time, perhaps hundreds of years ago, people had lived here. She'd found signs of it. Animals lived here, too. And now it was going to be home to him and her, and an asylum, and a hospital, she thought. And, especially, a jail. Enough. She had to go.

*　　*　　*

And a month later a boy and a dog ran through the streets of Jerusalem, strangers tied to each other by one rope, as if refusing to admit they were really *together*. Still, as if casually, they were starting to learn little things about each other. How ears prick up in moments of excitement – the power of shoes pounding against asphalt – the smell of sweat – all the emotions a tail can express – how much strength there was in the hand holding the rope, and how much yearning in the body pulling it forward . . . They had already escaped the busy thoroughfare, going deeper into narrow, curving alleyways, and the dog still didn't slow down. Assaf imagined that a huge magnet was pulling her, and a strange notion passed through him, that if only he could stop thinking, completely negate his own willpower, he, too, might be sucked toward that place with her. A moment or two later, he was jolted awake, because the dog had stopped in front of a green gate set into a high stone wall, and in a graceful motion, she stood on her hind legs, pushed the metal handle with her paws, and opened it. Assaf looked right and left. The street was empty. The dog breathed and pushed forward. He entered after her and was at once wrapped in a profound silence, the silence of the bottom of the sea.

Big yard.

Covered with snow-white pebbles.

Fruit trees planted in rows.

A round stone house, big and squat.

Assaf walked slowly, cautiously. His steps squeaked against the pebbles. He was surprised by how such a beautiful, wide space could be hidden so close to the center of the city. He passed a round well; a shiny bucket was tied to the well by a rope, a few big clay mugs set on a nearby tree stump, as if waiting for someone to drink from them. Assaf peeped into the well, threw a small stone, and only after a long moment heard the little hiccup of the water. Not far from the well, smothered in thick grapevines, was a shelter, and under it, five rows of benches. Five large stones stood in front of every bench, each chiseled into a kind of pillow on which to rest tired feet.

He stopped and looked at the stone house. A plant with purple flowers crisscrossed the walls, covering them, climbing all the way up the tall tower that rose above the house, and cascading at the feet of a cross at its top.

It's a church, he thought, surprised. The dog apparently belonged to the church. That's it, she's probably a church dog here, he thought, trying to convince himself, and, for a moment, managed to picture the streets of Jerusalem filled with lots of agitated church dogs.

The dog hurried, pulling him to the back of the house without hesitating, as if this really was her home. A little arched window was set into the top of the tower, like an open eye in the heart of the bougainvillea. The dog lifted her head to the sky and produced a few short, strong barks.

At first nothing happened. Then Assaf heard the squeak of a chair from above, from the top of the tower. Someone up there moved – the little window opened – and an excited shout escaped, a woman's voice – or a man's, it was hard to tell, the voice creaked as if it hadn't been used in a long time – one word escaped, perhaps the dog's name. The dog barked and barked, and the voice from above called her again, sharp and amazed, as if not believing its good fortune. Assaf thought that his little journey with the dog was about to come to an end, she would be going back home to the tenant at the top of the tower. It was over so quickly. He waited for someone to peep out from the window and tell him to come up, but instead of a face, a hand emerged, dark and slender – for a moment he thought it was a child's hand – then a little wooden basket appeared, tied to a rope, and the rope descended. The basket swayed at its end, a little airborne bulrush basket, all the way down, until it stopped right in front of his face.

The dog was nearly out of her mind with excitement – the entire time the basket descended, she barked and pawed at the ground, and rushed to the door of the church and back to Assaf. In the basket Assaf found a big, heavy metal key. He hesitated for a moment. A key meant a door. What was waiting for him beyond? (From one viewpoint, he was just the right person to handle this job. He had, behind him, hundreds of hours of training, preparing him for exactly this kind of situation: big metal key, tall tower, mysterious fortress ... also, a magic sword, a bewitched ring, a treasure chest, and a greedy dragon watching over it. And almost always three doors, and you have to choose which one you'll enter – behind two of them lie a variety of deaths and torments.) But here there was only one key and one door, so Assaf followed the dog to the door and opened it.

He stood on the edge of a large, dark hall; he was hoping that the proprietor would come down to him from the tower, but no one came, and no steps were heard. He entered. The door closed slowly behind him. He waited. The outlines of the hall began to paint themselves out of the darkness: a few high cupboards, chests and tables, and books, thousands of books, covering the full width of the walls, on shelves, on top of the cupboards, on the tables, and piled up on the floor. Huge bundles of newspapers were stacked next to them, tied with twine, each labeled with a little slip of paper – 1955, 1957, 1960 ... The dog started pulling again, and he was dragged after her. He spotted children's books on one shelf, and was confused and even alarmed – what were children's books doing here? Since when do priests and monks read children's books?

He swerved around a big square box in the center of the hall – perhaps an ancient sarcophagus. Perhaps an altar. He could imagine hearing the sound of motion from above, soft and quick steps, even the clink of forks and knives. Paintings of men in robes hung on the walls, haloes of light shining above their heads; their eyes, full of chastisements, fixed on Assaf as he passed.

The big space of the hall echoed around him and the dog, doubling their every motion, each breath, each scratch of claws on the floor. She pulled him toward a wooden door at the end of the hall. He tried to pull her back – he had some sharp intuition that this was his last chance to escape, and possibly to be saved from something. The dog had no more patience for his fear; she smelled someone she loved. The smell was about to become a body, a touch, and she yearned for it in all the depths of her doghood – the rope stretched and trembled, she reached the door, stood and scratched at it with her claws and whined. When she stood this way, on her hind legs, she was almost as tall as he was, and under the dirt and matted fur, he noticed again how beautiful and supple she was. His heart contracted – he hadn't had time to get to know her. All his life he'd wanted a dog and begged his parents to let him have one, knowing that there was no chance because of his mother's asthma. Now it was as if he had a dog – but so briefly, and only while running.

What am I doing here? he asked himself, and turned the knob. The door opened. He was standing in a corridor that curved around and probably encircled the entire church. I shouldn't be here, he thought, and started running after the dog as it leaped forward, passing three more closed doors, blowing like the wind between thick, white-painted walls. He reached a tall flight of stone stairs. If anything happens to me, he thought – and in his mind he saw the captain gloomily leaving the cockpit, going to his parents and whispering something in their ears – no one in the world would ever think of looking for me here.

Above him, at the top of the stairs, another door. Small and blue. The dog barked and whined, almost *talked*, and sniffed and scratched under the crack. Behind the door rose noises of joy and delight that sounded to him a bit like a chicken clucking, and someone inside, in a strange, old-fashioned dialect, 'Wait, my darling! The gate shall open soon, my heart's delight, there, there.'

A key turned in the lock, and the moment the door had opened a crack, the dog shot in, storming whoever was inside, leaving Assaf outside, behind the closing door. He felt disappointed – it always ended this way, somehow. In the end, he was always the one left behind a closed door. And just because of that, this time he dared – pushed the door a little and peeped inside. He saw a back bending over and a long braid emerging from a round, black knit cap. For a split second he thought it was a child with a braid, a girl, tiny and skinny, in a gray robe. But then he saw it was a woman, a little old woman, laughing and burying her face in the dog's neck, petting her with slender hands, speaking to her in an unknown language. Because he didn't want to interrupt, Assaf waited, until the woman pushed the dog away, laughing, and cried out, 'Well, my *scandalyarisa*, enough, enough! You must allow me to receive Tamar as well!' and turned back, and the wide smile on her face suddenly froze.

'But who –?' She was taken aback. 'Who are you?' she groaned, and her hands hovered at the collar of her robe, her face twisted in a mixture of disappointment and fear. 'And what are you doing here?'

Assaf thought for a moment. 'I don't know,' he said.

The nun was further taken aback and pressed up against the wall of bookshelves. The dog stood between her and Assaf, looking back and forth at them, licking her mouth in embarrassed misery. Assaf could imagine the dog was disappointed as well, that she hadn't brought him here expecting this meeting.

'Excuse me, uh – I really don't know what I'm doing here,' Assaf repeated, and felt that instead of explaining himself, he was, as usual, only making things more complicated, the way he always did when he had to untangle something with words. He didn't know what to do, to calm the nun down so she wouldn't breathe like that, too quickly, so the wrinkles on her forehead wouldn't quiver so much. 'This is pizza,' he said gently, signaling, with his eyes, to the box in his hand. He hoped at least this would calm her down, because pizza is simple and has only one meaning. But she pressed herself against the books even more, and Assaf felt his body, big and manly and threatening, and every move he made was the wrong one, and the nun looked so pitiful standing by the shelves, like a tiny, terrified bird, puffing up her feathers to threaten a predator.

Now he noticed the table was set. Two plates and two cups, big iron forks. The nun was expecting a visitor. But he

22

didn't know what could explain such tremendous fear, and such disappointment, really that of a broken heart.

'So . . . I'll go,' he said cautiously . . . but there was also that matter of the form and the fine. He had no idea what to do – how do you say such a thing – how do you ask somebody to pay a fine?

'Go? What do you mean?' the woman wailed. 'Where is Tamar? Why hasn't she come?'

'Who?'

'Tamar, Tamar, my Tamar, *her* Tamar!'

With impatience she pointed at the dog three times, who was watching the conversation with wide eyes, her eyes leaping back and forth like a spectator in a Ping-Pong match.

'I don't know her,' Assaf mumbled, carefully not committing to anything. 'I don't know her, honest.'

There was a long silence. Assaf and the nun stared at each other, like two strangers desperately in need of a translator. The dog barked. Both of them blinked as if they had awakened from enchantment. Assaf pondered, slowly, the thought crawling through his mind: Tamar is probably the same young lady the pizza man was talking about, the one with the bicycle . . . maybe she's making deliveries to churches? Well, now everything is clear, he thought, knowing nothing was clear but that it was really no longer his concern.

'Look, I only brought' – he put the white cardboard box on the table and immediately stepped back, so she wouldn't think, God forbid, that he intended to eat here as well – 'the pizza –'

'The pizza, the pizza!' the nun exploded in anger. 'Say no more about the pizza! I ask about Tamar and he speaks of pizzas! Where did you meet? Speak! Now!'

He stood, lowering his head between his shoulders. Her fear of him quickly evaporated as her questions hit him one after the other. It was as if she were pounding him with her tiny hands. 'How can you say that you "don't know her"? Are you not her friend? Or an acquaintance, or a relative of hers? Won't you look me in the eyes?' He lifted his eyes to her, feeling, for some reason, a little bit like a liar under her piercing gaze. 'You mean she didn't send you to me, to make me glad, to put me out of this misery? Wait – a letter! Of course, I am a fool – there must be a letter!' She leaped onto the cardboard box and began to dig through it, lifting the pizza and looking under it, reading the advertisement for the pizza place on the box with strange delight, her little face screwing up as if looking for some clue between the lines.

'Not even a little letter?' she whispered. And nervously fixed her silver hair, which had escaped from under the black knit cap and become disorderly. 'At least some message by heart? Something she asked you to remember? Please try, I beg you, it is very important to me – she told you to come and tell me something, didn't she?' Her eyes hung on his mouth, trying to pull the longed-for words from his lips with only the will of her wish. 'Perhaps she wished to send word that things went according to plan? That the danger has passed? Is this what she told you? Yes?'

Assaf knew: when he stood like that, he was wearing the expression that once made Reli, his sister, say, 'You got lucky with one thing, Assafi – with a face like that, you can only surprise people for the better.'

'Just one moment!' The nun's eyes narrowed. 'Perhaps you are one of them, God forbid, one of the villains! Speak! Are you one of them? You should know, young man, I am not afraid of you!' She practically stamped her little feet at him, and Assaf was stunned. 'What! Now you've swallowed your tongue? Have you hurt her? With these two hands, I will tear you apart if you have touched the child!'

Now the dog broke into a cry, and Assaf, bewildered, knelt beside her, petting her with both his hands; but she continued crying, her body trembling with sobs, looking a bit like a child who is trapped in a fight between his parents and can't take it any longer. Assaf actually lay down beside her, lay right down and hugged her, and petted and stroked her, and spoke into her ear, as if he had entirely forgotten where he was, forgotten the place and the nun; only tenderness for the depressed, frightened dog poured out from him. The nun fell silent, looking in wonder at the grown boy, concentrating in that moment, with his serious child's face, the black hair falling over his forehead, the acne on his cheeks – and she was moved by what she felt flowing endlessly from his body to the dog.

But at that moment Assaf remembered something. He lifted his head and asked, 'Is she a girl?'

'What? Who? Yes, a girl – no, a young woman your own age . . .' She was searching for her lost voice, freshening her face with light pats of her fingers, watching the way he comforted and appeased the dog, gently, smoothing over the waves of her sobs until he quieted them completely, until the spark of light returned to her brown eyes.

'There, there, you see? Everything is fine,' Assaf said to the dog, and stood up, and again retreated into himself a bit when he saw once more where he was and in what kind of trouble he was trapped.

'At the very least, you can explain one thing to me,' sighed the nun, a different sigh this time, full of more than disappointment and sorrow. 'If you do not know her, how, then, did you know to bring the Sunday pizza? How did the dog surrender herself to you and let you walk her on a leash? Why, she will not allow such treatment at the hands of anyone in the world, besides Tamar, of course. Or are you, perhaps, a sort of infant Solomon and know the language of the beasts?'

She raised her little sharp chin in front of him, her face demanding an answer, and Assaf, hesitating, told her it wasn't the language of the animals, it was . . . how to explain? The truth was, he didn't quite understand everything she was saying, she spoke energetically and in such odd Hebrew. She especially stressed her consonants and the ends of the syllables, the way old Jerusalemites speak, emphasizing letters Assaf didn't even know should be emphasized. Most of the time, she hardly even waited for his answers, just throwing more and more questions at him.

'But will you finally open your mouth?' she breathed impatiently, '*Panaghia mou!* How long can you remain silent?'

At last he pulled himself together and told her, tersely and succinctly, as he always did, that he was working at City Hall, and this morning –

'One moment!' she interrupted him. 'You are speaking too quickly now! I do not understand – why, you are too young to be employed.'

Assaf smiled inwardly and told her it was only a summer job, over his vacation, and she responded, 'Vacation? To where are you traveling? Tell me quickly, where is this wonderful place?'

So Assaf explained that he meant his summer break. Now it was her turn to smile. 'Aaah, you meant your summer *recess*. Well, well, then, continue, from just before that; please tell me how you managed to obtain such an interesting job.'

Assaf was surprised by the question – what did that have to do with the dog he brought for her? Why was she so fascinated by the history of what had happened before he came here? But it did seem to interest her. She pulled up a little rocking chair and sat on it, rocking herself gently, her legs slightly parted, hands resting between her knees, and asked him whether he was enjoying his work there. And Assaf said, Not really; he was there to write down residents' complaints about explosions of water pipes in roads and public areas, but most of the time he just sat and dreamed –

'Dream?' The nun sprang up as if meeting a friend in a place where everyone was a stranger. 'Simply sitting, dreaming dreams? For a salary? Aha! Who said you cannot speak? And tell me, what do you dream about?' She knocked her knees against each other in joy. Assaf was very embarrassed and explained to her he wasn't really dreaming, he was just, like, daydreaming, thinking about all kinds of things . . . 'But what things – that is the question!' The nun opened her narrow eyes, now sparkling with something essentially elfish; her face expressing such seriousness and profound interest that it completely confused Assaf, silencing him, because what would he tell her, that he was dreaming about that Dafi, whether he could finally manage to break things off with her and still avoid a quarrel with Roi? He looked at her. Her dark eyes were fixed on his lips, waiting for his words, and for one crazy moment he really thought he would tell her a little. Why not? he thought. Just for the hell of it. She won't be able to understand any of it anyway, thousands of light-years separate my world from hers, and the nun said, 'Yes? Have you gone silent again, my dear? Have your powers of speech suddenly disappeared? God forbid, you should silence a story at its first breath!'

Assaf muttered that it was nothing really, just a silly story. 'No, no, no.' The little woman clapped her hands. 'No such thing as a silly story exists, you should know that. Every story is connected, somewhere, in the depths, to some greater meaning. Even if it is not revealed to us.' But this is really a silly story, Assaf insisted seriously, then broke into a smile at the childish, sly way her lips pouted. 'Fine,' she said, pretending to sigh, and crossed her hands on her chest. 'Tell me your silly story, then. But why on earth are you standing? Whoever heard of such a thing?' – she looked in amazement around her – 'the host sitting and the guest standing up!' Quickly she jumped out of her seat to reveal a tall chair with a stern, straight back. 'Do have a seat, and I will bring out a jar of water and some refreshments – shall I cut some fresh cucumber and tomato for both of us?' –

And her to*mah*to, with the long *ah* – 'Why, it isn't every day that we receive such an important guest here, from City Hall! Sit quietly, Dinka, you know you will have some as well.'

'Dinka?' asked Assaf. 'Is that her name?'

'Yes. Dinka. Tamar calls her Dinkush. And I' – she bent to the dog and rubbed noses with her – 'I call her shrew, and rebel, and dear heart, and my golden fair one, and *scandalyarisa*, and ever so many more, don't I, my eyes?'

The dog looked at her lovingly, her ears moving every time her name was mentioned. Something unfamiliar, like a light, distant tickle, fluttered inside Assaf as well. Dinka and Tamar, he thought. Tamar's Dinka, and Dinka's Tamar. For the blink of an eye, he saw the two in front of him, cuddling with each other in soft, round completeness. But that really wasn't any of his business, he remembered, forcibly erasing the vision.

'And you? – What?'

'What, what me?'

'What is your name?'

'Assaf.'

'Assaf, Assaf, a psalm for Assaf . . .' she hummed to herself, and hurried to the little kitchen with quick steps, almost skipping. He heard her chopping and humming behind a flowery curtain; she then returned and placed a large glass jar on the table, in which slices of lemon and mint leaves were swimming, and a plate with sliced cucumber and tomato, and also olives and slices of onion and squares of cheese, everything dipped in thick oil. She then sat in front of him, wiped her hands on the apron tied around her robe, and stretched her hand out to him: 'Theodora, a native of the isle of Lyxos in Greece. The last citizen of that miserable island now sits to dine with you. Please eat, my son.'

Tamar stood for a long moment in front of the little barber-shop door in the neighborhood of Rekhavia and didn't dare go in. It was twilight at the end of a relaxed day in early July. She had been pacing the sidewalk, back and forth in front of the barbershop, for maybe a whole hour now. She saw her reflection in the glass of the big window and the old barber trimming the hair of three men as old as he was, one after the other. An old man's barbershop, Tamar thought. Suits me. Nobody's going to know me here. Two were now left, waiting their turn: one, reading a newspaper; the other, almost completely bald – what was he doing here anyway? – with watery, bulging eyes, chattered incessantly with the barber. Her hair clung to her back, as if begging for its soul. It had been six years since she had cut her hair, since she was ten. Even during the years when she wanted to forget altogether that she was a girl, she wasn't capable of giving that up. It was a convenient screen for her, and sometimes a little tent to hide in, and sometimes, when it spun around her, wild, full of air, it was her shout of freedom. Every few months, in a rare attack of self-adornment, she would braid it into thick ropes and coil it on top of her head, feeling mature and feminine and restrained, and almost beautiful. Eventually, she pushed the door open and entered. The smells of the soap and shampoo and disinfectant greeted her, and the stares of all the people sitting there. A heavy silence fell in the room – she sat down, bravely ignoring them, laid the big backpack by her legs. She put the huge black tape recorder on a chair next to her.

'So are you listening' – the man with the bug eyes tried, unsuccessfully, to pick up his conversation with the barber – 'to what she's telling me, my daughter? That they've decided to call my granddaughter, who's just been born, they're going to call her Beverly, and why? Just because. That's what her older sisters want, and –'

But his words hung empty in the room, condensing like vapor touching the cold. He went mute with embarrassment, suddenly conscious of his own baldness, as if something were dripping onto it. The men glanced at the girl, and then at each other, their glances quickly weaving strings of agreement. She's not okay, this girl, their looks said, she's not in the right place, and she herself isn't right. The barber worked silently, and once in a while looked in the mirror. He saw her quiet blue eyes, and the knuckles of his fingers went weak.

'Enough, Shimek,' he said, in a strangely tired voice, to the man who had gone silent long before. 'Tell me later.'

Tamar pulled her hair together and brought it in front of her nose and mouth, tasted it, smelled it, and kissed it goodbye, missed it already, its warm touch, the times it had tickled her neck, the weight it had when she pulled it up, the feeling that her hair made her bigger, enlarged her existence and her physical reality in the world.

'Take it all off,' she told the barber, when her turn arrived.

'*Everything?*' His thin voice curled up at its edges in amazement.

'Everything.'

'Wouldn't that be a shame?'

'I asked you to take it all off.'

The two men who had entered the barbershop after her

straightened up. The third, Shimek, burst into a choking cough.

'Sweetie,' the barber sighed, and a slight vapor misted over his glasses, 'maybe it's better for you to go home first and ask your mother and father.'

'Tell me,' she retorted, all of her being tensed to fight him, 'are you a barber or a school counselor?' Their eyes dueled with each other in the mirror. This toughness was new to her as well. She didn't enjoy it, but it was tremendously useful in the places she'd been hanging around lately. 'I'm paying for this, aren't I? I asked you to take it all off. End of story.'

The barber tried to object: 'But this is a man's barbershop.'

'Then *shave* my head,' she said irritably. She folded her arms across her chest and closed her eyes.

The barber looked helplessly at the men sitting on the chairs behind her. His eyes said, 'You're witnesses – I tried to persuade her not to cut her hair. From this point on, she is solely responsible for whatever happens!' and the men's eyes agreed. He passed his hands over his thin hair and pulled his shoulders back. He then held his big scissors, snipped at the air once or twice; he felt that something in the clacking sound was a little off, it sounded hollow and weak, so he snipped and snapped until it hit the correct pitch, the sound of the joy of his profession – then took one thick curl of hair, wavy and black as coal, sighed, and started cutting.

She didn't open her eyes, not even when he moved to the more delicate scissors, nor later, when he used the electric razor, and not even after that, when he made the last remaining hairs on her neck disappear with a sharp blade. She didn't see the men, focused on her, as one after another they put their newspapers down and leaned forward a little, looking, alternately, attracted to and appalled by the too-pink naked skull, like a chick, becoming exposed. On the floor lay the beheaded locks, and the barber watched carefully so as not to step on them. The room was pretty warm and stuffy, but she felt the air around her head become cool. Maybe this won't be so bad, she thought, and for a moment a smile passed over her lips. She heard Halina, her old voice teacher, who sometimes scolded her for neglecting herself: 'Hair needs attention, too, Tamileh! Treat it well and you are already happier, yes? Why not? You can do it – a little conditioner, some cream – it's not so terrible to be pretty . . .'

'That's it,' the barber whispered, and went to clean the blade with cotton balls soaked in alcohol, and messed around with his scissors' case. Anything, anything so he could stand with his back to her when she opened her eyes.

She opened them abruptly and saw an ugly, scared little girl. It was almost horrifying. She saw a girl from an institution, a street girl, a crazy girl. The girl's ears were too pointy, her nose too long, and she had huge eyes strangely set at a distance from each other. She'd never noticed how odd her eyes looked, and now the exposed, provocative gaze frightened her. Her first thought was of the sudden resemblance to her father, especially his features as he had aged in the past few years. Her second thought was that with the addition of some suitable clothes, further blurring her appearance like this, there was a chance that even her parents wouldn't recognize her if they accidentally passed her in the street.

In the barbershop, nobody was moving yet. She looked at herself for a long time with no mercy. Her naked head looked like an exposed stump to her. She had the feeling that now everyone could read her thoughts.

'You'll get used to it,' she heard the barber murmur, with compassion, from afar. 'At your age, it grows quickly.'

'Don't worry about me,' she said immediately, alert, refusing any tenderness that could crumple her; even her voice sounded different to her without her hair, higher, as if it had split into a few different tones and were coming to her from a new place.

When she paid the barber, he took the money with the tips of his fingers. She thought he was afraid she'd touch him. She strode slowly, very erect, as if balancing a vase on her head. New feelings arose from every move she made, and she actually liked it; the world's air moved in a strange dance around her head, as if coming closer to see who she was, retreating and then returning to touch.

She lifted the backpack onto her shoulders, took the tape player, and began to leave. She stopped for a moment at the door; an experienced stage animal of her kind knew that, in addition to everything else, she was in the middle of a performance. They saw a spectacle, frightening perhaps, but mesmerizing as well. She couldn't resist the temptation – she stood up tall, threw her head as if shaking back a grand mane of hair, a diva, and, with a gesture of grandeur, of a soul in storm, of Tosca in the final act before she jumps off the roof, she lifted her arm above her head, let it linger in the air, and then, and only then, did she walk out, slamming the door.

'Mushrooms or olives?'

He didn't know exactly when it had happened. When had Theodora stopped being suspicious of him, and how had he now come to be sitting in front of her, big fork in hand, preparing to eat the pizza? He was only vaguely aware of that moment – something happened in the room a few minutes ago, a different look passed over her eyes, and then a little door in her was open to him.

'Dreaming again?'

Assaf said, 'Mushroom-and-onion,' and she laughed to herself. 'Tamar likes olives, and you, mushrooms. She, cheese, and you, onions. She is little, and you are Og, King of Bashan. She speaks, and you are silent.'

He blushed.

'But now, tell, tell me everything! You were sitting there and dreaming –'

'Where?'

'In City Hall! Where! You never told me of whom you were dreaming.'

He stared at her: he was fascinated by the way her wrinkles were painted on her face; her forehead was covered with them like tree bark, her chin too, and wrinkle marks stretched around her lips, the lower lip slightly pushed out. But her cheeks were completely smooth, rounded, untouched, and now, because of his attention, a slight blush reddened them.

Her blush confused him. He straightened up and quickly turned the conversation to business affairs. 'So, can I leave the dog here, and you'll give her to Tamar?'

It was clear to him that she was waiting for him to say something very different, about reveries, maybe – She shook her head and announced decisively, 'But no, no! That's impossible!' 'Why?' he asked, surprised. And she responded quickly, slightly annoyed, 'No, no. I wish I could, but – do not inquire into matters beyond your comprehension. Listen here' – her voice softened at the sight of his disappointment – 'I would gladly keep my dear Dinka here with me, but she must go outside every once in a while, must she not? One must take her for little walks in the yard, and in the streets as well, yes? And in addition, she will likely want to escape to the streets once again to search for Tamar. What would I do? I do not leave this place.'

'Why?'

'Why?' She tilted her head slowly, back and forth, as if considering a problem between her and herself. 'Do you truly want to know?'

Assaf nodded. Maybe she has the flu, he thought. Maybe she's sensitive to the sun.

'And if the pilgrims of Lyxos suddenly arrive? What do you think will happen if I am not here to receive them?'

The well, Assaf remembered, and the wooden benches, and the clay mugs, and the stones to rest your feet on.

'Did you see the dormitory on your way in?'

'No,' because Dinka had run and pulled him up the stairs so quickly.

Now the nun, Theodora, stood and held his hand – she had a slender, strong hand – and pulled him to follow her, and called Dinka as well. As the three of them quickly descended the stairs, Assaf noticed a big scar, yellow as wax, on her wrist.

She stopped in front of a tall, wide door. 'Stay a moment and close your eyes.' He closed them, and wondered who had taught her Hebrew, and in what century. He heard the door open. 'Now open them.'

He saw a narrow, rounded hall in front of him, and in it, dozens of high iron beds lined up in two rows, facing each other. A thick mattress lay naked on each bed; a sheet, a blanket, and a pillow were folded carefully on each mattress; and on top of everything, like a period at the end of a sentence, rested a little black book.

'Everything is in utmost preparedness for their arrival,' Theodora whispered.

Assaf allowed himself to be pulled into the hall, gazing around him at every step; he paced between the beds. At every step, a slight cloud of dust rose. Light leaked in from high windows. He opened one of the books and saw letters of an unfamiliar language. He tried to picture the hall full of excited pilgrims, but here the air was even cooler and more moist than in the nun's room, as if it had a hand and could touch. For some reason, Assaf became uneasy.

He saw Theodora when he glanced up, and, for a split second, the strange feeling passed through him that even if he walked toward her, he would never reach her – he was trapped there, in clotted, motionless time. He almost ran back to her with one urgent question: 'And they – the pilgrims' – he saw the expression on her face and knew he would have to choose his words carefully – 'when are they supposed to actually come? I mean, when are you waiting for them? Today? This week?'

She turned from him sharply, coldly, like the point of a compass. 'Come, my dear, let us return, the pizza is becoming cold.'

He walked behind, confused and disturbed. 'And my Tamar,' she said, as they climbed the stairs, her rope sandals tapping in front of his eyes, 'she cleans the dormitory; once a week she comes to scour and sweep. But now, as you saw – only dust.'

Again, they sat at the table, but something between them had changed, become murky, and Assaf didn't know what it was. He felt agitated by something left unsaid, hovering there between them. The nun, too, was lost in her thoughts and wouldn't look at him. When she delved into herself in this way, her cheekbones were more pronounced, along with the long narrowness of her eyes, and she looked to him like an old Chinese woman. For some time, they ate in silence, or pretended to eat. Occasionally Assaf looked around: a small bed, piled with mountains of books. A table in the corner, holding an ancient black telephone, with a round dial. Another glance, and Assaf's eyes snagged on an object – it looked like a figurine of a donkey, made of bent, rusty iron wires.

'No, no, no!' the nun suddenly protested, slamming the table with two hands. Assaf stopped chewing. 'How is it possible to eat without talking? To ruminate like cows? With no conversation regarding matters of the heart? What flavor is there in your pizza, young man, without conversation!' and she abruptly pushed her plate away.

He swallowed whatever was in his mouth quickly, and didn't know how to get out of it. 'And you and Tamar . . .' He choked a little when he said her name. 'You and she talk, right?' His voice sounded too loud to him, artificial.

Naturally she sensed his miserable attempt to avoid talking about himself and stared at him scornfully; but he had already started something and didn't know how to retreat from it respectably. In general, he wasn't well versed in the art of small talk (sometimes, when he was with Roi and Maytal and Dafi, when wit and banter, or at least cheerful everyday chatter, were demanded, he felt like someone who had to turn a tank around inside a room).

'So she . . . Tamar . . . she comes to you every week, right?'

He could see she wasn't thrilled to have to answer him, but still, after he mentioned Tamar, a spark returned to her eyes. 'She has been coming here, to me, for one year and two months now,' she said, stroking her braid, with a touch of pride. 'And she works a little, because she needs money; lately, quite a bit of money. She does not take any from her parents, of course.' Assaf noted the slightest twitch of her nose when she mentioned Tamar's parents, but didn't ask – what business was it of his. 'There is plenty of work here with me, as you have seen: cleaning the dormitory, dusting the beds, and, of course, polishing the big pots in the kitchen every week . . .'

'But what for?' he actually burst into her words. 'All these beds, and the pots, too – when are they coming here anyway, the pilgrims, when –' And very wisely, he shut his mouth. He felt now that he had to wait. A familiar feeling was fluttering inside him: the moment he loved, in the darkroom, when a photo slowly rises out of the solution and the lines start to appear. Here, too, the things he heard, and what he could only guess, started to come together in some shape . . . Another moment or two and he would understand.

'And after we work, we sit, remove our aprons, wash our hands, and eat the pizza –' She giggled. 'The pizza! Why, it is only because of Tamar that I have learned to enjoy pizza . . . Then, of course, we talk about all manner of things – my little one speaks to me of the entire world.' Again he thought he heard a light sound of pride in her voice and wondered what this Tamar must have that Theodora was so proud to be her friend. 'And sometimes we argue, as well – fire and brimstone, but all in the most friendly manner.' For a moment, she seemed girlish to him as well. 'In the manner of very close friends.'

'But what do you talk about so much?' The question escaped from him with a kind of embarrassed urgency; his heart was crushed with an inexplicable envy. Perhaps because he remembered what Dafi had said to him just two days before, that whenever he was about to start a story she had a strange urge to look at her watch. 'About God?' he asked, and hoped, because if they were talking just about God, that would be reasonable, bearable.

'God?' Theodora was flabbergasted. 'Why . . . but it goes without saying . . . most certainly . . . God appears in our conversations now and again as well. How could He not?' She crossed her arms across her bosom and looked at Assaf wonderingly, considering, to herself, whether she hadn't made a big mistake with this one – and he recognized that look only too well, wanted to jump out of his skin to stop its rays. 'But, my dear, let me tell you the truth: I do not like to speak of God. We no longer associate with each other as we once did, God and I. He and I lead separate lives. But do we lack for human beings to speak of in this world of ours? And what of the soul? And love? Is love no longer significant, in your opinion, my dear? Or perhaps you have already solved all its riddles for yourself?' (Assaf blushed, and shook his head vigorously to say no.) 'And then we argue to high heaven – until the tower shakes! What about, you ask.' (Assaf understood that he had to ask, and nodded energetically.) 'About what do we not speak? We speak of good and evil, and whether we truly possess free will' – she flashed a gentle, teasing smile at him – 'the great freedom to choose our own path – or is it already determined for us in advance? And we speak of Yehudah Poliker, Tamar brings me his every recording, every new song! Everything here is taped! And then, suppose there is a very nice film at the Cinemathèque, I say immediately, "Tamar! You must go for me! There, take some money; bring a friend with you, perhaps, and then return to me quickly and tell me everything, scene by scene!" And this way, she can enjoy herself and entertain me as well.'

A new thought occurred to him: 'And you – have you ever seen a movie?'

'No. Nor this new thing, the television.'

The pieces started fitting together. 'And you – you said you don't go out, didn't you?'

She nodded her head, looking at him, smiling, following as the nascent thought dawned slowly upon him.

'You mean . . . you never leave here?' he said again, with amazement.

'Since the first day I arrived in the Holy Land,' she confirmed again, with that slight pride. 'I was a little lamb of twelve years when I was brought here. Fifty years have passed since then.'

'And you've been here for fifty years?' His voice sounded small to him, like a child's. 'And you never went –? Wait a minute, not even out to the yard?'

She nodded again. It suddenly became unbearable for him to be there. He wanted to get up, open a big window, and jump out and run off into the noisy street. He looked at the nun, shocked, and thought that she actually wasn't that old, not even that much older than his father – only because of her isolated life does she look like this, like a little girl who aged, instantly, without passing through life.

She waited patiently, allowing him to think all his thoughts about her, and then quietly said, 'Tamar discovered a very nice sentence in one of the books: "The sole cause of man's unhappiness is that he does not know how to stay quietly in his room." According to this, I am a happy person.' Her lips pouted a bit. 'Very happy.'

Assaf squirmed in his chair. His eyes were searching for the door, his feet tingling. It wasn't that he was unable to be alone in a room, even for long hours at a time, but only with the latest computer, a new quest game, and no one else there to give him the tips so he could solve the problems too quickly. Yes, that could hold him in a room for four or five hours easily, even without food. But to always live this way? All your life? Day and night, week after week? Year after year? For *fifty* years?

'Thank you for not saying anything,' the nun said. 'Silence is a sign of wisdom . . .'

Assaf didn't know whether he would be allowed to ask a question now, or whether he would have to be considered wise until the end of his visit.

'And now,' she said, filling her lungs with air, 'now it is your turn. A story for a story. But do not halt at every turn – throw your caution to the winds. *Panaghia mou!* Why won't you say a single word about yourself? Are you so important?'

'But what should I say?' he asked, distressed, because he didn't want to talk about God, and he didn't know much about Yehudah Poliker, and his life was so regular, and he didn't like to talk about himself anyway – what could he tell her?

Tell me a story from your heart,' she sighed. 'And then I will tell you a story from mine.' This is what she said.

And smiled a slightly pained smile. Suddenly it was possible.

Twenty-eight days before Assaf met Theodora, before he started working for City Hall, before he even knew a Theodora existed in this world and hadn't dreamt of a Tamar, Tamar left for the streets. Assaf, as he always did on his vacations, slept until noon, then got up and prepared a light breakfast for himself – three or four sandwiches, a two-egg omelet – and read the newspaper. He sent an e-mail to a Houston Rockets fan in Holland, and for one long, exciting hour participated in an online Quest for Glory game forum. In the middle of it, Roi called him, or some other boy from class (he himself almost never called others). Together they tried to come up with a plan for that evening, despaired, and concluded that they would just talk later.

His mother also called from work, to remind him to take out the laundry and empty the dishwasher, and to pick Muki up from her summer camp at two. In between, he watched a little of the National Geographic channel while doing his daily exercises, and went back to the computer, and the hours passed lazily, and nothing happened.

During these very same hours, Tamar shut herself into a tiny stall, covered with graffiti and obscene drawings, in the public bathrooms of the Egged bus station. She slipped off her clothes – Levi's jeans and the thin Indian shirt her parents had bought in London – she slipped off her sandals and stood on them, staying in her bra and panties, disgusted by the murky, thin air of the stall that hurried to cling to her flesh. She took a smaller bag out of her big backpack, and from that removed a T-shirt and some big blue overalls, stained and torn beyond mending, which felt rough against her skin. Get used to it, she thought, and fastened herself into them. She hesitated for a moment and removed the thin silver bracelet, which she had received for her bat mitzvah. This, too, was dangerous – her full name was etched on it. She took out a pair of sneakers and laced them up. She preferred her sandals, but she could tell she would need these shoes very badly in the next weeks, to give her the feeling of something holding her, keeping her shape together, but also so she'd be able to run faster if she was chased.

Then there was the matter of her diary, six hardcover notebooks sealed into an airtight plastic bag. The first one, from when she was twelve, was thinner than the others, still decorated with colorful drawings of orchids and Bambi and birds and broken hearts. The later ones, their covers smooth, were much thicker, the writing more cramped. They made the bag very heavy, and were a burden to her, but she had had to remove them from her house because she knew her parents would quickly get hold of them. Now she buried them deep into the big bag, but after a moment couldn't hold herself back. She dug out the first one and flipped through the pages, covered in childish handwriting. She smiled, unconsciously, as she sat on the toilet seat – there she is, in the seventh grade, the first time she sneaked out of her house when she went with two girl friends to Tzemah to the Tipex concert. What a crazy night that had been. She flipped forward: *Liat came to the party in a shiny black dress and was gorgeous!! Liat danced with Gili Papushado and was so pretty I wanted to cry!!* How old wounds never really scabbed over – they were ready to open again at any moment. (But now she really had to get out of here, to go.) She pulled out another notebook, from two and a half years ago: *It freaks her out, the way she is growing up, 'developing.'* (Hate *that word!!!* Their *words!*) *Who needs this?* She stopped and tried to remember just why she was writing about herself in the third person. She smiled, sorrowfully: it came back to her, the insane training she had forced herself to endure back then, to toughen herself up, give her thicker skin; she taught herself to withstand tickling, and on the coldest days would take off her sweater and coat, and her shirt, too, or would go barefoot outside, in the streets, in the fields – writing in the third person was a part of it.

*Love's tiny narrow places. Like that space between the*

*closet and the wall in her room, that she could still fit
into until a month ago, fold herself up in there for hours
– and it is driving her crazy that she will never be able
to go back!!!*

And on the next page – it was unclear what actions inspired
this school punishment – she wrote out, exactly a hundred
times, *I am an empty, shallow girl. I am an empty, shallow girl.*

God, she thought, resting her head on the back of the toilet,
I can't believe I was so screwed up.

But immediately after that, she discovered her first encounter
with Yehuda Amichai's book *Even a Fist Was Once an Open
Palm with Fingers*, and was filled with comfort by that child
who wrote: 'Little fish are born surrounded by a little protein
sac, and I know this book will be my little protein sac, for
the rest of my life.' A week later, decisively, conclusively:
*In order to have W.E., I vow, from this day forward and
for the rest of my life, to look at the world with constant
wonder.*

She smiled a bitter smile. For months the world had forced
her into wonder, and then rage, and, finally, complete despair.
And the only thing that had given her Wide Eyes lately was
the haircut.

She flipped through the book, forward, backward, laughing
a little, sighing a little. It was lucky that she had decided to read
her diary before she went on her way. She saw herself spread
out and exposed, as if someone had screened a complete movie
for her, made up of all the separate shots of her daily life. She
had to leave. Leah was waiting for her at the restaurant for
their farewell meal. But she couldn't. Couldn't go back out
on the streets again, couldn't face those looks they'd given her
since she'd shaved her head. At least here she was protected,
alone, surrounded by walls; and there, she was fourteen.
She had already started writing things backward that she
particularly wanted to hide:

*Poor Mom. She wanted to have a girl so badly, so she*

*could share everything with her. Tell her secrets, reveal to her the mysteries of femininity, how wonderful it is to be a woman, a gift of God, really. And what did she get? Me.*

Mom. Dad. She shut her eyes, pushing them away from her – and they shoved themselves right back against her. 'In every person's life are situations in which he alone is responsible for saving his own soul,' her father had said to her during their last fight. Enough, enough – get out of here – when everything was over she could think about this. 'As far as I'm concerned,' he had said, 'the matter is closed. I do not intend to lift a finger.' He looked at her with false indifference. But his right eyebrow trembled uncontrollably, as if it had a life of its own. Slowly, forcibly, concentrating with effort, she erased them from her thoughts. She mustn't think about her parents now – they would only weaken her, make her lose heart. They did not exist for her now – and feverishly she drew out a different notebook, one from about a year and a half ago. Idan and Adi had already become part of her life by that point, and everything started changing for the better – or at least she had thought so at the time. She read it, and couldn't believe that she was so occupied with such things until a few months ago. Idan said this and did that. He went to get a Franz Josef haircut and took her, and not Adi, to check out the hairdresser, 'because you are so much more practical,' he said. She didn't know if, coming from his mouth, that was a compliment or an insult – and she was amazed that anyone thought her practical. And the trip to the Arad Festival – someone stole the bag that held their three wallets, and they were left with a total of ten shekels. Idan took control – he bought a coupon book in an office supply store for nine shekels, and sent both of them to collect contributions for the Association Against the Hole in the Ozone Layer.

The dizziness of the joy she felt, to pull off such a scam, such a crime, in order to bring him the money they made – and what a decadent meal they ate, and still had enough left over to buy some weed. She smoked it and didn't feel a thing, but Idan and Adi wouldn't stop running around, reporting on their wild high. On the way back, on the bus, Adi sat with Idan two seats in front of her, both of them laughing hysterically the entire way.

Little asides were scattered through the nonsense, brief reports on events she didn't think seemed important then, which were like tiny whispers gathering to become a scream: Mom and Dad discovered that the Afghani wool carpet hung behind the door had disappeared. They fired the cleaning lady, who had been working for them for seven years, immediately. After that, a few hundred dollars vanished from her father's drawer – and there went the Arab gardener. After that, that thing with the car, the odometer showing evidence of a long trip while her parents were abroad on vacation. More shadows were sleeping beside the walls of the house, and no one dared to shine any light that might be too strong on them.

Someone pounded on the door. It was the washroom attendant, who shouted that she'd been sitting in there for an hour. Tamar shouted back that she would be there as long as she liked. She panted, startled by the rude disturbance.

When she started reading the last notebook, she was amazed – it was all there, completely in the open, in such detail: the plan, the cave, the grocery lists, the dangers possible and unlikely. She knew that she would have to destroy this notebook, make it disappear. It was too dangerous even to hide. She flipped through the pages until her eyes found the exact moment when she had allowed herself to feel something – the brief encounter, that night by the Riffraff Club, with the curly-haired boy. He had a soft gaze, and showed her his broken fingers, then ran away from her, as if she, too, might do something similar to him. From that point on, she armored herself, became stingy with words, and wrote like the clerk of a secret army unit, about operations, and problems, and dangers – what was accomplished that day, what needed to be achieved.

She closed the notebook. Her eyes glazed over in front of an obscene drawing on the door. She wished she could take the diary with her, *there*. She couldn't. But what would she do without it? How would she understand herself without writing in it? Her fingers numb, she tore the first page out and threw it into the toilet, between her legs, and after it another page, and another. One minute, what's that there? *I used to cry a lot and was full of hope. These days I laugh a lot, in despair.* Into the water – '*I will probably always fall in love with someone who is already in love with someone else. Why? Just because. Because I'm very good at getting myself into hopeless situations. Everyone has something he's good at.* She ripped – *My art? What, don't you know? – not to live for the moment but to* destroy *the moment itself.* She tore, she tore aggressively; all at once she stood up, dizzy. All that was left were the pages from the most recent days – the endless arguments with her parents, her screams, her begging, and the terrible knowledge unstitching her heart, her understanding that they really couldn't do anything; they couldn't help her, nor could they prevent her from going. They simply grew hollow, paralyzed by the disaster that had hit them like a magic spell, emptied them out. Only the shells of her parents were left, and now it was she alone who could do something, if she dared.

But when she gets to that place she's trying to find, she will very likely be searched. She will be searched, certainly, and someone will go through her stuff and try to discover who she is. Who am I? What is left of me? She flushed, and gazed at the torn pages, spinning, getting sucked in, disappearing: nothing.

Her spirits were low without her diary, and without Dinka.

She disappeared into the throng that streamed through the station. She saw her reflection in the windows of the restaurants, and in the glass of the hot-dog stands, and in people's eyes. She saw how her lips were pursed in front of her. They had looked at her completely differently until yesterday. And until then, she also encouraged those looks a little, because of the wink, the light, tempting invitation of what she wore, and of how she looked in what she wore. Tamar knew it as the exaggerated courage of the super-shy, the frightened daring that exploded from her, uncontrollably, like a hiccup out of her body: like the see-through shirt she wore to the ninth-grade graduation party. Or the shocking red shoes, the no-place-like-home shoes, she wore to the big recital at the academy. There were other similar incidents – and also the endless, agitated transitions between her days of neglect and abandonment in such matters (Halina once yelled that from now on she was forbidden to dress like some Orthodox girl in those Bnai Brak clothes), to her periods of glossy, well-groomed glamour and style, her purple period, the yellow period, the black . . .

She deposited her big backpack at the baggage check counter and clutched the smaller bag to her chest. From now on, this would hold her home. The guy working at the counter took one look at her and, like the barber, was careful that his fingers not touch hers; she picked up the little numbered metal tag from the counter.

She hadn't planned this in advance: and now, where will you put this tag? She almost laughed at herself – she now understood that she hadn't succeeded in foreseeing and planning everything: and if they find it on you, what will you say? And if one of *them* goes and gets the backpack from the baggage check, and looks in your wallet, and reads your diary, what then, you stupid, self-absorbed loser. She left, enjoying the self-flagellation, making herself tougher, so she could withstand whatever was waiting for her. But who knew what else would happen there, what unimaginable possibility hadn't occurred to her – what this new life would bring her way – or how reality would surprise her and betray her – as usual.


So he told her, Assaf told her the whole story again, from the beginning, from the job at City Hall arranged through his father's connections with Danokh, because Danokh owed his father some money for some electrical work at his house, but – Theodora stopped him again with a wave of her commanding little hand. She wanted to hear about his father and mother first. So Assaf had to stop, and he told her that his parents and little sister may have already landed in Arizona, in the United States, and mentioned that they had left on the spur of the moment because Reli, his older sister, had asked them to come right away. The nun was interested in hearing more about Reli, why she was so far away from home – so, to his surprise, Assaf had to talk about Reli as well. He described her in broad strokes – how special she was, how beautiful, how she crafted jewelry, she was an artist, and she designed a very special line of silver jewelry that was starting to become really successful abroad. He recited Reli's words and phrases, feeling how strange they were to him, perhaps because all this new success of hers was strange to him, perhaps because something there, in all her traveling, scared him. So he added, with slight resentment, that she could certainly be unbearable as well, Reli could, and hinted at her self-righteousness in everything, from the food she ate – or rather, *didn't* eat – to her ideas about Arab–Jewish relations, and how the country in general should look and behave; and so it came to pass that he talked about Reli quite a lot, about how she practically ran away from Israel a year ago, because she needed her *space*. He hated this word of hers, so he hurried to replace it, explaining that Reli felt she was simply *suffocating* here. Theodora smiled to herself, a deep smile, and Assaf immediately understood it; a breeze of understanding passed wordlessly between them, because there are some people for whom even fifty years in one room are not suffocating – and for some, a whole country is not enough *space*. Then she wanted to hear about Muki, too, who had gone on the trip with his parents, because she really couldn't be left here, and Assaf talked about her as well, and grinned; his cheeks went redder than usual, swallowing up even his acne, because the moment he said 'Muki,' the smell of her hair, just washed, wafted into his nostrils. He laughed and said that it always drove him crazy how since she was three, she had insisted on using one specific shampoo, and was careful to use a certain conditioner with it – really, since she was three – with her hair as soft as fog between your fingers, her blond hair. He laughed, and Theodora smiled again – and she'll stand in front of the mirror for hours, that little one, and admire

46

herself, certain that the whole world loves her. Whenever he or Reli would get annoyed by this ritual of self-adoration, their mother would tell them not to dare spoil it for her, to let the little one enjoy herself, so there could be at least one person in this household who loved herself boundlessly. Assaf suddenly realized he had been talking, uninterrupted, for quite a while. He got uncomfortable and said, 'That's it, a normal family. Really nothing special.' And Theodora said, 'Your family is exemplary; you should be very, very happy.' And he saw her delving deep into herself again. A light had gone off inside her. He didn't understand how he had chatted so freely with her. He told himself, Well, it's because she's so lonely here, maybe she hasn't talked to anyone for a long time, had a real heart-to-heart conversation. And then he thought, Oh yeah? And when was the last time *you* had one?

Then, of course, he remembered what was awaiting him tonight, with Roi and Dafi, and she leaned toward him a little and asked, 'Quickly, quickly – what did you think just now, at this moment? Your face, my dear – *pou pou* – a cloud passed over it.' 'Doesn't matter,' he muttered. 'Doesn't *matter*?' she retorted. She had a tremendous curiosity for his silly stories; perhaps they weren't so silly, if someone could be so interested in them. 'Nothing ...' He laughed, and squirmed in his chair, embarrassed. He really didn't want to start talking about such things – it never would have crossed his mind to talk about them before he entered this convent. Why, they hardly knew each other – it was as if some demon had entered him here, was changing him. But the nun threw her head back with fresh laughter, and he felt that even though she looked old, in some ways she was as young as a girl. Perhaps because she had never used up her youthful parts in living. Then it occurred to him: Why should I mind telling her about it, anyway? She's nice, and she's lonely, and I feel like talking a little.

And so, just as he was, he told her about Dafi Kaplan, and Roi and Maytal, and the nun listened carefully, watching his mouth, her lips soundlessly repeating the words he said. After five sentences, she grasped that Dafi wasn't the main story.

Assaf was amazed at how readily she understood what had been bothering him the most. 'But please, let us put that poor girl aside for a moment' – she waved impatiently – 'she is a flower without scent. I must learn of the heart of the matter: speak of the boy, your Roi, who no longer is yours, if I am not mistaken.' Assaf's eyes closed for a moment, because she'd touched the exact place that hurt. He took a deep breath and plunged in. He told her about his friendship with Roi, how they'd been like brothers since the age of four, how they would sleep one night at his house, one night at Roi's, or in the treehouse. Of the two, Roi was then smaller and weaker, and Assaf protected him from the bigger kids – the teachers said he was practically Roi's bodyguard. It continued in this way until about seventh grade, Assaf said quickly, skipping over eight years in one leap, and being brought back, gently but firmly. 'And *how* did it continue?' she wanted to know. So he told her about their elementary school days, when Roi clung to him, wouldn't let him befriend any other boy and invented an array of punishments any time he suspected Assaf of attempting to betray their friendship. The worst was the silent treatment: weeks would pass in which he refused to say a word to Assaf, yet still wouldn't move an inch away from him. Then there were Roi's horrible attacks of rage, like the time Assaf wanted to join the Scouts; Assaf eventually gave them up, with an aching heart. Even then, though, he was flattered that someone needed him and loved him so much. He was silent for a moment, swallowed, and brooded for a moment. And this is how it had continued until junior high, then everything changed. The details didn't matter – 'They *do* matter,' the nun said. He knew she would. He even gave her a teasing smile. It was already a game between them. She went into the tiny kitchen to put water on for coffee, and called for him to continue. Assaf told her how in the seventh grade, about three years ago, girls started to notice that Roi was good-looking. Because Roi really jumped in height, became tall and handsome, and then all the girls started falling in love with him. He loved them, too, all of them, and really toyed with them, Assaf said, trying not to sound too pious. The nun smiled at the red-and-blue wallpaper in her little kitchen. But the girls never tried to get him back for it, said Assaf, in wonder, elbows on the table, chin in his hand, almost talking to himself – if anything, the opposite! Imagine! They *competed* for his attention! During break, they would sit and talk about how he looked, and what clothes suited him, and how he should cut his hair, how his body moved when he played basketball. Once, by accident, Assaf sat behind the girls' tree in the schoolyard, and he couldn't believe what he heard. They spoke of Roi as if he were some kind of *god*, or at least a movie star. One girl described how she was plotting, in cold blood, to drop down one level in math, just to be in his class; another said that sometimes she prayed Roi would get sick, so she could go to the clinic and lie on the same examination bed!

Assaf looked at Theodora and waited for her to laugh with him about that girl's stupidity – but the nun didn't laugh. She only asked him to continue telling his story, and on he went, wishing that he could just shut up already, but it was out of his control. It kept rolling out of him, like a big ball of yarn unraveling – he hadn't spoken of this, in this way, for years, neither with a stranger nor with anyone close to him. It's probably this convent, he thought dimly, or the little room, which was something like the confessional he once saw in a church in Ein Karem. After this he would be himself again, and forget that day he ever sat in a room at the top of a tower and spoke of such nonsense to a strange nun. And Theodora said, 'Assaf, I'm waiting!' He talked about how, because of the girls, Roi became, in eighth grade, something like – how can I explain it to you – like the King of the Class, let's say. Assaf meant to explain to her what it meant, but she waved her hand and said impatiently, 'Yes, yes, King of the Class, of course I know, do continue, please.' And Assaf guessed in a flash that she had heard such stories from Tamar, about boys and girls, and thought maybe she enjoyed listening to him because it recalled her time with Tamar. When that occurred to him, the warm, new tickling moved within him again, and he imagined Tamar, somehow present in the room, unseen but seeing – sitting on the floor by Dinka's sleeping body, slowly stroking her head; perhaps he, himself, was also talking to her now, telling her how Roi became Rotem's boyfriend, the Royal Couple of the Eighth Grade. It was years, Assaf muttered, since Rotem – Roi had been through four or five other girlfriends since her, and these days it's Maytal. Because of her, because Maytal wants it, Roi has been demanding that Assaf fall in love with Dafi, even hinted that it was a condition of their continued friendship. Enough. Assaf shook himself. It didn't matter, it's nothing, nonsense, small details. Again he felt embarrassed, and terribly confused, for spilling his guts this way. 'Very, very important,' Theodora said tenderly. 'You still do not understand, *agori mou*? How shall I come to know you without the small details? How, then, will I tell you a story from my own heart?' When she saw that he wasn't convinced, she searched out his eyes and forced him to raise them to meet hers. 'For Tamar did not want to speak at all of herself as well, in the beginning – she too said, Why does this matter? and Why is this interesting? I labored to teach her that we have nothing more important than these small things, these trifles of ours. And, you should know, she is far more stubborn than even you!' Once Assaf heard that, he immediately stopped disagreeing with her. It was if his constricted throat came untied; even his voice changed, loosened up, and he spoke about Dafi, and about how she measured and calculated everyone by money or respect or success – as he spoke, he finally realized why being with her held no pleasure for him. She was always competing with everyone, anyone, checking the balance of success versus failure, profit against loss; listening to her, you got the feeling that all the people in the world were waiting at every moment for the chance to conspire against someone, to leap and devour someone the moment he weakened . . . 'There are such people in the world,' the nun said, the moment she felt him faltering in front of her, 'yet there are others as well, yes? Is it not true that for those others, life is worth living?' Assaf smiled and straightened up happily, as if with her little aphorism she had solved a very complicated problem that had been bothering him for a long time. He added later that even if Dafi were a completely different person, he still wouldn't fall in love with her; that he thought he would probably never fall in love. At least, not until after the army. He spoke, and was surprised by his own courage; he would say such things to only one person in the world, to Rhino, Reli's boyfriend – and even then, only rarely. And to this nun he's known for less than half an hour – what was the matter with him today?

He fell silent; the two looked at each other as if they had woken from some mutual hallucination. Theodora smoothed her hands against her head, as if trying to hold something inside; the big yellow burn shone on her wrist. For one moment the room was completely silent. Only Dinka's breath, as she lay sleeping, was heard.

'Now,' Theodora whispered, with a tired smile, 'after all this, why don't you tell me, finally, how you managed to come to me?'

Only then did he tell her the essential details of the story, efficiently outlining how Danokh had come to his office that morning and called him to the kennels, plus Form 76 and the pizza; it seemed funny to him all of a sudden, how he had run crazily through the city without knowing where he was going. He started to smile. Theodora's face stretched into a smile in front of him. They both peered at each other and burst out laughing; the dog woke up, lifted her head, and started wagging her tail.

'But this is astonishing,' Theodora sighed when she calmed down. 'The dog brought you to me . . .' She gazed at him for a long time, as if he was bathed in a new light. 'And you? You were the innocent deliveryman, an unconscious messenger . . .' and her eyes really sparkled at him. 'Who else would have been willing to walk in this manner, after a naughty dog, to buy the pizza and foot the bill, to completely negate his own will to hers? What a heart, *agori mou*! What a warm and innocent heart you possess . . .'

Assaf fidgeted in embarrassment. The truth was, he had felt like quite an idiot running after the dog that way, and was surprised by this new interpretation of his actions.

The nun hugged her small self and shivered in pleasure. 'Now do you understand why I asked you to tell me the whole story? Now I am reassured, because my heart is telling me that if anyone could find my heart's delight, it is you.'

Assaf said that was exactly what he had been trying to do since the morning, and if she could now give him Tamar's address, he would find her at once.

'No,' she said, and got up quickly. 'I am so very sorry, but I cannot do that.'

'No? Why?'

'Because Tamar made me swear.'

And as much as he tried to understand, and as much as he asked, she refused to answer. She walked through the room tensely, mumbling her excited '*pou pou*s,' shaking her head no no no, and spreading her arms helplessly. 'Believe me, my dear, if I could, I would even hope for you to – No! Quiet!' She slapped at her own hand angrily. 'Silence, old woman! You shall not speak!' Another disturbed circuit around the room with more angry breathing and a little tornado of emotions, and she again stood before him. 'Because Tamar asked me directly; you must not take offense, but I can tell you only that the last time she was here she asked me, made me swear, that if anyone should come in the next days and ask where she lives or, perhaps, what her family name is, or who her parents are, or in any way inquire after her, even if he is the sweetest, the kindest – she didn't say that, I say that – well, I am forbidden to respond.'

'But why, *why*?' Assaf exploded, and he stood up. 'Why would she even say such a thing? What could have happened to her –' The nun kept on shaking her head to say no, as if she was afraid he would pull the words out of him. They both raised their voices and moved in front of each other for one brief moment, long enough for her to raise a commanding finger to his lips.

'Now be silent.'

Assaf was amazed and sat down.

'Listen to me. I am not allowed to speak of her. I have made a vow; my hands are tied. But let me tell you a tale; perhaps, from this tale, you will come to understand something of the matter.'

He sat and tapped his hand against his knee. Perhaps he should go at once and waste no more time. But the word 'tale' worked on him like a magic wand, as it always did. The thought that he would hear a story from *her mouth*, with her facial expressions and the sparks of light from her eyes –

'Oh ho! You smiled, my dear! You cannot deceive me, this old woman knows how to read such a smile! You are a stories-child – I knew it from the first glance, just exactly like my Tamar! Well, then, I will tell you my story, as a gift, in return for the story you told.'

'So what'll we drink to?' Leah asked, forcing a smile. Tamar looked at her wine; she knew if she said her wish aloud, the words would scare her.

Leah said it for her: 'Let's drink to your success, and you'll both come back in peace.' They clinked their glasses and drank, looking into each other's eyes. The ceiling fans whirred, attempting uselessly to spread cool against the new heat wave pushing in.

'I'm dying to start already,' Tamar said. 'Because, these last few days' – she took a deep breath, and her eyes grew for a moment in her exposed face – 'I haven't been able to sleep for a week; can't concentrate on anything. The tension is killing me.'

Leah stretched her two strong arms across the table, and they linked fingers.

'Tami-mami, you can change your mind, you know. No one'll blame you – I'd never say a word about this crazy idea of yours.'

Tamar shook her head, pushing away every thought of giving up.

Samir came over and whispered something into Leah's ear. 'Serve it in the big bowls,' she ordered, 'and recommend the Chablis. And for us now, bring the chicken with thyme.' Samir smiled broadly at Tamar and returned to the kitchen.

'What did you tell them?' Tamar asked. 'The guys in the kitchen, what did you tell them?'

'That we're having a party for you. Wait – what did I say? Oh, that you're going on a big trip. Check out what they've got for you.'

'I'm going to miss it here so much.' Tamar sighed.

'You won't have food like this out there.'

'Now, look' – Tamar's face became hard again – 'I'm leaving the letters with you, in this envelope. They are already stamped and addressed.' Leah's mouth twisted, insulted. 'Look, Leah, it's no big deal, and it's not the money, I just wanted everything to be ready so you wouldn't have to go out to buy stuff.'

'And because you wanted to do everything yourself, as usual,' Leah corrected her, shaking her head as if to say, 'What will we do with this child?'

Tamar said, 'Enough, Leah. Leave it alone. You remember what to do with the letters, right?'

Leah rolled her eyes like a pupil forced to repeat some loathed material over and over. 'Every Tuesday and Friday. Did you put the numbers on them?'

'Here, on the side, on the round sticker, and before you send it –'

'Take the sticker off,' Leah recited. 'What, do you think I'm stupid? Some dumb broad off the street? Is that it?' She let out a slightly exaggerated laugh. 'That's exactly what I am.'

Tamar ignored Leah's usual self-deprecation. 'It is very important that you send them in order, because I really made up a story for them, with little jokes about all the kinds of people I'm meeting. It's pretty moronic, but it will keep them as calm as possible so they'll leave me alone.' Her lips narrowed mockingly. 'A story, with plot development and everything.'

'I don't believe it. You kept all that straight in your head, too?' and when she said 'head,' Leah's eyes slipped over the exposed skull, which seemed so horrible to her.

'Anyway,' Tamar continued, thanking Leah in her heart

for staying silent, 'it should put them to sleep for a month. That's around the amount of time I need, until the middle of August, and they'll be abroad for two weeks of it, anyway. The sacred vacation.' She smiled crookedly. 'This year, the excuse is that "life must go on, in spite of everything."' She and Leah looked into each other's eyes, sighed, and shrugged their shoulders, amazed, completely disbelieving the possibility of such a thing. 'The most important thing is that they'll leave me alone. They won't start looking for me.'

'It doesn't seem to me like they're rushing to do anything, anyway,' muttered Leah. She inspected the envelopes, reading Tamar's parents' names above the address out loud with her thick lips. 'Talma and Avner . . . nice names they've got.' She chuckled. 'Straight off public TV.'

'More like a soap opera, lately.'

Leah said, 'It reminds me of something I saw written on a wall once: I will kill my mother if she ever gives birth to me again.'

'Something like that.' Tamar laughed.

From the kitchen, Samir and Aviva carried in the main course. When she lifted the silver cover off her plate, Tamar saw, around the stuffed grape leaves, her name written with purple cherries.

'This is from all of us in the kitchen, with our love,' said Aviva, flushed from the heat of the pots. 'So you won't forget us wherever you're going.'

They ate silently, both pretending to enjoy it, neither of them with any appetite.

'What was I thinking?' Leah finally said, and pushed her plate away. 'You know I have that little storage pantry two doors down from here.' Tamar knew. 'I'm going to put a mattress on the floor there for you – don't tell me no!' Tamar didn't say anything. 'The key will be under the second flowerpot. So if you get sick of sleeping in Ha'atzmaut Park, or whatever you do, if the room service isn't fancy enough, come to my pantry and sleep like a human being for a night. What do you think?'

Tamar thought through each of the possible dangers. Someone could see her entering the storeroom and inquire into who owned it – Leah wouldn't give her away, of course, but one of the kitchen workers might say something by mistake, and they'd discover who she was and her plan would be exposed. Leah watched sadly the wrinkles scrunching over Tamar's white forehead and choked back a sigh. What's been going on with this one lately?

But, actually, the mattress in the pantry was a good idea, Tamar thought. Even a very good idea. She would only have to make sure no one was following her when she entered; no harm would come to her if she slept there for one night, to restore herself to a little humanity. She smiled – her sharp, intense, zealous face defrosted; all the sweetness of the world was in her for just one moment, and Leah melted. 'Come on, Mami, crash there – there's a tap, and a little sink; you could wash up. There's no toilet, though.'

'I'll manage.'

'Ah, it makes me feel good that I can help a little.' Leah was excited, and already knew that every morning she would hurry over to the pantry to see if Tamar had slept there the night before; she would leave little encouraging notes for her.

'Just promise me,' said Tamar, when she saw Leah's eyes grow moist, 'if you see me on the street – it doesn't matter if I'm working, or just sitting and resting on some corner – don't come up to me. Even if you are sure I'm alone, don't act like you know me, okay?'

'You're tough. Hardhearted,' Leah said. 'But if that's what you want, that's what you get. Just tell me how I'll pass by you without giving you a hug or bringing you food. And what if Noa is with me? You think she won't jump on you?'

'She won't recognize me.'

'You're right,' Leah said quietly. 'She won't recognize you like that.'

Tamar searched for comfort in her eyes. 'Is it that terrible?'

'You . . .' You're so naked this way that it breaks my heart,

Leah wanted to say. 'You're always pretty to me,' she finally said. 'My mother used to say that a beautiful person is always beautiful – even if he puts a shoe on his face, it will suit him.' Tamar smiled gratefully at her, covered Leah's big paw with her hand, and pressed it lovingly, because now the little sail of sorrow that had been stretched between them the whole lunch long billowed in Leah's direction for a moment; when her mother said that sentence, she certainly didn't mean her.

Tamar said, 'I don't know how I'd hold myself back if you ever passed by with Noiku. You know what I've been thinking about? This is the longest separation I've ever had from her.'

'I brought you her picture,' Leah said. 'Do you want it for the road?'

'Leah . . . I can't take anything there.' She held the photo hungrily, and her face became rounder, softer, wider, like a watercolor painting bleeding a bit, diffusing past the contour lines. 'What a little hummingbird . . . I wish I could take it. I would sniff her a hundred times a day. You know.'

Samir cleared the plates away and scolded both of them for not eating everything. He flashed a disturbed glance at Tamar's shaven head. They hardly noticed him: they looked at the photo and rejoiced, a mutual happiness.

'They talked about brothers and sisters in nursery school,' Leah told her. 'When they asked her if she had a brother or sister, what do you think she said?'

'That I am her sister?' Tamar smiled with pride, swirling inside that word like wine in a glass. They looked at the tiny girl, ivory and almond-eyed, for another long moment. Tamar remembered, word for word, what Leah had told her when they first started becoming close: that in the world of her former incarnation, the one she lived in until she was about thirty, she was hardly a woman. 'They treated me with respect there,' Leah said. 'But they treated me like a guy, not like a woman. I didn't feel like a woman then, never. And when I was a kid, I wasn't really a little girl, and I didn't grow up into a big girl, and not a woman, and not a mother. There was no woman in me until now. Now, at the age of forty-five, because of Noa.'

A thick man with silver hair and a red face started raising a fuss at one of the tables in the center room. He was angry with Samir for serving wine that was not sufficiently chilled; he yelled that Samir was ignorant and stupid, and Leah immediately leaped up like a lioness protecting her cub.

'And who are you?' the man said. 'I demand to speak with the owner!'

Leah crossed her strong arms across her chest. 'That would be me. What's the trouble, buddy?'

'You? Are you kidding?'

Tamar felt her guts freeze from the insult to Leah.

'You got a problem with that?' said Leah with deadly calm – but her lips became pale, and the long scars on her cheeks suddenly popped out. 'You think you can order the owner of the restaurant from the menu, too?'

The man became even redder, and the undersides of his eyes muddied. The woman at the table with him, buxom and bedecked with gold necklaces, lay a reassuring hand on his arm. Leah, with powers Tamar never had, immediately pulled herself together, sent Samir to the kitchen to replace the wine, and said the new bottle would be on the house. The stout man grumbled a little longer, but kept quiet.

'What a pig,' Tamar said when Leah sat down again.

'I know him,' Leah said. 'Some high-ranking military official, used to be a general or something. Thinks he has the whole country in his pocket, always getting into trouble and winning his fights with cash.' She poured herself more wine, and Tamar saw her hand was shaking.

'You never get used to it,' Leah admitted with a sigh.

'Don't you dare listen to him!' Tamar rushed to comfort her, as usual. 'Just think of what you've done with your life, what you went through and how you got there. You went to France, alone, and studied at that restaurant for three years –' Leah listened to her with a strange mixture of hunger and despair; the long scars on her cheeks pulsed as if blood was passing through them. 'And how you created this place, all of it, all by yourself; and the way you raise Noiku – come on! There is no other mother like you in the world! – What do you care about what a loser like that says?'

'Sometimes I think, if only I had a man,' Leah mumbled. 'Someone who'd take trash like that by the collar and throw him to hell. Like Bruce Willis –'

'Or Nick Nolte.' Tamar laughed.

'But he should be soft on the inside!' Leah lifted a finger. 'He should be sweet.'

'Hugh Grant, then.' Tamar giggled. 'Who will love you and spoil you.'

'Not him, I don't believe in pretty faces. You watch out for them – I've noticed you have a weakness for that! Now I' – Leah laughed, and Tamar's heart expanded, flooding with the knowledge that she had again pulled Leah out of despair – 'I need a Stallone. But inside, he should be like Harvey Keitel, in that movie we saw, *Smoke*.'

'No one in the world exists who's like that,' sighed Tamar.

'Someone must,' Leah said. 'You need one, too.'

'Me? I'm not into that right now.' She didn't even have the energy to start that conversation. Any thoughts of love or intimacy seemed dangerous to her now. Leah looked at her and thought, Why is she doing this to herself? Why is she destroying herself this way, so young? Suddenly Leah almost jumped out of her seat – oh, God, Tamar would be turning sixteen this week! Right? Am I wrong? Leah raced through the calculations quickly in her head – sure, it's this week. And she's not saying a word about it. And she'll be alone on the streets – how can you? How ... and Leah almost said something, but then Zion brought dessert to the table from the kitchen, and she said instead, 'What's with all of you today, you're coming out one by one.' Zion laughed. 'It's only for Tamar.'

Tamar savored the honey and lavender ice cream and regretted that she couldn't store it in her body to eat from, slowly, for the next month. She licked the last of it off her spoon, and Leah unconsciously mimicked her lip motions.

'Let's see if I got it all,' Leah said. 'When do you leave for the streets?'

'Now, I think. After lunch,' Tamar said, and shivered a little. 'I'm starting right away.'

'Are you serious?' Leah couldn't hold back a heavy sigh. 'And when will you call me?'

'First of all, I'm not calling anyone for about a month,' Tamar said. She knotted her fingers together and squeezed, hard. 'Then, after about a month, around mid-August, depending on my situation there, if everything goes well, I'll call and tell you to show up in your VW.'

'And then where am I taking you?'

Tamar smiled tightly. 'I'll tell you then.'

'You're something, you.' Leah shook her head and wished everything was over already and the *other* Tamar would return.

They got up and went to the kitchen. Tamar thanked everyone for the special lunch, and hugged and kissed the cooks and their assistants and the waiters. Leah proposed a toast to Tamar and success on the long journey awaiting her. They drank. Everyone looked at her with concern; she didn't look as if she was going on a journey. She looked like someone going in for surgery.

Tamar, a little dizzy from the wine, looked around the crowded, steamy kitchen, at the loving faces surrounding her. She thought of the many hours she'd spent here, her hands sunk to the elbow in a pile of chopped parsley, or stuffing grape leaves with rice, pine nuts, and meat. Two years ago, when she was fourteen, she decided to drop out of school and become a sous-chef for Leah. Leah agreed to it, and Tamar worked there for a few weeks until her father found out she hadn't been going to school. He showed up and yelled and threatened to bring in inspectors from the Labor Office if Tamar stepped into the restaurant ever again. Now Tamar almost longed for that shameful scene, to see her father so assertive and decisive, fighting for her. She returned to her despised studies, and met Leah only at Leah's house, where she would go to babysit Noa, the love of her life. But she still didn't give up the idea of cooking, because anyhow, she now thought, it's not as if I have a chance at my other career.

Leah escorted her outside. A thin trace of jasmine hovered in the alley. A couple passed by them, arms around each other, weaving a little, laughing with each other – They watched, looked at each other, and shrugged. Leah had taught her once that every couple has a secret that only the two of them know; if there is no secret, the couple isn't a couple.

'Listen, Tami-mami,' Leah said, 'I don't know how to say this, but just don't get mad, okay?'

'Let's hear it,' Tamar said.

Leah crossed her hands over her chest. 'If you want, I can save you from this whole mess – one minute, let me finish –'

Tamar raised her eyebrows in silence but already knew.

'Listen, I just have to make one phone call – to someone who still remembers me from those days.'

Tamar lifted her hand to silence her. She knew what it took Leah to pull herself away from her previous life, the difficulty of the withdrawal from everything she was addicted to, both substances and people. She also remembered well what Leah had told her once, that any contact with that world could screw it all up again.

'No, thank you,' she said, moved by Leah's offer.

'I just have to pick up the phone,' Leah continued, trying to sound enthusiastic. 'I'm sure the guy I have in mind knows about these scumbags. In one hour he'll go down there with twenty guys, surprise the hell out of them, and get him out of there for you.'

'Thank you, Leah.' She shouldn't even think about it. The temptation was too great.

'Some of those guys are just waiting for me to ask them a favor,' Leah said dejectedly, to the floor.

Tamar hugged her, reaching up to her and snuggling in her chest. 'What a huge heart you have,' she murmured quietly.

'Really?' Leah asked, her voice slightly choked. 'Too bad there are hardly any tits.' She wrapped her arms around Tamar, touching, with compassion, the shoulder blades sticking out of her skinny little body. They stood, hugging each other, for a long moment. Tamar thought that this was going to be the last hug she got before going on her way; Leah felt that, or guessed it, and tried very hard to give her the best hug, motherly and fatherly, that she could. 'Just take care of yourself.' She mouthed the words above Tamar's head. 'Because out there, nobody's going to take care of you. I should know.'

Tamar stopped one step before reaching the thoroughfare. Around the corner of the last house in the alley, she sent a frightened, challenging look at the street, scanning her zone of action. She couldn't find the strength to enter it; like an actor or singer, peeking, terrified, through a hole in the curtain before a premiere, trying to guess what would be waiting for her tonight. Out there. *In front of them.*

She was overwhelmed by the loneliness, fear, and self-pity she had been suppressing, in opposition to everything she had planned, with harsh care, for months; with that, and even a kind of masochism, she got on a bus. She went home, as she was, with her shaved head, in rags, in the middle of the day, and went to her yard. She prayed none of the neighbors would see her, and that the gardener wasn't working that day; she also knew that even if someone saw her, no one would recognize her.

As soon as she opened the gate, she felt the air around her warm up a bit and spiral awake; a big clump of the joy in life and love, covered with golden fur, leaped onto her; a big, warm, rough tongue passed again and again over her face. She felt a moment of amazement, of slight embarrassment – but what a relief, and a true feeling of salvation: the dog recognized her scent, her essence, without hesitation.

'Come on, Dinkush. I can't go through with this alone.'


'Once upon a time,' Theodora began, 'a long, long time ago . . .' and laughed at Assaf's surprised reaction to her storytelling voice. She settled herself in her chair, sucked on a piece of lemon to moisten her throat, and then, in a rush of speech, with eager gestures and shining eyes, she told him the tale of her heart. The tale about herself and the island of Lyxos and Tamar.

. . . One Sunday, about a year ago, Theodora was enjoying her siesta when her entire body was shocked by the explosion of a huge voice outside her window. It sounded like a whine or a whistle, until it became clear that it was the warm voice of a girl calling to her, demanding that she come to the window.

The voice was not calling to her exactly but to 'His Holiness, the Monk Who Is Living in the Tower!'

She quickly got up and opened her bougainvillea-framed window, and saw, right over the fence of the convent, a barrel in the schoolyard next door. A slight young woman stood on the barrel; she had black, wildly curly hair and held a megaphone in her hand and was speaking into it.

'Dear Reverend Monk,' the girl said politely, and was briefly silenced when she realized that the wrinkled face in the window was a woman's. 'Dear Reverend Nun,' she corrected herself, hesitatingly, 'I would like to tell you a fairy tale that you might know.'

Theodora remembered: it was the same girl she'd seen about a week ago, high up in her magnificent fig tree, straddling one of the big branches, writing something in a thick notebook, unconsciously munching fig after fig. Theodora was prepared – she aimed her slingshot, which she used to scare off thieving birds, at the fig-devouring girl and shot a sanded apricot pit at her.

She hit her mark. She allowed herself a moment of pride at once again discovering that she hadn't forgotten the art of aiming and firing from her childhood days on the island, when she was sent with her sisters to ambush the greedy crows in the vineyards. Theodora heard a yelp of pain and surprise from the girl when the pit hit her neck. The girl clapped her hand over the burning spot, lost her balance, and fell branch after branch until she hit the ground. Theodora experienced a moment of deep regret then. She wanted to run and help her up, to apologize from the bottom of her heart for the shot, and to beg the girl and her friends to stop stealing her fruit. But because she was a prisoner for life in her home, she didn't move; she only served herself the small, painful punishment of making herself watch the girl spring up off the ground and send her a scathing look. The girl turned her back to her, and promptly pulled her pants down, mooning her in a way that sent a shock through her heart.

'Once upon a time, in a faraway land, there was a small village; and near it lived a giant,' the girl began, speaking into the megaphone one week after that bitter incident. The nun listened, amazed, her heart fluttering with a strange joy, for the girl had come back.

'The giant had a big garden; and in it, a lot of fruit trees. There were apricot trees, and pear and peach and guava, fig, cherry, and lemon.'

Theodora passed a glance over her trees. She found the girl's voice pleasant. It held no resentment; on the contrary, her voice contained an invitation to talk; Theodora felt it right away. Not only was there this note of invitation; the girl spoke as if she were telling a fairy tale to a small child; the soft, soothing voice leaked into the depths of the nun's memory and rippled outward.

'The children of the village loved to play in the giant's garden,' the girl continued. 'Climbing the trees, bathing in the little stream, running through the meadows . . . Excuse me, Nun, I didn't even ask you – do you understand Hebrew?'

Theodora woke up from her sweet reverie, took a piece of paper from her desk, and rolled it into a little megaphone, and, with her slightly clucking voice, a voice that hadn't spoken loudly in years, informed the girl that she spoke, wrote, and read in perfect Hebrew; she learned in her youth, from Mr Eliasaf, a teacher at Takhkemoni High School, who used to tutor private students in order to supplement his income. When she finished her short, detailed speech, she thought she saw a glimmer of a smile in the girl's eyes.

'You haven't seen her when she smiles,' Theodora whispered to Assaf. 'With a little dimple here,' and she touched his cheek. He trembled as if he could feel the warmth of this girl, Tamar, on his cheek – this girl with whom he had no business at all – he had nothing to do with her dimple! In her heart, Theodora thought, You blushed, my dear! Aloud, she said, 'Your heart flies up when she smiles – no, do not laugh, I never exaggerate – your heart leaves your body and flaps its wings!'

'But the giant didn't want the children to play in his garden,' the girl on the barrel continued. 'Didn't want them to enjoy the fruit of his trees – didn't allow them to pick his flowers or bathe in his little stream. So he built a wall around his garden, a high, thick wall.' She looked straight into the nun's eyes. Her look was piercing and intense, a lot more mature than her age. Theodora felt tender yearnings slowly spiral inside her.

Assaf was listening, too, hypnotized, smiling unconsciously. He saw the picture in front of him: the little nun peeking out of her window, the wide, fertile garden ... and over the fence, standing on a barrel, the girl. To be honest, he was a little scared of girls who were capable of getting up on barrels, of doing those kinds of things. (What kinds of things? Deliberate, special, provocative – *original* things.) He could always spot them from a distance and cautiously avoid them: opinionated girls, decisive and self-confident. Girls who felt that the whole world belonged to them, for whom everything is just fun and games; who probably also feel that boys like him are clumsy, and a bit slow, and kind of boring.

Theodora looked at the girl on the barrel, however, and different thoughts arose inside her. She pulled a carved wooden chair, unused for years, to the window: the lookout chair for the pilgrims. A pile of books sat on it, and with one sweep of her hand she tumbled them to the bed. She sat upon the chair, stiffly, alertly; but in only a few moments her body melted, curved, and bent toward the window, until only her eyes peeked above the sill, her chin pillowed on her palms.

Theodora's garden was surrounded by a stone wall on the side facing the street; but only a high, ugly, chain-link fence separated it from the neighboring school. The fence didn't prevent the invasion of gluttonous students, driven to distraction by the scent of ripe fruit. In the morning, the pupils from the school; in the afternoon, the kids in the chorus that practiced there. Nasrian, her Armenian gardener – also her housepainter, carpenter, blacksmith, messenger, and mail carrier for her many letters – patched over the holes in the fence again and again, only to discover new ones each morning. The garden that had given Theodora great pleasure in the past now cost her a tormented soul, to the point that, more than once, in times of despair, she seriously considered cutting down all the trees – If I cannot have them, then they shall not have them!

Now, as the girl spoke to her, her exasperation was forgotten. She didn't know the fairy tale the girl was telling, but at the sound of her clear voice, a strange thought occurred to her: a thought about, of all things, her mother, who was always busy and tired, who always had a new baby tired to her back and never had the time to be alone with Theodora, just the two of them together. Then, perhaps for the first time in her life, she realized that her mother had never told her stories, or sang her songs . . . and with that, her mind drifted gently to her little village on the island of Lyxos, to the white-painted houses and fishing nets, and the seven windmills, the tiny little wooden birdhouses with diamond openings, built especially for the doves of the island, and the dark octopuses, hanging on ropes to be dried . . . She hadn't seen that village so clearly in years, the gardens in front of the houses, the narrow streets . . . They were paved with round stones, which the people of the island called monkey-heads – she hadn't thought of that nickname for almost fifty years. For almost fifty years, she had forbidden herself to return there for even one moment. She had built a fortress around that region, walled it in, because she knew the yearning and mourning would batter her heart unbearably.

'Take grapes,' she said to Assaf, almost soundlessly. 'Sweet sultana grapes, because now the story takes a bitter turn.'

About seventy years before Theodora was born, Panorius, the head of the village, a very rich and educated man, also an experienced traveler, decided to donate a huge sum of money for the building of a house in Holy Jerusalem for the people of his island. Panorius himself made a pilgrimage to the Holy Land in the Year of Our Lord one thousand eight hundred and seventy-one, and found himself on a boat, rolling around with hundreds of Russian peasants, in the filthy bunks Russia had built for her pilgrims. He passed hard weeks in the company of people who did not understand his language, whose habits and behavior seemed repulsive to him, even obscene. He fell prey to the hardhearted tour guides, who tormented the innocent pilgrims and robbed them of what little money they'd brought; when he grew sick, he couldn't find any doctor to treat him who could understand his descriptions of what ailed him. When he finally returned to the island, delirious and dying of typhus, he dictated a final request to his secretary on his deathbed: that in the Holy City a place be built where pilgrims from the island of Lyxos could stay in the Holy Land; a home where they could rest their tired heads, wash their feet after the long journey; a home where they would be spoken to in their own language, and even in the special dialect of the people of the Cyclades. He insisted on one final condition: that in this house should reside, forever, only one, a nun; a girl of the island, whose name would be chosen by lot. She would spend all her pure life in that house, and never leave it, not even for a brief hour. Her life would be devoted to waiting for the arrival of the pilgrims of Lyxos, and then seeing to their care.

The girl on the barrel continued her tale, but Theodora had already been swept away by a silent flood of memory. She remembered that day when the old men had gathered in the home of Panorius's grandson, for a third time since the house in Jerusalem was built, to draw a name. Since Panorius's death, two girls from the island had already been sent there: the first lost her mind after forty-five years; Amaryllia, the girl with golden braids, was sent to replace her. Now came an urgent need to replace the sick Amaryllia; rumor said she had fallen ill not only in body. At that hour, twelve-year-old Theodora lay naked and tanned as a plum on a cliff over her secret bay. Eyes closed, she thought of one particular boy who had lately started bothering her wherever she went. He made jokes about her triangular face, and her legs, which were always scratched; he called her a scaredy-cat and a little girl. Yesterday, when she returned from the sea alone, he blocked her way and demanded that she bow to him if she wanted him to allow her to pass. She jumped on him and they fought for long minutes in silence; only their panting and gasping could be heard. She scratched and beat at him and spit like a cat, and swore in her heart that she would fight him to death. He almost overpowered her – and then, at the sound of approaching wagon wheels, he got up and ran away. But when she picked herself off the ground, she found he had left something for her: a baby donkey he had sculpted from a long piece of iron wire.

So she was lying on the warm cliff, wondering what he would bring her today when she came back from the sea, remembering the strange and pungent smell of his body sweat as they fought, when she heard loud voices from afar. She sat up and saw a tiny figure running, yelling with all its power from the top of the mountain. She didn't understand the yelling at first; then she thought she heard something familiar. She pushed herself up on her knees. The tiny figure must have come out of Panorius's grandson's house. Theodora watched it, and discerned that it was a boy, a half-naked little boy, running across the length of the horizon, waving his arms and wildly yelling out her name.

She was sent away three days later. It was impossible to protest or object; even now the insult rose and bubbled in her

– her father and mother were as miserable as she about it, but it never crossed their minds to dispute the decision made by the old men of the island. Theodora remembered the farewell party they threw her; the white she-ass decorated with flowers and caramel candies in the shape of a tower in Jerusalem; also, the oath she swore: that never, ever would she desert the guest home, whose window looked west, toward the sea.

She could no longer remember the exact wording of the oath, but she saw now, again, as in a nightmare, the black-bearded face of the village elder and the fleshy lips of the priest who held her hand and branded her with a red-hot iron in front of the whole village. She knew she'd be able to buy her freedom by allowing a single cry of pain to escape her mouth, even a light moan – but when she glanced up, she saw, on a distant rock, the burning eyes of that boy, and her pride did not allow it.

The strange girl was on the barrel, still talking. Theodora took a deep breath, possessed by a shiver – she could almost smell the sea again, sailing on the first and last journey of her life, to the miserable port of Jaffa – she saw the long ride to Jerusalem, in an old bus that groaned like a human being – and she remembered the physical shock of amazement that filled her when, for the first time in her life, she was on land that was not an island.

It was late at night when a Bukharani street merchant dropped her off with her bundle in front of the convent gate, and she knew her life had ended. Sister Amaryllia opened the gate for her, and Theodora looked, horrified, into her glassy eyes, her face reduced to nothing: the face of someone buried alive.

In the two years she lived with Sister Amaryllia, not even one pilgrim came to the house in Jerusalem. Theodora grew into a lovely young woman, but Amaryllia reflected back at her, feature by feature and line by line, what was waiting for her when she became old. Almost every hour of the day, Amaryllia would sit on the high chair in front of the window facing west, presumably in the direction of the port of Jaffa, and wait. During the decades she was imprisoned there, she forgot even her family members, the letters of the alphabet, and the people of the island of Lyxos who had sent her there. She gradually eroded away into one narrow line, the scar of a white gaze.

And then, one month after she passed away and was buried in the convent yard, the horrible news came: an earthquake in the Aegean Sea, the Great Earthquake of '51. The island split in two – a great tsunami rose up and, in a few moments, took all its residents down to the depths of the sea.

But no, this is not what she wants to think about now, when outside, beyond the fruit trees, a clear, daring voice is dancing, walking her back to her childhood buried under fifty years and so much water. She didn't know why she was so willing to give herself over to the temptations of a voice that sounded like a song as it spoke. She pressed her fists to her eyes, hard, as if to escape the sight of the girl on the barrel; through the sparkles, she saw herself, the sharp, daring, feisty Theodora leaping and embracing her two best girl friends, and now – Where are you, laughing Alexandra, light mountain goat? Where are you, Katarina, who knew all my secrets? The people of the village floated up and rose to greet her, knocking on her closed eyelids, begging to be remembered: her sisters, her big brothers, the twin brothers, infants, struck blind one day when they looked into the sun during an eclipse. They, too, were gone, and also that stupid, beautiful boy.

She wiped her wet eyes on her sleeve and looked at the girl on the barrel, and over her fruit trees, and thought that, actually, she was behaving like a fool, even a villain. The trees bowed under the weight of the fruit, and no one but she ate from them; even after the pupils' daily plundering, masses of fruit were left rotting on the branches. She attacked the children because they stole from her, and she couldn't bear that; but if, perhaps, she allowed them to pick some, perhaps this ugly war could stop immediately . . .

A silence snapped her out of her thoughts. The girl had finished her story and was probably waiting for an answer.

Now, when the clumsy megaphone wasn't hiding half her face, Theodora saw how sweet she was; her eyes, revealed in that exposed, beautiful face, shone and teased at the same time, bold, honorable eyes that sliced through all the layers coating Theodora, her age and time and loneliness. Then she raised her paper megaphone and announced, her voice trying to sound serious, that she would be willing to begin negotiations with the girl.

'And this is how it began.' Theodora laughed silently, and Assaf stretched his arms, as if awaking from a strange dream. 'The following day, they came here and sat in my room: Tamar, with another boy and girl, her soul mates – and presented me with an exemplary, organized plan.'

In it, they listed each tree and every member of the chorus who wished to join in the arrangement; a schedule gave everyone a turn and said which weeks they were allowed to pick which fruit . . .

'And the war was over,' Theodora laughed, 'in a single day.'


Here it comes, Tamar thinks. After this moment, you won't be able to escape. She's dragging her legs and can't find a place to stand; the asphalt burns under her heels wherever she stops. To try and calm herself down, she recalls how she's actually been through many such moments in the past few months: the first time she dared approach someone in one of the dark market corners, asking him if he recognized the person in the photo she was holding. The first time she bought from one of the dealers in Tziyyon Square, a dwarf with thick hips and a colorful wool hat – for a moment, you could almost picture him onstage, playing the role of a friendly troll from Fairyland – her negotiation with him was short and to the point, and nobody would have guessed how her heart was beating like a drum. Money and merchandise switched hands, and she kept it in a bag, rolled up in a sock, knowing she now had enough for the first days of the operation –

But right now is still the hardest moment. To suddenly stand in the middle of the city, in the middle of traffic, in the pedestrian walkway of Ben Yehuda Street, which she'd walked through a million times like a normal, free person –

– walking with Idan and Adi, licking Magnum ice creams after chorus rehearsal, or as they sat and drank cappuccinos, laughing at the new tenor, that Russian boy who shamelessly dared to compete with Idan for the solos. 'Another mouth-breathing peasant from the Ural Mountains,' Idan muttered into his cup, flaring his nostrils lightly in the flutter that signaled both of them to burst into rollicking laughter until they cried. Tamar laughed along, even more loudly than Adi, perhaps so as to not hear what she was thinking about herself in that moment, and she kept laughing like that, for that entire period, because she couldn't get over the wonder that, for the first time in her life, she belonged to those who mocked, a small, united group that had been together already for a year, two months, one week, and a day. Three young artists, a rare oath of fraternity, whose members were loyal to one another, or so, at least, she believed.

And now she has to walk here all by herself, to find a location at an appropriate distance from the old Russian playing his accordion; to stop, within the normal flow of the street, to stand in a certain spot. Someone is already looking at her, slightly disturbed, circling her, with a disagreeable expression on his face. She feels like a little leaf that has decided to take a different direction from the current of the whole river – but she mustn't hesitate now, she mustn't think. Mustn't entertain the faintest notion that someone will recognize her and come over and ask, Are you crazy? How naïve she was – or stupid – to think that shaving her head and changing her costume would succeed in transforming her so completely . . . and, more than that, if someone were to debate for a moment whether or not it was actually her, why, then he would see Dinka and know. How foolish it was to take Dinka! All of a sudden all her mistakes spread out before her, a chain of foolishness and negligent planning. How had it happened? Look what you've done! Who did you think you were – you're just a little girl trying to play James Bond. She pulls up short, she stands and winces, as if absorbing a blow – but within herself: How couldn't you guess that this is exactly what would happen, and that in the moment of truth, all the stitches and holes would be exposed? You always do this, don't you? The moment always comes when your fantasies finally touch reality, and then the balloon that you are explodes in your face . . . People are milling around her on both sides, grumbling and jostling one another. Dinka barks softly, waking her up. Tamar straightens, bites her lip – Enough, stop feeling sorry for yourself, there's no time to hesitate now, and it's too late to turn back. Get out of your head and obey orders. You will put the big tape player on the stone flowerpot, push the play button, turn the volume up, more, louder – this isn't a room, it's a street, this is Ben Yehuda Street, forget about yourself for once, from here on out you're only an instrument by which to accomplish your mission, nothing more. Listen to the sounds, the beloved sounds, the sounds of his guitar, Shai's guitar, see his long golden hair falling on his cheek when he used to play for you in his room; let him wrap you up, melt your fears away, and at that right moment, that precise – *Suzanne takes you down* . . .

For long days, she had been trying to decide what song she should use to open her career on the streets. She had to plan that as well, of course. In the same way she planned and calculated the amount of drinking water in the cave, the number of candles and rolls of toilet paper. At first she thought she would sing something in Hebrew, something familiar, Yehudit Ravits or Nurit Galron, something warm and rhythmic and personal, something that wouldn't make her tense, that would mingle and mix with the street. At the same time, she was tickled by her constant temptation to dazzle them right at the start with something unexpected: Cherubino's second aria from Mozart's *Marriage of Figaro*, maybe; to announce, in that way, right at the first moment, a strong, clear declaration about who she was, and what her intentions on this street were, so that everyone would know at once how different and separate she was from everyone else here . . .

Because, in her imagination, she had limitless courage; in her imagination, she sent her voice out to the full length and width of the street, filled every gap and pothole there, immersing all the people in a softening, purifying solution; in her imagination, she chose to sing high, so ridiculously high as to blow them away right at the start with her high pitch, to abandon herself shamelessly to the floating exultation that made her feel a little lightheaded when she sang like that, drunk from the pleasure of the unbroken takeoff, from her darkest depths to the dizzying altitudes. And eventually, she chose 'Suzanne,' of all things, because she liked the song, and she liked the warm, sad, defeated voice of Leonard Cohen, and more than anything, she thought it would be easier for her, at least at the beginning, to sing in a foreign language.

But after a second or two of singing, something goes wrong: she already knows that she has started too softly, too hesitantly. No charisma, Idan decides from inside her head, chaining her down – what's wrong with her? She wishes it wouldn't spoil her singing, the one and only thing about herself she trusts in her whole complex plan. Now it seems much harder than she had thought – singing here really means opening herself up, exposing her innermost self to the eyes of the street. She struggles with herself, and sounds a little better – but it's so far from what she dared to dream about – that the whole street would hold its breath from the first sound, and be swept up by the whirlwind of her voice. Why, she had fantasized, in detail, how the window cleaner's gloomy, circular motions on the second floor of the Burger King would freeze; how the juice vendor would stop the juicer in the middle of a carrot's bitter cry . . .

But wait, one moment; don't despair so quickly; there is one man over there, by the shoe store, stopping and looking at you, still standing at a sufficient distance, careful not to commit, but still, he's listening to you. She pulls her shoulders back, making her voice full: . . . *she gets you on her wavelength* . . .

And just as it happens in a river, or on a street – when one branch gets stuck, others immediately cluster around it; that's the law, it's the physics of motion within a flow; another man stops next to the man listening noncommittally by the shoe store, and another, and more. Six or seven of them are already gathered there, and now it's eight. She tunes her breath, restraining the slight hysteria at the edges of her voice, and dares to raise her eyes and take a brief peek at the little audience, the ten people who are already gathered around her . . . *You want to travel blind* . . .

'Easy, easy, don't push, breathe from below, from your toes, the breath!' She hears the spirit of her tyrannical and adored Halina in her ears. 'God forbid you sing like that, from the throat – cchh! Ccchh! You're like that one, Cecilia Bartoli . . .' Tamar smiles in her heart. She misses her teacher. For her, she climbs the imaginary steps, from her throat up to the secret bird in the middle of her forehead; Halina, then, who actually has the look of a bird, quickly jumps up from her piano, her too-tight skirt rustling – one hand still playing, the other pressing on Tamar's forehead. 'There you go! Bravo! Now you hear it! Perhaps they will hear it in the audition as well.'

But Halina prepared her to sing in concert halls and elegant recitals, or in master classes with famous conductors or genius opera directors dropping in for a quick visit from abroad. Or for end-of-the-year chorus performances in front of an invited and prejudiced audience, with her mother's proud look (her father used to drive there unwillingly, and once she spotted him reading something that he held on his knees while she sang), and sometimes, a couple of her parents' friends would come, too, their faces soft and shining as she sang, listening to the girl they had known from birth, the one who was born screaming – even the midwife said, 'That one will be an opera singer, for sure!' And there was that photo of her at age three, holding the plug from the iron and singing into it . . .

And now this. Her fall. What else? It's a pity, it came too

fast; but wasn't it clear that this is what would happen to her here? Because we shouldn't forget, dear friends and parents, that this is she who is standing here; nothing about her is reliable, she has to betray herself just when she needs herself the most. That's the way it is, my sweet child, my poor, fucked child; you really have no one to count on, not even yourself. Especially not yourself.

The panic sobers her up – a little sobering rat running into the hollow of her stomach and biting into the lining. She is still singing, it's unclear how, but the bad thoughts quickly clutter into different words from the ones she's singing, into her familiar black hymns – the worst thing that could happen would be for her to sing them by mistake.

Don't stop, don't stop! she yells at herself, frightened when her voice starts shaking because of the quick, relentless heartbeats; her whole body is shrinking, her muscles clenching tightly; they can probably already hear on the outside what is happening to her inside. They can probably see her frightened, tremulous expression. It will all collapse in a few seconds, she knows – not only this miserable performance here but everything that preceded it, all of it loose and flimsy and hanging on by a thread. Good for you, dummy. You deserve it. You're finally starting to grasp what you've invented for yourself in your deranged mind – do you get it? Do you see where you've brought yourself? You're lost, lost. Now pack your things up nicely and quietly, quietly, go back home. No, no, keep on singing, she begs herself, please, please keep singing; she beseeches herself, as if she were a stranger, as if she were kidnapped; if she only had an instrument in her hand, a guitar, even a drum would help, or a handkerchief, like Pavarotti's, something to hold on to to make her body vanish. Her heartbeats become a straight line of internal drumming. Something inside her is, with Satanic efficiency, recruiting everything that can negate her from the inside, all the bad looks ever thrown at her, every whisper, the humiliations, the sins, and the long insults, a procession of rats marching by. Look how quickly the street exposed the lie that you are. No: how quickly *reality* exposed you. Not your imagination, the hallucinations that you usually inhabit, because this is *life*, honey, real life, concrete, the existence you are trying to be accepted into, again and again, as a member with equal rights; and it rejects you again and again, like a body rejecting an organ transplant. 'Again, you're breathing from chest and not from diaphragm,' Halina determines dryly, and with a squeak of her zipper closes up her black handbag and turns to go. 'Your voice falls completely into your throat. I told you a thousand times: don't force the throat! I don't want you like Mussolini on the balcony!' What would Idan say if he passed by here now? 'Don't call us, we'll call you.' Let it go; he won't pass by here, and do you remember why? That's right, because our Idan is now in Italy – oh, don't think about *that* now, please, please – Idan and Adi and the whole chorus, a month of performances all over the Boot. Today they will sing in the Pergola, and at this very moment, by the way, at this hour – they are rehearsing with the Florence Symphony Orchestra. Let go of it now, concentrate; remember, for example, that this is how you will have to survive, and that without this money you won't be able to eat tonight. Until yesterday, they were in Venice, at La Fenice. I wonder how the performance went, and whether they went later to see the Bridge of Sighs and have some fruit gelato in the Piazza San Marco. They had worked for this trip for almost half a year, the three of them; she still couldn't have imagined then how the world would turn on its head. Forget Venice now, be with 'Suzanne,' give your whole self to the song. But what if Idan and Adi managed to arrange to sleep together in Venice – I mean, with the same host, I mean, in neighboring rooms?

The thought chokes her. She falls silent in the middle of a word and simply stands mute. The guitar on the tape recorder continues alone, accompanying 'Suzanne' without Suzanne. Tamar shuts down the stereo and collapses to the stone flowerpot. She is sitting with her head between her hands. People look at her for another moment, then shrug and start to scatter, wrapping themselves up in the street's skin of estrangement and indifference. Only one older woman, moving heavily, wearing poor clothes, approaches her: 'Girl, are you sick? Have you had anything to eat today?' Pity and concern are in her eyes, and Tamar works to try and squeeze out a small smile. 'I'm okay, I got a little dizzy.' The woman digs through her purse, searching between used bus tickets – Tamar doesn't understand what she's looking for in there. She pulls out a few shekel coins and puts than by her side on the flowerpot. 'Take it, sweetie. This is from me – get something to eat. You shouldn't live this way.' Tamar looks at the money. The woman seems a lot poorer than she is. She feels like a liar, feels that she's taken advantage of the woman. She disgusts herself.

But then she remembers she's here on a mission, in a show she is writing – and directing, and acting in. Above all, she hopes, with all her heart, that someone is watching her from the side and sees exactly what she wants to show him. The girl in the show has to take the coins left on the flowerpot, count them, put them in her bag, and smile to herself in relief, because now she will have money to buy food.

Dinka lays her head on Tamar's knees and looks into her eyes. Her big, doggy, motherly head. Oh, Dinka, Tamar cries in her heart, I don't have the courage to do this. I am not capable of giving myself up like this, to strangers. Enough, Dinka exhales into Tamar's palm, *phumph* – first off, there is nothing you can't do. And second, could you please remind me who was the only one from the whole class who took her shirt off during the closing number of *Hair* at the end of the year, in front of the whole audience? Tamar is embarrassed – it was different there, how can I explain it to you? Dinka lifts her eyebrows a little, her face mocking and inquisitive. Tamar gets annoyed – even you don't understand. Then, it was exactly the posture of the frightened, the arrogance of the shy, the deliberateness of those who are scared of their own shadow; it's always like that, you know – those 'slalom passes,' as Shai calls them. And I no longer have strength for them . . . Then make a pass like that here, as well, Dinka decrees, decisively shaking her head away from Tamar's hold. Show them the arrogance of the shy – give them that slalom. And what if they laugh at my singing,

Tamar begs, what will happen if I blow it again? Who will want me?

But they both know that her greatest fear is what would happen if she succeeded, if her plan came to pass and brought her closer, step by step, to those who are supposed to capture her.

'Come on,' Tamar says, suddenly full of shaky bravado. 'Let's show them who we are.'


At two in the afternoon, exactly four weeks after Tamar's failed premiere, Assaf left the convent; the sun attacked him, and he felt like someone who, for a long time, had been in another, very distant world. Theodora escorted him to the stairs descending from her room and urgently insisted he find Tamar, and quickly. He had a lot more questions to ask her, but understood that she would not give him any more details about Tamar, and he no longer had the patience to remain there, in the close room.

His body was tense and electric, and he didn't know why. Dinka trotted by his side, glancing at him with curiosity every once in a while. Perhaps dogs smell these things, he thought. They smell nervousness. He started running. And she woke to him and ran by his side. He loved running. Running calmed him down; he liked to think while he ran. His gym teacher had tried to convince him on more than one occasion to participate in track meets; he said that Assaf had the breath and the pulse and, mainly, the endurance to qualify for the team. But Assaf didn't like the tension of competition. Not only because of the rivalry with boys he didn't know, but also because he didn't like to do things in front of an audience. It was funny – in the 60-meter run, he was always among the last (the teacher called it 'late ignition'); but in a 2,000-meter run and, even better, the 5,000, he had no competitors, not even among the seniors. 'The moment you have it, you have it, eh? All the way to the end. Guaranteed.' His teacher once said that, admiringly; Assaf treasured that little sentence in his heart like a medal.

He now started feeling that all the running he had been doing was finally turning into *it*, the right running, well tuned and beautifully paced. He ran, and his thoughts became clearer; he somehow knew he had unintentionally been trapped in a little whirlpool – nothing really dangerous, but still, he had apparently entered into a zone of compressed reality – electrified and highly charged.

They ran side by side, relaxed, easy running – the rope hung loose between them, and Assaf was almost tempted to let go of it completely. He thought this was the first time they had run together like this, like a boy with his dog – he glanced aside and saw her there, her tongue hanging out, her eyes shining, and her tail erect. He adjusted his steps to match hers, and was filled with warmth at the pleasure of his new synchronicity with her. He could imagine that she, too, felt this way, that she knew they were companions in a journey. He smiled to himself; there was something in it that he hadn't known for years, that he had already forgotten to yearn for – something like friendship.

But when he thought again about the girl, Tamar, his temporary peace of mind deserted him, and his pace lengthened. Every new thing he discovered about her, every little fact, every minor detail, seemed, for some reason, immense to him, full of hidden meanings. (Dinka, surprised, hurried after him.) Since the morning, from the moment he had first heard about her, he felt a new being forcibly trying to push itself into his life and cling to it at all costs, send roots down into it. Actually, Assaf didn't really like such surprises; usual, daily life seemed too full of the unexpected as it was. Besides, he remembered, suddenly worried all over again, glancing at his watch, he was supposed to dedicate a little time to his private affairs and figure out how he would get Roi off his back. Plus, he really had no intention of running around half of Jerusalem chasing down some anonymous girl to whom he had no connection and never would. What business of his was her life, anyway? He knew about her only by a strange coincidence, and if you think about it, at least he knew Dafi and didn't have to learn about and get used to her faults. This new girl, whose dog

really is very cute, who likes pizza with cheese and olives . . .
He couldn't remember how this train of thought began.

Suddenly Dinka passed him and started running faster. He
didn't understand what had happened; he lifted his head and
looked around and couldn't see what she was chasing – he
was the only person running on the street. But he had already
learned to count on her senses and guessed that she probably
saw or smelled something that was hidden to him. It was as if
a powerful internal engine had ignited – she made sharp turns
down streets and into alleys, and burst into Ha'atzmaut Park,
through bushes and grass; she ran like a storm, her big ears
pushed back by the wind. Assaf flew after her and marveled
again at a dog's sense of smell, the way she was capable of sens-
ing a person without using her eyes. He also wondered what,
exactly, he would say once Dinka led him to this person.

'Gotcha!' somebody said behind him, leaped on his back
forcefully, and pushed him to the ground, hard.

Assaf was so shocked that for a long moment he just lay
there, unmoving, not thinking. He could feel the man on top
of him twisting his hand behind him and almost breaking it
– and only then did he yell.

'Go ahead, yell,' said the man, sitting on his back. 'You'll
cry soon, too.'

'What do you want from me?' Assaf moaned in pain. 'What
did I do to you?'

The man pushed his head hard into the ground – dirt got
into his mouth and nose, and he felt his forehead scratching
against something until it bled. Two strong fingers pressed
hard against the sides of his cheeks and forced his mouth
open; immediately after that, other fingers invaded his mouth,
searching for something, then leaving. Assaf lay stunned. He
saw ants running around in front of him, and a cigarette butt;
everything was enlarged.

Then some paper or a formal ID was shoved under his
nose. He crossed his eyes, but couldn't see anything, it was
too close. His eyes were blurred by tears. The guy who was
sitting on his back grabbed Assaf by the hair and pulled his
head back painfully and shoved the paper under his nose again.

Assaf thought his eyes were going to pop out of his sockets and vaguely saw the photo of a smiling, dark-skinned guy on a police badge. He was relieved for a moment, but only for a moment.

'Get up! On your feet, you're under arrest.'

'Me? What for, what did I do?'

Assaf's other hand was then twisted back behind him, and he heard a click he knew only from the movies – handcuffs. He was handcuffed. His mother would die.

'What did you do?' A low murmur of laughter behind him. 'Soon you'll tell us *exactly* what you did, you little shit. Up. Get up.'

Assaf tucked his head as far as he could between his shoulders and was silent. His guts were going crazy, he was afraid he'd shit his pants. He suddenly lost all his energy. (It always happened that way to him: when someone spoke so rudely to him, or anyone else, his will to live would evaporate for a moment. It was as if he would run out of himself, losing any passion for existence, when people spoke like that.) Dinka, on the other hand, was full of fighting spirit. She stood at a distance and barked with all her strength, in a terrible rage, but didn't dare come closer.

'I said, up on your feet!' the man roared, and grabbed him by the hair again. Assaf had to get up. His hair was almost pulled out by the roots – the sharp pain again brought big tears into his eyes. The man went through Assaf's pockets, searched in his shirt as well, and quickly patted him down over his back and between his legs, searching for something – a weapon, maybe, or something else. He was so frightened he didn't dare ask the man anything.

'Tell the world goodbye,' the man murmured. 'Go on, move your ass, and if you try anything funny, if you act up at all, I'll crush you right here. Got it?' He took a little walkie-talkie out and called for a police car. With that, he pushed Assaf to the park's exit.

Assaf walked, handcuffed, through the streets of Jerusalem. He lowered his head and prayed that none of the people watching him now knew him or his parents. If only his hands had been cuffed in the front, he could raise his shirt to hide his face like the suspects on television. Dinka followed them, and every once in a while burst into a series of raging barks; each time, the man threw curses at her and threatened her with kicks. Assaf still couldn't believe that he was really a policeman, because of his violent hatred for him and Dinka.

But he was a detective, and he walked Assaf, as if he were leading a slave procession, all the way to the police car waiting by the parking lot of Agron Street. The police car drove them to the station in Migrash haRusim; the two policemen spoke with the detective who caught him. 'I recognized the little shit right away,' the detective bragged, 'because of the dog. The orange collar. They thought they could fool me.'

When they arrived at the station, the detective took him into a side room. JUVENILE INVESTIGATION was written in blue marker on the door. The room had very thick walls, and Assaf thought, This is so no one will be able to hear my screams when he tortures me. But the detective left him in there with Dinka and locked the door.

There was a metal desk in the room, two chairs, and one long bench by the wall. Assaf stumbled to the bench and sat on it. He had to go to the bathroom, but there was no one to tell. A big fan was moving slowly on the ceiling. Assaf forced himself to think about the child riding a camel in the Sahara Desert. The thought tried to escape him, but Assaf focused, with all his powers, on the child riding the camel: at this very moment, in the great Sahara Desert, in vast spaces without end or horizon, a huge camel procession moves slowly forward (he usually took his ideas for these thoughts from the National Geographic channel). Toward the end of the line, a little boy sits on one of the camels, swaying and bobbing with the camel's rhythm. His face is covered because of the dust storms; only his eyes peer out, examining the land before him. What does he see? What's going through his head? Assaf swayed with him on the camel, surrounded himself with the silence of the desert. He could always escape there, even within the noise of the drill at the dentist. And not only there: right now, an Icelandic deck boy is sailing over the North Sea on a huge gray fishing boat; he spent the whole morning washing the remains of dead fish from the deck, and now he leans over the metal railing, watching the icebergs rising like mountains above the ship. Does he like those long voyages? Is he afraid of the captain? When will he see his home again? Assaf focused on them – he didn't exactly know how it helped him calm down, but it always worked, kind of like his discussion groups on the Internet, but without any direct connection to anyone. It was as if all those lonely people scattered throughout the world, in some mysterious way, created a secret net, transferring strength to one another in times of need. Like now. At least the shameful storm in his belly had subsided. He straightened up a bit. It would be fine. His mother was rubbing his back softly, caressing him, reminding him that everything would be all right, that in her secret contract with God it clearly stated that he would always, always be fine. He even managed to smile at Dinka. It will be fine, you'll see. Dinka stood up, and in an ancient movement, whose history is as long as the history of the friendship between man and dog but was completely new to the two of them, came and laid her head on his knees and looked into his eyes.

He couldn't even pet her, with his hands cuffed behind his back.

Tamar gets up from the stone flowerpot and stands, silent and trapped in thought. It seems, for a moment, as if she has stolen away to a far place, and her eyes grow even bigger and are gazing into the air. Only those who believe in supernatural things would say that lightning passed through her brain in that instant and that, without understanding it, she was seared by a strange, vague prophecy: soon, four weeks from today, she would lose her Dinka, and the dog would later be found searching through the streets frantically, and one boy, a stranger, would follow her, step by step, over the entire face of Jerusalem.

One moment of fog, and the sharp flash in its depths, and then Tamar blinks and smiles with her eyes at Dinka, and forgets. Now she only hopes that no one will remember the last few embarrassing moments. She rewinds the tape and finds the accompaniment she is looking for, listens to the opening notes, moves the tape player so its sound has as wide a reach as possible.

Because here is that moment again when the exodus must come, the deviation from the mass, that is, she has to detach herself from the flowing anonymity, the daily, nervous, protective anonymity of the street. She simply has to be exceptional, and look – you're surrounded by dozens of indifferent people, and the smells of the shwarma being cut, and the fat dripping into the fire, the shouts of the vendors in the bazaar above you, and the squeaking accordion of the Russian who perhaps used to be someone just like you, a kid in some conservatory in Moscow or Leningrad, and perhaps he, too, had a teacher who called his parents in for a meeting and lacked the words to express her excitement. She lifts her head and chooses a point of focus in the space around her. It's not a Renoir painting hung in the rehearsal hall, and not a chandelier with golden filigree that probably hangs in the Pergola. It is a little sign announcing VARICOSE VEINS CURED IN THREE MONTHS, GUARANTEED! She likes this, of all things. It suits her now. So she closes her eyes and sings to it:

> The water is wide; I cannot get o'er,
> And neither have I wings to fly.
> Give me a boat that will carry two,
> And both shall row, my love and I.

She can feel how the street splits in two, even without opening her eyes; it isn't split by its length or width, but into the street that existed before she sang, and afterward. She has the clear, confident sense that she doesn't have to look – her skin feels it: people are slowly stopping where they stand. Some of them turn around and return, hesitatingly, to the place where the voice is coming from. They stand. They listen. They forget themselves in her voice.

Of course, many don't slow down, and don't even notice any change in the din of the street – they go, they come back, they are burdened and embittered. An alarm whines in one of the stores. A beggar woman passes by, pushing an old baby stroller with whistling wheels. The window cleaner on a ladder at the second-floor window of the Burger King doesn't stop his circling motions; but still, with every moment, another person joins the circle around her. One row of people already surrounds her, and another is gathering; Tamar feels herself in a double embrace. The circle is moving in an unconscious, unnoticed motion, a huge creature with tens of legs; the people are turning their backs to the noise and protecting her from the street. They stand in different positions, leaning forward slightly; someone accidentally lifts his eyes and meets the gaze of the person standing next to him. They smile for a moment, and a complete conversation passes through that tender smile. Tamar notices all this, but vaguely. She understands the looks in their eyes from previous performances she's had with the chorus, the good ones: that look of someone remembering something he used to have and lost, that he would like to be worthy of again.

> Down in the meadows the other day
> A-gathering flowers both fine and gay,
> A-gathering flowers both red and blue,
> I little thought what love can do.

She finishes with a barely heard note – stretching like a thread becoming thinner and thinner, weaving into the mad swell of the wheel of life surrounding her, becoming stronger again now that her song is fading. Those standing around her clap their hands eagerly. One or two sigh deeply. Tamar doesn't move. Her neck is flushed, her eyes silently, soberly alight. She stands, and her hands are pulled down by the sides of her body. She wants to leap in joy and relief, because she did it, and she was so close to giving up. But even now, she remembers that singing is not what brought her here. It was depressing to remember that singing was only the instrument, the bait. No, that's wrong – Tamar herself is the bait. She looks around, her eyes shining and full of gratitude, but also inspecting. She scans the crowd – from the first glance, it seems to her that not one of the many people around her is the one who was supposed to swallow the bait that is her.

Now she realizes that in her agitation before the performance she forgot to put out her hat for the money; and she has to bend over in front of everyone in her uncomfortable overalls and search through her bag, and of course clothes and underwear pour out of it, and Dinka insists on shoving her nose in the bag and sniffing through it. By the time Tamar finds her beret – until about a year ago she loved to wear hats – until Idan told her what he thought about hats – almost all her audience has scattered.

But some stay, and they approach her, some confidently, some shyly, and put coins into her wrinkled hat.

Tamar hesitates over whether she should stay here and sing some more. She knows she can, she has the courage – she even feels the desire to continue singing, a familiar feeling of conquest and greatness that possessed her from about the middle of the song, but with a power she never knew singing in closed concert halls. Whoever knew that her voice was really so big?

She also knows that if the man or one of his messengers was around, she would feel his presence. He would already be standing somewhere in one of the outer rows of the circle that had gathered around her, looking her over, the way you inspect innocent, unworried prey, calmly considering how to trap it.

She was standing in the heart of a waterfall of golden sunshine. Tamar shivered, gathered up the money from her hat, and started to move away with Dinka. A few people tried to talk to her. One boy raised her hopes; he wouldn't let go of her, there was something cruel and rough in the line of his mouth, and for a moment she stopped to listen to him attentively. But when she realized he was only trying to pick her up, she shook him off and went on her way.

She sang five more times that day – once in front of Hamashbeer, twice near Gerar Behar Center, and another two times in Tziyyon Square. She added a new song every once in a while, but made sure never to sing more than three at a time. She refused to sing more, even when the applause was hearty, the reactions enthusiastic. She had a goal, and when she finished singing and the thing she was expecting didn't happen, she turned off her tape player, collected her money, and tried to disappear. The main thing had been accomplished: now people will talk about her. She scattered herself like a rumor. She couldn't do more than that, only hope that soon, quickly, the rumor would reach the ears of the man she was waiting for – her predator.

He closed his eyes, leaned on the wall; the ceiling fan squeaked in a regular rhythm, and outside, people came and went: policemen, criminals, ordinary citizens. Assaf didn't know how long they would keep him in here like this, and when, if ever, they would come to look after him. Dinka lay by his feet on the cool floor. He got off the wooden bench and sat beside her on the floor, leaned against the wall. They both closed their eyes.

Immediately Theodora's voice swarmed around him, and he dove into it, searched for comfort in it; he was still quite confused by the agitated leaps between her stories, between times and countries and islands. But he remembered quite well how she had sat, bent over and introspective, after she'd finished her story; she seemed, to him, like an old, gnarled root. His heart felt pity for her. If she were his grandmother, he would probably get up and hug her without thinking twice.

'But I lived,' she told him, as if she was responding to his soul's movement toward her. 'In spite of everything, hear me now, Assaf, I have lived this life!' When she saw the doubt in his eyes, she banged on the table and fumed, 'No, my dear! Please remove this look!' She rose slightly out of her chair in anger, and emphasized every word with care: 'On that first night after I learned of the terrible fate of Lyxos, when the dawn came and I saw that I had not died of agony or loneliness, I decided to live!'

She was only a girl of fourteen then, but she understood her situation clearly and, above all, with no self-pity. The past had vanished behind her, and no known future awaited her. She knew no one, not here or anywhere else. She knew nothing about the country she lived in, and she didn't speak the local language. Assaf thought perhaps her belief in God must have helped her, but she explained to him that she never had believed very deeply in God – even less so after the disaster. She had a big, empty house, a generous monthly pension coming in from a bank in Greece, and a harsh oath she knew she would never break, if for no other reason than out of respect for the dead who had sent her here.

'This was my situation,' she told him, dryly and restrained. 'I had to decide, on my own, what my fate would be, from that moment and for the rest of my life.' She stood up and paced around the room; she finally stopped behind him and laid her hands on the back of the chair. 'I decided completely. Do you hear me? If I was destined never to emerge from this house and into the world, I would bring the world into it.'

So she did. She ordered the convent's servant in those days, Nasrian's father, to go out and buy every book in Greek he could find. He found mainly old sacred scriptures in the cellars of Greek churches, and they didn't interest her much. So, on her fifteenth birthday, she gave herself a present: she hired a private Hebrew tutor and started studying both ancient and modern Hebrew with him. She was quick to learn and hungry for knowledge, and after four months of studying with Mr Eliasaf, she started buying books from Hans Flueger's Book Merchants, books about the land of Israel, the country in which she had so unwillingly arrived and in which she was imprisoned. She learned everything the books could teach her about the Arabs and the Jews and the Christians living with her in the same city, so near, yet completely invisible. When she was sixteen, she hired another private tutor for Arabic, literary and conversational, and read the Koran and *The Arabian Nights* with him. The booksellers in the Orthodox neighborhood of Mea Shearim started sending her wooden crates full of books of the Mishnah and Talmud, and their interpreters. These didn't interest her much, but sometimes, at the bottom of the crate, she would discover a non-kosher, forbidden book about scientific inventions or the lives and habits of ants, or about some famous painter from the sixteenth century, and she would devour it hungrily. When these scraps no longer satisfied her, she started purchasing old, torn copies of books from the Dr Hugo Bergman Zionist Library. She also paid Eliezer Weingerten, a book distributor, very generously, so he would immediately pass on to her every book about the new subjects her heart was so drawn to: the Napoleonic Wars, inventions and scientific developments, astronomy, the days of prehistoric man, and the travelogues of well-known adventurers.

It wasn't easy, of course: she had to learn how to match the words she read to so many things she'd never seen with her eyes: what, for example, is a 'telescope'? What is the 'North Pole'; what are 'germs' and 'opera,' 'airport' and 'basketball'? 'Can you believe it – that only at the age of eighteen did I learn of New York, and who Shakespeare was?' Her face wrinkled in wonder, and then she whispered, as if only to herself, 'Not for fifty years, since I first entered this house, have I seen a rainbow with my own eyes.'

When she was nineteen, she bought the Mikhlal, the youth encyclopedia; others came after it, in three languages, dozens of volumes – but Theodora never forgot the waves of intoxication flooding her during that joyous six months as she read, day and night, entry by entry, the whole of creation.

After this period, she became possessed by a great lust for knowledge, above all, of the present, especially world politics. Every morning she sent Nasrian's father to buy a newspaper in Hebrew and a newspaper in Arabic, and she read them, with a dictionary and gritted teeth; this is how she became acquainted with David Ben-Gurion and the ruler of Egypt, Gamal Abdel Nasser. She learned that smoking causes lung cancer, and excitedly followed, together with the rest of the world's citizens, the process of educating Rajib, the Indian child who had been raised by wolves until the age of nine. Slowly, with great effort, she started cutting a path through the bush of facts and new names, to picture the world, but above all, to beat down her ignorance, the ignorance of a girl from a tiny cycladian island, the tiniest and most forgotten in the island chain around Delos.

'And still,' she told Assaf, and her fingers rested above her eyebrows as if she was pressing down a headache that had started to emerge, 'for all the happiness that it brought me, I was sad, and filled with longing – because it all was words and only more words!'

Assaf gazed at her, not understanding what she meant. So she, as whenever she was impatient, slapped her hand against the table. 'And how do you explain green and purple and burgundy to someone who is blind – *now* do you understand?' He nodded. But he still wasn't sure – 'So I was, *agori mou*: licking the peel, but never biting into the fruit itself . . . What, for instance, does a baby smell like after its bath? What does a man feel when a fast train passes in front of his face? How do the hearts of all the people sitting in a theater for a magnificent play beat together?' He now started to grasp what she was saying: her world was made entirely of words, descriptions, written characters, dry facts. His mouth opened a bit, with a wondering smile: why, this is exactly what his mother had warned him would happen if he spent all his time in front of the computer.

'You know, in those days, I also established the Republic of the Mail, right here in this room,' and she told him about the correspondence she had been maintaining for over forty years, with scholars and philosophers and writers from all over the world. At first she sent them simple questions, ashamed of her ignorance and apologizing for her nerve. In time her questions began deepening, widening; and the answers became more detailed, personal, and heartfelt. 'And besides my professors, you should know, I also correspond with quite a few innocent life prisoners, like me.' And she showed him a photo of a Dutch woman who was wounded in a terrible accident and bedridden for the rest of her life, and all she saw were a few branches of a chestnut tree and a part of a stone wall; and also a photo of a Brazilian man, who was so fat he could no longer pass through his bedroom door, and from his window, he saw the shore of a small lake (but not the water); and an old peasant from Northern Ireland, whose son is serving a life sentence in England, so he imprisoned himself of his own volition in one room, until his son went free; and many, many others.

'I correspond regularly with seventy-two people in the world,' she said with modest pride. 'Letters come and go. I write to every one of them at least once a month, and they write to me, and tell me everything about themselves – even their most intimate secrets . . .' She laughed and her eyes shone slyly. 'They must think, a little old nun sitting at the top of a tower in Jerusalem – who could she tell?'

Only after many years of reading and study and research did it occur to her that she never had had the privilege of reading even a single children's book – young Nasrian (who had already replaced his father, whose legs had grown old) started visiting the appropriate shelves in the bookstores. She read *Pinocchio* for the first time at the age of fifty-five, and *Winnie-the-Pooh* and *Lobengulu, Zulu King*. They weren't her own childhood, nor were they set in the landscapes in which she had grown up, but her childhood was submerged in the depths of the sea and she could never bear to return to it. One night she laid her hands on *The Wind in the Willows*, and whispered to herself with amazement and joy, 'There. My childhood has just now been born.'

'By the way, you should know' – she laughed – 'that until that moment there was not even a single wrinkle on me! I had the face of a baby until I started to read those books!'

Now that she had a childhood, she had to start her adolescence, so she read novels like *David Copperfield*, *The Demon from the Seventh Grade*, and *Daddy Long Legs*. The iron door that had been slammed in her face on the island now reopened, and Theodora, an old, knowledge-hungry girl, entered her sleeping, cobwebbed halls: her soul, her body, passion, yearning, love; everything came alive as she delved into the stories, and sometimes, after a night of feverish reading, she would drop the book she was reading and feel how her soul rose and swelled within her like milk boiling in a pot. 'During those hours,' she told Assaf almost inaudibly, 'I would almost plead for a single pinprick of salvation, to pierce the burden, the damned skin of words wrapped about me.'

'That was Tamar?' Assaf asked without thinking, in an epiphany he immediately regretted, because Theodora practically shook, as if he had carelessly touched her in her soul's depths.

'What? What did you say?' She stared at him for a long moment. 'Tamar? Yes, perhaps, who knows ... I never thought of it ...' But something curled up inside her, as if Assaf had been taunting her deliberately, explicitly telling her: You brought everything books could teach you, with words and letters, into your room, and suddenly a flesh-and-blood girl burst in, strong, alive, dynamic.

'Enough.' She shook herself. 'We have spoken enough, my dear, and perhaps you should have left already.'

'I still don't understand something: she –'

'Go find her, and then will you understand everything.'

'But explain!' He almost slammed the table like her. 'What do you think happened to her?'

Theodora took a deep breath, hesitated for a moment, and then said, 'How can I tell you without telling you . . .' She got up, uneasy, and began to pace, glancing at him every once in a while, scrutinizing him the way she had in the first moments of their meeting, to see whether he was worthy of hearing and knowing, whether he was trustworthy. 'Listen, this may be just the nonsense of an old foolish woman.' She sighed. 'But the last few times she came to me, she was already speaking of different things. Bad things.'

'Like what?' Uh-oh, Assaf thought, here it comes.

'She would say that the world is not good,' she said, and

planted her hands on her bosom. 'The world is rotten at its core, and you cannot trust anyone, not even those closest to you; everything revolves around power and fear, self-interest and evil, and that she does not fit.'

'Doesn't fit what?'

'Here. In the world.'

Assaf was silent. He remembered the bold girl on the barrel, the girl who he was certain was arrogant and mocking – but she is also a little like me, he thought with wonder, and took her off the barrel, gently.

'I would tell her the opposite: how, on the contrary, her life will be good and beautiful; she will love somebody, and he will love her, and they will have children with joyful faces; she will travel the world and meet interesting people, and sing on stages, in concert halls; they will cheer . . .'

The words grew cold in her mouth, she sank into herself again, trapped. What does she know, Assaf thought with compassion – she herself doesn't know of any of these things she's promised Tamar, closed up in this house for fifty years – what does she know?

He remembered the disappointment and heartbreak on her face when he came here and she saw he was not Tamar; he knew, for certain, how important Tamar was to her – no, not only important: necessary, like water and bread, the flavor of life.

'And most recently – nothing. I no longer knew what was happening. She did not open her heart as she once had; she came, and worked, and sat with me, but didn't speak. She sighed often. She was keeping a secret from me. I do not know what is happening to her, Assaf . . .' Her eyes and the tip of her nose reddened all of a sudden. 'She became thinner, and lost her light. No longer was there light in her beautiful eyes.' She lifted her face to him, and he was shocked to see a thin line of tears in her wrinkles. 'What do you say, my dear? Will you find her? Will you?'

\*     \*     \*

At nine in the evening she bought two pitas of Jerusalem Mix and a Coke, and sat at the entrance to an office building to eat. She gave Dinka one portion and devoured the other. They both delighted in the food, inhaled and exhaled and eventually sighed together, satiated. Tamar licked her fingers and thought that it had been a long time since she had enjoyed a meal the way she'd enjoyed this one, bought with the money she earned by singing.

Later, the thoughts returned. People hurried by her, and she tried to shrink into a little anonymous bundle. Now she wanted time to turn backward, so she could be the Tamar of a year ago, a year and a quarter; to lie on her stomach on her bed, surrounded by the stuffed animals that had been with her since birth and clutch the phone receiver between her shoulder and ear, her legs swaying and crossing behind her back – the girls in the movies did that, and so did she; she finally had somebody to do that with – and it was such a pleasure to lie there and talk to Adi about Galit Adlitz, who was seen kissing Tom, with tongue and everything; or about Leanna, from chorus, who agreed to go steady when some boy from Boyer High School asked her. From Boyer, imagine! Not an artist! And they were both properly shocked by it, confirming to each other, in this way, their mutual loyalty to art, meaning, to Idan.

An old man, leaning on a cane, dressed with old-fashioned elegance, slowly passed by and saw her – his lips wriggled in amazement, like a fish. She saw herself in his eyes: a too-young girl at a too-late hour, in the wrong place.

She cradled herself as closely as she could. The day had been long and exhausting, her first day on the street, but she had to get up and make a few more rounds, so if anyone had noticed her and had been tracking her from afar, he could approach her again, under cover of the dark.

More than a few approached. All the time, people talked to her, making remarks and suggestions – she had never been so soiled by so much obscenity, by such abrasive anonymity. She quickly learned that she must not answer – not say even one word, just hold on to her bag and big tape player and keep walking. Dinka, of course, helped keep harassers away, because when she growled from her gut, even the boldest of men would suddenly evaporate.

But the one she was waiting for, the one of whom she was most frightened, did not come.

She went down to the market Jerusalemites call Ha-khatulot Square and passed between the booths, lit with spotlights, secretly caressing the heavy hangers of harem pants and Indian shirts. She loved the square, even though Idan and Adi had deemed it nothing more than a 'poor man's Piccadilly.' Her hips would begin to sway in a different, elaborate rhythm when she walked through the booths with hookahs and exotic oils and colorful stones. She tried on the Bukharan caps, and the fat vendor teased her about her pointy, Ashkenazi head; one boy, a world-class expert (so he said), offered to write her name on a grain of rice, and she said her name was Brunhild. A beautiful young man in shorts with a turban on his head sat on the ground, holding the smooth leg of a girl in his hand, gently painting on it a henna tattoo. Tamar stood and watched, a little envious. She pulled herself together and walked away, passed once, and twice, through the booths, inhaling the thin smell of incense and the clouds of weed that billowed up here and there. She pretended to be deeply interested in the candle booth, in all the shapes and colors, hoping that the slight shiver she'd been feeling in her back for the past few seconds was telling her that someone was inspecting her, but when she turned around, no one was there.

One street over, on Yoel Moshe Salomon, a performance was in progress: a girl, about her age, whose golden curls peeked out from her colorful knit cap, held two ropes in her hands. Burning wicks were attached to the ends of each rope, and she danced with them, crossing and sliding them against each other in long, round motions; another girl sat behind her, staring, leaning against the wall of a store, keeping a monotonous tempo going with a tambourine.

The girl was completely intent on the motion of the ropes, and Tamar couldn't keep walking, charmed by the girl's absolute concentration, which she understood so well. She also wanted to know what it looked like, what they see in you from the outside when you are entirely absorbed in yourself. What of yourself do you abandon to their eyes? The girl's eyes were blue and beautiful, and mulishly following the two little flames; her eyebrows quivered up and down with childish wonder, and Tamar thought they were similar in that way, she and the girl, because Tamar also 'sang with her eyebrows.' The two little flames crossed the night skies; there was something touching about them, so daring, so precarious. Tamar then remembered where she was and why; without moving, she cautiously and systematically glanced to the sides. She didn't know exactly whom she was looking for. She thought she was looking for a man, that was as much as she had been able to gather over the last month: it's a group of young men, very tough – one of them was supposed to approach her on the street and ask her to come with him, on the condition, of course, that she could first walk over the coals, meaning, prove she could capture an audience. Tamar knew she had passed that test. It was her only great achievement to date.

The rope girl's mouth fell open a little in self-forgetfulness, exposing her snow-white teeth. She started to increase the tempo, and the tambourine tempo increased as well. Tamar's eyes hopped from person to person; quite a few young men were standing there, but she couldn't decide if any one of them was eyeing her differently, with some significance. Two small punks with spiked hair suddenly jumped out from the audience in front of the performer and started yelling right in her face; they weren't even yelling words, just barking rudely, like animals. It distracted the girl for a moment – and the two ropes got twisted and sank to the ground, ashamed. The girl sadly took off her knit hat; her golden curls tumbled out in slow motion. She wiped her sweat and stood lost, as if she had been woken up from a dream. The audience gave a single, united sigh of disappointment and scattered. Not one of them gave her any money for all the effort she had made up until that moment. Tamar approached her and put a five-shekel coin, one that she earned that day, in the hat. The girl smiled at her, tired.

Up the street, Tziyyon Square was also crowded and full of life. Boys were skateboarding in the plaza below the bank. There was no chance of singing there, because the Breslevs showed up with huge speakers thundering Hasidic tunes from the roof of their car. Tamar sat in a corner by the bank and curled up, all eyes, hugging Dinka closer to her. Dozens of boys and girls were running around; some kind of unpleasant fuss and buzz emanated from them, a mechanical hum as they stretched out in lines all over the square, as if they were zooming along invisible rails. They went, they came back – they were looking for something urgently. Some of them stood by the railings, talking tersely to a bearded guy. She saw the dwarf with the thick hips and the cheerful woolen cap, almost hidden by a group that surrounded him: hands touched pockets, concealing fingers closed over something. A tall boy in denim overalls like hers, but wearing nothing underneath, approached her. 'Sister,' he said, and knelt in front of her so that he was level with her face. He had a nipple ring. 'H. I've got H.' She shook her head emphatically, no, no – she was set for the first week – and he didn't make a big deal out of it, stood up and moved on. She shrank, shocked, not by what he said to her, but by what he had called her.

She closed her eyes hard and opened them, and the square was still there. The Breslev Hasidim were dancing in the center of it: seven grown men with long hair and flying beards, in snow-white clothes and big white yarmulkes. She already knew from her previous nights here that they would dance like that until midnight, with continuous leaps of madness and heated passion. Two voluptuous young women in scanty T-shirts passed by her, their arms linked, and stopped to watch. 'Look at them,' one of the girls said. 'And they're like that without Ecstasy – they're on faith.' Dinka pushed closer to her. Suffering terribly from the noise, she turned her back to the square, cradled by Tamar's bosom, and tried to fall asleep. Poor Dinkush, Tamar thought. She doesn't understand what I'm doing. This must be a nightmare for her.

A young woman approached her, holding a thermos and a plastic cup. She asked Tamar if she wanted tea. Tamar didn't understand this unexpected tenderness, it sounded like someone speaking in a foreign language. The woman crouched down and sat by her on the sidewalk. 'There are cookies, too,' she said with a smile. A new thought made Tamar sit up suddenly. Her heart started beating. Perhaps her predator was actually a predatress; she'd heard rumors that quite a few girls were in the business, too. But this woman really wanted to help her. She said she was from a group of volunteers that come to make contact with, and just be there for, the kids in the square. She poured hot tea for Tamar, who wrapped her two cold hands around the cup. An almost embarrassing wave of gratitude rose in her. She ate a cookie, too, and refused to talk. The woman patted Dinka, scratching her just the way she liked, and gave her a cookie as well. 'I've seen you here before,' the woman remembered. 'About two weeks ago?' Tamar nodded. 'I also saw when you bought from that guy, the short one, and I saw how the undercover cop chased you. Tell me, do you think you might want to meet someone who's already been through this?' Tamar withdrew into herself – the last thing she needed was to be saved from the streets when she hadn't yet managed to get onto the streets.

'I'm giving you our phone number,' the woman said, writing it on a napkin. 'If you want to talk, or you need any help, or want to meet with your parents at our place, we'll be there.' Tamar looked at her, and for a moment forgot herself in the good green eyes. She almost dared to ask whether she had seen a guy here in the square who played guitar, a guy with long, honey-colored hair that fell over his eyes, a very skinny and tall and terribly miserable guy. She didn't say a thing. The woman nodded, as if she had received some signal from Tamar but it hadn't got all the way through. Then she touched Tamar's arm lightly, smiled a real smile, and left. Tamar was alone again, and lonelier than before.

Not far from her a group of boys sat, beer cans in their hands, wearing only undershirts – how were they not cold? A stocky boy approached them – 'Hey, brother,' 'Hey, bro.' 'Anybody out here?' 'Go by the pool club, the Arab's around,' and they slapped their palms together and pulled in for a quick hug, their hands slapping twice on the other's back, one-two. Tamar watched them and carved it into her memory. He's been living in this world of body language for at least a year. That's probably how he speaks now. With what language would he speak to her? How would he treat her when he saw her?

And why isn't she joining one of the groups? Why is she paralyzed, trapped like this in the farthest corner of the square? At this stage in her plan, she had thought she would have somehow met up with a group of kids and perhaps found the place she was trying to reach through that group. From the outside, it looked so easy to join; especially if you were a girl, you just trailed along the margins of the group, and then they would start to notice you, and you'd talk, laugh a little, flirt a little, smoke something together, and that's it – you'd already be sucked in, and would crash with them at their squat in a public park or on some roof somewhere.

But it wasn't happening for her. Not today – maybe tomorrow. Maybe never. She couldn't join in yet. She pulled her knees into her stomach; the thoughts climbed over one another, stinging and biting her in exactly the place that hurt. Perhaps it was just her reserve with strangers, her thoughts whispered, she'd always had such a damned hard time bonding, mingling with others, compromising on a mutual language to share. 'You can call it snobbery,' she whispered suddenly, passionately, into Dinka's fur, 'the truth is, it's just my miserable soul. What do you think, that I don't want to connect with other people? I can't truly connect with anyone; it's how I was made. It's a fact. It's as if my soul lacks that part that can stick together, like a Lego piece that really sticks to someone else. Everything eventually falls apart for me. Back to zero. Family, friends, everything.'

The candy-apple man passed for the tenth time that night, offering her one, not giving up. He was old, with a yarmulke and a tired smile. 'Take it, only three shekels, it's healthy.' She said thank you and didn't take it. He stood still for a moment and watched her. What does he see in her – what do others see? A girl with a shaved head in overalls, with a backpack, a big tape player, and a dog. The casino had started operating for the night, over by the garbage cans: a skinny man in cutoff pants and a sailor's bowed legs turned a cardboard box over onto the trashcans and started shaking dice in a plastic cup. 'Who bets on the biggest seven? Who goes for seven times three?' She was shrinking with loneliness, more and more. She lashed into herself. You don't belong anywhere anymore, not at home, not with the chorus, not to the closest friends you ever had; one more minute and you'll disappear completely and no one will notice it. No, no, it's really better not to start doing this now. Look, Dinkush, it's not that I think they shouldn't have gone to Italy because of me, that's not it, because what could they do if they stayed here? She giggled, picturing Idan perched on the railings in the square, associating with these people – 'Hey, bro.' 'Whassup, man' – but it's the way they treated it from the first moment they knew. I only tried to mention it to them, to explain a bit – and the way that they both, together, immediately –

Obliterated me. She choked over these words in her throat; the Breslev Hasidim changed the tape. Now they were playing trance music, and danced to it like wild goats, hands and legs and beards waving in every direction. The music shook the ground she was sitting on. The square started to spin. A few boys and girls joined in the dancing now; they were fluent in this music. She tried to remember the short course she went through with the old albino – he looked at least forty to her – whom she had met at the Submarine two weeks ago: 'Acid is what you take for trance.' His shirt was open to his navel, exposing a smooth red chest that looked practically cooked. 'But E goes with house music, because the people who dance to it are more, like, upscale – there's lots of pose to it. And with techno, you'd want –' She couldn't remember what techno went with anymore. She mainly remembered his spongy hands, covered in fake-hippie silver rings, which stubbornly tried to climb onto her thigh.

The Breslev Hasid kids were running around, excited,

between the dancers. Another girl approached Tamar, sat next to her crosslegged and silent. She was wearing jeans and a home-knitted white sweater, but her sneakers were torn and her pupils too large. Tamar waited. Perhaps she was the one? Perhaps now, now it would begin. 'Can I?' the girl finally asked in a high-pitched voice, and started petting Dinka. And Tamar knew, she sensed it, that this girl was not one of *them*. She petted Dinka for a long time, as if it satisfied a craving; inhaled her scent and made noises of affection. For a few moments she abandoned herself wordlessly to Dinka. She then stood up heavily, and told Tamar, 'Thank you.' Her eyes were shining, and Tamar didn't know whether it was from joy or tears. She walked a few steps away and then returned. 'Me? I went out and worked the streets so I could get my dog out of the kennels in Shoafat,' she explained to Tamar in a voice that was completely childlike but slow and lingering. 'I made a hundred shekels, and went immediately to pull him out of Shoafat. A week later, he got run over by a car. Just like that, in front of my eyes' – and with that, she walked away.

Tamar hugged Dinka anxiously. She didn't want to stay there another moment, so she got up and walked away, but slowly; and when she reached the center of the square, she stood briefly, making herself as visible as she could. Perhaps it would happen now. Somebody would come up to her and tell her to follow him, and she wouldn't ask any questions and wouldn't argue. She would follow him obediently to whatever was waiting for her. The square was full of people, but nobody approached her. Crouched over by the railings, mumbling to himself, stood that curly-haired boy; he had been a guitar player once, and they'd broken his fingers. She remembered him in his last incarnation, playing accompaniment in a recital at the music academy. Now he came here almost every night and hung around on the edges of the groups. She heard a rumor that once, about a year and a half ago, he was the star player here, a musician of divine grace, their breaker of box office records, until he thought he'd get smart and run away. When he felt her looking at him, he slunk off, his shoulders pulled almost up to his ears. Tamar sighed to herself as she thought that now Shai had probably been the one to replace him.

She made it out of the illuminated, noisy square, and took a deep breath of relief. She squatted and pissed in a courtyard, between stacks of construction wood. Dinka stood watch. She smelled the warm steam coming up from between her legs. She looked at the wood planks, whitened by the moonlight and reflecting on the piles of trash. The sounds of the square reached all the way there. She stood, pulled her overalls up, and for a moment surrendered to the strangeness of the place, the iron cutting machine standing by the cement mixer, the two looking like a pair of giant bugs. How can a coward like me be *doing* this? she thought, surprised.

Now she only wanted to lie down and fall asleep and escape, even from herself. She wished she had someplace to wash, to scrub herself clean of the day. She hesitated for a moment: Leah had a place prepared for her, and she knew treats would be waiting there – some great meal packed away, still warm, with expensive chocolates for dessert; and probably a funny little letter, too, with a painting by Noiku, something that would restore to her some of her humanity. But Tamar had decided that morning that she would not go there. Everything, everything must be hers alone, only hers. Why? Because. What does Theo say? Don't inquire into matters beyond your comprehension. She walked more quickly. Her lips moved as she argued with herself: Just explain to me why you shouldn't go to Leah's storeroom. I don't know. Just so you won't put Leah in danger? No comment. Or maybe so you can believe even more than you already do that there is no one, no one in the world, you can count on except yourself?

She crossed King George Street and circled around and around the tall, crumbling building where her father's office was located. The streets seemed empty. She moved like a robot now. Went in, went down the stairs to the bottom floor, to the bomb shelter, and found the key she had hidden above the door frame. She opened the iron door. A thin mattress and light blanket waited there for her, and one more thing. She had laughed at herself when she brought it over last week, yet now she clung to it as if it could purify her. Her brown stuffed teddy bear, missing an ear, which she had slept with every night since she was born.

A key turned in the lock. Assaf leaped from the floor to the bench. The detective entered and saw his panicked jump, and Assaf immediately felt guilty for something. A handsome young woman in uniform entered with the detective. She told Assaf her name, Sigal or Sigalit – he didn't quite catch it – and added that she was a police investigator, with a special certification in adolescent counseling, and that she was going to have a conversation with him and the detective. She asked whether he would like a relative to be present during the interrogation, and Assaf almost yelped a terrified 'No!'

'Well then, let's begin,' said the investigator pleasantly. She looked again at the open file in front of her, asked Assaf a few general questions, wrote down his answers, and explained his rights in detail. At the end of every sentence, hers or his, she would smile at him, with a smile that split her face in two. Assaf wondered if her rule book said she was required to smile. Eventually she said, 'Perhaps we should first hear what Moti has to say to you.'

The detective, whose face clearly registered disgust at her touchy-feely manner, sat across the table noisily, spread his legs, and stuck his thumbs in his belt loops. 'All right,' he growled, 'spit it out – suppliers, dealers, amounts, kinds of dope, names. I want information and no bullshit. You got that?'

Assaf looked at the woman. He didn't understand a thing.

'Answer him, please,' said the investigator. She lit a cigarette and prepared to write down whatever he said in his file.

'But what did I do?' Assaf asked, and was embarrassed by how his voice almost curled into a whine.

'Listen, you little –' the detective started, but the woman cleared her throat, and he licked his upper lip quickly and clenched his jaw.

'Now listen to me carefully,' he said after a moment. 'I've been on this job for seven years. And I have a photographic memory, you ask anyone – and I saw your stinking dog, not a year ago, not two years ago, just under a month ago. There was a girl attached to it, maybe fifteen or sixteen, curly, big black hair, about a meter sixty, with a nice face, actually.' The detective was now speaking mainly to the investigator, undoubtedly trying to impress her with his photographic memory. 'I had her in my hands, in the middle of a deal with the dwarf in Tziyyon Square, and if it wasn't for that dog, that mo –'

Throat clearing. Lip licking. Deep breath.

'Now just look at this,' and he pulled his pants leg up, exposing a hairy, muscled calf with signs of a bite and stitches still clearly visible on him.

'To the bone. I've already gotten ten shots because of that dog, that motherfu – that stinking dog.'

Dinka barked in protest.

'Shut up, you stinking piece of shit,' the detective spat at her.

'But what did I do?' Assaf asked again. His focus was completely lost: a meter sixty? Meaning, about to his shoulder. Black hair and curls, and actually a nice face.

'*But what did I do?*' the detective imitated him, mockingly. 'You'll hear what you did: it's whatever you and her and the dog did. You're this close. This! Close!' The detective made a squinching motion with three of his fingers. 'What do you think, we're idiots? You will give me her name, immediately!' And he slammed both his hands on the table as hard as he could. Between his hands and his power at the table, Assaf jumped in fear.

'I don't know.'

'Don't know what?' The detective got up and paced around him in the room. Assaf watched nervously. 'You were just strolling along the street, no big deal, and saw this big, expensive dog, and just like that, it agreed to come with you for a walk?' Suddenly he jumped at Assaf, grabbed his shirt, and shook. 'Talk, motherfuck –'

'Moti!' the woman shouted, and the detective loosened his grip. He gave her a bitter look and shut up, still bubbling with anger.

'Look, uh, Assaf,' the woman said in a polished voice, 'if you didn't do anything, why were you trying to escape?'

'I wasn't trying to escape. I didn't even know he was chasing me.'

The detective, Moti, spit out venomous laughter. 'Who is he kidding? I chased him through half of the city, and now he's giving me, "I didn't know!"'

'Then perhaps –' The investigator raised her voice over the boiling detective's. 'Will you tell us how exactly you got the dog from the girl? What do you think, Assaf?'

'I didn't get it from her, I don't even know her!' Assaf cried out from the bottom of his heart. The investigator pursed her lips in hesitation.

'But how can that be?' she asked again. 'Just tell me, you seem to be a reasonable kid. Do you really think we would believe that a dog like that just came up to you and let you take him by a leash? Would it let me? Would it let Moti?'

She gestured lightly toward Dinka, and Dinka gave her a furious growl.

'You see? You had better tell me the truth.'

The truth! How hadn't it occurred to him? Probably because of the fear and the pressure and the humiliation of the handcuffs, and more than anything – because of the feeling he knew from other places, that even if he wasn't really guilty, he would be punished, and justifiably, for *something*; even if he wasn't clear what it was for, something he had probably done sometime, and now it was time to be punished . . .

'In my shirt pocket.' He had no voice, and he said again, 'In my shirt pocket, look, there's a piece of paper.'

She looked at the detective, and he approved her approach with a nod. She searched and found the paper.

'What is this?' She read it, and read it again, and gave it to the detective. 'What is this?'

'From 76,' Assaf said, sucking power from the words. 'I have a summer job at City Hall. They found this dog, and

I was supposed to look for her owners.' He said owners, luckily, not letting slip the fact that he knew her name, the curly-haired owner's name.

The woman turned and looked at Moti. He chewed his lip vigorously.

'Call City Hall,' she ordered him. 'Now! From *this* phone!'

Assaf gave them the number, and told them to ask for Avraham Danokh. The detective dialed, his hands jerking violently. There was a silence. Assaf heard Danokh's sharp voice in the receiver.

The detective said he was a member of the Jerusalem police and that he had caught Assaf walking a dog in the center of the city. Danokh laughed his thin, bitter laugh and said a few words Assaf couldn't make out. Moti listened, filtered out a 'thank you,' and hung up. He looked at the wall sternly, his lips pursed.

'So, what are you waiting for,' the investigator scolded. 'Release him already!'

The detective turned Assaf around brutally. Assaf heard the sound he so yearned for, the sound of handcuffs being unlocked.

He massaged his wrists like they did in the movies (now he understood why).

'One minute,' Moti said. He tried to harden his voice, so they wouldn't see his defeat. 'Have you found anyone yet who knows her?'

'No,' Assaf lied easily. It didn't matter what she did, he wasn't going to turn Tamar in to this guy's hands.

'Listen, we really apologize for the misunderstanding,' the investigator said. She didn't look at him. 'Perhaps you want to get something to drink from the cafeteria? Do you want to call anyone? Your parents?'

'No, eh . . . yes, I want to call somebody.'

'Please do,' she said, giving him a real smile for a change. 'Dial nine first.'

Assaf dialed. The detective and the woman spoke in whispers. Dinka came and stood by him; her head barely touched his leg. With his free hand he scratched the fur on her head.

Someone picked up the phone on the other end; noise filled the receiver.

'Hallo,' a voice yelled.

Assaf yelled back: 'Rhino?'

The detective left the room. The investigator stared at the wall as if she wasn't listening.

'Who is it? Assaf? Is that you?' Rhino yelled, trying to be heard over the noise of the machines. 'What's up, my man?'

Just then, when he called him 'man,' Assaf suddenly found himself on the verge of a breakdown.

'Hey, Assaf, I can't hear you! Assaf? Are you there?' Rhino called him *A*-ssaf, with the emphasis on the first 'A,' which drove Reli crazy.

'Rhino, I . . . I'm a little . . . something happened . . . I need to talk to you.'

'Wait a minute.' Assaf heard him yell out to Rami, who worked for him, to turn off the metal sharpener.

'So where are you?' Rhino asked from the new silence.

'At the – it doesn't matter. I have to see you. Will you meet me at Sima's?'

'Now? I already had lunch.'

'I haven't.'

'Wait a minute – let me see . . .' Assaf heard him giving orders to his workers. From what he heard, he understood that of all the days he could have come to Rhino he had picked a busy one. He listened to the instructions and smiled: a bust of Herzl, a woman on a swan, three big Buddhas, and six statuettes that would be presented during the Israeli Academy Awards ceremony. 'Okay.' Rhino returned to him. 'I'll be there in fifteen minutes. Don't worry. And don't do anything stupid. I'm coming.'

A big weight started rolling off Assaf's chest.

'A friend of yours?' the investigator asked affectionately.

'Yes . . . Not exactly, a friend of my sister's . . . Never mind.' He had no intention of telling her the whole complicated story. She walked him outside; it was completely different to walk past the policemen and other officers as a free, innocent man.

'Tell me,' he asked her as they stood outside, before they parted. 'The detective, he said something about that girl being in the middle of a deal. I'm just curious – what deal?'

She squeezed the cardboard file she held close to her body and looked right and left; she was silent. Now that he was free, he could see that she was really pretty. It's not her fault, he thought, she was only doing her job.

'I'm not sure we should talk about that,' she finally said, with an apologetic smile.

'But it's important to me,' Assaf said, quietly and firmly. 'So I will at least know what he suspected me of doing.'

She looked profoundly at the pointed toes of her black shoes. At last she said, 'It had something to do with drugs. She was buying drugs from someone in the center of the city. Apparently it wasn't a small amount. But really, you didn't hear anything from me, you understand?'

She turned and left.

Assaf passed through the guard's booth and went down to Jaffa Street, walking slowly, thinking slow thoughts; everything stopped cold. All that running since morning, and Theodora's story, and the little excitements, all the tiny hopes that rose up, here and there, inside him, all his foolish illusions – he felt as if he had taken a punch in the stomach. Sometimes, when taking photographs, something like that would happen to him; he would take a shot of a man sitting on a bench, not noticing that far behind him there was an electric pole; only when he developed the picture would he see a huge pole rising out of the man's head.

And what a pole! Dinka was moving closer to him, carefully rubbing against his thigh. She seemed ashamed to him, because of her relationship to Tamar. 'Dinka,' he said quietly, so only she would hear, 'how could she have anything to do with . . . Why is she messing around with . . . ?'

The words soured in his throat. He kicked an empty beer can as hard as he could. Quite a few in his class were already smoking cigarettes, and then there were those five guys who were caught taking bong hits in the bathroom. And of course, rumors running constantly throughout the corridors about other people, too, who didn't get caught. Those guys had started coming back from trance parties, in Ben Shemen Forest, or on Nitzanim Beach, speaking a new language. He sometimes felt as if everyone around him, more or less, had already experimented. Maybe even Roi, who had been smoking cigarettes openly for two years now. Assaf always pushed the rumors away from himself; he didn't want to know about it; it made him tense to think that things like that were happening to people he knew, to kids who had been in class with him since kindergarten, and now it was happening to Tamar as well, whom he didn't know but whom he already knew a little bit about –

'No. Explain to me so I'll understand.' He became angrier and angrier and spoke to Dinka in a loud whisper – and she seemed used to such street talk – 'How can it be that a girl like her is on drugs, and taking so much?' But what do you actually know about her? he responded to himself. You hardly know her. You were so sure, you just assumed, instantly, that she was just like you. And, as usual, you instantly started inventing some little story about you and her. Am I right? Am I right?

Dinka walked beside him, her head bowed, her tail drooping; walking like that on the side of the road, they looked like two mourners. The rope dragged on the ground between them. Assaf opened his hand and let it fall to the ground, but Dinka stopped, as if she were amazed and scared by his action, from the hinted intention of it. Assaf immediately bent down and picked it up.

Heavy and defeated, he walked toward the market, to Sima's Restaurant, willing himself to cling to the picture in his mind, of her standing on the barrel and telling the tale of the Giant's Garden. The more effort he put into keeping the image fixed, the more he felt it slipping away from him – he couldn't understand her, and he didn't want to have anything to do with her.

But something in his heart contracted a little at these thoughts. Perhaps it was the look Dinka had given him when he let go of the rope just now. Perhaps it was because he felt that if he gave up on this whole thing right now and brought Dinka back, and told Danokh that he had tried and had got beaten up, and even arrested, and he was sick of it – if he did that, he would not only be giving up the possibility of seeing, just once, what she looked like, this Tamar, but he might, you could say, actually be abandoning her.

Nothing happened on her second day on the streets, either. She sang three times in the Walking Street, once in the entrance to the Klal Building, and twice more in Tziyyon Square, so different in the daytime that it was almost delightful. Faces started to pop out of the crowd: store owners she already knew, the juice man, who sent over a big cup of mango-peach and told her that when she sang, his fruit gave more juice; the women soldiers patrolling the area had started smiling at her; and the Russian with the accordion came over and told her about himself, and begged her to please wait until he finished his set before she started singing, because she was taking all his income.

By the time she had finished a dozen performances, she knew not only how to sing but what numbers worked. 'Sixteen Going on Seventeen' from *The Sound of Music* had always seemed saccharine and schmaltzy to her, but people loved it here; it always brought a loud round of applause, and money, too. The same went for another old standby – 'Leaving on a Jet Plane,' by Peter, Paul & Mary – so she sang that one over and over, shifting it around for herself with the 'Little Prince of the Second Platoon,' or with something warm and melancholy by Shalom Hanokh. On the contrary, the one time she dared to sing Barbarina's aria from *The Marriage of Figaro*, the pride of her auditions, from the platform of the Old Knesset, people left in the middle – people laughed in her face. A few boys stood behind her and imitated her. Still, she kept it up all the way to the end, and watched how, one by one, people would detach themselves from the crowd like grapes from a bunch on the vine; every person, as he left, gave her a little pinch of insult, as if she wasn't good enough for him. She then had a short, sharp argument with herself (with Idan, actually) about whether she should remain faithful to her own vision at any cost or adapt herself to the tastes of the audience – 'Surrender to the mob, you mean,' Idan corrected her. She decided that, for her purposes, she was allowed to compromise, to be a little flexible (he tapped the table with his thin, pale fingers, looked upward in deep thought, and didn't say a word). And even enjoy it – why not?

She slept in her shelter again that night. This time, she was almost tempted by Leah's storeroom; it began to appear in her mind as a palace full of superb food, with waterfalls for washing in and delicate silk sheets – but she knew there might be a chance, tiny, yet bigger than yesterday, that her predator was watching her. He, or one of his messengers. It was very likely they had seen her singing this morning and reported to their boss; he probably had told them to go back and check up on exactly who she was, whom she was hanging around with, whom she was talking to, and to make sure she wasn't a police plant or something.

Because of this tiny, insistent worry, she returned on the second night to her stinking shelter, with the cockroaches scurrying around all night. She lay awake and thought thoughts: she passed from city to city over the map of Italy, and counted the days on her fingers, and she knew tomorrow was her day. She heard the rustle of tiny legs on the walls and on the floors around her, and beat back the waves of self-pity storming through her. In every person's life, she remembered bitterly, there are situations in which he is solely responsible for saving his own soul. She couldn't close her eyes until dawn.

'Abandoning her?' Rhino roared, his mouth full. 'What do you mean abandoning her? You don't even know her!'

'I know enough . . .'

Assaf stuck his face in his plate of stuffed vegetables so Rhino wouldn't see the dramatic change in his complexion.

'I can't believe it,' Rhino said. 'Your parents leave you alone for ten minutes and you're already messing around with girls.'

'I'm not!'

The people at the next table stopped in the middle of a political argument and looked at them.

'I'm not!' Assaf whispered again, angrily.

Rhino leaned back and inspected Assaf profoundly, with new appreciation. 'Assaf,' he said, 'you'll start shaving soon.'

'Where did you get that from?' Assaf said, touched his cheek briefly, and felt the fuzz. 'I still have some time.'

'But what are we going to do about this?' Rhino asked, and started to pull shishkebab off the skewer. Assaf watched him and pondered one of Reli's theories: that one mustn't ever eat more than six mouthfuls during a meal, because a stomach is satisfied after those six and any additional swallow is excessive, gluttonous. And Rhino sat here in front of him – for a second lunch, he was doing pretty well.

'I'll keep walking with the dog,' Assaf said, 'and maybe, eventually, we'll find her.'

'A girl that's on drugs, Assafi.' Rhino used his heavy voice, laying every word down like a sack of cement.

'I know. But –'

'Not just a girl who takes a puff here and there –'

'Yes, but –'

'A girl that's buying from a dealer in the city – pills, you said?'

'I don't know. How should I know? I don't understand anything about it.'

'And what do you think you're going to do when you find her? You'll tell her to stop and she'll stop, just like that?'

'I haven't thought that far ahead.' Assaf shifted in his chair. 'I only want to give her the dog. It's part of my job, right?' He did his best to look unquestionably official, without much success. Dinka lay down beside them, her tongue hanging out, her alert eyes focused on them, passing from one to the other.

'Listen.' Rhino leaned forward and emphasized his words

with the slice of pita in his hands. 'I got two guys in my workshop who've finally gotten clean. You know what getting clean means? It means relapsing at least three times – they get clean and then go back to using and get out of it and fall back into it. It's the same thing every time – they fall off the wagon and then have to go through the entire mess all over again – the police and detox and rehab – and even now I'm not one hundred percent sure that they're immune from getting back into it.' The pita slice bobbed up and down in front of Assaf's eyes. He rubbed his temples hard and felt how hot his skin was. Rhino was right. He should just walk out of this entire story now. But – the girl on the barrel, how could he give her up?

'Listen to me, Assaf. Forget about her. Stop daydreaming. You don't know how hard it is for an addict to kick her habit.' Rhino put down the pita and the fork, and rubbed his heavy palms against each other. 'I've been swallowing all these stories – I'm using, I'm clean – since childhood. Half the people in my neighborhood were users. Do you know what 'jonesing' is?'

'I've heard of it. Not really.'

Everything Rhino said was making Assaf depressed. Not just that – it was strange that he was delivering these formal sermons. He usually didn't speak much. Rhino loosened his belt to give the food room, and also so he could take a deep breath. 'Jonesing is what happens in the first days of withdrawal. Are you listening to me? I'm talking about the four or five first days, when a user's body starts to scream in pain because it isn't getting its fix.' He leaned forward and spoke quietly, his eyes squinting at Assaf. 'It's like being without food and drink for a month; it simply tears a human being apart, from the inside. You've never seen it, how a man gets sweaty and gray, his hands and legs twitching –'

The whole time Rhino spoke, Assaf shook his head to say no, as if trying to push the words away from him.

'So, what do you say?' Rhino asked him when he was finished. 'Are we forgetting about this?'

Assaf took long sips from his Coke, put the glass down,

114

didn't look at Rhino. He simply couldn't bring himself to say the word.

Rhino looked at him curiously. His wide chest exhaled the air locked inside it. 'I understand,' he said with a sigh. 'We have a complication here.' He bit into something and stopped. The fork looked like a child's utensil between his fingers. Assaf's mother, who was an expert on fingers, always said that Rhino had the most masculine fingers she'd ever seen.

'And you?' Assaf dared. 'You never took drugs?'

'Never.' Rhino leaned back, and the chair groaned. 'I was this close to trying it, and didn't. I had another addiction. You know.'

And he told Assaf, for the umpteenth time – but there was something familiar and reassuring about it – how, in his childhood, since he was six, he would go with his father to synagogue on Shabbat, and once there would run away, to the tree next to the YMCA Stadium, and sit on it from nine in the morning until the game started at half past two.

'I would watch the game, go back home, get a horrible beating from my father, and then start waiting for the next Shabbat.' Assaf pictured him, small and burning with excitement from between the trees' branches, and smiled.

'Do you understand?' Rhino laughed. 'Now I think that maybe it wasn't even the game that interested me so much, not as much as the anticipation; waiting there for five hours and thinking, It's coming, any minute it's going to happen – that's what I liked more than anything. That was the drug. And the moment the game was over, I felt complete emptiness until the next week. But how did we get on this?'

Assaf smiled. 'We got talking.'

'Well, fine,' Rhino said, and Assaf felt him change tactics. 'Why am I attacking you? You've had enough of that from the bastard with the handcuffs.'

They ate in complete silence for a few more minutes. Rhino ate a lot and drank a little water, and ate again, and drank again. Assaf finished everything on his plate. Gradually, the tension between them dissolved. Then they looked at each other, full and satisfied, and smiled. Normally, they got along better in silence.

'So, what have the old folks been telling you?' Rhino asked.

Assaf said that they hadn't called yesterday, but probably would today.

'I wonder if your mother managed –'

'– with the door of the airplane bathroom,' Assaf finished, and they both laughed. She had been practicing at home on the handle that opened the dishwasher; Rhino had told her it worked on almost the same principle. Her deep apprehension regarding the door had become a family joke.

'So you're telling me you still haven't heard from them,' Rhino inquired again, and looked for something deep in Assaf's eyes.

'No. I haven't, really.'

'Ah.'

Rhino didn't like the notion of this trip. He suspected Assaf's parents weren't telling him the whole truth. 'And what about Reli?' he asked, as if it meant nothing.

'I think she's okay.' Assaf regretted having already finished his food, not having a full plate to stick his face into.

'She's coming back with them? She's not coming back?'

'I hope she is. I don't know. Maybe.'

Rhino was downright inspecting his face, looking for clues. But Assaf had nothing to show him. He had his own deep suspicions that there was some secret they were hiding from him because of his close connection to Rhino; they decided too easily not to take him, then they bribed him with the promise of a Canon.

'Because I' – Rhino lit a cigarette and sucked at it with pleasure – 'I've been having this feeling, all the time.'

'No, no,' Assaf said quickly. 'You'll see, it'll be okay.' He remembered the long period when Rhino had quit smoking because Reli demanded it. He knew that smoking now was another bad sign. 'Don't worry. They'll go there and talk to her, and she'll come back to us.'

'To us' also meant to Rhino, of course. Especially to Rhino.

'She's found someone else over there,' Rhino said in his low basso, and exhaled upward. 'She found some geeky American. She's going to stay there, I'm telling you; I feel these things in my bones.'

'She won't,' Assaf said.

'I've been fooling myself, for nothing.' Rhino stubbed out his cigarette cruelly, even though he had smoked only a quarter. Assaf knew, by how much he had spoken during the meal, that Rhino was in an unusual state of mind. It was a little embarrassing to see him, with all his size and strength, exposed this way, so helpless. Assaf suddenly understood that Rhino no longer had any control over it. 'Look at how many years I've continued to delude myself,' Rhino said, very slowly, as if he was enjoying hurting himself. 'Look at what love is.'

They both went into a panicked silence. Assaf felt that word of Rhino's burning through him, perhaps because it had never, ever been used in their conversations.

And the word was there, fluttering like a living creature, a chick that had fallen from Rhino's bosom, and someone had to pick it up.

'The girl,' Assaf muttered, without thinking, 'the dog's girl. She had a friend, a nun who for fifty years has been –' and shut up, because he felt it was a little insensitive on his part to talk like that, about his own concerns, while Rhino sat, tormented, in front of him. 'You'll see, she'll come back,' he said, strangely, weakly, because what else could he say except to repeat those words over and over, like a prayer or an oath? 'Where will she find someone like you? My parents say that, too, you know.'

'Yes. If it was only up to your parents . . .' Rhino nodded his head, then stretched out his full size, looked up and to the sides, sighed. 'Look. Your dog's asleep,' he said.

Dinka really had fallen asleep. Assaf had been sneaking her shishkebab and fries during the whole meal. They don't usually allow dogs here, Khezi the waiter told Rhino, but for Mr Tzahi . . . Assaf and Rhino stayed a little longer, to sit and chat; they talked about all kinds of things, getting away a little from what had passed between them earlier. Rhino told him about the new statue he was casting today: by that sculptor, the famous but crazy one, who quarreled with every foundry in the country; he fought with Rhino every time, sometimes coming to blows – it's the same story with every sculpture. But when he returns to the workshop a year later, saying, with his crooked smile, that he has new work, Rhino just can't say no. 'That's how artists are.' Rhino laughed. 'You can't try to reason with their minds, because they can't either. These guys have no fear of God – they're taking orders only from themselves. So what are you going to do – argue with them?' His laughter was quickly smothered; maybe he remembered that jewelry is also an art.

The people at the next table got up to leave. 'Turkish coffee, Mr Tzahi?' the waiter asked Rhino, and Rhino ordered it for both of them.

'No,' said Rhino, when the little cups arrived. 'You still haven't learned how. This is how you drink it –' and he sucked up the coffee with a whistle, his lips, thick and almost purple, pursed like a kiss. Assaf tried to imitate him, but only drew air. Rhino smiled. Assaf looked carefully. It was 'the smile that melted every woman on earth,' his mother had announced, annoyed that only one woman on earth, Reli the Fool, was indifferent to it. Stone, stone, a heart of stone.

'So then, what are we going to do about this?' Rhino asked, indicating the dog. 'You don't mean to give the girl up, do you?'

'I'll walk around a little more today, until the evening, and then I'll see.'

'And until tomorrow?' Rhino smiled. 'And until you find her, huh?'

Assaf shrugged. Rhino looked at him at length and sucked in his cheeks. During the Gulf War, Rhino had bought a ten-thousand-piece puzzle of the Swiss Alps and brought it to Reli and her parents, to try and ease the tension of the evening hours between the shelter siren and the All Clear. Reli broke down first, on the first evening. Assaf's mother followed her, retiring two days later, saying that even Saddam's missiles were better than this Swiss torture. His father continued for a week. Rhino kept after it for a month, for the principle of it, and stopped only after he started imagining that he was developing a slight color blindness, especially with shades of blue. Assaf, who wasn't even eight then, finished the puzzle a week after the war ended.

'Listen now.' Rhino thought for a moment, his fingers playing with the military chain around his neck. The edges of his undershirt had gone green from the oxidized bronze dust. 'I don't like that you're going around like this – and your folks will have me for lunch if you lose a fingernail. Am I right?'

'Right.' Assaf also knew that Rhino wouldn't forgive himself if something bad happened.

'You've been lucky so far, only one sadistic cop got you. It could be somebody else next time.'

'But I need to look for her,' Assaf repeated stubbornly, thinking in his heart, 'find her.'

'Here's what we'll do.' Rhino pulled a red marker out of his overalls, with which he marked the statues. 'I'm also writing down my cell number, and my numbers at home and at work.'

'I know them.'

'It's better if they're all in one place. Listen to me well and don't tell me later that you didn't hear me: if there is the smallest problem – and I mean the tiniest, I don't know what – if someone's harassing you, or walking half a meter behind you, or you just don't like somebody's face, you go to the nearest pay phone. At once. Promise?'

Assaf made a face that said, 'What, am I a baby?' but inside he didn't really object.

'Do you have a phone card?'

'My parents left me five – eh, seven.'

'On you, I mean, do you have one on you?'

'They're at home.'

'Take it. Don't save money on my account. Now, who's paying for the meal?'

'Shall we do the usual?'

They cleared the table, positioned their arms in front of

each other. Assaf was a strong figure of a man, and every day, in two sessions, did 120 push-ups and 140 sit-ups. Now, for a few moments, he squeaked and groaned, but he still had no chance of beating Rhino.

'But it's getting harder and harder every time,' Rhino said gallantly, and paid the waiter.

They stood up to go. Dinka trotted between them, and Assaf was secretly pleased to see the three of them together this way, he and Rhino and the dog in between. Outside the restaurant, Rhino went down on one knee, just like that, knelt on the dirty sidewalk and looked into Dinka's eyes. She looked at him for a moment and immediately moved her head, as if his gaze were too close, held too many emotions for her.

'If you don't find the girl, bring the dog to me. She's smart. She'll have friends in my yard.'

'But the form, the fine . . .'

'It's on me. What, do you want the City Hall vet to inject her with something?'

Dinka licked his face.

'Hey, hey.' He laughed. 'We've only just met.'

He got on his motorcycle. 'Where are you going from here?' he asked; the helmet mashed his face down for a minute.

'Wherever she takes me.'

Rhino looked at him and laughed from the depths of his stomach. 'What can I say, Assafi? To hear a sentence like that from you . . . this dog has certainly succeeded where your parents and Reli failed. "Wherever she takes me" . . . the days of the Messiah have come!' He started his bike with a roar, making the street tremble; the bike moved away, he stuck out his leg, waved an arm, and disappeared.

The two of them were left alone.

'What now, Dinka?'

She watched Rhino until he disappeared, then sniffed at the air. Perhaps she was waiting for the fuel fumes to evaporate. She then turned around, stood erect, lifted her head, raised her nose. Her ears poked forward a little bit, toward something beyond the houses surrounding the market street. Assaf already knew the signs.

'Rruf!' she said, and started running.

On the third day, already tired, legs dragging after a sleepless night in the shelter, they went back out on the street, before the offices opened in the building where she was hiding. She bought Dinka and herself breakfast in the Dell' Arte Café, and they both ate in the empty courtyard of the club next door, the Experiment. Tamar's heart ached for Dinka, who looked so ragged. The sheen of her fur had disappeared, the golden waves of her beautiful coat. Poor Dinkush. I dragged you into this without even asking. Look at you, trusting me with closed eyes. I wish I understood exactly what I was doing and where I was going.

Yet, as always, when she stood in front of an audience, she was quickly made whole.

She sang in Lunz Street, and the audience that gathered around her wouldn't let her go, asking for more and more. Her eyes shone: as each performance passed, the familiar urge became even stronger in her – she couldn't believe it would be aroused in her here as well, and with such intensity – the need to get them, to sweep them up into her from the very first note. Immediately she heard Idan and Adi screech: 'But a piece of music has to develop slowly, to ripen! There is no such thing as instant art!' And she thought, They don't know what they're talking about. Here, it wasn't golden chandeliers and velvet walls. No one here was going to wait for her to 'ripen': the street was full of temptations that could attract the people passing by as much as she did. Every twenty meters, someone stood playing a violin or a flute, or throwing torches into the air, and every one of them desired, at least as much as she did, to be heard, and discovered, and to be loved. On top of that were the hundreds of shop owners and vendors and falafel and shwarma sellers, people standing behind store counters, and peddlers in the bazaar, the coffeehouse waiters and the lottery-ticket hawkers and the street beggars, and each one of them constantly calling out with a mute, insistent cry, 'Me, come to me, only to me!'

Of course, in the chorus, there had also been quarrels and jealousies and competition for the good parts. Each time the conductor gave someone a solo, three others announced their resignation. But it looked like child's play now, compared to what she saw on the street. Yesterday, for example, when she saw that the circle forming around the two Irish girls with silver flutes was much larger than hers, she felt a pinch of jealousy much more bitter than the one she'd felt when Atalia from the chorus was accepted at the Manhattan School of Music in New York.

Today, as she bowed gracefully in front of her audience's lit-up faces, in front of their hands applauding her enthusiastically, she knew she truly wanted to play the game here according to its rules, to fight for her audience, and tempt them – to be daring and amazing and of the *street*. She even thrilled to the street as an arena of unending struggle: a war of existence waged at each moment beneath the cheerful, colorful, civil appearances. She knew that to survive here, she had to free herself from her delicately refined tastes, to be a guerrilla fighter in developed urban territory; and this is why she took five big steps away from Lunz and positioned herself in the middle of the Walking Street, sent a wink in her heart to Halina, who had always complained that she didn't have any of the ambition that was so vital for an artist, that she was spoiled and refused to fight for her proper place, avoiding competition of every kind – and now, look at me, in the center of the universe – would you believe it's me?

And she sang, in the richest and clearest voice she had yet achieved since coming to the streets, Billie Holiday's 'God Bless the Child.' As she was about to start the second song, the Russian accordionist suddenly started playing 'Happy Birthday to You' very loudly, and the Irish girls with the flutes from down the street joined in, as did the blind violinist from Lunz Alley who played ersatz Gypsy music, and to her surprise, even the three men from Paraguay, with their guarded faces and their exotic, gloomy instruments – they all came and surrounded her and played for her. She stood in the middle, her heart overflowing, deviating insanely from all her rules of caution, smiling joyfully to the audience around her, to all the strange faces that shone with genuine affection as they understood why the Russian was bowing to her; it almost swept away the painful thought of how she had spent her last birthday with Idan and Adi at the top of the tower on Hatzofim Mountain, how they had sneaked up there at midnight and stayed awake until they saw the sunrise . . .

When they finished the number, she didn't sing another song. She detached herself apologetically from the audience, went up to the Russian, and heard what she figured she would, that yesterday a woman had showed up, tall, kind of butch, with scars all over her face, and 'give fifty shekel that we should play you this song today. Well, fifty shekel in every hand, so we don't ask nothing.' He looked at her warily: *What is it, Tamarutschka, I don't play good?*

*You played superbly, Leonid. Top marks.*

She left, thinking that the world was a good place, or at least had some potential, as long as people like Leah lived in it. She considered the description of Leah that had come from Leonid's mouth and wondered how she herself almost didn't see those scars anymore, what Leah called her stripes, and thought that she had been saved from at least one torment today: that of sitting by the phone waiting for someone to call and wish her many happy returns. Her reverie was broken when she realized she had come to the platform in front of Hamashbir. She didn't like performing there – she didn't even like being there, between the traffic and the vendors and petition tables and the noise of the buses. She turned around. She wanted to go back to the Walking Street, but still, she hesitated. Something stopped her. She didn't know what it was. She became nervous and uneasy, probably because of the birthday celebration – but also because of some internal muddle, new and unexplained. She walked, drawn back – and now grew suddenly angry at Leah, who had thrown such a party for her in the middle of the street, in front of everyone

– and what if things got complicated later? Someone would start investigating who the scarred woman was who had paid Leonid and the others. She walked aimlessly, getting angrier and angrier. What did she need a birthday for, while she was in the middle of matters that were far more important?

With evident reluctance, she decided to sing one song, no more, and walk away. And of all the times and places, this is where it happened, and without her being prepared for it: she, who had aimed for this, waited for this moment so desperately, she who had remained so alert, guessing countless times at what shape it would take, who would be the messenger of her predator – she didn't grasp what was happening when it came.

She finished singing and collected the coins. The people scattered, and she was left with a feeling she already knew, the strange combination of pride in doing a good show, for succeeding once more in charming them; and mixed with it, the distasteful sense that crawled into her after everyone had walked away and she was stuck in the middle of the street, knowing she had just abandoned some very private part of herself to strangers.

Two old people, a man and a woman, who had spent the performance sitting on a stone bench to the side, stood up and tottered toward her. They gripped each other tightly, and the man leaned on the woman. They were small and wrapped up in clothing that was too heavy for such a hot day. The woman smiled shyly at Tamar, her smile almost completely toothless, and asked, 'May I?' Tamar didn't know what she wanted and said yes. She was moved by the way they stood there, clinging to each another.

'The way you sing. Oy! Oy!' The woman put her hands on her cheeks. 'Like in the opera, like a cantor,' she said, and her chest rose and swelled. She touched Tamar's arm and patted it excitedly. Tamar didn't usually like strangers to touch her, but she felt all her soul being drawn to the soft hand.

'And he –' The old lady nodded toward her husband with her eyes. 'My husband, Yosef, he has almost no more eyes to see and hardly can hear with his ears, and I am his eyes and

ears, but he heard you. Isn't it true you heard her, Yosef?'
And she nudged him with her shoulder a little. 'Isn't it true
you heard her singing?'

The man looked at Tamar and smiled vacantly, and his
yellow mustache split in two.

'Excuse me for asking,' the woman said sweetly, and her
soft chubby face suddenly moved very close to Tamar's face,
'but your parents, do they know you are like this, alone in
the street?'

Tamar still didn't understand what she wanted, still didn't
suspect anything. She said she had left home 'because it was
getting a little difficult there,' and smiled a little apologetically
for having to expose such a good woman to the harsh facts of
life. 'But I'm okay, don't worry.' The old woman still looked
at her piercingly, and grabbed Tamar's wrist with her doughy
hand, encircling it with unexpected force, and for the blink
of an eye the image flashed in Tamar's mind of the Wicked
Witch checking to see if Gretel was fat enough yet – but the
image vanished as quickly as it had appeared, in front of the
puffed-up, friendly face.

'Not good,' the woman murmured, and glanced around.
'It is not good to be like this! A girl alone, and there are all
kinds of people here and nobody to take care of you. And
what if someone wants to steal your money? Or, God forbid,
something worse?'

'I can take care of myself, Grandma.' Tamar laughed,
wanting to leave now; the concern surrounding her was a
burden and plucked at all her sore strings.

'No friend or brother to guard you?' the woman sput-
tered. 'And where do you sleep at night? You shouldn't live
like this!'

It was at this point that suspicion first woke in Tamar,
fluttered in her stomach, whispering to her to not say too
much. She couldn't believe the flutter – the old people looked
so innocent and friendly – and so she laughed now again, but
it was a different laugh, forced. She repeated herself, saying
that she really didn't need anyone to take care of her. She
turned to leave. But the woman hung on to her – Tamar

was amazed that the gnarled fingers possessed such violent force – and she asked whether Tamar was eating enough – you look so thin, sweetie, just skin and bones – and Tamar, already more alert because of the 'sweetie,' said she was doing just fine, thank you. The old woman stayed silent for another moment. Tamar saw her lips forming some final question, and then it came, sharp and cutting: 'Tell me, *maideleh*, perhaps you want someone to protect you while you are here?'

She had already backed off half a step away from them. They had really started disturbing her – they were surrounding her very closely, like smoke; but this was a new kind of question, this last one, and it came from a completely different place. Tamar stopped and looked at the two in surprise – but the thought started to swell up in her brain: This is it. It's them – how impossible – but these were probably the people she had been waiting for, his messengers.

But it couldn't be! She shook herself, smiling at her foolishness. Look at them, two poor refugees; but they were asking the right questions. No, it's impossible, look at them, Granny and Grandpa, full of goodwill and concern – what connection could they have to that horrible man?

'What? What do you mean?' she asked, her eyes larger than usual. 'I don't understand.' She knew she had to be smart now, very alert, not too excited and not too frightened; only her heart – they could probably see from the outside how hard it was beating through her overalls.

'Because we, Yosef and me, know a very good place, like a home, where you can live, and there is good food, and you will also have friends, and it's very happy all the time. Right, Yosef?'

'What?' Yosef asked; he seemed to keep falling asleep behind his dark glasses, and only her nudging woke him up.

'That we have good food.'

'Well, yes, the best food there is. This is because Henya is cooking,' he explained, with a nod toward his wife. 'So the food is good, and you get to drink and to sleep – everything is good!'

Tamar didn't hurry. Something in her still refused to believe it, or was afraid to believe it; something in her eyes was still begging them to prove her wrong, because if this was really it, if they were really his messengers, then everything was about to start. Now. And she would have no control over what was going to happen. And she knew that instant that she didn't have the courage to do it.

'So what do you say, cutie?' the woman asked her. Tamar could see her lips trembling with excitement.

'I don't know,' Tamar said. 'Where is it? Is it far?'

'It's not so far.' The old woman cleared her throat, and her hands started to wave in front of Tamar. Perhaps it was the excitement. 'It's right here, just half a moment, but we'll take a taxi, or somebody will take us, just say already, say yes or no. All the rest – we'll take care of it.'

'But I . . . I don't know you,' Tamar almost shrieked in fear.

'What is there to know? I am Grandma, and he is Grandpa. Old people! And there is one son, Pesach, who is the manager there, and he's a fine boy, believe me, cutie, he is gold.' Tamar looked at them despairingly. This really was it. That was the name Shai had given her when he'd called from there. Pesach, the man who had hit him, who had almost killed him with beatings. The old woman continued. 'And he has this place exactly for children like you.'

'Place?' Tamar asked, playing dumb. 'Are there more children?'

'But of course! What did you think, you will be alone there? You have there kids who are actors, A-plus! And some they do *gymnastica*, like the circus! And there are musicants with violin and guitar, and one that does a show with no talking, like the one – what's his name from the television? – Rosen! And the one that's eating the fire, and a girl that's walking with only hands, woo-hoo!' She shook her head in awe. 'You will have so many friends there, you will be happy all the day!'

Tamar shrugged. 'It actually sounds nice,' her lips lied, but her voice barely registered.

'So we go, then?' The old woman's mouth trembled and

her face blushed eagerly. Tamar couldn't look at her all of a sudden – she seemed like a fat spider, a spider so quickly weaving her web around the ant. Her.

The old woman took Tamar's arm, and together they walked back down to the Walking Street. They moved very slowly because of blind Yosef. The woman didn't stop speaking, as if trying to flood Tamar with words so that she wouldn't understand exactly what was happening. Tamar's heels were burning. It would be so easy, right now, to just detach herself from the old woman's arm and simply walk away, and leave for good. She would never have to feel this cool, loose skin against hers; she wouldn't get entangled in this web the woman was excreting around her.

And she would never reach that house that she had been searching for for months.

Tamar sorrowfully looked around, as if she would never walk on the street again and wouldn't see the stores and the people and everyday life. In a whiny voice, Eeyore's voice, she thought to herself, Many happy returns of my birthday, and thanks so much for the wonderful gift.

'Do we must take the dog?' the old woman squawked with dissatisfaction when she suddenly noticed that the big dog dragging along behind them belonged to Tamar.

'Yes, she's coming with me!' Tamar answered quickly, and deep in her heart hoped they would say that she couldn't bring a dog, and then she would have a good excuse to get away.

'It's a woman, the dog? Female?' The old woman twisted her mouth. 'And what will happen? She'll be pregnant and have puppies and we have a party?'

'She's . . . she's already old. She can't get pregnant,' Tamar whispered, and her heart pitied Dinka, having to go through such humiliation at her age.

'So, what do you care?' the woman tried again. 'Leave her here. What do you need her for? And we must feed her, and she will get sick and bring dirt.'

'The dog is coming with me!' Tamar cut into her; for a moment she and the old woman looked at each other, and Tamar now saw what was hiding under the wide smiles and fat, motherly wrinkles – a sharp look, gray as steel, a battle veteran – but the old woman lowered her eyes first. 'You don't need to shout like that. What did I say? What is it, such nerve to shout at us, and we're doing you a favor . . .'

And Tamar knew, knew, knew this was it.

They continued in silence for a few more minutes. Near Ha-khatulet Square a blue, dirty, beat-up car started gliding toward them. Tamar didn't notice it at first – then she started wondering why the Subaru was coming so close to them, and then her throat started to choke in terror. The car pulled up next to them; the old woman looked to the right and left quickly.

The driver, a young dark guy with one deep wrinkle plowing the center of his forehead, got out of the car and glanced at Tamar, his eyes hot and full of contempt. He opened the front door for the old woman, as if he were driving a Rolls-Royce. The woman waited until her husband had squeezed himself into the back seat, then pushed Tamar in after him.

'Straight to Pesach,' she ordered. The driver released the parking brake and the car leaped forward. Tamar turned her head and saw the street diminishing behind her, closing quickly like a zipper.

II

THE GIANT WORE A black net tank top and held a toothpick in the corner of his mouth. He was talking into two telephones at the same time: into the one on the table, he yelled, 'I told you a hundred times already! Always check in the morning! So check the sack in the other car to see if he took the knives!'; into the other one, a cell phone, he said, 'So where am I gonna find you a glass box now?' He lifted his head and saw Tamar; without shifting his gaze from her, he slowly moved the toothpick in his mouth from left to right.

Tamar stood still. Her hands gripped the stitches of the overalls bottoms. She had met so many shady, sinister people in the past few weeks, and every time she got scared, she calmed herself down by thinking that they were only the preface to *him*, that she should save her fear for the crucial moment. Now, standing in front of him, she was surprised – he seemed almost harmless, a kind of huge, fat, sweaty teddy bear. But she still couldn't keep her legs from shaking.

He wore a thick black ring on one of his fingers, and Tamar was hypnotized by his pinky, with its long talonlike nail. She wondered if the call that had brought her here had been made on the telephone on this table, if it was in this room that those fists had struck, and if that horrible cry had come from here.

The old man and woman, his father and mother, hovered around him; they presented Tamar to him while he spoke on the phone, then smiled at him from either side of her, a suggestive smile, one that held a promise, as if they had bought him a precious gift. He was taller than both of them, even sitting; he filled the room with his body, making Tamar feel odd – her tininess felt ridiculous. The names 'Meir' and 'Ya'akov' were hanging on a golden chain that fell on his wide chest – probably the names of his children – along with something that looked like an animal's long tooth. Into one telephone he snapped, 'Just watch him – keep an eye on how he throws – he already screwed up on me, cut someone the day before yesterday in Akko,' and into the other he growled, 'And the lunatic can't just get into a wooden box, or some cardboard from the supermarket?'

Dinka sat, uneasy, at her feet. Shifting position now and then, Dinka then stood, something she didn't usually do when she waited for a long time. Tamar looked around carefully: a big metal cabinet to her right. Bars on the windows. A torn poster, half falling off the wall. 'You wanted to blow your mind? Well, you blew it.' The man finished one conversation with: 'I'll tell you one more time – you will check, the whole time, that no one's behind him, so no one ends up with a knife in his head.' He had a bald red spot on the crown of his head, a long braid down his back, and heavy, dark bags under his eyes. He hung up one receiver, and the muscles moving under the skin of his arms looked like bread loaves. Into the other telephone: 'Then go to a pet store – there's probably something over there in the mall. Buy her an aquarium, let's see her squeeze into that – just don't forget to bring me a receipt!' He exhaled slowly, as if to say, 'I have to think of everything,' looked at Tamar, and asked what she could do.

Tamar swallowed. She could sing.

'Louder, I can't hear you!'

She could sing, she sang in a chorus for three years, she was a soloist, or at least she had been, she corrected herself silently, until the trip to Italy.

'They told me you sing in Ben Yehuda Street. Is that true?'

She nodded. Two scratched-up photos were stuck up on the wall behind him. He seemed twenty years younger in them, almost naked: red, shiny, and wrestling with another man, probably in some competitive match.

'So what's the deal – you ran away from home?'

'Yes.'

'Okay, okay, don't tell me, I don't want to know. How old?'

'Sixteen.' Today.

'You came here of your free will, right?'

'Yes.'

'Nobody forced you to come, right?'

'Yes.'

He took papers and thick books out of the crammed drawer in his desk, looked through them until he found a page with faded printed letters on it, a copy of a copy. She read: *I, the undersigned, am honored to announce that I have come to Mr Pesach Bet Ha Levi's Home for Artists of my own free will and volition, and under no outside influence; and herein commit to honoring the rules and regulations of this organization, and to obey the management.*

'Sign here.' He pointed it out with a thick red finger. 'First and last name.'

A moment of hesitation. Tamar Cohen.

Pesach Bet Ha Levi peered down and read it. 'Everyone suddenly becomes "Cohen" around here,' he said. 'Who are you kidding – show me ID.'

'I don't have one.'

'So some other proof, something.'

'I have nothing. I got out fast and I didn't take anything with me.'

He cocked his huge head in doubt. After a moment he decided to let it go. 'Fine, we'll keep it like this for now. All right: I can provide you a place to sleep, a room and a bed. Two meals every day, one in the morning and hot in the evening. The money you earn from singing you give the home to pay for your food and rent. You get thirty shekels a day from me, for smokes and sodas and other petty cash. But I'm warning you, nicely, don't even think about slipping one over on me. Want to know why?'

Tamar asked why.

He tilted his head back slightly and smiled beyond the toothpick at her. 'You look like a delicate girl to me, so maybe it's better not to get into the details. The bottom line is: You don't cheat Pesach. Do we understand each other?' For a split second Tamar saw what Shai had been talking about, the quick, almost undetectable metamorphosis between the two completely different people inside him. 'Not that no one has ever tried.' His smile widened a millimeter; his cold eyes pierced her, deep into her soul, into the darkness of her secret. 'There's always one smart-ass who thinks he'll be the first to succeed –' She saw the curly-haired boy by the railings in the square, dragging himself along slowly, broken-fingered and hollow. 'But whoever's tried, well, let's just say, he isn't trying anymore. He isn't trying anything anymore.' His eyes, Tamar thought anxiously, something is wrong with his eyes. They're not connected to him. To anything. She didn't know how she could stop the shameful shaking of her legs.

'Get a blanket and mattress from the last room at the end of the hall, by the electrical boxes, and look for a room. There are lots of empty ones. Food in the dining hall, second floor, every night at nine o'clock. Lights out at midnight, sharp. Hey – what's the deal with the dog?'

'It's mine.'

'So she stays with you the whole time. I don't need somebody getting bitten here. She's got her shots?'

'Yes.'

'What about food?'

'I'll take care of her.'

'Good. Somebody explain to you what you do here?'

'No.'

'Later. One thing at a time.' He returned to his phone, started dialing, and stopped. 'One minute. Another thing: do you use?'

She didn't understand. Then she understood.

'No.' He just better not look in her bag, she thought. She had half a bundle – enough for five days – in there, sealed in plastic.

'You better not use here. If I catch you, even once, I'll take you straight to the police.'

His mother, standing by his side, nodded energetically.

'I'm not using.' But he confused her, that was for sure. Everyone here used, that's what she thought, that's what Shai had told her on the phone, when he told her about this place and begged her to come and save him.

'Because,' Pesach raised his voice, 'here we stick to art. You keep all the rest of that garbage out of here. Are we clear?' Tamar was struck by the idea that he wasn't talking to her but to someone eavesdropping, hidden in the room or beyond the window.

'Wait, wait, wait.' He put the phone down again. He inspected her. 'Are you like this all the time?'

'How?'

'Quiet. No one can hear you.'

Tamar stood ashamed, her arms limp.

'So how can you sing if you can't talk?'

'I sing. I sing.' She raised her voice, trying very hard to fill herself with life.

'Let's see, then. Sing for a minute.' He stretched out his big legs.

'Here, now?'

'Sure, here. Do you think I have time to go to a concert?'

She stiffened at the insult: she had to audition? Here? But then she reminded herself what she was going to do here and suppressed her little internal rebellion. She closed her eyes and focused.

'Well, sweetie, do we have to bring in a warm-up act? I don't have all day.'



So she sang to him. Instantly – 'Don't Call Me Sweetie' by Korin Alal. She shouldn't have chosen this song, but she didn't even think for a minute – the song just burst out of her uncontrollably, like a shout. Perhaps because he called her sweetie so dismissively; she would never have dreamed of singing that kind of song a cappella, leaving herself practically naked in front of him. And yet – just because of the rage burning inside her, she sang brilliantly from the first moment, and the piercing silences between the lines accompanied her as well as an entire orchestra. She sang with passion, and moved in time to the music, and took the correct breaths, and she knew, in complete despair, that she was making her first major mistake with this man. She wanted to stop, but knew if she stopped, she would lose the chance to stay here. But she shouldn't have sung a song like that, speaking so directly, provocatively, because when she sang, 'Don't call me sweetie / it gives me a rash / it turns me into a chocolate fish,' their eyes were dueling, as if she had declared war on him. And when, in the song, she sang about the one who understood she had no choice but in the wisdom of the little flowers, it was as if she was revealing to him that she wasn't only the delicate little girl he saw in front of him, that she was hidden under a false bottom. Why the hell didn't she choose to introduce herself with another song, why hadn't she started with something quiet and sad – 'Evening Falls between Cypress Trees' or 'My Simple Coat' – surrendering, yielding; why did she have to provoke him, to draw special attention to herself in the very first moment? It's that curse again, she thought dazedly, while singing; it's the arrogance of the shy, the hasty courage of the terrified. Because when he negated her with his 'sweetie,' as if she were just another girl, she simply had to show him what set her apart, within, when she was ignited to sing – when suddenly the singer, the one who can't be scared off, bursts out of her like a torch . . .

It was because of this singer, probably, that she even stopped being angry with herself after the first moment; she abandoned herself to the internal gallop of the song, the bitter power in it – she danced and moved and burned with closed eyes. Her arms were thrown, powerfully, to her sides – her knees bounced wildly to the rhythm, almost without moving from her place. She tuned herself against the sound coming from the deepest place inside herself, at the farthest distance from the fat red man slouching back in his chair with the toothpick in his mouth, and along with it, later, an expression of surprise, and a faint smile; he leaned back and clasped his hands behind his neck –

When she finished, she just turned off. Turned herself off. She couldn't be ablaze in front of him without her shield; she was too certain that everything she wanted to hide was already out in the open. The room continued to echo for a few seconds more, her fusing streams of energy.

'You're not bad . . .' said Pesach Bet Ha Levi. He took the toothpick out of his teeth and sucked it, and screened her with a mixture of suspicion and amused respect, then looked at his mother, who smiled toothlessly and nodded through the whole short performance. 'What do you say, Mamaleh? She's something, that little one, isn't she?' His father was sitting, asleep, on a bench behind her. Tamar tried not to listen to the conversation. She hoped for a normal bathroom around here where she could take a shower, first thing. He's only a small-time crook – she courageously repeated to herself what Shai had told her on the phone, calling from this very room. Only a small-time crook who'd found a little, original niche in the world of crime; but my life – Shai sighed in the middle of his speech – he ruined my life. Big time.

'We're done here.' Pesach started wrapping up. 'We'll see where we put you tomorrow morning.'

'I'm sorry, I don't understand.'

'Don't worry. Go now. Get settled in, rest up. Perhaps this was easy for you. Until now. The hard work starts tomorrow, and that's when you'll be told where you'll be, in what city.'

'I'm not going to be in Jerusalem?' She tensed up. This possibility had never occurred to her.

'You'll go wherever you're told. Clear?'

Again, his empty eyes. The eyes of a dead man. She shut up.

'Go on, sweetie, time's up.' His eyes left her; he wiped her from his thoughts and went back to dialing numbers on both telephones.


She walked out of Pesach's room, with Dinka behind her.

She still didn't know where she was, what this place was. The tiles laid in the floor of the corridor were broken, crooked, and sunken; the ground showed through in a few places, and weeds and thorns poked out. You could see where, as soon as people left the place, nature had returned with a vengeance – Tamar thought her family had gone through a similar process. The corridor went on and on. There were signs on the walls: TO SPECIALIST CLINICS, TO LOBBY, SURGERY, CHILDREN'S INTERNAL MEDICINE. She peeped behind a half-open door and saw an iron bedstead, a mattress and blanket rolled up on it. Perhaps someone was sleeping there, and perhaps not. The floor was stamped with the rusty marks of many beds. Pipes and electric wires hung from the ceiling. Another sign reading OXYGEN with a torn Madonna poster next to it. She found the room at the end of the corridor. She had to struggle with the door to push past the weight of the mattresses piled behind it. The air was dusty and compressed inside. She pulled a mattress off the pile; it was striped and very heavy, and covered with large stains. She tried to put it back and take another, but whatever had come out of there wouldn't go back in. Blankets were piled on top of the mountain of mattresses; she climbed it, pulled two blankets out, trying not to smell them. The smell of dust and urine rose with her every motion. There were no sheets. She would have to touch those blankets, sleep under them. Their smell would stick to her skin. Never mind, she reminded herself despairingly. The important thing was to get *him* out of here. That was why she had to get in here anyway, really get in, in her entirety.

She dragged the mattress back along the corridor. It weighed almost as much as she did; it came down heavily on her back, doubling her over, dragging behind her like a train of poverty. The one advantage to it, she thought, was that she wouldn't bump into Shai face-to-face before she was really ready for it. Dinka ran around her, trying to get under the mattress, but each time she tried she was pushed away by it and she whined. Every few moments Tamar would stop, open one of the doors, and peep in under her hunched back. Each room had a bed or two in it and looked inhabited. She saw a guitar leaning against the wall in one of the rooms. Her heart leaped in her chest – maybe this was his room. The room was empty, and graffiti was smeared on the wall in charcoal: *If the world doesn't understand me, the world is not the world.* She thought it was like him to make such a statement, but the jeans thrown on the bed were far too short for his long, long legs. She closed the door and opened the one after it. Empty beer cans and heaps of cigarette butts. Two green Maccabee Haifa scarves hung, crossed, on the wall. Someone sat there, his naked back to her; the thin white back of a boy concentrating on a Game Boy – he didn't notice that she had opened and closed the door.

It pulls you in so hard, Shai had told her during that phone call, with unusual force. You end up wanting to get sucked in, to fall apart and shatter into your smallest fragments. It's as if you're dying to see how low you can go – that's the impulse that takes you over, and you have no will, no nothing. Things crash so quickly, Watson . . . At that point, when he said her secret nickname, her eyes closed with indescribable pleasure, as if it erased everything he had said a moment before. She hadn't heard him call her that for long months. She didn't know how much she had missed it. A moment later, she heard the first slap, and after that – the beatings, the fists, and him crying out.

She shut the door. When she turned to keep going, bowed under the mattress, her lowered eyes saw a pair of big, bare, dark feet, the feet of a girl with thick toes and nails painted a shining purple. A loud voice, full of laughter, said, 'Why, you're completely buried there, let's lift it together.'

She didn't see her face, just felt that someone was coming up behind her, bending down, and taking up the burden of the mattress, sharing it with her. She suddenly felt relieved.

'Where are we going?' Tamar asked.

'Second floor.'

Tamar was silent. Her legs searched for the stairs. She climbed one, and two, the mattress floated on her back. She and the girl started swaying forward and backward under the weight of the load, and again went back down to the corridor and stood still for a moment. They started climbing again, and swayed, and Tamar heard a burst of laughter behind her. 'You know what it reminds me of? Two years ago we did Don Quixote in a school play, and me and two other girls were the horse, and we were walking just like this, each one with her head in the other's ass, and suddenly the sheet ripped open and this is how everybody saw us.' The memory intensified her rolling, infectious laughter, and the mattress jiggled and shook and was pulled backward, and after a moment, the two of them fell, the mattress on top of them. They crawled out and lay on it, shoulder to shoulder, without looking at each other, and laughed till they couldn't breathe, both of them. Tamar, with all her heart, dove into the laughter of this strange girl.

'Sheli,' the girl said, wiped her tears against the back of her hand, and rubbed her arm against Tamar's.

'Tamar.'

'Hey, Tamar.'

'And this is Dinka.'

'Hey, Dinka.'

Tamar saw a big laughing face by her side, cratered with old chicken pox scars, teeth with big gaps, and a smile full of grace, topped with fluorescent green, Brillo-pad hair.

'Let's try it again.' Four silver earrings hung from each of Sheli's round ears, and a silver stud shone in her nose as well; she had a big eyebrow ring, and a large tattoo of an archer stood out on her stomach as she stood. She stretched a strong hand out to Tamar and pulled her up. It became clear that she was a head and a half taller than Tamar.

'Well, here I am.' She shrugged, almost apologizing for her height. 'Complete, uncut, unabridged. Back to the mines!' They both crawled under the mattress again and lifted it together. It took them about ten minutes to get it up the stairs; they were laughing so much, they collapsed and stood and groaned, and their eyes teared with exertion, and by the time they made it to the second floor, they were already exhausted and a bit tangled together.

Sheli opened the door. It was a smaller room than the others. The floor tiles were broken and missing here as well, and the PVC pipes and electrical wires hung down from the ceiling, but the bed by the window was made, the blankets on it folded carefully. A colorful Mexican tapestry hung stretched on the wall, and a book, *The Bird of the Soul*, rested on the bed. Some kind of shelf, supported by red bricks, was under the window; on top, a few colorful stones and a thick red candle, and books leaning on each other. Tamar's eyes clung to them with hunger.

'"Do you find the rooms pleasant?"' Sheli asked with a smile.

'"Truly? I do not find the rooms pleasant,"' Tamar quoted back, and was rewarded by a merry sparkle from the eyes in front of her.

'"Well, will you not stay with us?"'

'"I will and I'll stay with a willing heart!"' – Tamar smiled – '"because the neighbors are fine in my eyes,"' and received a smile as wide as a hug from Sheli.

'Welcome to Hell,' Sheli said. 'Make yourself at home. How long has it been?'

'Been since what?'

'Since you left home.'

For a moment she hesitated. Sheli was being so generous with her, and Tamar was almost tempted to tell her the truth.

'Hey, hey, I'm not the police.' Sheli laughed. 'You really don't have to tell me anything.' But Tamar saw her shining, cheerful eyes darken a little.

Tamar longed to tell her the truth; she felt suffocated by the burden of her secret. But she had no choice. 'Sheli, don't be insulted. I need a little time.'

'Take your time, baby. We'll be here for a while. I think we'll be here for the rest of our lives.'

Tamar, who had started spreading her blanket on the mattress, stopped. 'The rest of our lives? Why?'

Sheli lay back on her bed, lit a cigarette, and swung her legs up on the little iron railing at the edge of the bedstead.

'Why, why?' Sheli's lips pursed toward new cracks that had plowed the length and width of the ceiling. 'And now, Tamar, our listener from Jerusalem, asks, "Why?" And really, why? Why did my mother decide, at the age of forty-five, to marry such a repulsive man? Why did my real father die on me when I was seven? Is that nice, is that ... sporting? And why do fleas like to live in mattresses?' she asked, smacking at her tanned thigh.

'No, really,' Tamar said, approaching her bed. 'Why ... why do you say it's for the rest of our lives?'

'Scared, huh?' Sheli said quietly, and with compassion. 'Never mind. Everybody is like that at the beginning. Me, too. You think you've come here for a week, two weeks – it'll be like a summer camp, sure, that's it, an art colony for all the good boys and girls who have cut Mommy's apron strings for a taste of freedom. You stay. And then you stay, and you stay, and even when you run away, well, eventually, you come back. This business sucks you in. It's hard to explain to someone new. It's like a nightmare you can't escape.'

Tamar went to her bed and sat down.

'I don't envy you,' Sheli said, sitting up, her legs sprawled out. 'You're still at the stage when it hurts, when you still miss home – suddenly you smell something in the air, and you remember the omelets mother used to make, with a finely chopped salad on the side. Right?'

Tamar lowered her head. It wasn't the salad for her, actually. When was the last time her mother had stood in the kitchen? When was the last time she had said a single sentence Tamar couldn't anticipate or that wasn't straight from some family TV drama? When was she *there* at all, her real self, without the layers of self-pity wrapped around her? Without every facial expression or hand gesture mourning the fate that brought her to this family. When did she ever stand up for her own opinions with integrity, in front of Tamar, or in front of Tamar's father? And when the hell was she ever really a *mother* to 'all these Tamars,' as she called her with a sweetly cutting sigh, yes, yes, *all these Tamars*, who yearn and constantly quarrel with one another – and with no warning, she was hit by an unexpected yearning for her father, and shivered; for a minute, she was drawn, against her will, into the unfinished business between them – she was, again, on one of their nighttime strolls, just the two of them walking quickly and in silence for an hour, an hour and a half. He needed a lot of time before he was willing to peel away the tough rind of his childish, twisted arrogance; to finally stop teasing her, cutting into her every sentence with some sarcastic comment. Only then would she meet him, so briefly, meet the man he had buried, systematically and cruelly, so deeply inside himself. She remembered that once, a year ago, no more, he had stopped her with his hand at their front door and blurted, 'Talking to you is like talking with a man.' She knew that was the greatest compliment that could come from his mouth, and kept herself from her automatic response, to ask him why he didn't have one friend, one man he could pour out his heart to.

'I'm already past that part, thank God,' Sheli said, from very far away. 'I've erased them completely from my life, both of them. They're dead, as far as I'm concerned. Now I'm my own mother and father. Hell, I'm a complete PTA meeting!' and she threw her head back again and the peals of her laughter rang in the air, even though now they rang a bit too loudly. She nervously searched through one of her bags and pulled out a new pack of Marlboros.

'Do you mind the cigarettes?'

'No. Do you mind the dog?'

'Why should I? Her name's Dinka? Let it be Dinka. Dinka – isn't it kind of like Alice's cat, Dinah, in *Alice in Wonderland*?'

Tamar smiled. 'You're the second person in the world to ever guess it.' The first one was Idan, of course.

'Don't look at me like that,' Sheli said. 'If I was getting my high school diploma this year, I'd definitely be majoring in literature.' She pointed toward the dog. 'Come here, Dinka,' and Dinka stood and approached her as if they had known each other for years. 'Come to Mommy, and to Mommy's mommy, and to Daddy's mommy.' She lit the cigarette and blew smoke out of the side of her mouth. 'What eyes she has . . .' she whispered. 'She understands everything.' She pressed her face into the dog's fur. For a long moment there was no movement in the room except for Sheli's shoulders, shaking slightly. Dinka stood, beautiful and noble, looking straight ahead. Tamar turned her face to the window – sprays of light came in diagonally through the torn window screen, and thousands of dust motes flew in, blowing in constantly. Sheli shifted on her bed and sat with her back to the room. 'It's contagious,' she finally said, in a voice that cracked. 'When someone new comes with the smell of home still on her, it attacks you, too. Fucks up all your defense mechanisms.'

Tamar sat on her bed and played with her toes. Then, in a swift motion, she lay on it full length, feeling the hollows and the hills, and the prickles of the rough blanket.

'Congratulations,' Sheli said. 'That's the hardest step here. It's like going into the sea, the moment the water reaches your you-know-what.'

'Tell me,' Tamar asked, 'how come there's hardly anyone in the rooms?'

'Because they're all out performing.'

'Where?'

'All over the country. They'll start coming back early tonight. Some spend a day or two on the road, but they all return here. And everyone is here on Friday night, always.' She blew a smoke ring and traced a smile inside it. 'Like a big, happy family.'

'Ah.' Tamar digested this new information. 'How are the guys here?'

'Oh, there's all kinds. Some are fuckable, especially the guys who play – they're really hot – and some just suck. Most of them are pretty psycho. They won't talk to you and can't even tell if you're there, they're high most of the time, and when they're not' – she waved her hand holding the cigarette – 'you had better keep your distance. If you give them any trouble, they'll eat you alive.'

'High? But that guy Pesach told me –'

'That drugs are off limits here? *Sure,*' she said, stretching the word out, her voice rough. 'He's covering his ass.'

'Really?'

'"Really"? You're so cute, I swear.' Sheli scrutinized her briefly, her eyes dissecting. 'You don't belong here, you know. It's not like' – she searched for a word, and Tamar irritatedly finished the sentence in her head – 'like in your books.' But Sheli didn't want to hurt her; she flashed a smile and cautiously sidestepped the words, avoiding any friction. 'C'mon, who do you think sells it to the guys at marked-up prices? Who? And who makes sure that there will always, but always, be pipes and works available here? Not him? Not his bulldogs?'

'Who are his bulldogs?' Tamar asked faintly.

'The guys who drive us around. They guard us during the performances. You'll get to know them only too well. But he doesn't know anything, understand? He's clean. He's just in it for the art, and to keep us off the streets, and to give some poor orphans a hot meal every day; he's a would-be Yanush Korczak. But not a day passes when they don't try and sell to me, and they'll try to sell to you, too.' Sheli tilted her neck back slightly and looked at Tamar. 'Well, maybe not at first. First they need to check out just who and what you are. Tell me . . . do you use?'

'No.' She had smoked once on that trip to Arad, and that was it. She never took it, even when she was offered it here and there. She had a hard time even explaining why. It had something to do with the connection between internal emotions and strange substances.

'You're lucky. Me neither. I have character. I don't touch it. Some weed once a week, just to kind of cleanse my soul, and sometimes when it's really, and I mean really, shitty, I'll do a little crystal; but that's it. Heroin? Never touch the stuff, not even if they put it here in front of me, not for a million bucks. I wouldn't touch it with a ten-foot pole. *Nada!* My life is fucked up enough – I'd rather be fully conscious of every step on my way down to the bottom.'

Tamar wanted to ask about Shai – whether Sheli had seen

him here, whether she knew what condition he was in these days, whether he was even alive. It took a lot of effort, but she stayed silent. Sheli was very nice, but Tamar was plagued by the thought that Pesach might have sent her here to discover who she was. It made no sense, it was disgusting to even suspect Sheli of that, but she had trained herself over the last month to suspect any person she met, so she wouldn't make any mistakes. The worst part was that Tamar knew Sheli could easily sense this thin cover she was now using to protect herself.

'There's something I don't understand,' she said after a long silence. 'Why does he run this place, Pesach? What does he get out of it?'

'Art, of course.' Sheli laughed, blowing a cloud of contempt toward the ceiling. 'He's running his own private producing company with his own artists. He organizes it, and books shows and drives around and holds the whole country in the palm of his hand, cell phones, big boss, tough guy, *impresario de crapola*. He really loves it. And don't forget, he cuts coupons all day.'

'What do you mean?'

'Money.' Sheli started rubbing imaginary bills and drooling imaginary spittle. 'Money . . . *dinero* . . . *masari* . . . *gelt*.' She had the talent to squeeze humor out of every gesture, and Tamar, even in her bleak mood, couldn't help laughing.

'But it's not . . . there's got to be something else going on here, right? Otherwise, what is all this for?' Tamar waved her hand, indicating the room, the whole abandoned hospital. 'He can't be doing all this just for the few shekels we earn on the street. Do you really think this is it?' Because even if Pesach preferred to be just . . . a small-time, if successful, crook . . . one piece was still missing from the puzzle around her; she couldn't figure out what it was. Something having to do with work and profit. Some counter-argument about the gap between the amount of effort that she felt went into this – all the organizing, running a huge home here, and transporting kids to different cities – versus the amount of money that this Pesach could earn from hats placed on sidewalks.

Sheli fell silent for a moment. She curved her lips around the cigarette. 'Now that you mention it . . .' she murmured, and Tamar wasn't sure she was being honest.

'What? Don't tell me you never thought of that.'

'What do I know? I thought, I didn't think. What does it matter? Perhaps at the beginning you think a lot, yes, your brain is working overtime. Later, I told you – you just get sucked in.' She pulled her knees to her stomach, and her chest sank. 'You get up in the morning, they take you to do a performance, two performances, ten performances. In one day you go from Tel Aviv to Holon, to Ashkelon, to Nes Tziyona, to Rishon Le Tziyyon; you try not to listen to the guy sitting in the front seat, his guard dog. Hearing his voice is enough to make you feel like calling Darwin up and telling him, 'Hey, mister, bad call – man didn't evolve from the monkeys, it's the other way around.' She instantly did a perfect imitation of a monkey scratching his chest, searching for lice, picking one out, looking at it, considering it for a second, and then crushing it between puffed-out lips. 'Once or twice a day they give you something in a pita, and you eat – in the street, in some dirty yard, in the car – between the performances. You sleep, they wake you up, you perform. You don't know if you're in Bat-Yam or Netanya, it's all the same shit, all the streets and squares look alike. All the audiences are the same: all the boys are named Din, and the girls, Ifat – unless it's the Russians, and then it's Yevgeny and Mashinka. All the rest are just cheap, nameless bastards. The day before yesterday, this one scumbag put a twenty-shekel bill in my hat and bent down and took fifteen back in change. Can you imagine? He was lucky I didn't kick his ass. After a few days like that, you can't tell morning from night, can't tell if you're coming or going, can't remember your name, your rank, *or* your serial number. You finish a set, ah, very nice, applause; you collect the money and go to the rendezvous point, and the car is waiting for you. Or sometimes he's waiting for someone else to finish in another city, so you have to bake in the sun for an hour –' The longer she spoke, the more pinched and resentful her face became, making her look

149

a lot older than her age. 'Eventually, the car pulls up – your limousine, your Lamborghini! Ha! The fucked-up Subaru. You creep inside and fold yourself up as small as possible and sleep for another hour, so as to not get depressed by a conversation on the theory of relativity with the sausage in the driver's seat. By the end of the day, you don't remember where you went, or what you did, or what you're called. When they bring you back at night, you barely have the energy to eat the mashed potatoes that Pesach's mommy burned. And you crawl upstairs and go to sleep. You see?' She flashed a wide, glamorous smile. 'This is what I've been talking about: the fascinating lives of the megastars, the shining world of bohemia!' She fluttered her lashes three times and gave a little curtsy, indicating the end of the performance.

Tamar was silent for a long time. She felt her muscles stiffening, as if to absorb the blows of the days to come. 'So how come you're here today?' she asked.

'Today I had to meet with my juvy officer.' Sheli laughed. 'Some fart with a certificate who is sure she's God's greatest gift to the world since the toaster. But at least I get a day off once a month, so I can hear her say, "But, Sheli, tell me, why do you refuse to help us help you?"'

'Why a juvy officer? What did you do?'

'What did I do? What *didn't* I do?' She hesitated a little and laughed. 'My God, it is so obvious you're new – you don't ask questions like that here. Here, you have to wait until they tell you themselves; if they don't say anything – you don't ask. But you asked, so I'll tell you: I committed no murder, except on the few packs of Marlboros I transferred to my legal custody without proper compensation. Did you fall off your bed?'

'No. You stole cigarettes?'

'Someone stole my wallet the day I ran away; by the time I reached Holon Central Station, imagine! I was left with nothing. And, more than food, more than drink, if I don't have my cigarettes, I go absolutely crazy. How did I know they had cameras and detectives and all that shit?'

Dinka barked. A shadow fell over them. Pesach stood in

the doorway, filling the entire space with his body. Tamar
was terrified by the thought that he had been listening to
them for a few minutes. He had to duck his head to get in
through the door. His eyes resentfully scanned the two girls,
sitting on their beds facing each other, their arms wrapped
around their knees, hugging them close.

'You've started a club here already?' he growled.

'Why, is it forbidden?' Sheli taunted him.

He sniffed the air. 'You watch your mouth. And be careful
not to burn the mattress.'

'Why not? Do you need the fleas for something, too? Wait
a minute! Maybe you'll start a flea circus as well, like Charlie
Chaplin!' and she did an excellent imitation of a flea jumping
from one hand to the other.

'You . . .' Pesach leaned on the wall and rubbed his back
against it in an almost imperceptible motion that, for some
reason, made Tamar's stomach contract. 'You never learn
your lesson, do you?' Again, he spoke very slowly, as if
he were spelling out every word. 'One day, honey, one
day you'll cross the line, this much, just this much –' he
pinched his index and thumb together – 'and suddenly you'll
be in a situation that you will most certainly find very, very
unpleasant.'

She saw it happening now, how without any outward
change the fat teddy turned into a wild bear with long claws.
His skin, she thought in amazement, it's as if his skin has dried
up on his face.

'So why don't you do it now and get it over with,' Sheli
snapped, and turned away from him – and received Tamar's
instant worship.

'Believe me, you're very close, very, very close. One day
you'll get on my nerves, and then we'll see what happens to
you, big hero, we'll see you the way you were when you came
back that one night, bloody and beaten up and crying for us to
please, please, take you back. Do you remember that, or have
you forgotten already?'

Sheli concentrated on her cigarette and watched the smoke
rings she blew toward the ceiling.

'So you better keep quiet, and don't spoil the new girl for me. And you better go down, both of you, to the kitchen and help with supper.'

'With the mashed potatoes, you mean,' Sheli corrected. He shot her a murderous look and walked out.

'How can you not be afraid of him?' Tamar asked.

'What is he going to do to me? He needs me, he won't give me up.'

'Why?'

'Do you know how much I bring in every day? Probably five hundred shekels.'

'Five hundred?' Tamar gasped. 'Just from singing?'

'I don't sing.' Sheli laughed. 'I do impersonations, kind of like a singer-stand-up artist, like Rita, Yudit Ravitz, that kind of thing.'

'So why don't you work alone?' Tamar asked. 'Why do you have to give him the money?'

'Because being alone on the streets is not a walk in the park. You can get by for two or three days, people leave you alone, checking to make sure you're not a narc or something. But then the real shit starts – Believe me, I tried. You heard what he said. I came crawling back.'

Tamar thought about all she had heard. After a moment she asked, 'Do Rita.'

'For you? A private show?' Sheli said. 'No problemo.' She stood on the bed and took a deep breath . . . Tamar started to smile.

She did Rita, and Madonna, and finally Tzipi Shavit singing 'Everybody Went to the Jambo.' She couldn't sing – Idan would have quaked with disgust – but she had a cheerful, sparkling talent, combined with a healthy, unapologetic rudeness, and Tamar laughed until she cried. She thought that with Idan and Adi, the laughter was completely different, all from the head.

Then, all at once, Sheli's energy evaporated. She stretched out full length on the bed, said, 'Night,' pulled the blanket over her head, and, in a few seconds, started snoring.

Tamar sat on the edge of her bed, a bit surprised at the

quick finale. She then nodded to Dinka and whispered, 'Let's go.' She decided to help in the kitchen, because she was a little scared of Pesach. Also, because she thought that the more she walked around this place, the more she would understand, to prepare herself for what was expected of her.

They woke her at six the next morning. A skinny guy with thick sideburns shook her rudely. 'Come on, get up, we're moving in a half-hour.'

She felt as if she hadn't slept a wink the entire night. She'd kept glancing at the clock until three in the morning, waited to hear the outer gates open. She thought that perhaps he would arrive later, perhaps he was performing in a faraway city. Now she wearily pulled on her clothes. Then she stopped and looked in her bag, checked where she had placed something last night, and saw the change; she looked through it cautiously. The one shekel coin she had hidden yesterday, between two socks, wasn't in its place. She searched and found it at the bottom of the bag and knew that someone had taken her bag last night, after she fell asleep, and looked through it for clues. It was lucky that she had hidden the plastic-wrapped bundle in her panties. She was lucky she'd remembered to leave her bracelet, with her name engraved on it, at the baggage check.

Sheli still slept, trying to shrink as much as she could, dreaming, perhaps, that she was small and gentle. Tamar looked at her. She thought about how Sheli had welcomed her the day before, how naturally she took her up to the room and talked to her and made her happy. She didn't make a big deal of anything, not of Tamar's suspicions or the usual boundaries she set in approaching new people. I am very grateful, she thought, lacing up her sneakers, very grateful for people who know how to be easy with me.

She and Dinka went downstairs to the first floor. A few of the faces she had seen at dinner the night before were up and walking around. The corridor was full of action. Pesach marched past everyone like a general before a battle; he held a big red book in his hands and flipped through it again and again. 'You.' He pointed to the guy who had woken her up, the skinny one with the sideburns and an Elvis pompadour. 'You take the guy with the sticks. First to Netanya, half an hour in the Walking Street; then you go by the old post office – know where that is? Where Sharon Cinema used to be? Good. Then you *fly* to Kfar Saba, to the square by the mall. He finishes his business over there and, boom, straight to Herzliya, to – whatchamacallit? – Beit Ha-Etrach, is that what it's called? The patch of grass there, by the main street. There. And watch out: you get there by half past twelve, not one minute after. Got it? Now: you stay there with him for twenty-five minutes, not a minute more, why do you need more than that? How long can a guy walk on stilts, anyway? And from there, like a rocket, you take him to Ordeya Square in Ramat Gan. How many have you got already, four? Not enough. Wait one minute.'

He pulled out his cell phone and dialed. 'Khemi. Listen, Khemi, until when are you with your girl in Herzelliya, at Citizen House? For how long? Why? How much time does she need to pull scarves out of her nose? I don't accept that. Magic or no magic, you disappear by twelve on the dot, not one second after. Why? Because I'm putting someone else in there at half past and I need at least a half-hour gap in between. Why? You still don't know why? . . . Okay! The lightbulb went on! Bravo. So don't argue with me! Go!'

He continued in this fashion, sending out the boys and girls, organizing the drivers who took them, reminding each one what to take, running after the sword swallower, who, as usual, had forgotten the bag with his swords; ordering the girl who made balloon animals to put a tape player next to her, with music, to keep the audience entertained in the meantime; tapping the pale guy with the violin on his shoulder and telling him to try smiling at least once an hour, because the audiences don't like funeral faces. The corridor became emptier and emptier, until Tamar was almost the only one left. She already feared she would have to spend another whole day in this gloomy place.

'Now you. We're sending you to Haifa. C'mere, Miko. You have a special passenger today! Take her to the Ha Carmel Center first. Find a good place for her – it's her first time out of town and she's a class act.' Pesach winked at him. 'So be gentle with her, okay? Then take her to Neve Sha'anan, to – what do you call it – the Ziv Center –' He talked on, and Tamar stopped hearing him. She had the ability to stop hearing whenever outside voices became too irritating. It used to drive her mother crazy. Where are you disappearing to when you do that? How do you do that? When you make that marble face, your eyes become like, I don't know what, like they're covered with skin, like a parrot.

'And if you have time on the way back, squeeze another one in on Zikhron Ya'Akov, and in the Walking Street over there.' She heard Pesach from afar. 'About how long do you sing for, sweetie? Hey, wake up! Where did you go!'

Tamar said about half an hour.

'Fifteen minutes isn't enough for you? Fine, today you'll do half an hour. I want you to feel good about it. Tomorrow, we'll see. That's it, four performances. That's enough to start with.'

Miko was the man who had driven her here yesterday, with Pesach's mother and father. He went to the Subaru without a word to her; she followed. She didn't know where she was supposed to sit, beside him or in the back. She sat in the back seat, knowing that this would make him feel like a cab driver. She didn't care. Dinka stuck her head out the window and breathed the cool air with pleasure.

Tamar was glad to be out of Jerusalem, to be on the way to somewhere, in transit. She felt slightly important, as if she were a famous artist being driven in a special car to a performance. In her mind, she waved to the throngs of adoring fans who gathered on the sides of the street and threw hothouse orchids to them from her bouquet.

They drove in silence. Tamar wondered when Miko would explain to her what she needed to know. He didn't say a word. He was constantly pressing the buttons on his cell phone, playing shrill, staccato tunes, one after the other; he flipped between the dozens of different rings the device offered for almost an hour, and Tamar's head nearly exploded. The once or twice she tried to ask him questions, he ignored her. When Tamar was six, she had lived by the train tracks; then, she divided the world into two kinds of people: the kind of people who wave back to a little girl standing by the tracks and those who don't. Miko was undoubtedly of the second category. Every once in a while, he looked at her through the rearview mirror. His eyes were black and burned her – he despised her. She didn't know why, and after a short time, she didn't care, either.

'Now listen to me,' he suddenly said rudely, 'this is how it goes. I pull the car over in some street by the center. You walk around for, like, ten minutes, and then you start performing. If you see me in the audience, you don't drop any sign that we know each other. And most important – if someone asks you, you don't know anything about me. You came to Haifa last night on a bus, you slept in Central Station, and you didn't talk to anyone. Clear?'

Tamar nodded without looking at him.

'When you finish singing – you sing, right?'

'Yes.'

'Finish up, take the money, walk around for another five, ten – no more than ten – minutes. Only through side streets, never on the main drag. Got me?'

'Yes.'

'After ten minutes, you go back to the car and vamoose. Got it?'

'Got it.'

'One more time: if there's a cop around or anything fishy, don't come close to the car, and if you see me, you walk right by as if I was nothing. Air. You get in only if it's a thousand percent clear. That's it.'

They came to a small, quiet street, that went down toward the sea. Tamar saw low houses and a row of pine and cypress trees shading the street. Miko parked the car and even slid a parking permit under the windshield wipers; she imagined he was doing that only to prevent any possible contact with the police. 'Now, this is Ha Broshim Street. Remember the name. On the corner there's the supermarket and the gym. Don't forget. Move. Go on. Move.'

Just like that, without a blessing for the road, without anything, she stepped out to the street.

She got hoarse as soon as she started singing and had to stop for a few minutes. She was scared. She was going to spoil it for herself again, right here. While she was clearing her throat, she thought that it wasn't good for her to be getting used to singing without warming up her voice first – it causes damage in the long term. But the words 'long term' sounded empty to her, they had nothing to do with her life, because, for now, she existed only in the short term. She started singing again. She sang 'Your Wreathed Forehead' and 'Guard Your Soul.' She didn't like her singing here, she wasn't connecting to the words, and as much as she tried, the performance wasn't taking off. She grew uneasy – she was afraid Pesach might hear about it from Miko and fire her on the spot. The thought drove her crazy: that she could be dependent on Miko's professional opinion! She also knew exactly the reason for her failure: when she sang in Jerusalem, the street lit her up, almost always; and even when she couldn't forget her goal for one moment, she sang out with freedom and joy. Now, with Pesach's huge engine behind her, she felt like a canary in a cage.

As a finale, she sang '*Los Biblicos*' in Ladino, a song the audience knew as 'A Rose Is Blooming.' The simple warmth of the tune revived her spirits a little; the people walking around started smiling at her. Something familiar returned, flowed in her again, and so she spontaneously decided to sing Leah Goldberg's 'Marionettes.' She knew it from Noa's children's tape, which she loved, and her voice jumped and danced:

*'In masks on a balcony carnival night*
*That a streetlamp forgot to keep with its light*
*They carelessly met.*
*He spoke and she listened;*
*She's Pierrette, he's Pierrot . . .'*

She smiled with her eyes at a young man who stood there, barefoot, intently absorbing her voice. He was almost shocked by her smile, and approached, drawn to her. *'And perhaps she's not Pierrette,'* she sang to him, rolling her eyes,

*'Perhaps, perhaps, simply*
*She's a puppet, Marionette,*
*Who's being pulled by a string . . .'*

They applauded her enthusiastically and asked for more. But she didn't feel like singing an encore. She wanted to keep moving, to understand what was going on around her, in what kind of show she was participating, and what exactly her role was.

When she finished, the man, barely more than a boy, came up to her. He was thin and delicate, wearing a djellaba and tiny beads in his hair, his eyes fiery, completely high. He told her he had to take her with him to the Galilee, immediately: there was this one cave with divine acoustics created for her voice, and he had to hear her there. When he said 'cave' she saw hers for a second, the one with the mattress and a folding chair, and the guitar leaning on the wall. Who knew if she would ever manage to get back there? Who knew whether she would ever manage to take Shai there with her? She smiled her polite smile at him and shook her head no. He wouldn't let go. Just come and see it – his hand grasped her arm tightly, stroking it a bit – God made it just for your voice. What do you say, little flower? Just sing one song for me over there . . . Tamar yanked her arm out of his hand, hard. Her gray-blue eyes became metallic. I said, Let go of me! He looked at her and saw something that made him back off. He left.

She wandered through side streets for a few more minutes, feeling like a prisoner being transferred from one jail to the next. People walked around her, talking; cars were going by. Everyday life was so close, you could reach your hand out and touch it. She saw everything as if from behind a wall of glass. Miko didn't look at her when she got into the car. She handed over the bag with the money. He weighed it in his hand.

'That's it?'

'That's what they gave me,' she said, and was angry at herself. Why am I apologizing to him?

'Because if you're keeping any for yourself, it's over for you. You know that, don't you? We have ways of checking.'

'I didn't take anything,' she said quietly, and stared him down, straight into his eyes, until he had to look away.

He started the car. Again they drove in silence. Tamar tried to understand what was going on. During the performance, she had seen him passing through the people listening to her a few times. She didn't understand whom he was supposed to protect her from, and why there was this great fear of the police – and why did Pesach explain to someone over the phone that morning that he needed a half-hour gap between performances? She tried to concentrate. When the man with the cave in the Galilee harassed her, Miko didn't dive in to help her out. So what was his job during her performance? There was no logic to it. They drove her to Haifa, they warned her and scared her, she sang, nothing special happened, and now she was being driven to perform somewhere else. What was all this for?

She called on her father for help – he could help a little, at least, with what he understood: overhead versus income, investment risk, profitability . . . his mantras, his little suit of armor. She thought about the five hundred shekels Sheli earned every day. Now, let's assume that not everybody made as much as Sheli. Let's say that, on an average day, each one of the artists earns – she did the arithmetic in her head. It got complicated. Numbers had always confused her, and her stomach revolted at those calculations, their calculations. But she didn't give up. She closed her eyes and calculated, multiplied by the number of girls and boys she had seen in the corridor that morning. Her eyes widened: she came up with almost ten thousand shekels a day. That was a lot of money. But something was still missing.

The performance in Ziv Center also went over peacefully. She sang even worse, preoccupied with these troubling riddles; but the audience here was even more excited. She couldn't explain it. Sometimes it was like this – and sometimes it went the other way. It was always a bit depressing – because when they applauded, it only proved yet again how big the gap was between what she felt inside and the way things looked in the eyes of outsiders. She actually knew it well: the particular depression that came after a performance, when she felt that the love encircling her accentuated her loneliness even more, when she felt what depressed her more than anything – that no one understood her.

How did Shai put it, two years ago after some show? – 'Sometimes, it's more insulting when they love you for the wrong reasons than when they hate you for the right ones.'

People came up to her afterward, as usual, and shook her hand enthusiastically, and asked her questions about herself, and fussed over her; it was pleasant to be fussed over like that.

There was a policeman there; he stood to the side at a distance. But he was busy with another gentleman, elegantly dressed, who spoke to him agitatedly, waving his hands. He was probably telling him that something horrible had happened. The policeman listened, wrote something down, and didn't look at her once.

'It was a little better this time,' she blurted when she gave Miko the money, and was ashamed of how eager she was to try and make him happy.

After that, she tortured herself for the whole ride over that sentence: It was a little better this time. What was better? What? That they gave her more money? Actually, the previous performance had been a little better. So what? If they didn't give you a lot of money, did it count less? And if you earned less than Sheli, were you worthless? You toady.

For the first time since she had come to the streets, she really felt as if she had sold herself. She vowed that she would never, ever again apologize if she didn't earn much, not to Miko, or Pesach, or anyone like them, and, in general, not to anyone in the world. She sat up straight in the back seat of the car and raised her chin. The movement reminded her of Theodora, and she drew energy from that thought, and she swore: her role, her destiny, was to sing. And all the rest – was their business.

On the beautiful boardwalk of Bat Galim she sang 'Sweet to Die on the Sea' in Portuguese. She had hardly worked on it before, but the moment she saw the sea, so close to her, it flared up inside her, and she went with it and sang, entirely free, an experienced, ripe singer delivering her song. After that, she took a sharp turn, the familiar pleasure of the slalom, and burst out with 'Benny Benny Bad Boy,' and her hands fluttered like flames of fire; she danced and leaped the way she would never dare to do at parties. She was Riki Gal on stage, with her wildness and bursting passion for life, the halo of blond hair disappearing into clouds of purple smoke . . . A guy and a girl, not much older than she, perhaps a couple of soldiers on vacation, began to dance enthusiastically next to her. She sang to them and made them jump, she danced right in front of them. She finally understood something Halina hadn't been able to teach her for years – not to run away from the excitement she aroused, not to stare out into the empty space beyond them as if she had nothing to do with what she was inciting in them. Ever since she had gone to the streets, performance by performance, she had, without a doubt, become more daring. She didn't hesitate to look straight into the audience's eyes, to smile, to shine her light into them. It had already happened, more than once, that she, with no shame, sang a whole song for one person in front of her – maybe someone she liked, who she thought would understand this song. She would set her sights on him, and focus them, and flirt a little. Sometimes she could feel the real embarrassment she was causing by her mature, piercing look.

It also excited her to think, to feel, how each of them was trying to guess what she was, who she really was, trying to figure out her story. This, too, was a completely different experience from performing with the chorus, one among all the good girls in matching costumes. When she sang in the streets, she would feel, in her body, against her shivering skin, how people gazed at her, searched and dug into her, their imaginations stitching tales and hallucinations onto her body: She's an orphaned girl who's being abused and has to earn her living; she's a rock star from a provincial town in England and she fell in love with an Israeli guy who then left her, so now she has to pay for her ticket back; she's the new discovery of the Paris Opera Youth Workshop, who is conducting an anonymous trip in far-off lands to build up her strength and endurance; she's a girl sick with cancer who decided to spend her last year living the wild life of the streets; she's a prostitute who, during the day, sings with this pure voice . . .

Something swept through her performance on the seashore, between her imagination inflaming her and her vocal daring. It was the first time in her life she had ever sweated from singing, and she enjoyed it so much. Even after Miko had signaled her once, and twice, to finish, she decided to sing another song, ignoring his murderous look, and sang 'Stupid Stupid' by Eti Ankri, hugging herself, swaying to the rhythm of the waves and the rhythm of the soft, lying tune, hiding waspy stings in the words that she could relate to so easily –

> Stupid, stupid, stupid, stupid,
> Look at what you've come to, stupid.
> Stupid, stupid, stupid, stupid,
> Even the blossoms have dried –

Tamar danced around herself, lightly, in self-forgetfulness and bitter pleasure –

*Your thinnest veins,*
*Your cracked dreams,*
*You erected them in strange fields*
*And they hack into your body . . .*

Afterward, after her audience had scattered, she saw an older lady clumsily walking around in terror near where she had sung, looking for something, on the ground, between the bushes, under the benches. 'Here, I am standing right here,' she muttered when she lifted her eyes and saw Tamar. 'Maybe it fell? Maybe they took? But how? Tell me, what is it, what is it? I was just one moment here to hear a song, suddenly I see – gone! Gone!'

'What's gone?' Tamar asked, and her heart started sinking.

'My wallet, with all the money and documents.' She had a fat red face; her nose was embroidered with burst blood veins, and a tower of bleached-blond hair rose from her head. 'Today I get three hundred shekels from boss for wedding of my daughter. Three hundred! He never gives such money! And here I go to hear you, only one minute I stay – oy, I'm an idiot! Now – gone. Everything gone!' Her voice died in sorrow and amazement.

Without hesitating, Tamar handed her all the shekels in her hat. 'Take them.'

'No, you shouldn't. You mustn't!' She stepped back, touched Tamar's slender hand affectionately. 'You mustn't . . . you need food . . . you're a little bird . . . and you give to me? No, no, not good . . .'

Tamar shoved the money into her hands and ran away. She stormed along the beach. The moment she entered the car she said, 'No money. There's nothing. I made about seventy shekels and I gave it to that woman.'

His eyes glittered darkly. 'What woman?'

'That Russian woman you stole from.'

Silence. Miko turned around. He turned very slowly, until she saw his entire face in front of her. Everything seemed to move in slow motion, there was a lot of silence around; she saw the deep wrinkle in his young forehead, his short, curly hair, his thin lips. And then he hit her. He slapped her once, and then again. She flew against the seat, once to the right, once to the left. Dinka rose up and started to growl threateningly. Tamar put her hand on the dog's head: Calm down, calm down. The world was spinning in front of her, falling apart and coming back together again heavily. She heard him driving; the landscape started to run together. She saw Miko's muscular back, intense and alert. She tightened her lips with all her strength and contracted her stomach muscles; but tears started sliding down her cheeks. She didn't wipe them away. She estranged herself from them. *Stupid, stupid, stupid stupid, all your softness is now hard.* She hummed it over and over, turning the words into a single continuous sound inside her, like an alarm, and then a scream. You couldn't hear anything outside. She dove into herself, blotting out the exterior world, all the impossible burdens heaped on her shoulders. She escaped. No one felt her go. She ran away, and made it into a big room, with a piano and Halina. That was the shelter she needed now. Little Halina, with her glasses slipping to the tip of her long nose, with the spark of a sharp look shooting out over the rims. Halina, clenching her little tyrant's palm into a fist, ordering Tamar to focus her voice on the tip of her thumb, on the nail covered in red polish: 'Llll – a!' Tamar sang out, in her head, concentrating hard. 'Nnn – o!' Halina hums in response: 'My nail doesn't feel you at – aaall!' 'Lll – a . . .' 'A little more resonnn – ance . . .' and it helped. It caressed the empty places inside her head; the sound streamed through her like hot blood; it calmed her down and reminded her of what she truly belonged to, and of where she was entirely at one with herself.

After a moment, she felt his eyes stabbing her through the rearview mirror. 'That's the last time you use that word, got me? It's the last time you even think that word in your head. You owe Pesach seventy shekels. You'll sort that out with him. But if you say that word one more time, you're finished. You own mother won't recognize you when I'm done with you.'

\*     \*     \*

After that, they drove in complete silence. Her head hurt from the slaps, her soul was shouting, her cheeks burned from both the smacks and the shame. It had been about ten years since anyone had hit her. When she was little, her mother sometimes got angry and would slap her; her father would then hurry to stand between them; once, when her mother really lost control (Tamar couldn't remember what she had done to provoke such an eruption) and chased her throughout the house, she heard her father yell from his study, 'Talma, not in the face,' and a warm spring of gratitude for his attempt to protect her surged through the terror of trying to escape.

Now she thought, Perhaps he was just afraid that she would have marks.

His greatest fear, always: that someone might see.

She forced herself not to think about what had just happened. She knew if she thought about it she'd cry. She pulled herself together, spurred herself to action, busying her brain with feverish calculations: If Miko picks pockets at every one of her performances, and gets two or three wallets; and if she has four or five performances every day, at least – and there will be days when there are ten performances – if twenty or thirty, or even fifty, girls and boys live in the home ... if there's one or two hundred shekels in every wallet, sometimes perhaps a thousand – her head started spinning. A successful small-time crook, but maybe not so small-time. Her clumsy calculation came to upward of tens of thousands of shekels a day. It didn't sound quite right to her, but even after she counted a second time, she came to a similar total. Her palms started to sweat. She tried to translate it to an easier, more comprehensible language. She told herself that Pesach Bet Ha Levi made more in one half-hour than what she earned in a year of working for Theodora.

They came to Zikhron Ya'Akov at five in the afternoon. Tamar felt ragged and broken. She could hardly get out of the car. She didn't think she could stand in front of strangers and sing without crying.

But she stepped out. It was a performance, and she had to

do it. It had nothing to do with Miko and Pesach and the filth they tried to wrap around her. You have a performance. Perform. You will perform in any condition, and if you don't have the strength to do it for yourself, do it for Halina. She'll never forgive you if you give up. 'Imagine, an actor fights with his wife at home – what, you think he's in the mood to play Hamlet? And still, he plays Hamlet!'

She dragged herself to the Walking Street and wandered around for a few moments, looking at the window displays. She saw her reflection in them – a thin girl with a shaved head and huge eyes, with a mouth that looks, tonight, like an upside-down crescent.

She walked between the people, between families, small and large; a light evening breeze started blowing. Kids ran around, chasing each other. Their parents called out to them lazily to stop. Tamar furtively dipped into these little moments of grace – *Look at what you've come to, stupid / All your softness is now hard.* In the coffeehouse that spilled onto the sidewalk, a young, good-looking father sat with his son, who was five or six years old. The boy asked his father to let him read the newspaper on the table, but he didn't know how to read one, and he got tangled up, the huge pages sticking to his face, and he rolled around laughing. His father patiently explained how to do it, showing him the proper motions, repeating them again and again.

A cord of love bound the two, and Tamar almost stepped forward to ask the father if he would allow her to be his son's governess forever, for all eternity – she even knew the songs from *The Sound of Music* and everything! Yearnings for Noiku ran hot through her, for Noiku's contagious joy in living and her peachy cheeks; the way the two would go crazy together, and how the kitchen looked after they baked a surprise cake for Leah; the way they performed on Leah's bed together, turning up the music full blast and making the faces of two rough rockers from the Ohio State Women's Penitentiary – and Noiku only three years old! What fun it would be when she was seven, and seventeen! Tamar could be her best friend, her sister, her guide, her closest soul mate.

She immediately took down, in her head, an urgent question for Theodora, one of those questions you could talk about only with Theo: If a person – any person – decided to enclose himself in armor, seal up and protect his soul, for a certain amount of time, in order to be able to execute a difficult mission – whatever it might be – after the mission has ended, will he be able to be himself, to go back to exactly the same person he was beforehand?

Dragging her legs, she came late to the place she had decided on: the sidewalk in front of Aharonson House. She found a comfortable place for Dinka to lie down, by a huge potted vase with grapevines growing out of it, and made sure they could maintain eye contact. She then stood in the heart of an imaginary circle she sketched around herself, lowered her head, and started getting in the mood for the performance. It was hard for her, standing there. Almost as hard as the first time she sang, in the Walking Street in Jerusalem, a million years ago.

Then surprisingly – for her as well – she opened her mouth and sang. Her singing was strong, stronger than usual; her voice was completely outside her, outside everything happening to her. It remained so clear and pure, she could hardly believe it. She even felt the wonder that her voice could remain so separate from what she, herself, was going through. She was completely unfocused through the first two songs, mainly concentrating on trying to get close to it, to her voice, to make it her own again. It was a strange experience. For the first time in her life, she felt a kind of resentment toward her voice, which seemed to insist upon staying clean while she was getting so filthy. Almost without thinking, she changed her prearranged plans, moved, instead, to sing Kurt Weill. Halina called them 'man-hating songs.' She sang of Jenny, the used-up maid, the depressed prostitute, dreaming of a ship with eight shining sails and fifty-five cannons and dozens of pirates who would reach the shore of her town's port in front of the crummy old hotel she was working in, and destroy, in a storm of fire, the town and the hotel and all those who had abused her. It wasn't the first time she had sung this song, but now, it was grabbing her by the roots; she knew she was singing from a new place inside herself, from the bottom of her stomach, from the earth. In her head, she sang along with Marianne Faithful, who had taught her to sing Jenny. Marianne Faithful, whose singing Shai adored, particularly from the period after the drugs; they would both listen to her smoky, burnt voice in his room, and Shai said that only someone who had really burned in her life could sing like that. Then, Tamar thought sorrowfully, she would probably never sing that way, because what could possibly happen to her in her life?

Her hands started to move; her face, the face that had absorbed the slaps, regained its expressiveness. Her voice flew through her body like her blood, reviving, in its flow, her hands, her stomach, her feet, her slightly heavy breasts. Warm circles slithered through her body, and she moved them through herself temptingly, lightly intoxicated. She sang to herself, for herself; it was almost as if it didn't belong to the people around her anymore, and they felt it. Probably because of that, they also wanted to peek into what was happening inside her, but she didn't give it to them – as far as she was concerned, they were surrounding her now only by coincidence. She sang, rolling her voice deep inside her, through her darkest caves. She had never dared sing to those places, not with such ugly, burnt, thirsty pain. Now – she reached down that far, she submerged her filthy self, full of choked cries, of loneliness and poison, until she felt it rising up. It was being pulled out, saved from herself – and she was rising alone with it, slowly: who she was now, what she had lost in the past year, and what was growing, slowly, inside her, in spite of everything.

Vaguely, she noticed it – more and more people had gathered around her. A lot of people – she never had had such a big crowd. She had already sung for over her half-hour, but couldn't detach herself – not from them, but from the new places she had found within herself.

For a finale, she sang the solo that had been taken from her, her beloved solo from Pergolesi's *Stabat Mater*. She chose to end with this, above anything else, with the pure, crystal-clear sounds. Nobody laughed this time. Again, her singing was her only absolute, the only thing that was completely her. A thousand classes hadn't given her this concrete insight: her voice was her place in the world, the home she leaves in the morning and returns to at night, in which she can be herself in her entirety and hope to be loved for all that she is and in spite of all she is. If I had to choose between happiness and singing well – she wrote in her journal once, when she was fourteen – I have no doubt which I would choose.

One moment of grace, tranquillity, and internal conciliation – and she started to wake up and remember where she was. She saw Miko's curly hair as he crept through the rows of people, screwed up her eyes tight, and sang, and knew this voice of hers was now making one person in the crowd forget himself for a moment; and she knew then what it meant to be, as she rolled the words out, 'accessory to the crime.' And she kept on singing.

When she finished, she almost collapsed, completely dizzy with exhilaration. She slowly tossed her hat down to the ground and collapsed to the side for a moment, pressing her whole body against Dinka, clinging to her, pulling strength from her. People crowded around her, yelling 'Bravo!' The hat was brimming with shekels, and a twenty-shekel bill blinked greenly at her, for the first time in her career. She gathered it all up and put it in her bag, but they wanted more, shouting together in rhythm, 'More, more, more!'

She was powerless – too many emotions coursed through her, and they saw it and still didn't give up – they now knew they would get the last of her, her nectar. She blushed, confused, shining as if she were glistening with morning dew. They cheered and she laughed. Now she was in a different public space, an arena of arousal and excitement; it was dangerous. When she performed with the chorus, she was well protected by all sides, protected from the possibility of humiliation, of falling apart, that moments like these some-times had. At most performance halls, the curtain descends, hiding the intoxication of finishing a show from the audience;

here, there was no curtain, she was standing among them, and they shamelessly fed off what was in her, that she could feel only when she was being sucked at like this by them. It was powerful, the excitement, being sucked like this, so powerful she got scared for a moment – perhaps she had already given too much of herself, and whatever had been taken from her would never be returned.

And because of that, she sang a modest little ditty for her encore, a French children's song about a shepherd and a shepherdess – the shepherd finds a small kid in the valley and brings it back to the shepherdess, asking nothing in return except a kiss on the cheek. The song cleared her head, brought her back down to earth. She saw Miko dart away from there, quickly, the pockets of his pants bulging. Her eyes searched the crowd, seeking the source of the next outcry. Guilt pierced her heart – how could she stand it, and not confess right there, right now, in front of everyone? But she was on a mission, she had a role to play. She repeated these words to herself again and again, while she sang the simple tune, and that alone kept her seeming innocent and sweet and enchanting; only by her rich experience did she manage to prevent herself from singing what someone else inside her was yelling, loudly – How could you, you, with all your brave principles and criticisms of the world . . .

'Not bad,' Miko chuckled when she handed over the bag as if it were infected with some contagious disease. 'See, you learned something. Just make it shorter next time.'

He counted it silently – only his lips were moving. 'All *right*,' he told her through the mirror. 'You made a hundred and forty shekels. You're welcome every day.'

She turned her head away from him, disgusted. She was afraid she would puke right there. A brown wallet was bouncing on the passenger's seat next to him; for the blink of an eye she saw a tiny photo in it – a picture of that laughing boy from the coffeehouse.

\* \* \*

She had already started to doubt she would ever see Shai there. One week after her arrival at the abandoned hospital, she understood exactly what Sheli had been talking about on the first day: she was sucked into it. Long hours passed during which she didn't think about why she was there, or for whom. She rarely thought about her former life, like a tightrope walker who mustn't look down at the abyss beneath him. She banished any thoughts of her parents, about people she loved, about the chorus, even about Idan. She had gone thousands of kilometers all over the country that week, with a total of nine different drivers, by her count. She went to Beersheba, and Safed, and Afula, and Nazareth. She learned to eat in the car, without surrendering to the familiar dizziness of her nausea; and to sleep at any possible opportunity, at any moment of the day, curled up like a ragged cloth on the back seat. She learned to sing five and six and seven times a day without ruining her voice; mainly, though, she learned to keep quiet.

Her and her big mouth. Miko had begun her education with those two slaps. Later, she learned not to say anything, even to the other boys and girls; and, as Sheli had warned, to be very careful with questions. Everyone in that home was a wounded soul in one way or another. Every one of them had escaped some disaster. And under the rudeness and loudness of the big group, certain rules of behavior were carefully adhered to, and these contained more than a little compassion and nobility: any questions about the home you left behind, whether you had escaped or were banished, aroused waves of renewed pain, opened closed wounds that might have already started to scab over; and any questions about what would become of you, where you would go from here, what awaited you in your life, your expectations, awakened both despair and fear. She grasped very quickly, and intuitively, that the past and future were off limits here: Pesach's home existed in the dimension of a permanent, continuous present.

It was just as well. She worried that any unnecessary word would give her away. Maybe that was what imposed on her friendship with Sheli a certain restraint and reserve. Sometimes, early in the morning, or late at night – before

Sheli would, as she said, 'crash like a sack of potatoes' – they would exchange a few words, their experiences of the day, both feeling how much they wanted to say more, to talk about real things. But they would stop themselves, say no: they, too, just like everyone who came here, had known betrayal from those closest to them. They, too, had learned a lesson: that there are situations in which you can't really trust anybody. In which – how did someone put it once? – in which every person has to save his own soul.

In those moments they would exchange pained looks, full of words: You and I, we're both lonely guerrilla soldiers, trying to survive behind enemy lines, careful not to deposit our secrets into the hands of a stranger. Even if she is as sweet as you, Tamar – as you, Sheli. Me too. It's a shame. Perhaps someday. I wish. In another life. In another incarnation . . .

Not everybody was as lonely as she. She noticed some friendships there, and couples; there were even three big family rooms, full of smaller and larger groups of people. Off the dining room there was a room that served as a kind of club, where the boys and girls would play Ping-Pong and backgammon. Pesach even donated a high-tech coffeemaker and promised he would bring in a computer soon, one you could even compose music on. She heard that there were sometimes parties in the rooms at night, and she knew people were smoking together, jamming. From her usual vantage point, as an outsider, she noticed with what joy they would meet each other in the dining room at night – the approach; the hug, hands wrapping around each other's back, a tap, and another one – 'Hey, brother, what's up?' 'What's up?' For a moment, she, in her loneliness, would envy even this.

But her reason for coming here remained as far off and unattainable as on that first day.

When she was still living at home, only in the planning stages of this, she was sure she would constantly be in action here, thinking, cracking clues, pulling evidence together to form some answer – but from the moment she entered the home, her brain slowed down, became sluggish and heavy, gaping, so dumb that she experienced long moments of panic, afraid she would stay this way for good, would be carried forward in this magic circle of performing and sleeping, and gradually forget what she came for.

She had to wake herself forcibly from this desperate, hypnotic illusion. Slowly, with effort, she put the pieces of the mosaic together: there were artists in this place, twenty boys and girls, or thirty, or fifty – you couldn't tell, they came and went, they were gone for long days and then suddenly reappeared. Sometimes she felt as if she were in a crowded train station, or a refugee camp. She didn't know whether all the others had come to this home the same way she had. As far as she could tell, they, too, had heard rumors about this place and had very much wanted Pesach's 'talent scouts' to discover them. She was surprised to find people whispering, all over the country, about this unique residence and its romantic aura of all that was artistic and bohemian. People from Tiberias, Eilat, Gush Etzion, from Kfar Giladi, even from Taibe and Nazareth, had heard of a place where, if they take you, you get to perform hundreds of times in the street, all over the country, gaining experience and confidence – and you emerge hungry, a stage animal – a lot more than after four years in some fancy art school. None of them ever spoke about Miko, his friends and their trade, out loud. The artists lived with the crooks, spent many hours every day with them, ate and drove with them, performed near them, and, as if they didn't see or hear it, never said a word about what was really going on. Tamar felt it happening to her, too: she was training herself to be the three monkeys. Once, coming back at night from a performance in Nes Tziyyona, lying down, folded up and hungry in the back seat, she thought she was starting to understand how people got used to living under oppressive dictatorships, for decades; they disconnect themselves from whatever is going on around them. If they could truly comprehend their situation, tell themselves with stark honesty whom they're cooperating with, they would have no choice but to die of shame.

Because she couldn't confront Miko's actions, and those of his friends, she was able to see only the artists: mimes and magicians and violinists and flutists. She saw one gloomy-faced girl who played the cello, wearing glasses and a red cloche hat that she never took off. Tamar wondered how one runs away from home with a cello. She saw a Russian boy who specialized in riding a high unicycle; Tamar remembered seeing him perform in the Walking Street before she had come here. She saw two brothers from Nazareth who performed magic tricks on high stilts, and an Ethiopian boy who drew marvelous illustrations of black angels and golden unicorns on the sidewalk. One American boy, a lapsed yeshiva student, sketched stylized, cruel caricatures of people on the street in charcoal; he constantly sketched everyone around him, even in the home, and people had finally gotten used to the agitated pencil motions. A religious, red-haired boy from Gush Etzion, always seeming confused because of the murky look in his eyes, knew how to swallow and blow fire. Those two girls from Beersheba, who appeared to be sisters, maybe even twins, were mind readers, or at least that's what they claimed – Tamar tried never to come too near them. No less than ten jugglers lived there, and they all threw and caught balls, sticks, bowling pins, apples, torches, and knives. One tall guy with shifty eyes had developed his own unique skill: he mimicked the body language of the people in the street, how they moved and how they walked: he would follow behind them as they crossed over the circle of his performance, almost clinging to their backs, aping them, without their knowledge, to the cheers of spectators. One night, during supper, Tamar realized that, sitting in front of her, was the girl she had once seen near Ha-khatulot Square – the one who danced with the two burning ropes; and next to her was the contortionist, a mean-looking girl from a kibbutz in the north, who once, after Friday supper, amazed them all by folding her long body into a Coca-Cola carton. She saw a very young teenager, almost a kid, who resembled Effi from *Where's Effi?*; he was an artist at blowing bubbles, of all shapes and sizes. She saw one Jerusalemite, with a pale face and greasy black hair, who called himself a 'street poet,' and could, within seconds, compose rhymes for whoever paid.

Other singers like her lived there, and she even exchanged a few words with one of them on the drive to Ashkelon; they discovered they were even singing a few of the same songs (the Hebrew ones at least). She saw rappers who beat rhythms out on empty paint cans, and someone who played the saw, and another who could play whole compositions on wineglasses by rubbing his fingers against the lips of the glasses. She saw at least five other guitar players like Shai, but from what she heard sometimes while passing by the rooms, not one of them could play like him. Every once in a while someone would pronounce his name with a kind of respect; yet an echo of mourning would always accompany it, as if they were talking about a man who was no longer alive.

And him? Shai? She didn't see him.

One night she woke up, to the sounds of shouting. She lay still for one moment, confused; she thought she was at home and tried to connect all the shadows to her familiar objects. The shouts grew louder. Uneasiness filled her. She looked at the clock: half past two. Suddenly she remembered where she was. She jumped off the bed, ran to the window; below, there was a car, and three men trying to pull something out of it; no, someone, someone who didn't want to come out. He clung to the door with his hands – they pulled him and hit his hands. One of them was Miko. She also recognized Shishko, who looked like Elvis. She pressed her forehead to the window, trying to see every detail, but the men surrounded the car and blocked whatever was going on down there from view. They cursed under their breath, and every once in a while threw a punch through the window with their fist, probably trying to knock out the resisting body. Tamar screamed silently, and without feeling it, she beat her fists against the window frame until they bled. Then Pesach came running out from the building, looked worriedly up at the windows, then returned to the building and switched off the light over the entrance. Now it was even harder to see what was going on. Pesach approached the car, stood a moment in front of the open door, leaned his forehead on its roof, and Tamar hoped he was talking to whoever was inside, trying, patiently, to convince him to come out. But then, in a slow, almost lazy motion, his elbow moved backward, and then the big arm struck, once. One blow, and everything became quiet. Tamar stood, shaken, at the window. One of the men took something out of the car; it looked, at first, like an object – a rolled-up rug; he carried it easily on his back and brought it inside. As he stood at the entrance of the building, Tamar saw, for one moment, the outstretched hands of the boy thrown over his back. Only one person she knew had such long fingers.

Days passed. Who knows what places the boy riding the camel in the Sahara Desert had reached on his journey through Assaf's fantasies. Assaf himself had already started working in City Hall during those days of late July. He sat, bored, for eight hours every day, in the empty room next door to the Department of Water, answering phone calls, giving out what small details he knew, toying idly with the dream team he was putting together for Fifa '99. He didn't know that, in a few days, a big, lost dog would enter his life, and a girl, also somewhat lost, would storm in after it, and that, from that moment on, he would no longer wonder what the deck boy, sailing on the ship in the North Sea, was doing, but instead keep wondering, 'Where is Tamar?'

On one of those evenings, when Assaf was still dragging his feet with Dafi Kaplan, smiling tiredly at Roi's rude jokes, counting the moments until the evening would be over, Tamar returned to the home in the middle of supper. She had been in Bat Yam, or Netanya – she didn't quite remember. She hurried to her room and changed her clothes. As usual, she left Dinka there. If she did actually meet Shai at dinner, she better not have Dinka, who would jump on him joyfully, in front of everybody.

She washed her face in the rusty sink in the room and looked into the triangular fragment of a mirror hanging on the wall. Her hair had grown a little; little spikes, very black, had started sprouting on her skull. She thought it actually suited her; she spent the next moment or two unusually busy with thoughts about her looks, yearning for a long bath and sweet lotions, and Halina trying, with all her might, to turn her into a beautiful woman. She was still smiling to herself when she came to the dining hall and was taken unawares.

Because the moment she walked in, she saw him, and quaked – he was so thin and miserable, a faded copy of himself. She didn't stop moving, passed straight in front of him, stiffly, her eyes piercing the floor, her face white. Shai stared right through her. Maybe he was confused, maybe high. One thing was clear: *he did not recognize her*. That was an unexpected blow, harder than the rest of it: even he wouldn't save her from the curse of being a stranger. He sat, closed off in himself, rocking a little, as if he were praying. She saw he was wearing the blue vest she liked, and that it was now dirty and torn. He played with the mashed potatoes in front of him, touching them with his fork, then moving them away. Tamar forced herself to eat the cold portion slapped on her plate (Mamaleh was always angry when people showed up late). She thought the whole room had suddenly dipped into silence, and that everyone was looking at her and at him.

Sheli burst in, excited, even taller in her new yellow Doc Martens. Her hair glowed green, and she suddenly sparked everyone to life. She hurried over to Tamar, approaching her, as she always did, with the same initial joy. 'Let me sit next to you, oh, come on, move over! I have something *amazing* to tell you –' She started in on her story, but immediately saw Tamar's distant eyes. With a slight contraction of pain, Sheli gave up on her, 'No problemo,' and she sat silently for a moment. She then turned and started chatting with the guy sitting on her right with the same expansive cheer: today, some important manager from the local station had approached her during her performance in Ashdod; he'd offered to sign her to a three-year contract, with a further possibility of traveling to New York ... but as she told the story, she started to

wonder why Americans would be interested in hearing impersonations of Iggy Waxman and Sarit Khadad, and her face fell
a bit. Tamar steadily chewed through the mash of food. Then
she slowly lifted her head. Her eyes flashed at him. He looked
at her, because she was new. Then, slowly, his pupils dilated
and his face began to crumple.

She dropped her head immediately. Nobody must notice
the connection between them, no one must see that they
knew each other from their former lives. She tasted cold
omelet, pushing it to the edges of her plate. Next to her,
Sheli was becoming grumpy over her own stupidity. She said
she was the mother of all fuck-ups if she was really able to
buy that crap, help me, here, Dickhead is going to take me
to America – yeah, right! He'd showed her a business card
with gold embossed letters, drugged her with words, and she
ate it up. She'd spent an hour with him in some stinking hotel!
and now, to punish herself for being such an idiot, she'd run
away again, immediately. She'd go to Lifta and finish her life
like a dog, that was all she deserved. The guy next to her tried
to calm her down.

It was a noisy night; slices of bread were flying at the
nearby tables. The kids were merrier than usual tonight;
perhaps because Pesach wasn't there – neither were any of
his bulldogs. At the table by the door, a few boys had started
singing a loud, off-key rendition of 'Who Knows Why the
Zebra Wears Pajamas,' and the others joined in, playing on the
tables with their forks and spoons. Mamaleh started shouting,
threatening that she would tell Pesach everything, and one
tall boy, the mimic, jumped up and started dancing with
her, bowing to her and pulling her so they moved cheek to
cheek, until he got her to smile. Tamar touched her forehead,
then slid a finger down her left cheek. She blinked twice. She
touched her right cheek. Then, as if by accident, she lifted
one finger in the air, touched her right earlobe, fluttered her
fingers twice on her chin. She went through another five or
six of these motions, patiently, slowly, even though her heart
was pounding like crazy.

Shai never took his eyes off her. His lips moved as if he was reading aloud. He really *was* reading aloud. This was the first miracle she had hoped for: that in spite of the long time that had passed, he would remember; that, in spite of everything that had happened to him, and all the drugs, he would still remember their secret finger language.

'I came to take you out,' her fingers said.

He buried his face in his plate. She saw how dirty and stringy his beautiful wavy hair had become, how thin his wrists.

He then straightened up in his chair and looked at the ceiling for a minute. She saw he was trying to remember. He hesitatingly touched his right cheek, touched his chin, the tip of his nose. He messed up once, and sucked in his lips, making the sign that erases everything. He repeated his previous motions, and wrote to her, letter by letter:

'They will kill us both.'

The guy talking to Sheli to her right became excited. He was the saw player. 'Lifta? With the Russians? Are you crazy? They're more fucked up than anyone!'

'Oh yeah? What do they have that isn't here?' Sheli asked, and burst out in a laugh. Her behavior was strange today, trembling, exaggerated – but Tamar didn't have any attention to spare.

'Those guys use *vind*,' the guy explained. He was lanky and hairy, with a monkey's upper lip. '*Vind* means screw in Russian, because the stuff drills right through your brain, *trrrr*, like a screw.' Sheli shook her head doubtfully; her green hair also trembled, always glowing wherever she was. 'No, listen to me: it's like neon mixed with cough syrup in peroxide, it's the lowest of the low. Heroin is like weed next to it. It just bombs you out of your skull. It's the world's cheapest high.'

'I've never touched the shit,' Sheli said, shrill laughter rolling out of her. 'The only high I get is from jogging.'

In the middle of the tense conversation with Shai, Tamar still remembered how, on the first day, Sheli had said she never touched heroin, only weed.

With her fingers she spelled out: 'I have a plan.'

He started to answer her. One girl noticed his strange gestures and nudged her friend to look. Tamar bent over her plate and shoved the cold omelet into her mouth; Shai seemed simply to be playing something, with his fingers and his imagination.

He said: 'I use.'

Tamar immediately answered, almost without lifting her head from the plate: 'Said wan sto' – You said you wanted to stop. Their sentences were short and practical. She immediately saw that in spite of everything, he was able to understand her, even in half words. That was an encouraging sign; the same thing had happened when, as children, Tamar and Shai were forbidden to talk to each other at the table in an effort to keep them from their private world where no strangers were allowed. In those days they had to be satisfied with signaling only the beginnings of words to each other: I wan go sle; or wh crap foo tod.

Shai waited two full minutes before he answered: 'Can't alo.'

'Togeth.'

He leaned his head in his hands, as if his head weighed a ton. Tamar remembered a song she sang with the chorus; the words were by Emily Dickinson, the title 'I Felt a Funeral in My Brain.'

His fingers suddenly shook so badly Tamar was afraid everyone would see what was happening. He wrote: 'You can't alo.'

She answered: 'I can.'

He said: 'Run awa fr here.'

Tamar responded: 'Only with you.'

All at once he gave a loud sigh. He stood up quickly, and when he tried to hold on to the table, he almost pushed the glass off. Silence blanketed the room. He tried straightening the glass on the table, but his fingers couldn't quite grab it; the glass was dancing – it looked as if it were covered in slick oil and trying to elude his grasp. He had to hold it in both hands to make it stand still. It took perhaps three seconds, but it seemed to take forever. All eyes were on him – so tall, and skinny, swaying like a bamboo stalk in the wind. His whole face broke out in sweat; everyone stopped eating and talking, and just stared. He stepped back and tipped his chair over, waved his hand in a gesture of giving up, of despair, and ran out of the room. Tamar gorged herself on mashed potatoes, omelet, bread, anything, just so as not to lift her head and see their eyes now.

Someone said quietly, 'If that man doesn't get off it now, he's finished.' Ah unpleasant silence fell over the room, perhaps because the future had been mentioned, the future one mustn't speak of, their nonexistent future.

A girl who probably hadn't been there all that long asked who that guy was, the guy who just ran out – they answered her that he was burned out; a walking burnout, said one boy. But who, what was he, she asked, and Tamar froze in her chair. Who *was* Shai? What *was* he? They're already mourning him. It made her sick to see how easily even someone like Shai could become fodder for gossip. Just try to summarize him to them – try to squeeze into a two-sentence headline the wonderful complex that is Shai, all the conflicts in him. 'But he never talks, does he?' the new girl asked, with a kind of freshman nerve, and a few voices answered her. Tamar felt their excitement in talking about him, felt what an intriguing enigma he was to them. Yeah, at the beginning they thought he was a mute – but he played guitar like the devil; only he can't without drugs. But when he's playing and using, the money pours in. They even want him on TV; Dudu Topaz himself heard him playing on the street and invited him on his show, but Pesach didn't allow it, said he wasn't ready for such wide exposure . . .

'He's Pesach's Jimi Hendrix,' said one of the other players, and Tamar heard familiar jealousy in his voice. There was always a trace of jealousy in the voice of whoever was speaking about Shai. 'He's also Pesach's Jim Morrison. Tons of talent, except for the fact that he's so completely flatlined.'

She couldn't eat any more, not even in order to hide her state. She sat, frozen, praying that no one was watching her now. She was in shock, not only over Shai's condition, but because of his absolute refusal to accept her help. This was exactly what Leah had warned her about: he would be unwilling to go, incapable of working with her, or even of just cooperating. But he asked me to come! Tamar argued angrily when she sat with Leah. He, himself, called and begged for someone to come rescue him! Leah went over it again, explaining – he will be frightened to death to make the tiniest change in a life that's already fallen apart, and he will be scared to death of losing the security of the constant supply of drugs that he has there. Terror started gathering like clouds inside Tamar's brain; here, this was something she didn't plan for in advance. How would she get him out of here without his own cooperation? Perhaps even against his will? Something sank in her stomach, and kept sinking . . . There you have it, my dear child, you were held completely imprisoned by your dreams, and there, finally, is the great weak point in your lunatic plan.

Because she had planned everything, every detail, for months, with an almost insane precision. She had repeated her plan over and over, trying to guess at and anticipate every step of the process, any problem that could crop up after she came here and found him; with the same inexorable precision, she planned how she would then take care of him all by herself after she rescued him from this place; she calculated exactly how many boxes of candles and packs of matches she would need in the cave. She remembered to prepare a can opener and mosquito repellent and bandages. The one tiny thing that never crossed her mind was how she would get him out of here if he didn't have the will, or the guts, to leave.

Amazement at her own blindness now swept over her. How had it happened? How could she have ignored all the warnings, as if she were setting herself up, on purpose, to fail? She got up, put her plate in the sink. A few boys and girls were already outside in the yard, sitting on the ground. She saw Sheli's green loofah of a head resting on the shoulder of a tall, wide boy; another guy with an Indian face and a long braid took out his guitar and started to sing. She opened a window to breathe a little, and the song wrapped itself around her. She couldn't resist its dark, sad rhythm:

> Cheap white ecstasy
> For the masses
> Blue LSD
> Take out your cash,
> Make anarchy,
> Break your routine,
> Release the madness,
> Get arrested . . .

And the boys and girls around him chimed in, singing, 'How – can – you – do – such – a – thing, how – do – you – do – such – a – thing.'

And the boy:

> 'No more miracles
> And no rose hope
> Dying and rotting
> Making revolution, oh yeah . . .'

He repeated the song from the beginning, in all its monotony; she stood and moved to it, hating the words, stealing strength from the music, thrashing herself with the repetitive refrain: How could you do such a thing? How could you forget to plan the most important part?

It depressed her so much, discovering again, as usual, the strength of the force that sapped her from inside, her rat platoon, her Fifth Column. She didn't know what she would do now. Give it all up? Go home with her tail between her legs? One more black rat scurried by, leaping for her attention through all the usual, familiar stops on the path, rubbing his behind in the roadmarks, snickering at her in loud squeaks: You won't succeed at anything ever in your life! You airhead! You dreamer! Something will always be slightly damaged when you try to make it real, when you try to realize your dreams, when you try to connect your imagination to your real life . . . Now the whole pack gathered around him, squeaking in a wild chorus: This is exactly why you will never have a serious career as a singer, because you will always fail yourself as soon as you're tested! The most you'll get are a few secondary roles – Barbarinas at the beginning, and Marcellinas when you get old, and perhaps some Frasquita in between. You will wander all your life, lonely and miserable, from amateur chorus to amateur chorus at community centers; at best you might be a chorus conductor. And, by the way, you will never truly fall in love either, that's for sure. Because, did you forget? There's that missing Lego part in your soul. You won't have kids either, clearly, and I'll tell you why . . .

These thoughts, above all, brought her back to her senses. Tamar sharply cut the rat dance short, mustered what was left of her strength, and fought back. She tried to understand her mistake as reasonably as possible. She thought about it, with honesty, with utter clarity, and without being cruel to herself; and after a moment, she answered herself that if she had thought then, when she was still at home, that Shai wouldn't cooperate with her, she probably wouldn't have gone on this journey.

So it was actually good that she hadn't thought about it. It was if her brain had helped her by hiding this obstacle from her . . . Strange. She straightened up a little and took a deep breath: strange how she had managed to recover from this attack of bitterness, how she rescued herself from the jaws of her own cruelty. Something new had happened to her: the unfamiliar winds of tranquillity blew through her, she felt something like self-confidence. It would probably disappear in a minute – but she would treasure it always, she would remember that place in her body where she felt it, where it was created, and would try to return there, to produce it within herself when the next attack came.

Meanwhile, she couldn't forget she was stuck here, all alone, with no allies, and she had to think for both of them, meaning: to create the conditions under which Shai would run away with her. She had to confront him with a completed, indisputable plan. These thoughts refreshed her a little; now she felt as though she was coming back to life after a long day's sleep. She wondered where Shai was. In what room, in what dark bathroom was he now squatting, preparing the fix for himself that would get him through the night?

Sheli watched her from the yard with a big smile, too big. She called her to come down and hang out a little. Sheli's eyes were shining; something in her natural joy seemed sharp and glassy. Tamar felt she lacked any remaining energy to see or talk to people tonight. She had to be alone. It occurred to her, vaguely, that as a friend she should take Sheli back to the room now, to keep guard over her so she wouldn't fall apart and shame herself. But she had no more strength for anything. She signaled Sheli: 'I'm going to sleep,' flashed a smile, and dragged herself heavily across the room; just as she was, in her clothes, without washing the day off her, without even petting Dinka, she fell on the bed and lay there.

What's going on here? she thought, exhausted. How did this all start? How did this all suddenly become my life, my reality? There comes a moment, she thought, when you take one tiny step off the beaten path and you have to follow one leg with another, and before you know it, you find yourself on an unfamiliar route; every step is a reasonable one to take, more or less; it is born, evolved from the previous one, but suddenly you wake up inside a nightmare.

An hour passed. Two hours more. She couldn't fall asleep. Huge waves crashed through her brain. You are here, you're next to me, she mumbled, as if she were attacked by fever, her thoughts running in circles. I will get you out of here; she transmitted the message to him silently, praying he would read her mind. I don't know how, but you'll see, I will get you out, with or against your will, and I will keep you and get you clean and bring you back to what you once were, my brother, my brother . . .

III

AFTER LUNCH WITH RHINO, Dinka walked him to a neighborhood he didn't know, behind the market. They passed between little yards, with white-painted railings. Assaf peeked through a wooden gate and saw a huge geranium burning red, growing through an old pile of tin. He decided he would come back here sometime, when everything was finished: his experienced eye checked the flow between areas of light and shade, framing pictures, drawn to a black cat lying between fragments of orange glass, pointed like the scales of a dragon, on top of a wall. Here and there, in the yards against the walls, were old armchairs, mattresses, too. Big jars full of pickles sat on the windowsills. Assaf and Dinka passed by a synagogue, where people in work clothes were praying the Minkha to a tune he knew, the tune of his father and grandfather. They passed an ugly slab of concrete – a public shelter covered with colorful children's murals – another synagogue, a very narrow alley covered by a weeping willow like a canopy –

This was where Dinka stopped, sniffed the air, and looked at the sky like a man who wants to know what time it is and has no watch.

Suddenly she decided. She sat by a bench under the willow, put her head on her paws, her eyes pointed forward. She was waiting for someone.

Assaf sat on the bench. He waited. For whom, for what, he didn't know, but he was already getting used to this kind of situation. Someone would come. Someone would appear. Something would happen. And he would discover a new thing about Tamar.

He just didn't know which of the two Tamars it would be

– Theodora's Tamar or the detective's? Perhaps there was yet another Tamar, a third one.

Long moments passed. A quarter of an hour, half an hour, and nothing happened. The sun began to sink, still generating the heat of late summer days. But a breeze blew through the narrow alley, and all of a sudden Assaf felt how tired he was. He had been on his feet since morning, and spent most of that time running; but the fatigue wasn't only from running. Physical exertion never exhausted him in that way. There was something else, a constant excitement burning inside him, as if he had a fever (even though he wasn't feeling sick; if anything, quite the opposite).

'Dinka,' he said quietly, not moving his lips. People were passing through the alley and he didn't want them to think he was talking to himself. 'Do you know what time it is? Close to six. Do you know what that means?' Dinka's ears pricked up. 'It means Danokh closed his office two hours ago, and the veterinarian went home, too, and I'm not taking you back to that place tonight. So that means you'll have to sleep over at my house.' He started rejoicing over the idea as he was talking. 'There's only one problem: my mom is allergic to dog hair. Luckily, they're abroad, my folks, so just be careful not to shed –'

The dog barked and stood up. A very skinny young man, with a slight stoop, came out of the shadow of the weeping willow. Assaf stood up. The guy said in a high-pitched voice: 'Dinka!' and ran to her, dragging one leg. Something looked strange about the position of his head, as if he were tipping it back – or perhaps he could see only out of one eye. In his hand he held a heavy plastic bag with YEHUDA MATZOS printed on the side. When he saw Assaf, he stopped. They caught each other off guard.

The guy stepped back, probably because he expected to see Tamar and got Assaf instead; Assaf, because he saw the young man's face. The whole left side of his face was covered by a huge burn, red and purple, marking his entire cheek, his chin, and the left part of his forehead; his lips seemed unnatural as well, at least up to the middle, thin and a bit stretched out, and lighter than the other half, as if they had been reshaped with surgery.

'Sorry,' he muttered, and started to retreat quickly. 'I could have sworn it was a dog I know.' He limped away, his back to Assaf, his black yarmulke shining.

'Wait!' Assaf hurried after him with Dinka; the guy only sped up, not turning his face around. But Dinka passed him, leaped on him, and barked with joy, her tail wagging in excitement, and he had no choice. She was so happy that he had to stop and bend down to her; he grabbed her big head in his hands, and she licked him. His whole face. And he laughed in his strange, high-pitched, fractured voice.

'But where is Tamar?' he asked quietly, perhaps speaking to Dinka, perhaps to Assaf. Assaf, from behind him, said he was also looking for her; the man then stood and walked back to him, again standing in front of him with the same slightly tilted stance, and asked him what he meant.

Assaf told him the story. Not the *whole* story, of course, only the little story of City Hall and Danokh and the kennels. The guy stood and listened. As Assaf spoke, he unconsciously turned his head even more, in tiny increments, until he stood completely in profile, his uninjured side toward Assaf. This is how he stood, as if he was looking unintentionally into the branches of the willow in front of him, trying to pull together some conclusions while also observing nature.

'Why, it's a real blow for her to lose that dog,' he finally said with conviction. 'What will she do without her dog? How will she manage?'

'Yes,' Assaf said, searching. 'She must be very attached to her.'

'Very attached?' The guy laughed shortly, as if Assaf had said something nonsensical and outlandish. 'What do you mean, attached? She can't take a step without the dog!'

Assaf asked, feigning indifference, if he had any idea where she could be found.

'I? How should I know. She . . . she doesn't talk, just listens.' He kicked a stone by the curb. 'She – how can I explain it to you – you talk to her and she *hears*, so what choice do you have? You pour out everything freely. She's great.' His voice, Assaf thought, he had such a thin voice, it was like a little boy's, and there was something whiny about it. 'You tell her things you never told anybody else. Why? Because she really wants to hear you, you know? She is *interested* in your life.'

Assaf asked where he had met her.

'Here. Where else would I meet?' He gestured toward the bench. 'She passed by with the dog, and I used to sit here, like this, at about this time. I always go out in the evening. It's the best,' he said, swallowing the words hastily. 'I hate the heat.'

Assaf was silent.

'And before, sometime, maybe three months ago, I walk up, and I see her sitting, like, in my place, but she didn't mean to. She still didn't know about me. I'd already turned around to go, and then she called me. Saying –' He hesitated. 'Asking me something. She was looking for somebody –' He hesitated again. 'Whatever. It's private. Anyway, we start to talk, and since then not a week goes by that she doesn't come here, sometimes even twice a week. We sit, we talk, we eat something Mother makes.' He showed Assaf the big plastic bag in his hand. 'There's food here for Dinka, too. I save it up all week. Can I give it to her?'

Assaf thought Dinka wouldn't want to eat any more after the restaurant, but he didn't want to insult him. The young man took a smaller bag out of the big plastic one, and a good sturdy bowl, and poured a mixture of potatoes and bones into it. Dinka looked at the food, and looked at Assaf. Assaf gave her an encouraging wink, and she lowered her head and started to eat. Assaf was convinced she took his hint.

'Say, you want coffee?'

It would be his third cup today, and he wasn't used to drinking coffee, but he hoped that more conversation would come along with it. The guy pulled out a thermos and poured coffee into two plastic cups. Between them, on the bench, he spread a little cloth printed with flowers, laying down saucers of salty pastries and waffle cookies, and a plate of plums and nectarines.

'I'm used to doing this, for her when she comes.' He smiled apologetically.

'Did she come here last week?'

'No. And also not two weeks ago, and three, and a month. So I worry. Because she's not just someone who disappears on you or dumps you without saying anything. You understand? I can't stop thinking about it – wondering what could have happened to her.'

'And you don't have her address or anything?'

'Don't make me laugh. Not even her family name. I asked her a few times, sure, but she has her principles of privacy and all that. Well, you know how it is, they're very sensitive about it.'

Assaf didn't understand. 'Who's "they"?'

'They, people like her, in her state.' *The drugs*, Assaf thought, and his heart sank as he imagined her in one of those situations that Rhino described. He bit into a salty pastry, trying to find comfort in it.

'That's funny.' The man giggled with pleasure. 'She also always starts to eat from the pastries first.' Something about him was completely exposed; he was like a child who hadn't yet learned how to maintain the appropriate distance from strangers. He hesitated a moment and stretched a skinny, weak hand to Assaf.

'Victorious.'

'What?'

'My name. Victorious. Take more. Mother makes these herself.'

He said 'Mother' in a warm, intimate voice. The situation was odd, but Assaf felt nice sitting with him there, on the bench under the willow. He took another pastry. He wasn't crazy about salty stuff, but the thought that Tamar liked these cookies, ate pastries exactly like these . . .

Dinka licked the bowl and stretched out, heavy and long.

Then it dawned on Assaf: 'So, you come out here every day with cookies and coffee and wait for her?'

Victorious looked aside and shrugged. 'Not every day. What, every day? You think I come here every day?' A long silence. And then he said, casually, 'Maybe every day. What do I know? It's only so if she comes, I'll be ready.'

'And you've been waiting like this for a month?'

'Why not? Is it hard? I happen to be between jobs, so I'm usually free. Do I mind coming down here in the evening to wait a little? You pass the time.'

A man walked down the road, in their direction. Victorious saw him coming long before Assaf or Dinka did. He immediately turned, twisting his body to the side and arching backward until he had almost turned his back to the road. The man passed; he was old and deep in thought, and didn't notice them.

Assaf waited until his steps had faded into the distance. 'And you and Tamar, you two would talk?'

'Do we talk? Are you serious?' Victorious spread his hands out with pride, as if he were presenting a wide sea. 'Believe me, you can't talk like this with anybody in the world, because people, right away they look at you funny. Am I right or wrong? From the moment you meet they think he's like this, he's not like that, they think how you look on the outside is the most – understand? But take me, for example. To me, outer looks don't change anything ever, *ever!* Do you agree with me? That the most important thing is what's inside the person? True, yes? And that's why I'm telling you – I don't have friends, and don't need friends.'

He quickly pushed two more cookies into his mouth, between his torn, stitched lips. 'Because for me, personally' – he said, a little later – 'what's important to me is knowledge, yes? As much knowledge as possible. That's why I study. Don't you believe me?'

Assaf said he believed him.

'No, because you looked like . . . Listen, I think, what's most interesting to me is stars.'

'What stars? Famous people?' Assaf asked hesitatingly.

'What famous people? What people are in your head?' Victorious laughed a long, silent laugh, hiding half his mouth with his hand. 'In the sky! Now tell the truth – did you ever think about stars? Seriously think, I mean? Did you ever think?'

Assaf admitted that, no, he never did think about stars. Victorious slapped both his spread-out hands on his thighs, as if he had again, for the thousandth time, discovered more despairing proof of human beings' lack of understanding. 'Did you even know there are perhaps another million suns? And galaxies? Did you know in the universe you have another million! Not another poor star, like our earth, not another system like our solar system – galaxies, I'm talking about!'

He got very excited talking about that, and his other cheek, the healthy one, also became red. Three boys passed by, pumped up over some game. Victorious immediately turned and tilted his head, as if he was sunk deep in thought.

'Hey, Victorious,' they said, 'what's up?'

'Cool.' He didn't move from his thinker's pose.

'What's up with the stars? How's the Milky Way doing?'

'Cool,' Victorious said again, gloomily.

'Count them good,' one boy advised, bouncing his ball very close to Victorious's leg. 'Better keep track of those stars.' He moved in close to Assaf. 'Know why Victorious never goes to watch Wimbledon?' Assaf stayed quiet – he thought a fight would break out soon.

'Because he's afraid he'd have to look both ways!' The boy screamed with laughter, and demonstrated it while the other two laughed with him. The boy stretched his hand out and snatched a nectarine from the plate, took a full bite, and the three of them walked off laughing.

'And I subscribe to every journal on the subject!' Victorious continued, as if their conversation hadn't been interrupted. He puffed himself up a little to restore his wounded honor. 'In English, too! Don't you believe me? For two years I study English in the Open University, a correspondence course, fifteen hundred shekels – my mother paid that for me as a gift – you don't even have to leave your house, you only have to go there for exams. But I didn't go. What do I need their exams for, and their grades? But come and see my room, you'll see all the issues of *Science* and *Galileo*, in order, stacks of them! I've filled two and a half shelves already! And next year, God willing, Mother said she will buy me a computer, and then I will be a member of the Internet, and there I will find all the knowledge. You don't even have to leave your house. Everything comes to you, complete. Powerful, huh?'

Assaf nodded quietly. He thought that if it wasn't for Tamar, he would have passed by him, seen his face, perhaps recoiled a bit, then felt a little sorry for him, nothing more.

'So, did you talk about all this stuff with Tamar?' Assaf asked eventually. 'About galaxies, and all that?'

'Sure!' The smile spread over his whole face, into the purple stain. 'She . . . what do you think! She wants to hear about it again and again, how the quasars go, and holes in time, and pulsing stars, and the universe expanding, and how this, and how that, and do you get it? Because, that girl, she's never seen one star in her life! You see? And maybe it's because of this. Maybe because of her psychology she wants to know so much, if you follow my logic.' Assaf thought he must have missed some critical sentence during the conversation. Victorious didn't stop. 'She sits here for half an hour, an hour, won't let me stop. When I come home after Tamar, I go straight to bed, I'm finished. Well, actually' – a forced laugh escaped his mouth, exposing, for a moment, crooked teeth – 'maybe it's me. I'm not used to talking a lot about this, because, to tell you the truth, Mother, she's not really interested in the scientific stuff.'

Assaf still lagged a few sentences behind; there was some mystery to his words, or perhaps just confusion.

'Now,' Victorious said, and bent toward Assaf a little, 'when I was a child, very small, I had a little accident. Nothing serious.' Again, he spoke quickly, but with a kind of indifference, as if he were talking about someone strange and far away. 'Mother was cooking something. Soup. She knocked a boiling pot on me by mistake. It happens. Wasn't her fault. And then I was in a hospital for a year or so, plus some surgery here and there, and it was all a big mess. But since that time I've learned what a human being is. I swear to you. I became like a psychiatrist. On my own, no books, no nothing. And because of this, I can understand her from the inside, and I can also help her, even without her feeling that I'm trying to help her. Got it?'

Assaf shook his head to say no.

'Because they, they have their pride, and you need to talk to them as if it's nothing, as if it just *comes* to you, like it's every day that you sit in the street with someone and explain the scientific stuff. Got it?'

Assaf asked warily who 'they' were. He already knew the answer, but it was as if he had to hear the exact word again, and to feel the same pain strike him deep in the gut.

'Them, you know, people who have problems – it's important to let them have their pride, because, between you and me, what do they have except their pride?'

'And you saw her in a . . . difficult situation?'

'No.' Victorious laughed. 'It's normal for her. It's how she was born. She doesn't know any other situation.'

'What are you talking about?' Assaf cried out, finally waking up from his daze. 'How was she born?'

'Blind.'

Assaf jumped off the bench, simply jumped and stood still. 'She's blind? Tamar?'

'Didn't they tell you? Look at the dog. It's a guide dog.' Assaf looked: right, sure, she was the exact same breed, a seeing-eye Labrador, or a semi-Labrador, at least. Not really, though, not exactly. He opened his mouth to say something, but he thought Dinka was staring at him especially profoundly. Her eyes didn't let go of him; it was as if she was trying to communicate something to him, warn him. Assaf thought he was going crazy. Blind? And Theodora didn't say anything about it? And the pizza man said she was riding a bike! And how did she elude the detective?

Victorious smiled with satisfaction. 'I amazed you now, didn't I?'

A woman's voice called out from far away: 'Victorious, it's almost seven, come in the house!'

'That's Mother,' Victorious said, and got up at once and started gathering the remaining cookies. He poured what was left in the coffee cups on the ground and wrapped everything, the cups, plates, napkins, Dinka's bowl. Assaf still didn't move. He was standing still, amazed.

'Okay, I'm going in the house.' Victorious lifted the bag up onto his shoulder. 'Do you feel like coming tomorrow, too? I'll be here. We can talk again. Why not.'

Assaf stared at him.

'In another hour, hour and a quarter,' Victorious said, and pointed his finger upward, 'look at the sky. The greatest show in the universe!'

Assaf asked which stars you could recognize at first glance. He wanted to buy some time; he thought he was starting to guess something. Victorious raised his hand and showed where Venus would appear, and the North Star and the Great Bear . . . Assaf wasn't listening. Something wonderful, even exalted, took shape for him. Something about Tamar, and her courage, every once in a while, to do really crazy things, to make up and follow her own private rules. Victorious continued explaining, and Assaf sneaked a peek down and met Dinka's conspiring gaze. Obediently he returned his eyes to the sky. He thought of Tamar's generosity, with Theodora and with Victorious. It wasn't generosity having to do with money – it was tricky to explain. It was generosity of another kind.

'Me?' Victorious said, somewhere beside him. 'My dream? That soon, God willing, there will be travel to space. Spaceships will go like buses from Central Station.' He put his hand over his mouth like a bus driver and announced: 'Spaceship to Mercury, departing in ten minutes! Spaceship to Venus, leaving now!'

'Will you go?' Assaf asked.

'Maybe yes, maybe no. Depends.'

'Depends on what?'

'On how I feel that day.' He patted Dinka again. 'Okay, I'm off. If you find her, tell her – Victorious, he is collecting information for you all the time. You tell her. You won't forget, right? Victorious, that's my name.'


When he got home, life, meaning all those things he had escaped from that day, collapsed on top of him. There were five messages on the answering machine from Roi, one from Danokh, one from Rhino, and one from his parents saying they had landed already and everything was okay. Assaf finally went to the bathroom and read half an issue of *Name of the Game* without really absorbing the words in front of his eyes. Then he took a shower, and called Danokh at home and told him he had been running after the dog for a whole day. He asked for permission to follow her ('Her?' Danokh asked, surprised. 'It's a bitch?') for another day, and permission was granted. Then he called Rhino to let him know he was still alive. Assaf admitted that his sleuthing work still hadn't uncovered any great leads – but he couldn't tell Rhino that, for some reason, he had the feeling he was gradually closing in on Tamar.

Only then, in the middle of talking to Rhino, he remembered and was shocked by something Victorious had told him. Some very important information. Assaf had actually meant to ask him about it once they got a little deeper into their conversation, but in the middle of everything that had happened, he forgot about it.

'Assaf, are you still there?'

'Yes. No. I remembered something I forgot.' She's looking for someone, Victorious said, then got scared – he had probably revealed some secret of hers, because then he said it was a 'private' matter. Whom was she looking for? Why didn't I ask him? How could I miss a thing like that?

'Have you heard from your folks?' Rhino buzzed into his ear.

'Not really,' Assaf said, confused, and hung up. He was relieved that he had spoken to Rhino before having a long conversation with his parents.

Dinka wasn't hungry. He arranged a place for her and lay beside her on the rug stroking her fur, trying to figure out whom Tamar was looking for. They both passed out in complete exhaustion like that for an hour or two. When they woke, the house was completely dark, the echoes of a telephone ring vanishing in the air. Assaf made himself some Mjadra instant rice, adding a few hot dogs with ketchup to the meal and finishing it off with half a watermelon. For some reason, he didn't feel like eating out of the full pots of food his mother had left him; he enjoyed taking care of himself. He took the plate into the living room, breaking house rules, and ate, staring at the sports channel. He watched a replay of a league game from two months ago, and let the whirlwind of the day subside. The phone rang three times. He knew it was Roi and didn't pick it up until it was really too late to go out. Then he answered.

'Assaf, you loser, where are you?'

Assaf heard a lot of noise in the background: music, laughter. He said he got stuck at work. Roi burst into loud laughter and immediately ordered Assaf to get off his ass and come down, now, to Coffee Time, because Dafi was waiting for him, and she was pissed off.

'I'm not coming,' Assaf said.

'You're *what*?' Roi couldn't believe what he had heard. 'Listen good, Zero: Maytal and I have been going around town for three hours now with your Dafi, who, by the way, is looking like the bomb tonight, portable porn-movie, tight black top, snaps and all, so don't give me, "I'm too tired from work"! What do you do there all day anyway except scratch your balls?'

'Roi,' Assaf said quietly, with a tranquillity that surprised him, 'I'm not coming. Tell Dafi I'm sorry, it's not her fault. I just don't feel like it tonight.'

Silence. He heard the wheels of Roi's brain turning. He knew how they worked. Roi sounded a little drunk, but he was still sharp and knew that Assaf had never spoken to him like that, with that tone in his voice.

'Listen closely to me,' Roi said, in a whisper bubbling with venom, and Assaf thought that someone else had already spoken to him like that today. He couldn't remember who, he only remembered that someone had wished him ill. Of course, the undercover cop. 'If you are not here in one quarter of an hour, on the dot, you're finished. You got me, you little shit? Do you understand what I'm saying? If you're not here, you're *dead* to me.'

Assaf didn't answer. His heart was beating hard. They had been friends for twelve years. Roi was his first true friend. Assaf's mother talked about how, during that first year of kindergarten, before meeting Roi, Assafi had been so lonely; and she was so happy when he came home that one time with lice, because it was a sign that he at least had had contact with another boy.

'You'll be alone,' Roi whispered, and Assaf was amazed by the strength of the hatred in his voice. Where had it been hiding all these years? 'No one in class, no one in the world will even piss in your direction, and you know why? You really want to know why?' Assaf shrunk, preparing for the blow. *'Because I'll stop being your friend.'*

It didn't hurt.

'Look, Roi,' Assaf said. He thought he sounded a bit like Rhino now, speaking quietly, heavily, in a manner that left no doubt. 'The thing is, you haven't been my friend for a long time.' He hung up the phone. Enough, he thought, feeling nothing. It's over.

He went and sat by Dinka. She gazed at him with her expressive eyes. Later, he lay down on the carpet and put his head against her, feeling her breathe. He wondered what would happen now, whether he would really notice any change at school. He thought not; for the past few years, he'd actually been pretty lonely the entire time he spent with Roi, and everyone, whatever stuff they did, going to parties, laughing at jokes, playing basketball for hours, going out on Friday nights, when they would sit for whole evenings in smoky coffeehouses and stuffy rooms. What did those guys really do during those dozens of endless evenings? Knocked back a few beers, hit on girls, smoked a lot of cigarettes, and drank a little vodka; and he? He would contribute a few sentences to the conversation every once in a while, about teachers and parents and girls, and when they were smoking a hookah he'd take a few puffs and say that it tasted good. And when they danced, he would always be the one stuck to the wall next to one of the other boys, and would chat with him until the boy managed to summon up the courage to ask some girl to dance and never came back. Vacations were the same, only worse; the endless rounds around town, from one coffeehouse to another, from one bar to another; and he? What did he do? He spent most of the time trying hard to hide what he really felt from them. He did the bare minimum required to save face, and always, after such a mind-bogglingly vacant evening, he felt like a beanbag filled with thousands of foam balls. Strange; he was in fact lonely, he just had never thought of himself that way. Other boys and girls were lonely. Nir Chermetz, for example, who had never had a single friend in class. Or Sivan Eldor, the snob. Assaf always pitied them for not belonging; but who was he? What did he have?

It occurred to him that he almost never spoke to Roi about photography. Roi knew that Assaf, for three years now, went, every other Saturday, to his photography course, and went with his class to the Judah Desert, and the Negev, and up north, and showed his pictures in exhibitions (even though he was the youngest of them by at least ten years); but Roi never asked, was never interested, and, it went without saying, never went to any of the shows. It seemed strange that Assaf had never once thought of telling him, for example, about the pleasure he got from taking a good photo, from waiting for three or four hours in a wheat field by Mikhmoret, until the shadow fell exactly on some old bus station, with its cracked concrete, the caper bushes bursting through. Somehow conversations with Roi never had the room for these things. Certainly not in a foursome of the two couples. He thought of Tamar. He thought he would like to tell her about it, to describe the amazing change photography had brought to his life, how it had opened his eyes to see things, and people, and beauty in the little things, the so-called boring things. He would like just to sit with her sometime in a beautiful place, not a coffeehouse, and talk, really talk to her.

At the same time Assaf knew – he didn't nurture any illusions on this score – that the storm she had unleashed on his life would end as soon as he met her, as soon as he faced the usual battery of tests, of his conversational skills, his wit, his cynicism and acidity, his ability to shine and be glib; and he knew – what he had known with utter sobriety, for years – that only one situation in the world, in the universe, existed in which anyone could fall in love with him: only if she, accidentally, happened to run the entire 5,000-meter course by his side. It struck him that perhaps he really should change his tactics now and give in to his teacher's pleas and compete. Maybe he'd find a girlfriend among the long-distance runners.

These thoughts filled him with anxiety. He stood up, drank three glasses of water, and absently checked the mail. Then he saw it: a green envelope from the Ministry of Education, Department of Exams – they had been waiting two months for this, and it arrived the moment his parents went abroad! His fingers shaking, he opened it: 'Dear Student, we're pleased to announce that you have successfully passed the Final Examination in English . . .'

He shouted with joy, and the phone started ringing, joining in. For a moment he was afraid that it was Roi again, but it was his father. Shouting happily from Arizona, across continents and oceans: 'Assafi, how are you?'

'Dad! I was just thinking about you! What's it like there? How was the flight? Could Mom open the handle in the –?'

They spoke over each other as usual, and laughed and shouted. Every second costs a fortune, Assaf thought, and was angry that his enjoyment of this conversation had a limit – one of these minutes was probably a half day of work for his father – maybe . . . two ceiling fan installations and three toaster repairs, at least. Never mind, to hell with money – he wanted to hug them, smell them, take them in as much as he could. It's probably Reli's phone bill any-way, and Reli has a lot of money now, right? The thought freed him, and he laughed all the way to Arizona as his father described the wonders of the flight and the road. Assaf said everything was normal at home, don't worry, I'm eating well, keeping the house clean. He suddenly felt the way he had a few years back, when he would still come to their bed on Saturday mornings to cuddle and play. 'Dad, listen, the results from the Ministry of Education arrived today –'

'One minute, Assafi, don't say one word! You tell that straight to your mother!'

The noise of setting the receiver down and steps walking away ... it was probably a very large house, and quiet, with the silence of the sea in the middle of it ... Assaf tried to guess what conversations were flowing along the parallel phone lines. Maybe someone in Alaska is proposing marriage to someone in Turkey ... maybe Phil Jackson, at this moment, is offering Papi Turgeman from Ha'Poel an invitation to play for the Lakers next season ... and then, suddenly, his mother was on the line, with the abundance of her body and soul, and her rolling laughter. 'Assafi, my teddy bear, I miss you so much, how will I survive these two weeks?'

'Mom, you passed the exam!'

Silence, and after it, an explosion of screaming and cheering. 'Has the letter arrived? An official letter? Did you check the signature? They said I passed? Shimon, did you hear that! I did it! I have my high school diploma!'

And while they were there in Arizona, dancing and hugging each other and squandering half a year's salary, little Muki sneaked over to the telephone. 'Assafi?' she said cautiously, making sure that the amazing distance she had traveled had not changed anything about him at least. 'What country are you in?'

And he explained to her that he hadn't gone anywhere, it was she who had traveled. She started talking about the flight, and how her ears hurt, and the puzzle she got from the flight attendant, and what's in America. There's a squirrel in America, she said, and proceeded to describe it in detail. Actually, you could probably import herds of squirrels into Israel for the price of this conversation, but Reli was paying for it anyway, and maybe not just Reli. More about that in a minute. So Assaf sat back and listened to Muki talk about the Guatemalans they bought there for her, little fabric dolls that the children from the country of Guatemala put under their pillows at night, how they tell one problem they have to each doll, and in the morning, the problem is gone. Assaf, who would have gladly passed his problems on to such a magical Guatemalan doll, gently asks Muki to give the phone back to Mom, because there is one important topic left to discuss, and they still haven't talked about it.

'What can I tell you, Assafon?' his mother said in a more cautious tone. 'We met him.' Silence. Assaf waited – but he already knew.

'He's wonderful, Assafon. He's gentle, he's charming, and I think his mother must be one of us – at least half. He's everything Reli needs, and he's got a huge house here, you should see it, with a real pool and a Jacuzzi, and a crazy Mexican woman who cooks for him. Reli's already taught her to prepare our cholent. He's very important in some computer company here . . .'

Assaf folds up, sitting on the couch; his fingers cling to Dinka's fur. How will he tell Rhino? How will Rhino stand it? Everyone betrayed him. Well, Rhino had suspected this the entire time, that the reason they went was to meet Reli's new man.

'Assafi? Are you there?'

'Yes.'

'Assafon, teddy bear, I know exactly what you're thinking now, and how you feel, and what you wanted to happen, but it's probably not going to happen. Are you there?'

'Yes.'

'I don't need to tell you how much we love Tzahi; he will always be like a son to us, really, our son, but Reli has made her decision. That's it. It's her life. And her choice. We have to accept that.'

Assaf wanted to scream at Reli, and shake her, and remind her how Rhino had taken care of her through her bad spells, before she'd become such a hot shot; how he'd loved her with blind devotion from the first day of high school, and throughout the service, and for another two full years after that, through all her craziness and all the times she needed her *space*, how he had gradually become like a big brother in their family, helping Dad when he had too much work, helping Mom with everything she needed, from picking up her groceries to painting the house. That was what finally pushed Reli over the edge: she felt he was marrying her parents, not her. Well, Assaf thought bitterly, his parents certainly – well, you couldn't say they used Rhino, but they were very nice about letting him help them with a thousand and one things. Rhino did all of it with love and by choice, and Assaf remembered how he had even given up a partnership in his father's surveyor's office. Instead, he decided to open a casting and foundry workshop, mainly for Reli, because of her initial excitement about it – work that was so manly and physical yet had such a strong connection to art. How could you negate ten years like these? Aside from that, Assaf was losing Reli now that she had finally made her decision. That wasn't so bad. But losing Rhino hurt, because Rhino would certainly cut all his connections with the family; so as not to be reminded of her a hundred times a day, he would cut them out of his life. Assaf, too.

Assaf didn't remember how the conversation ended. Probably less joyfully than it had begun. Afterward, he unplugged the phone. He was scared Rhino would call back to check whether they'd called. Assaf didn't know what he would say if that happened, how he would soften the blow. He wasn't a good liar. He stood up, he sat down, he wandered through the apartment, a ball of nerves. Dinka watched him, puzzled.

In situations like these, when he was this upset, his mother would come up to him or behind him, grab him, capture him in her thick arms, look deep into his eyes, and ask, 'What are they seeing now, these beautiful eyes?' When he avoided her gaze, she would say, 'That bad, hmm?' and order him to 'report to HQ,' and pull him into her little parlor and shut the door. She wouldn't let him leave until he told her exactly what was bothering him. But even if she were here now, she would be playing a pretty suspicious

role in this particular mess – everything was so complicated and murky and troublesome. He had to do something,
something that would change everything at once, something
to fix, or at least balance – just a little bit – all that was
rotten and screwed up in the world. Something that Tamar
would do in such a situation, perhaps. Yes, an idea, à la
Tamar.

It came to him in a flash; he knew precisely what to do,
discovered it, invented it: he climbed up to the attic and went
inside, grabbed a bucket of white paint, the last remainder of
their most recent house painting, and a big roller. He took
a ladder from the pantry and settled it on his shoulder,
whistled to Dinka, and walked out of the house. He walked
briskly, avoiding people's faces, until he reached his school.
He crept into the yard through a hole in the fence by the water
fountain.

Last year they'd had a teacher, one Chaim Azrieli, an old
man, gentle and childless, to whom they gave absolute hell. Roi
was the ringleader of the gang, and Assaf tailed along behind
him with the others. He never did anything especially mean,
but he was part of the whole group, of the general mockery.
And this teacher had been especially nice to him, too – when
he discovered Assaf's interest in Greek mythology, he brought
him a book of myths Assaf hadn't heard of and said that it was
a present.

Then, on the last day of school, they wrote graffiti about
him on the school's outer walls. They did it the night before the
year-end party, a group of ten boys. Assaf was the ladder: Roi
climbed up on his shoulders and wrote in black paint. Since
then, every time he walked by the school during vacation,
Assaf saw the graffiti. Everyone who passed by that way
saw it – Chaim Azrieli, too, probably. He lived only two
blocks away.

Now Assaf mixed the paint, adding some more water,
and climbed the ladder. The yard was empty, lit by one
streetlamp. Dinka sat, her head following the brush as it
covered the graffiti with a shiny white stripe, word by word:
CHAIM AZRIELI: BRUSH YOUR TEETH!!

The next morning, feeling purified and refreshed after a full night's sleep, Assaf went on his way, with an easy heart and his bike.

In the middle of the night, he had felt a big warm body – not the cleanest – tossing and cuddling up to him in bed. Without opening his eyes, as if it had always been like this, he hugged her, learning from her how she liked to sleep, curling over into a crescent, pushing her back into his stomach, her nose softly blowing into his open palm. Every once in a while she shivered, as if she were dreaming about a hunt. In the morning, the two of them opened their eyes and smiled at each other.

'Is this how you sleep at home?' he asked her, and didn't wait for an answer. He got up happily, whistling to himself in the bathroom, combed his hair carefully, and did what he hadn't in months (mostly because his mother was always nagging him about it), spread a huge amount of Oxy over his pimples.

He had already taken the bike – an old Raleigh he had inherited from Rhino – out of the garage last night. He hadn't ridden it in months – he had to pump the tires, oil the chain, and wipe a thick layer of dust off the front light and reflector. As he rode it through the clear early morning, Assaf was happy; he whistled to Dinka in his heart and sang out to her. She bounded along by his side, now close, now farther away, all the while giving loving looks. He had cut the rope off last night; and now the two enjoyed the new range of motion between them: she ran independent of him, she even disappeared for a moment behind a parked car, then returned of her own volition.

He let her lead, of course. He had already learned it was the best thing. He pedaled and whistled, noted how well trained she was in running alongside a bicycle. In his imagination, he already saw her running between *two* bicycles along some distant path, through a wide green meadow, looking at the two riders with that same longing expression.

Still, it seemed to him that she was running less purposefully this morning – trying one way, moving back the other way . . . not that he minded getting lost behind her – through the yawning streets as they woke up, between the milk crates and stacks of newspapers on the sidewalk, past the jets of water from shop owners hosing down the sidewalks in front of their stores, past a dog sitter who was walking five at a time with five leashes, all of whom barked jealously at Dinka.

Little by little she drew him toward the city gates and outside. Assaf wondered if she was taking him to Tel Aviv, or what. She ran by his side, galloping lightly, amused, leaping from her back legs to her front legs like a horse on a merry-go-round – unlike those horses, she abruptly switched direction. Assaf saw how it happened to her: her nose received a particle of information, one of the thousands of smells and memories filling the air. One of them broadcast a message to her with a stronger signal than the others. She stopped, returned to the spot where she had sensed it, stood and inhaled it; she decoded it inside the dark cell of her nose. She then burst forward into a new direction, running with all her might.

He didn't know the area, and as usual he had no clue why she had brought him here. Sometimes, when he passed by here on the bus to Tel Aviv, he would see the valley spread out at the side of the road; it never occurred to him that anything – or anyone – was there. Now he was going down a steep path, walking his bike, a carefully packed little knapsack on his shoulders – because who knew when or where he would eat his next meal.

Here Dinka seemed less sure of herself. She ran forward and came back, circling hesitantly and, it seemed, at random. She would pause and smell the four points indecisively. Once, she galloped enthusiastically up a sand dune covered with garbage and scrub brush only to stop at the crest, surprised, look right and left, then return to Assaf, her tail drooping between her legs.

At one spot the path was blocked by a pile of stones. Assaf hid his bike behind a bush, underneath a big cardboard box he had noticed along the way. He climbed the stone heap and crossed a little meadow where the fennel grew so high and thick that Assaf nearly vanished and Dinka was no more than a running line of bushes splitting in two. The meadow ended, and he found himself in front of houses. Ruins.

They were built of big, heavy stones; wild bushes grew thickly through the walls. Assaf walked quietly; the only sound was the twittering of birds. Grasshoppers hopped over his feet. He went up and down through little arched stairways connecting the houses and peeked into the houses themselves. He assumed it was a deserted Arab village, whose inhabitants had fled during the War of Independence (according to Rhino). Or were cruelly banished (Reli). The houses were made up of empty, cool, shady rooms – all filled with piles of refuse and filth. Each room had a hole in the ceiling and huge holes in the floor. Assaf looked closer and saw that another kind of room ran underneath, perhaps a water cistern of some sort.

He walked through the ghost village, almost tiptoeing, as if he were paying his respects. People used to live here, he thought; they walked and talked here, along this path; their kids ran around and played, and they never in the world imagined to themselves that the world would turn them on their heads like this. Assaf always avoided thinking too deeply about this kind of thing, perhaps because of the duet that started playing in his mind whenever he came too close to political issues: those endless debates between Rhino and Reli. Even here they were with him in the blink of an eye, arguing. Reli muttered that every deserted village like this was an open wound in the heart of Israeli society; and Rhino would patiently respond that if it had been the other way around, then *her* house would look like this, and which did she prefer? As if standing in for his mother's ritual, banal last word on their debate (her attempt to make peace), a dove flew over Assaf's head, mottled and very fat. It landed on a porch railing, having cleared the height of a solitary wall without a house behind it. When its feet touched the railing, Assaf flinched: it seemed that her weight might make the entire porch collapse, and the whole wall with it.

The camera, he thought, of course. Why didn't I think of bringing it today!

Outside one of the ruins, he saw a pair of sneakers hanging by its laces on a jutting piece of stone. He climbed the stairs, peeked inside, and saw two boys, asleep.

He moved away immediately and stood outside for a moment, amazed: what were they doing here? How could anybody live in this filth?

He walked two steps down; then climbed one step back up. He felt a little scared, and embarrassed as well, for peeking into their lives this way. He stopped in the doorway and looked. The two boys were very skinny; one was rolled up inside a blanket stained with white paint; the other, almost completely exposed. Both were sleeping on yellow foam mattresses burnt and charred around the edges. Empty bottles of Vodka Stopka rolled along the floor, and the air was thick with flies and their loud buzzing. Someone had overturned an iron bedstead in the middle of the room, over the big hole, probably so he wouldn't fall into the pool of water underneath.

The boys slept on either side of the hole, pressed against the wall; at first glance, they seemed younger than Assaf by at least three years. He thought it was impossible that kids could live this way.

He turned again to go. He couldn't bear it. Besides, what could he do for them? As he turned, he managed to step on a tin bowl on the ground, and it flipped over; when he tried to step lightly over it, he knocked down an iron hanger in the window – a chain of tiny accidents that made a lot of noise. The guy who slept closer to the doorway drowsily opened his eyes. He saw Assaf and shut his eyes again. After a time, he struggled to open them once more. His hand reached under the mattress and emerged with a knife.

'What do you want.'

The voice was a boy's voice; he spoke slowly, weakly, in a Russian accent. There was no question mark at the end of his sentence. He couldn't even rise from his mattress.

'I don't want anything.'

Silence. The boy lay on his back, his bare chest white and

211

smooth. He looked at Assaf, his face expressionless – without any fear, any threat, any hope.

'Maybe there is food,' he asked.

Assaf shook his head, no. But then he remembered. He took out the two sandwiches he had made himself that morning and came closer. The boy didn't rise up, only reached a hand up. His other hand remained on the knife.

Assaf stepped backward. The boy sat up slowly. It was clear every motion was extremely difficult for him. His hands shook slightly. He pressed almost the entire sandwich against his mouth; only then did he feel that the sandwich was wrapped in wax paper. He removed it, peeled off whatever he could, then pressed it against his mouth again. He then closed his eyes and chewed for a long time, moaning softly. His feet appeared from under the blanket. The toes were black. A Russian book with a colorful cover was lying on the concrete floor by the mattress. Newspapers were stacked against the walls, the floor littered with toilet paper and junk food wrappers. Lots of wrappers. And a needle.

The boy finished the sandwich and patted his mouth, using the wrapping paper, with a well-mannered gesture inconceivable in the middle of that devastation.

'Thank you.'

He looked at the other sandwich Assaf was holding; his mouth moved in gnawing motions. 'Put it down for him,' he told Assaf, pointing to the sleeping boy.

Assaf circled cautiously around the edge of the hole and placed the other sandwich next to him. As Assaf bent down he saw a black gun on the other side of the mattress, by the boy's head. He saw it for only a moment and wasn't sure if it was real or a toy. The sleeping boy didn't even open an eye.

He walked back and stood by the doorway. 'I'm Assaf.'

'Sergei.' Silence. He nodded heavily, like an old man. 'Little Sergei. There is also Big Sergei, sleeping over there. Perhaps you have more food?'

Assaf said no. Then he thought maybe his bubble gum would help. He gave him the whole pack and the two chocolate bars. The boy asked Assaf to split them with his friend.

This time, next to Big Sergei's mattress, Assaf saw tin foil from a cigarette pack, stretched out and carefully ironed, two straws, and a few burnt pieces of toilet paper next to it. Assaf gazed at it all for a moment: a year ago, a few students from the eleventh grade had got caught smoking heroin in the school bathroom. That was the rumor, and Assaf passed it along like everyone else, because they were, for him, only empty words. Later, someone from the eleventh grade had explained it all in the yard: how you take the tin foil and light toilet paper under it, and how the dope balls up on the foil from the heat, and then you can run a flame along underneath it and inhale.

Big loud graffiti, in Russian, lined all the walls; each long line of words was written in a different color. Assaf asked what it was.

'This? A story. A writer used to live here. He's dead now.'

Dinka, who had been walking around the outside of the house the entire time, looking for something, now climbed the stairs. Sergei heard her steps and clutched his knife. When he saw her, he smiled. 'Dog,' he said, and for the first time, warmth blew into his voice. 'In Russia, I had one like this.' Then he lay back down and watched Dinka, his eyes wide. Assaf didn't know how to prolong the dying conversation. 'What's this book?' and he pointed to a book lying by the mattress.

'This? Like, Dragons, D&D.'

'Really?' Assaf got excited. 'There's D&D in Russian?'

'There's everything in Russian,' the boy said, gasping heavily. 'In the place where I came from, I had a *grupa* of D&D . . . How do you say it in Hebrew?'

'A group?' Assaf guessed.

'Yes . . . group . . . D&D . . .' His eyes closed.

'One minute,' Assaf said.

Who are you, how did you get here, how have you been brought to such a state, what have you eaten in the last week except junk food, maybe you're sick, you seem sick, where are your parents, do they even know where you are, how come they aren't turning the world upside down and inside out to find you, what will happen to you tomorrow, where will you be in a month, will you still *be* at all?

Instead of all that, he said, 'I'm looking for a girl.' He still had a slight hope that Dinka knew why she'd brought him here. 'She's little, with long hair, black. She was with this dog.'

Sergei opened his eyes slowly and looked at Assaf as if he had already forgotten him. He rose up on his elbows and blinked at the square of light in which Dinka was sitting. Assaf thought his eyes were focusing for a minute.

He lay back down again; his arms couldn't hold up the weight of his head. He closed his eyes, didn't move; flies sat in the corners of his mouth, picking at the crumbs of the sandwich. Assaf waited a few more minutes, disappointed. Through the arched window, he saw blue skies, the side of a mountain, and a few pine trees. A moment passed. He turned to go.

The boy's voice stopped him in the doorway. 'She came here,' he said without opening his eyes, and the hair on the back of Assaf's neck stood up. 'Maybe a month ago? Maybe two months? I don't know. She's looking for someone, a child maybe? A guy? Came with a picture like this, photo, do you say photo in Hebrew?' Assaf nodded, and the boy continued: 'Asking if we know, maybe it's her friend, I don't know.'

Assaf listened quietly. His mouth went dry; a pain began to drone deep in his heart.

'One was here – his name was Paganini.' The boy spoke in a dreamy, floating voice. 'He played violin, playing, playing, until a gas balloon exploded in his hands, and no more playing.' He was silent for another long moment. Assaf was afraid he had fallen back asleep and wouldn't talk again. But the boy continued, his eyes closed. 'And he, Paganini, saw her guy playing guitar in the Walking Street.'

'And Paganini? He knew the . . . her guy?'

'No . . . didn't know. How could he? But her guy, he play very good, very good, Paganini said.'

Assaf knew he mustn't think about what he was hearing here

yet, only listen. Forget it, this guy of hers who plays the guitar so well, forget all about it.

The boy was now filled with a little life; he tried to sit up again, and succeeded for a moment. 'And when he play, the guy, there are a lot of *musikanti* there, giving concerts together, like artists, in the street like this. Like, a *group*. And everybody is little, kids, but it's also a little mafia. I don't know. Complicated . . .' He surrendered to his weakness, lay back, and continued: 'I remember her' – his voice murmuring between the deep breaths of a sleeper – 'she's little . . . not afraid of anything, came here alone, yelling to me, Get up, get up, look at his picture . . .'

He snored a little. Assaf waited a few minutes more; carefully, he tiptoed out of the ruins, still forbidding himself to think or feel anything. She has a boyfriend, but that's okay. She's looking for him; she's probably been running all over town looking for him. That's fine. It's none of my business. I only need to give her back her dog. Come on, Dinka. Let's go.

But his shoulders dropped, and all the passion left him.


Got to call Rhino, he thought as he plodded after Dinka. This is getting too messy. And didn't Sergei say something about the mafia? What mafia? Why the mafia? I can't handle this on my own anymore. I shouldn't have gotten in this deep.

When they reached the meadow with the tall fennel bushes on the way back, Dinka stopped. Again, Assaf saw it happen: as if a transparent butterfly of scent fluttering through the air had alighted on the tip of her nose, then flown off again, showing her the way, down a new path.

She made a sharp right turn, then bolted, stopped, looked at Assaf expectantly, wagged her tail hard; if she had suddenly raised a sign with FOLLOW ME! written on it, it couldn't have been more clear.

The curved path turned into a cobbled road, paved with well-cut stone. Pomegranate trees grew along both sides, and lemon trees and figs and high cactuses. A little stream flowed along next to it, and it was beautiful; almost unbelievable to think that such beauty could exist here, and a few meters away, two boys were lying in piles of filth.

A little pool of water sparkled at him behind some thick bushes, open like a good eye, blue-green in the light of the sun; the water was clear, combed by ripples of wind, and swelled over into the flowing stream that Assaf had passed earlier.

Dinka looked at him and barked joyfully; she looked at him and at the pond, and at him, and barked again.

Dinka, he said, I'm not in the mood for guessing games right now. You'll have to explain yourself. He stepped onto the slippery stone surrounding the pool's edge – perhaps something was there that belonged to Tamar, he thought. He suddenly felt scared – perhaps Tamar was in there.

He peeked again, cautiously. His fear sketched horrible things for him to find in the depths of the water, along the bottom of the pool – but there was nothing there, and nobody.

He then searched the bushes, moved branches aside, checked here and there. He found two old needles, a torn newspaper, a towel, rotten watermelon peels, and the entire time Dinka ran around him, standing on her hind legs in front of him, getting tangled up in his legs. She almost knocked him in twice, barking in unusual excitement, as if she were trying to rescue him from his despondency.

He knelt down in front of her, and they looked at each other, nose to nose. She barked, and he spread out his hands, grasped her head, looked into her eyes in feigned despair, yelling into her barks, 'What, what, what?'

She shook herself away from him, pulled her head out of his hands, and stood at the edge of the water – She looked at him as if to say, 'Well, if you can't take a hint –' and jumped in.

She made a huge splash, and he was covered in cold droplets. Dinka sank for a moment, then rose up, floating; her intelligent head turning this way and that above the water, and underneath, her body, dark and drenched. She swam in the little pool in the intense, frightened manner of swimming dogs, with that troubled and concentrated look they have, as if swimming were very hard work for them.

So this is what you wanted? For me to join you? But what if somebody comes by and sees me, he thought, and answered, Who's going to come by here? The two Sergeis are asleep – they can hardly move. And it's so beautiful here. And the truth is, it wouldn't hurt me to clear my head a little bit – he immediately took off everything except his underwear and jumped in. And froze. All his body parts leaped up in a roar – his body lifted halfway out of the water – he inhaled the air from the whole valley around him and dove down, touching the slippery stone on the bottom of the pool with his hands, rising again to absorb the sun.

Dinka swam around him in little circles, and he felt how sorry she was that she didn't have more ways of expressing joy. Her tail cut through the water again and again, spraying him with frozen drops, and Assaf – whose mother always claimed he had the most remarkable powers of recovery, and he never quite understood what she was talking about – jumped on her and held her under – she escaped and butted her head against his chest, and they chased each other from end to end, crossing over in diagonals. Assaf grabbed a round stone from the mud and threw it in, and Dinka dove in after it and brought it up in her mouth, inhaling and exhaling sprays of water and air, and they embraced like two long-lost brothers who haven't seen each other for thirty years.

'Does she come here?' Assaf asked, his face resting against hers, his hair falling over his forehead. 'Does she come here to be alone? Do the two of you swim here? Or was it only after she came to talk to those two, the two Sergeis, that she got into the water? Hey, where's the stone?'

She was a dog, and he was a boy. They didn't have a very evolved mutual language, but in the depths of his heart, he felt that she had given him this swim as a gift, and that perhaps, in her dog's brain, it was her way of thanking him for not giving up, for continuing the search for her Tamar.

\*    \*    \*

Later, he closed his eyes and floated on his back. The sun dazzled through his eyelids. There is someone, he thought, in a pleasant stupor, that one person in the world . . . I wonder what she'll think of me when we meet . . .

There is someone, he thought, and his eyelids became heavy, someone who once swam in this pool, in this water, and it touched her the same way it touches me now . . .

He floated away and disappeared into a sunny dream; he knew something was bothering him, the new fact he had discovered not long ago, a few minutes ago, but as always, he succeeded in putting it out of his thoughts. There would be time for that later. It wasn't going anywhere. He tried again to imagine what she, Tamar, looked like. He put together what he had heard about her from Theodora and the detective. He heard Dinka panting and getting out of the pool, and after a moment, he was sprayed again with frozen drops as she shook the water off her fur.

The coldness reminded him. She was looking for a guy. A shadow passed over his eyes, blocking the sun for a moment. What did you think, a bitter voice muttered within him, that she would wait for you? A girl like her isn't alone, not for one minute. She's probably surrounded by guys all the time. And she doesn't have just any boyfriend but some guitar player. Assaf envisioned him at once, from the top of his head to the end of his guitar strings, some hunky guy with a movie-star smile, another Roi; witty and arrogant, who could make girls laugh and drove everyone crazy when he played his guitar.

Okay, he told himself with closed eyes, refusing to surrender to the jealousy that erupted in his heart, okay, fine, so she has a boyfriend. So what? What do I care about her boyfriend? I am looking for her so I can give Dinka back to her, boyfriend or no boyfriend. It's none of my business.

He dove deep into the water and stayed there as long as he could, trying to chill the poison in his blood, baffled by what was happening to him. Why was it so painful for him to think of her with a boyfriend? It may well be like this forever, he thought, bitterly: him looking for her, and her looking for someone else. Rhino wants Reli, and Reli wants the American. Why can't you give the world a little thump on the side, the kind you give to a toolbox full of screws and nails, and then everything could fall into its rightful place? When he started to suffocate from lack of air, and after the cold had shrunk the new pain inside him, he rose to the surface and let the sun do its best to comfort him.

It warmed his belly, stroked his chest; the thoughts scattered again in soft circles . . . and perhaps I will continue to look for her for weeks, months, perhaps even years, and in twenty years, let's say, I'll find her and knock on the door of her house, in one of those fancy neighborhoods, and her doorman will open and say, 'Yes, who are you?' and I'll say, 'I have something for Tamar.' 'You?' he'll say. 'How could *you* have anything to do with Tamar? Tamar doesn't meet with just anybody; every moment in her life is dedicated to profound thoughts about good and evil and free will, and besides, she's in a very bad mood these days because she just separated from her first husband, the famous guitar player . . .'

'Look at the body on that one!'

'Be honest, you want him, don't you?'

'Hey, since when do faggots come here, anyway?'

Assaf opened his eyes and saw three boys standing around the pool.

'Good morning, sugar, did you sleep well?'

'Did you dream about how we gave it to you last night?'

He found himself making the necessary motions to stand. The water came up to his neck. He was cold. He tried to swim to the edge, but one of the boys walked there – pretty slowly, even with a limp – and by the time Assaf had placed his fingers on the stone to pull himself out, the boy's shoe was ready and he stepped down. Assaf swam to the other side, but one of them was there, too, shoe waiting in the air. Assaf began to swim from one side to the other, back and forth. He knew he didn't have a chance, they wouldn't let him get out, but he wasn't thinking straight. Meanwhile, poor Dinka was standing far away, barking madly, trapped, because one of the boys, the one who looked like the oldest of the three, held her collar tightly and pressed her head against his leg so she couldn't turn her head, bite, or even move.

For minutes they played with him like this in utter silence, anticipating him each time he tried to climb out of the water. Eventually, when he was about to despair, they stepped back and let him out. He stood there, almost naked, shivering from the cold, surrounded. This was very bad. The worst thing that had ever happened to him. He didn't know what they would do to him, or to Dinka.

The big guy came closer; he held Dinka so tightly she whined; he was practically dragging her behind him.

'So what's going on, sister?' He smiled at Assaf. 'You thought you'd make a Jacuzzi out of our private pool?'

Assaf lowered his head, and made his most dim-witted face.

'Say, sister,' the guy inquired, his voice too soft, too considerate, 'you probably pissed in our private pool, too, didn't you?'

Assaf shook his head fervently, and muttered that he didn't know it was private.

The guy whistled long, in astonishment. 'And you didn't see the sign? The DEATH PENALTY TO ANY MOTHERFUCKERS WHO GO IN WITHOUT PERMISSION sign?'

Assaf's entire body shook. He really hadn't seen any sign.

'No shit, really?' the tall guy asked, amazed. 'No sign? Avi, do me a favor and help our sister see it.'

The boy named Avi pushed a stiff finger under Assaf's chin, pressing hard until he was forced to raise his head.

'Now look, my heart. Do you see it now? With the golden frame? With the picture of Cindy Crawford in her sparkling bathing suit?'

He didn't see it. He said that he saw it.

'Should we throw her in, Herzl?' Avi proposed. He was a little guy, wearing a baseball cap turned backward.

'Maybe we should take off her panties,' the third one

proposed, the boy with the limp and big moles all over his face.

'What for, Kfir? Do you feel like doing her?'

The two young guys laughed. Assaf didn't move. This is the end of me, he thought. They're going to rape me.

'No,' the tall one said, the older one. Herzl. 'I have a better plan for motherfuckers like her. Why don't you give her back her clothes, but take a look to see if there's anything in her pockets that might serve as some minimal fine for swimming in our private pool, with suspicion of pissing.'

The one with the limp picked up the clothes, rifling through the pants, and found the three hundred shekels that was supposed to pay for Assaf's lunch in the City Hall cafeteria until the end of his parents' trip, the money he had saved so carefully for the 300 mm lens for the new Canon.

They threw his clothes at him, hard. The belt buckle hit his lip, and he felt a warm stream of blood start down his chin. Without wiping his mouth, he first put on his pants; he could hardly get his legs in. The three were standing and watching him. The silence worried him. Anything could happen in this moment of stillness, and Assaf knew that the really tough part was only beginning now. He got so muddled by his shirtsleeves that he eventually gave up and stood half naked, the shirt in his hands. He swallowed. He didn't know how he would do it, how he would make himself talk.

'Go on, sister,' the big one said, confused, and pushed Dinka closer against his thigh. 'Why are you still blocking the view?'

'The dog,' Assaf said, without looking at him.

'*What* did you say?'

'I need her.' He didn't have the courage to lift his head. His voice wasn't even passing out of his vocal cords, but squeaked from a different place, somewhere in the neighborhood of his elbow.

The two younger guys stared at Assaf in silent disbelief. Then they looked at the tall guy and opened their mouths to snigger, waiting to be told what to think.

He produced a long, long, quiet whistle. 'Her, you said? I

thought it was a male. A bitch is even better for us.' He passed a finger over the orange collar. 'You even went to the trouble of getting her a license, thank you very much.'

'I need the dog,' Assaf repeated. He actually mined the words out of a frozen mass he felt in the hollow of his stomach. Dinka looked at him again. Her drooping tail started wagging a little, hesitantly.

The two boys caught sight of a glimmer in Herzl's eyes and started to laugh. They howled with laughter, slapping their hands against their thighs. Herzl raised a hand – not a hand, a finger – and they shut up.

'Tell me, you fucker,' he said, for once genuinely surprised. 'Wouldn't it be a shame to ruin your ugly face? Wouldn't it be a shame if we let Kfir here sexually abuse you, with him on probation and all?'

'Come on, then . . . let's fight,' Assaf muttered, and thought he must be insane. He had no idea where that phony sentence had escaped from.

The tall guy took one step forward, then put his hand behind his ear. 'We didn't hear you,' he said, and smiled a thin smile.

'You and me,' Assaf whispered. His lips became white, he could feel their whiteness; his whole body was white. 'Let's fight. Whoever wins gets her.'

Again, the two boys cackled and screamed, and grabbed at each other, and exchanged high fives. They jumped around him, yelping, seeming like two cheetah or wolf cubs whose father was teaching them how to tear apart living prey.

Herzl gave Dinka to Avi and approached Assaf. He was a head taller and at least a shoulder wider. Assaf dropped the shirt he was still holding. Herzl stood in front of him, his arms spread, his hands inviting him to come closer.

Assaf's legs hardly moved, but he started jerking into some frozen, fractured circuit around the guy. Herzl was turning in front of him. Assaf saw the muscles sliding along the long arms in front of him. He hoped it would end quickly. Whatever it is, let it end quickly, let it not be too painful, too humiliating. It bothered him that he was half naked. He vaguely remembered how in moments of danger the body releases adrenaline that's supposed to strengthen muscles, quicken reflexes; and he thought, sadly, that he probably didn't possess this substance. On the contrary, his head became foggier and foggier; he had the feeling he was actually *anesthetizing* himself, partly to dull the pain that would soon come, but mainly to dull the humiliation.

Herzl poked his fist out, teasingly, as if he were trying to wake him up, and Assaf flinched and almost fell. The two other guys screamed with pleasure; they circled them the entire time, jumped, and ran around very close. One of them thumped Assaf on the back of his neck. At this the big one straightened up, flicked his finger like some gang leader from the movies, and said that if either of them got involved, then he, Herzl, would personally smash him up. Assaf felt the guy's odd integrity melting his heart within his anaesthetizing fear.

But in the same moment, the guy moved forward – not even very quickly, just the opposite, with a kind of professional assertiveness. His arm captured Assaf's neck with immense power; Assaf, who was pretty strong himself, never knew – had never known – that such a thing existed. The boy bent Assaf down, inch by inch. Assaf felt the warmth of the strange body near him; heat rose from the boy like from a stove, the smell of smoke came from his armpits. Assaf's neck began to squeak, and gradually, the life was squeezed from his body and his eyes stopped seeing.

Then the guy let go. Assaf stood, hazy from pain, dizzy from suffocation, aware only that Herzl was turning him gently around so that Assaf would face him the way a nurse in a clinic positions your arm for a shot. The boy organized everything, arranged Assaf just so for what was to come. Assaf was thinking, but he couldn't change anything, couldn't move or run, and then the guy kneed him in the balls, just like that, and when Assaf bent over with a deep moan, he encountered the same knee again, smashing him in the nose.


Afterward, who knows how long afterward, the weird sketch

moving in front of his eyes, which had seemed at first the scribblings on blue paper of a disturbed child, slowly connected and turned out to be the branches of a bush under which he was lying.

'What do you mean, dead?' he heard a distant voice say. 'It's just his face that's gone.'

'Not his face, psycho, his nose; look how much blood came out.'

Assaf raised a hand, one of the hands that was placed somewhere by his side. It weighed a lot. He slowly separated its fingers. That took time, too, and he touched his nose. His nose was very wet, and full of unfamiliar bumps. Later, he found the nostrils, and all the rest. His mouth had gotten some of it, too. His upper lip hurt and pulsed; one tooth, up on the side, was a bit loose.

But for some reason, nonsensically, he felt relief.

Perhaps because all his life he had feared getting beaten up by a thug like that, by someone who has no God, as Rhino had said in a different context. It so terrified Assaf that he grew afraid of all the thugs, even those who were a lot smaller and weaker than he. It was as if he had accepted it, as a matter of fact, that he had no chance against them, that they would always humiliate him. Though Assaf had fought, more than once, with boys in his class, he knew they were boys like him, and there would always be some ultimate law they would never break while fighting. But the punks – he turned corners to avoid them when he saw them coming down the street, and kept his distance from them in the clubs on Friday night, and refused to answer when they shouted insults at him and his friends. He learned to walk that walk – transparent and fake-proud – when he passed by them in the street, and once, on a bus, he got up and left because one of them told him to get up and leave. He didn't even argue, just got up, left. There wasn't a day in his life when he didn't remember the heat of that humiliation.

And now, half-faint and crushed as he was, it was over, and he was almost free of it. He didn't understand exactly what had happened, only that something had happened, that he had now passed through a great obstacle that had been embittering his life.

'Come on,' said the tall one. 'What were you scared of? Let's go.' They turned to leave. Assaf got up – that is, he dragged the upper half of his body up into a half-upright position. A crazy biker kept riding around the inside of his head, as if it were a Wall of Death.

'I need the dog,' somebody said nearby. Probably in Hebrew. It might have even been Assaf himself.

'What did I hear?' The tall guy stopped, slowly turned around. Assaf tried to focus his eyes. Maybe there were two guys at this point? The two tall guys turned toward him and slowly merged into one tall guy. Assaf focused hard and saw the collar around Dinka's neck tightening again in the big fist. Her head was actually tied to his leg.

'Come – on – let's – fight – for – the – dog – again,' said whoever had decided to speak on Assaf's behalf, in complete opposition to his reason.

The light smile widened. 'Did you hear the dwarf?' He looked at his friends, and they smiled flatteringly at him. 'The dwarf wants a rematch.'

Assaf stood up. It was strange to have crossed beyond fear. He had absolutely no idea what was happening to him. This inner stubbornness clung to him as if, having overcome fear, he might as well see what it was like when someone walks up and takes you apart from top to bottom, over and over again.

Herzl moved in. The dance began again, Assaf and Herzl turning in circles around each other. Assaf heard the sound of his own breath, as if he had dived underwater. Fragments of thoughts flew through his brain . . . something about magic and how it was a pity he couldn't use it here. One very useful kind of magic is called 'Summoning.' You have to press *magic*, and then *target*, and then the magic creates a special beam that brings the object to you or, in this case, to Dinka. There is also another magic, 'Shrinking,' that shrinks your enemy by half. But where are they when you need them? Then something blurred in front of him – he didn't see what – and he felt a fist in his chest, near the sternum. It wasn't a hard hit, just a mocking warm-up punch, no more than what two guys exchange when they meet. In his condition, though, it was enough. He stumbled backward and fell. It was so simple to fall, to give in to the laws of gravity and weight; the natural law that someone like that will always beat someone like him. That someone still didn't attack him. He was waiting for Assaf to get up. A few moments later, after Assaf had managed to collect his limbs and stand, he got tangled in a bush and fell again. His knees simply folded under him, he had no control over it. He just lay there, gasping for breath – it was becoming ridiculous – he lay there, on his back, waiting for a hit, a kick, something to knock him out of the game completely. A fly buzzed over his nose; streams of pain flowed constantly, passing through his back, from his knees, into his balls. The tall guy approached him, gave him a hand, and helped him to stand up. They looked straight into each other's eyes for a moment. It was the first time Assaf really saw him clearly, not through his fear; he was at least three years older than Assaf, with a long, gloomy face, sculpted and handsome, a finely cut nose, and a very thin mouth.

'What's the matter, sister?' he said. 'We didn't drink our chocolate milk today? Mom ran out of Gerber food?'

Assaf tried to kick him – it was a miserable attempt. He saw himself from the outside, saw how slowly he was moving, how much energy he needed to just lift his knee a little bit. Herzl caught his foot easily by the ankle and, without much effort, lifted Assaf up and threw him backward. Assaf fell on his back; the wind was knocked out of him the moment he hit the ground. His bones knocked against one another. Herzl pounced on him, flipped him over, facedown, and started bending his hand backward. Assaf couldn't breathe. He gasped, swallowed earth, bellowed, perhaps even cried.

Herzl said in his ear, strangely quiet, 'If you don't shut up right now, you can kiss your arm goodbye.' Assaf murmured something. 'Can't hear you,' Herzl said, tight-lipped.

'I,' Assaf whispered voicelessly, 'have to have the dog.'

The other guy twisted Assaf's hand another centimeter

back. Assaf imagined the ping of the sinews and tendons and all the other flesh starting to tear – any second now . . .

'Shut up, I'm telling you.' The voice above him suddenly turned into a raspy growl. 'I'm giving you one last chance.' Herzl blew in his ear heavily, and for the first time, Assaf could feel effort coming from him as well.

'Kill me, I don't care.' His voice sounded to him thick and slow, like in a melted cassette tape. 'But – I – need – that – dog – I – can't – without – the – dog.'

No answer came. Suddenly it became very light as well – Assaf was almost floating – nothing could stop him from taking off now . . .

In the silence that followed, he heard a very odd chuckle, as if somebody said somewhere in space, 'I don't believe it.'

The pressure on his arm disappeared. Assaf thought that was it, maybe he had ripped his arm off and it was now that moment, the split second, before the pain reaches the brain. But the guy wasn't on him anymore, and Assaf's hand was lying behind his back, still attached. He started to feel it again, it came back to him in a wave of biting ants. He heard talking around him, something like an argument, a few shouts, and thought maybe someone from the outside had come to save him at the last moment, the way it happens in the movies. He couldn't follow it exactly. Streams, no, waves, of pain from all over his body were crashing against one another at the base of his skull. He closed his eyes and waited, passive. The entire time, he thought, someone very close to him kept mumbling stupidly that he needed some dog.

'Because I said so!' he heard Herzl spitting the words far away from him. 'Because I decide, you fucking retard. Did you hear me?'

'But what will I do with her now?' the other's voice whined, probably Avi's. 'If I let go of her, she'll bite.'

'She won't bite,' Herzl said very quietly, stating an irrefutable fact. 'She'll go to him.' In a moment, Assaf rose up on his elbows. Dinka was by his side, above him. He saw her tongue coming closer to him, gently licking his face. Again, he lay down, and didn't move, allowing himself to lose himself in her touch. Farther up on the side of the hill, he saw the three boys moving away, out of the valley. They had already forgotten about him. The two younger guys were doing something – probably fooling around: they were picking up big stones, almost small boulders, and throwing them at each other, dodging and hooting with joy. The older one, the one who had smashed his face in, walked in front of them, erect, distant, lost in thought.

Assaf held on to Dinka, leaned on her, and rose up. He stumbled to the pool and washed his face gingerly. He saw his reflection in the water and prayed that before his parents came back, he would grow a thick beard. Dinka was reflected in the water by his side and rubbed herself against his body, whimpering – a cry of longing he had never yet heard from her, a voice of comfort. He sat down heavily on the edge of the pool, with Dinka by his side, trying, unsuccessfully, to ignore the rhythmic pulsing of pain. A few minutes later, it came back to him, along with the throbbing aches – something Herzl had said, something about thank you . . . Herzl had thanked him for something . . . what was it? He splashed his face again and moaned at the sting of the water. His hand traveling on Dinka's back suddenly stopped. That was it: Herzl had said thank you for the license – but Danokh, at City Hall, said they had found her with no signs of identification. Assaf started to emerge from the fog of pain, his thoughts fumbling forward as if they were in a room full of smoke. He groped through her fur, found her collar, and touched the metal tag; since he had met Dinka yesterday, he'd touched the tag quite a few times and somehow never thought it might be her license – and if it hadn't been for Herzl –

He shook the tag off her moist fur, and tilted it into the light. Dinka stood patiently, turning her head to the side, allowing him to check. He closed one eye and tried to focus.

'Egged Baggage Check 12988.'

He looked at Dinka, amazed. 'And all this time, you didn't say anything?'

\*　　\*　　\*

228

Assaf hid behind one of the columns of the Central Station, watching the line. Three young guys ran back and forth behind a wide counter, yelling and joking with one another and the customers, briskly distributing packages to whoever came forward with a tag like the one in Assaf's hand. One of the men, the one who wore a conductor's cap, worried him: he was the most serious and organized of the three, and each time he gave someone the parcel which had been deposited, he asked to see ID – that is, he took the ID and studied it carefully, comparing it to the names written on the official roster, which was stained with a splash of tomato juice. The two others were less strict: they took the tag, went to the huge shelves on the other end of the room, pulled out the desired package, and handed it to the tag owner without asking for anything.

Assaf joined the line. There were seven people in front of him. The line moved quickly, and he knew that it didn't matter, his luck would bring him directly into the hands of the one with the conductor's cap. He had no clue what he would do when the guy asked for ID and saw that his name didn't match the one written on the list. He stood there, trying not to think about what had just happened to him by the pond. He knew that if he even allowed himself to think about it – the beating he took, the money stolen, his dream for a telephoto lens that would now have to be postponed so many months – he would simply lose his mind in anguish and anger. He tightened all his aching muscles and hardened himself, decisively ignoring the recent past and near future. He was on duty now. He was on a mission. Meanwhile, the three baggage clerks were discussing the match this coming Saturday. The guy with the hat was a Ha'Poel fan, and the other two, Beytar fans, and they were laughing at the first guy loudly, telling him that on this Saturday, just like every one of the last millennium, Ha'Poel didn't stand a chance. 'What do you mean they don't stand a chance?' he kept saying in a growing rage. 'It all depends on whether Danino is healthy this Saturday. Who's next? Who's next?'

'Yeah, and it also depends on whether Danino can keep up with Abuksis.' The second guy laughed. 'And it *also* depends on whether Danino can avoid getting red-carded,' the third joined in, to help serve up this feast of humiliation. 'In other words, forget it!' At this point, there were two people in front of Assaf in the line. He left the line and walked to a newsstand. He had a few coins left in his pocket, poor remnants of what had been there. He bought a *Yediot* and threw the news section into the trash, stood to the side and read an article in the sports section about the coming game. He felt comfortable hiding his swollen face behind the newspaper for a few minutes. He read the article all the way to the end, again and again; he was sorry the baggage clerks weren't Ha'Poel basketball fans, because that was more his sport. Then he went to the bathroom and washed his face in cold water for long minutes, restoring it somewhat to its familiar form.

Six people were in front of him when he got back into line. He rubbed the tag for luck until it was warm; he was sure everyone could see how nervous he was. In Dragonfire, his favorite game, there were four main characters – a magician, a warrior, a knight, and a thief. He had already been a warrior this morning; now he would be a thief. When his turn came, the man in the hat – of course – reached a hand toward him. 'Move it, let's go, quickly!' 'Sure,' Assaf cried jovially, 'I want to make practice at two!'

The hand stopped above the tag, suspiciously checking his bruised face. 'Why, who are you for?'

'The reds, who are you for?'

'You're my brother.' He leaned toward Assaf and winked. 'But what's going to happen if we fuck up Saturday like last time? What'll we do? Where can we possibly run to?' He indicated the other two with a nod of his head. 'And what if Danino doesn't play?'

'They're giving him another checkup Wednesday,' Assaf reported with authority. 'So maybe he's got a chance – what do you say? Look on the bright side!' He tried to look as enthusiastic as possible.

'It's hard to know.' The other guy scratched his head, as if

Danino were lying in front of him on the table, waiting for his verdict. 'If it's a torn tendon, we're screwed.' He took the tag and turned toward the shelves. Five, ten, fifteen steps. Assaf tapped his fingers on the counter. The guy was looking and looking, moving bags and suitcases around, and couldn't find it. Assaf vigorously scratched Dinka's head. Magician, warrior, knight, and thief. The thief has to count on his sharpness and agility, his escape skills and his cleverness. *Choose the thief if you want to use his cunning and dexterity to keep your hero out of trouble.*

'When did you leave it here?' he yelled from the end of the room.

'Eh . . . my sister left it here a while back.'

It wasn't a good answer, but he didn't have a better one.

'Got it.' He pulled out a big heavy gray backpack. He could hardly pull it out from between two suitcases. 'It's been lying here for maybe a month already. Did you forget about it? Just show me some ID.'

Assaf smiled sweetly and glanced around quickly to see any possible escape routes. The bag was on the counter, maybe ten centimeters away; Tamar was within a hand's reach. He played his last card: 'But Shandor might not play for Beytar.'

'*What?* What did you say?' The man's eyes lit up with love and a new hope. 'Shandor is injured?'

'Didn't you hear?'

'What? You mean it? Did you hear that?' he yelled to the other two. 'You're going down!' and in his joy he pushed the bag into Assaf's hands. 'Shandor isn't playing today!'

'Shandor?' One of them laughed. 'Where did you get that from? He was practicing yesterday, I saw him with my own eyes!'

'Pulled a muscle,' Assaf said confidently, taking one step back, pressing the precious bag to his heart. 'Happened after practice. Read the paper.'

The Ha'Poel fan smiled brightly, and was already taking care of the next customer. To be honest, Assaf wasn't certain if it was Shandor or someone else, Ya'acobi, who had been injured after practice, in the dressing rooms – but someone had pulled a muscle, and why not make a man happy?

He rushed away with Dinka, hugging the bag in his arms, trying not to attract too much attention to his pained limp and that face; in the last hour, he had started getting scared – well, not scared, really, concerned – that someone might be following him. He had no apparent reason to think so, but still – perhaps because of what Sergei had said to him in the ruins, perhaps because he was finally starting to grasp that Tamar was tangled up in something really dangerous – every once in a while he felt the back of his neck tingling, as if someone was looking at him, checking up on him – every once in a while, he heard steps behind him, and when he turned around to check, there was no one there.

His bike was waiting for him on the platform of the Nations building, white with the dust from Lifta's paths. He took the bike lock off and pedaled off slowly, aching with every movement. He had the bag now, and he tried to forget his pain by pretending that the weight on his back was Tamar, that she had fainted, and fallen, without knowing it, into his care. Dinka ran after him, in front of him, at his side, sniffing excitedly at the signals the backpack sent her. He got off his bike when they reached Sakar Gardens, looked around in every direction. His gaze traveled the length of the green. Still nobody there. He waited, though, his eyes following a beautiful hoopoe that flew over the grass – while he scanned his surroundings (the whole time, Dinka watched him, tilting her head to the side with a questioning look, as if she was wondering who had taught *him* to do these things as well); then, with an almost unnoticeable step, he threw his bike down and disappeared into the bushes.

He sat on the ground, placed the bag in front of him. He decided not to hurry. He wanted to prolong this moment, because, after all, it was a kind of first date. First he read the note tied to the bag, with the date of its deposit at the baggage check. He calculated: about a month ago. A little less. She had probably left the bag and then disappeared. But why didn't she leave the bag at home? Maybe there were things in it she was afraid her parents would see. Now he remembered how Theodora's nose had twitched when she mentioned Tamar's parents. But what exactly did she say? He closed his eyes and beamed a laser into his memory – uncovering word after word: '. . . because she needs money; lately, quite a bit of money. She does not take any from her parents, of course.' He thought about it for another minute and sifted his mind for everything he had ever heard about her, from anyone who had ever said anything about her. He searched for clues that would explain why she wouldn't take help from her parents, and couldn't find any. He left it in the Open Questions file.

Then he tried to think about where he had been the date she deposited the bag; it amused him to think of a time when he knew nothing of her – it was kind of like those many years during which his mother and father had lived in the same city and known nothing of each other. They might even have bumped into each other on the street, at the movie theater, and never imagined that there would come a time when they would have three kids together.

But really now, what was he doing, that day she deposited the bag? He checked the date again. It was still just the beginning of summer vacation. What could he have been doing? His life then seemed so empty to him now, compared to the last two days that had been electrified with Tamar.

Not only empty: he thought that until she had come into his life, he had been doing things almost mechanically, auto-matically, without questioning his actions, or really feeling; and now, since yesterday, everything happening to him, every person he met, every thought he had – it was all connected, and rooted in one deep center, full of life.

He opened the bag. He did everything very slowly. It was exciting to open the buckles of the backpack, because it was she who had closed them. In one minute, he thought, he would encounter something from her life. It was too much. Everything was too much. He laid the bag down for a moment, open, in front of him. Dinka had no such patience; she gasped and panted and kept trying to shove her nose into the bag. He reached inside, and his hand felt the wrinkled, slightly moist touch of clothing that had been packed away for a long time. He suddenly realized what he was doing and stopped, embarrassed. What was he doing? Why, he was invading her most intimate privacy. Quickly, before he could pause, he pulled out long Levi's, a colorful, very wrinkled Indian shirt, delicate sandals. Carefully, he spread them on the ground, looked hypnotized. These clothes had touched her – they had been on her body, they had absorbed her scent. If he wasn't so embarrassed in front of Dinka, he would smell them, just as Dinka did, with cries of yearning.

And why not?

He saw at once that she really was tiny. The detective had said a meter sixty; yes, he thought, she would just about reach his shoulder. He stood up straight, took a deep breath, folded his legs under himself, looking, insatiable; suddenly – how did his mother put it? – he felt full of joy, to the very tendrils of his ears.

His hands traveled carefully through the other clothes in the bag. He touched a paper bag and pulled it out, placed it to the side, searched a little more; he found a delicate silver bracelet at the bottom of the backpack, passed a finger over it. If he had a bit more experience in detective work – or with girls – he would have tried to search for signs on it, aside from the flowery engraving all around it; he, of all people, because of Reli's experience in jewelry making, should have checked more closely. But who knows? Perhaps it was just because of Reli that he immediately put the bracelet away, placing it back into the bag, and missed seeing Tamar's full name engraved inside. Later, many weeks later – when he tried to remember his strange journey toward her, one of those endless mental reconstructions in which people think, If I had done this, then that wouldn't have happened – he decided that he was actually very lucky not to have discovered her last name on the bracelet at that moment, because if he had, he would have searched for her parents' address in the phone book and gone there; her parents would have taken Dinka from him and paid the fine, and everything would have ended there.

But at that moment, he was thinking of only one thing: what

was in the sealed paper bag in front of him. He didn't dare open it, because he felt, or guessed, or hoped, that something important was inside, since she had felt the need to wrap it up like that. He felt the bundle – he thought there were books in there; perhaps her photo albums. Dinka was crying: There's no time! He opened it and looked inside, and a little groan escaped his lips. Notebooks. Five. Some thick, some thin. He put them to one side, stacked on top of one another, a small, condensed pile. He reached out his hand, as if it was not his hand, and grabbed one. He flipped through the pages quickly, in front of his eyes, not daring to read them. Pages and pages covered in a cramped, curving, hard-to-read hand.

Diary, it said, on the cover of the first notebook. Between happy Bambi stickers and drawings of broken hearts and birds. The letters were rounded and childish, and three lines sprawled across the bottom: *Do Not Read! Private! Please!!!*

'You don't say,' Assaf murmured. 'Are there special situations when you're allowed to read somebody else's diary?'

Dinka looked the other way and licked her lips once.

'I know. But maybe it will say where she is. Do you have a better idea?'

Dinka passed her tongue over her lips again, and sat straight and deep in thought.

Assaf opened the diary. On the first page he saw a red double frame, words shouting inside it:

*Father and Mother, please, please, even if you have found this notebook, please do not read it!!!*

And underneath, in big letters:

*I know that you've read my notebooks a few times already. I can tell. But I truly beg you, don't touch this notebook. Do not open it, please. I'm asking you to respect my privacy for once in my life. Tamar.*

He closed it. The request was so touching, so desperate, he couldn't refuse her. It also shocked him to think her parents were capable of peeking into her diary. In our house, he thought, a little arrogantly, I could have left such a diary (if I wrote one) open on the table and my parents wouldn't dream of looking through it.

His mother had her own private diary. She wrote in it almost every day. Every once in a while – but lately, less and less – he would ask her what she wrote in there. What does she have so much to write about, anyway? What was going on in her life? She said she was writing down her thoughts and dreams, her troubles and joys. When he was younger, he had asked her many times if he could read it. She would smile and press the notebook to her chest and say that a diary is a private thing; it was a matter between her and herself. What? He was amazed. You don't even let Dad read it? – imagine, not even Dad. Assaf remembered now how many years he had kept himself busy with the main riddles of the diary: What did she have in there that she didn't let them see? And was she writing about him as well? He asked her, of course, whether she was writing about him. She laughed, her wide, rolling laughter, throwing her head back a bit, shaking her mane of curls; she said that she could recite for him, by heart, everything she had written about him, gladly. So why *write* it? he yelled, angry. In order to believe it, she said. My happiness.

When his mother said 'My happiness,' she always meant having him and Reli and Muki; his mother had stayed single for many years (in her opinion, at least), and by the time she met his father, she was sure she would never marry. Then, all because of a major blown fuse and troubles with the safety switch, that sweetie walked into her life, that round, smiling electrical genius who agreed to come immediately, almost in the middle of the night, and fixed everything. As the repairs dragged on, she felt the need to entertain him; so she stood next to him, asked a question or two. She was surprised because he started telling her about his mother; that is – really, he started from the beginning, confessing that he simply *had* to leave his mother's house and rent his own apartment, but his mother wouldn't let him go, it was as if she had a set of claws. He didn't look at Assaf's mother as he spoke. He seemed shy to her, inexperienced with women. Because of that, his forthrightness surprised her (it surprised him, too). The moment she asked him one right question, from the heart, streams of conversation and thoughts and hesitations that had probably been sealed in him for years burst out. She stood by his side, in front of the open fuse box, a littler taller, and wider, than he – held up a candle, and felt – and this was the moment for Assaf and Reli and even Muki in the last year to shout together – that he was blowing all her fuses!

As the years passed, Assaf stopped thinking about her diary. He willed himself not to think about it. He got used to seeing his mother, usually in the evening, curled up in her little room, her HQ, sitting on the old couch in her wide sarwal pants, with a long, untucked shirt over them, leaning on the big pillows 'like a great Eastern lady' – in her own words – but sucking on her pen like a schoolgirl and writing.

Now, for some reason, the feeling bubbled in him, as it had years ago: perhaps, weeks, months ago, she had written in there what Reli would tell her, in secret, from America. Perhaps her diary knew the truth about Reli's new boyfriend before Rhino and he had suspected it.

He opened the notebook again. Dinka gave him a quick look from the side. He imagined he heard a low, threatening growl from her and closed it.

'I'm not her parents,' he explained to her, and himself. 'And I don't know her. So it really won't matter to her if I read it. Do you understand?'

Silence. Dinka looked at the sky.

'I'm actually doing her a favor, so I can bring you to her, right?'

Silence. But it was a little softer. Yes, it sounded reasonable to him, he could continue with that line of logic. 'I have to use everything I can get, any hint, every available piece of information, to find out where she is!'

Now she whined, pawing once at the ground with her claws, the way she always did when she was embarrassed. 'Look,' he went on, 'she won't even know I read it. I'll find her, and then I'll give you to her!' He was getting more and more worked up from the force of his own words. 'More than that – she'll never have to see me. We'll be like two strangers – strangers for life!'

At that Dinka stopped pawing the dirt, turned her entire body toward him, and stood, her brown eyes searching deep in his. Assaf didn't move. He had never seen such a look from a dog's eyes. 'If you say so,' her look said, with a sort of doggy smile, and Assaf blinked first.

'I'm reading it!' he announced, and turned his back to her. First he riffled the pages, just to get used to the idea of what he was doing. He thought he could detect a light scent of hand lotion, maybe from the very hand that had pressed against the pages. Then he ran his eyes over a few lines, not reading, just to acquaint himself with her letters. He saw childish handwriting, and little sketches of snails and mazes penciled in the margins.

Abruptly, decisively, he jumped inside:

*. . . but how come Mor and Liat, everyone, they all know exactly what they'll do, and where they'll work, and who they'll marry. And she is constantly sunk in her own stupidity and her imagination, clueless how to make her future start, now! She's afraid the woman in her dream was right, that anyone who is lazy and dreamy like her will have a mistake-life – a MISTAKE-LIFE!!!*

He put the notebook on his knees, baffled. Whom was she speaking about here? But the writing – the words themselves, the rhythm of the thoughts, the outburst at the end – gave him a strange shock. He flipped through a few more pages and a lot of short passages. A description of a madman she'd seen on the street, of an orphaned kitten that Dinka adopted; a page on which only one line was written: *How can you even live after you know what happened in the Holocaust?* Suddenly he saw letters in a foreign language. He looked closer: it was Hebrew in mirror-writing. He didn't have the time to decode it, but after he flipped the page, he thought she might have had a special reason to encrypt what she had written there. Stubbornly he read, struggling through every word: *Sometimes she thinks that perhaps there is a world* – it would take him hours to read through such a page. He went back to his bike, and with the little screwdriver that was always attached to the back of his shoe ('A screwdriver is like a handkerchief,' his father had taught him. 'You never know when you're going to need it.'), he took the mirror off, went back to the diary, and read quickly:

*that perhaps there is a world in which the people go out in the morning, to work or to school, and in the evening, each one returns to a different home; and there, in every home, each person is kind of playing his role. The father role, or the mother, or the child, the grandma, and so on, and so forth. And all evening they talk and laugh and eat and fight and watch TV together, each one of them behaving precisely according to his role. Later, they go to sleep, and in the morning they get up and again go off to work or school and come back in the evening, but this time to a different home, and there, everything starts all over again: the father becomes father to a different family; the girl is a girl in a different family. And because they forgot, during the day, what had happened the previous evening, they always think they are in their own home, the right home, and this is how it goes for all their lives.*

Slowly, he put down the notebook. This idea filled him with excitement and unease. He thought, of course, about his own house – what if it were true, what if, every evening of his life, he was going to a different home, meeting different people there, complete strangers, and calling them father and mother? No, he immediately pushed the thought away. This could never happen with us; he would recognize how his mother smelled among a thousand different mothers, and the touch of his father's hand on his cheek and all his dumb little jokes, not to mention Muki – he could recognize her with his eyes closed among a thousand six-year-old girls.

He opened another notebook, a later one, flipped through

the pages, and closed it. Her strange idea wasn't letting go of him. Perhaps she was a little bit right after all. Because, if she was completely wrong, then why was he feeling, as if from a great distance, something like a tiny blister on his heart?

He turned the page:

*But she is not pretty.* Not *pretty. It doesn't matter what anyone says or what reason they have for lying to her. Liat once told her, about two years ago, 'You're almost beautiful today.' At the time it was the biggest compliment she had ever gotten, because the 'almost' proved it was real, it was for her. But, thinking about it now, she feels like screaming, because external beauty will determine her destiny!!!*

(But she is pretty, Assaf protested, remembering how Theodora had described her – even the undercover detective had to admit it. Assaf felt a little sorry for her now, and felt a strange relief along with it, because perhaps she wasn't so stunning after all . . .

*after school, she went to Café Atara. A mature woman was sitting there; she was about forty years old, with short, straight hair to her neck, and thick black unfashionable glasses, and truly terrible skin. She sat and stirred her coffee with a spoon for maybe half an hour without drinking it. But she wasn't daydreaming: she looked too nervous. After that, she took out a book, which I thought was in English, and read for at least another half an hour. But when I walked by her, I peeked at her and saw it was actually in Hebrew, and she was reading it from the end to the beginning! I'm writing it down, for the record, to remember that the world is full of mystery! I am also not as naïve as I was as a child. I know that every person in the world has his own secret games – so here's another thought for today's gymnastics class: what if the world underwent some kind of mutation – and all clothes disappeared, evaporated – no clothes, that's it! And*

*everyone had to go naked everywhere, to restaurants, to
school, to concerts. Brrr! By the way, the woman in the
café seemed like a journalist or judge to her. It was quite
clear to her that this is how she herself would be in about
twenty-five years – a wise, sad old judge, with no one
coming to sit down next to her.*

Assaf was embarrassed. It's one thing to open up someone's
diary in order to search for clues leading to her – but it was
a completely different matter to peek like this into someone's
soul. But that peek had already done its work: something in the
words, in the sadness and the loneliness, made it impossible for
Assaf to break away from them. He opened another, thicker
notebook. If he had a few quiet days, he would sit and read
them all, from beginning to end, and become absorbed into
her life. But Dinka was restless again, as he was – what he was
discovering in the diary made his need to find her even more
urgent, intense. So he flipped quickly, moving through another
notebook; he saw that the handwriting had changed, matured.
There wer no more snails sketched in the margins. He lingered
in front of another page of mirror-writing:

*3.3.98 I & A laugh all the time, about everything. They
have a lightness that she does not possess. She once did,
when she was a little girl – she is almost certain she did. I
& A weren't always so cheerful, either. It's as if they have
learned how to play the role of 'happy person.' Perhaps it's
different for them, because she has something they don't.
Thoughts are especially black today. Rats everywhere.
What happened? Nothing. Does there have to be a reason?
Yesterday, she visited Theo. They spoke about* Wings of
Desire. *What a divine film! When – if – she grows up, she
will make surrealist movies in which anything can happen.
The idea that angels can walk next to people and hear their
thoughts is deliciously scary (also just scary). We had a long
argument over whether there is life after death. T doesn't
believe in God, yet is still certain of life after death; that
there is no point to her life in this Vale of Tears without*

*a promise of some life after it. I sat quietly and listened*
*until she finished speaking, then I told her that it's exactly*
*the opposite with me! I mean, I have to know that life is*
*only here and now, and I hope there is no such thing as*
*reincarnation!! To think I would have to go through this*
*all over again!*

He shut the notebook again, as if he had just seen an open
wound. He wasn't confused, even for one moment, by the
frequent changing of 'I' to 'she.' Tamar, she was so – he
searched but couldn't find the word. So smart, probably, but
also sad, very sad. She had no illusions. She touched the wire
with bare hands, and her sadness wasn't an ordinary sadness,
the kind that was familiar to him, for instance, when Ha'Poel
lost a game or he got a bad grade. It was a completely different
kind of sadness, like that of old people who already know
everything about life. Assaf knew this sadness every once in
a while, in brief flashes. He couldn't describe it with words,
and preferred not to try, because once you put something into
words, it stays for good, like a final verdict against you. And
yet, if Tamar were here, he would speak with her fearlessly,
and finally try to give it a name, that thing that always waited
behind the thin veil of life and the everyday and his family.
He didn't like thinking those thoughts, even when he was
protected by his mother's strongest hugs. They would attack
him every once in a while, as he sat alone in his room, or before
falling asleep at night – suddenly he would be trapped in a
cold thought, as if he were falling, dropping into a pair of
gaping jaws.

Tamar, he felt, was writing about those very things; she
was the only person in the world ever to describe them
clearly, soberly: to describe what was elusive and scary. He
sat, sliding and thumping his fists against his thighs, now
closing the notebook, now opening it again, as if closing and
opening a dam to adjust the floodgates between the notebooks
and himself. Even though nothing had changed in the world
immediately outside these bushes, Assaf was all of a sudden
lost and bewildered, hovering in the space of the universe,

like a lonely human snowflake, desperate for assurance that somewhere in that empty space hovered another like it, named Tamar.

He also knew, without deluding himself for a moment, that the difference between him and her was that she, apparently, was not afraid of those thoughts, or at least didn't run away from them. Not like him; he always peeked and ran, remembered and forgot. She talked about her black thoughts, her herd of rats, as if she were talking about old acquaintances; sometimes even with a smile. He almost had the impression that she enjoyed wallowing in them, in a strange way. And when he saw the page on which she had written one hundred times, like a punishment, 'deviant' he felt like scratching it out with a big X and writing 'rare' above it. If I bring Dinka to her, he thought passionately, she will be so happy! And he knew he wanted to do more than that for her, much more.

He stood up, sat down, closed the notebook, opened it. His whole body tingled and burned. Dinka watched him. He thought her eyes were actually searching his out: Now do you understand what I've been talking to you about this whole time? Suddenly he wanted to get up and go; he had to run, to discharge the effervescence in his blood, also all the words rushing in his head, because she was something else, Tamar – more than smart, more than sad, more than rare. She was *thrilling*! That was the word he was looking for – he'd found it. His mother liked to say that after a watching a good movie: 'Now, that was thrilling!' Just the word itself, from his mother's mouth, used to excite him, before he ever really understood it. He felt it again, exactly, that *thrill*, in what Tamar wrote, as if someone had come and stirred up everything he had in his heart, in his head, in his guts.

Dinka was barking *No time, no time!* Assaf kept jumping back and forth between notebooks, his heart sinking with the knowledge that he didn't have the time to read them all. He found the fifteen-year-old Tamar here: suddenly things were lightening up; the oppressive sadness disappeared, and he met a happy girl, even cheerful. Oh good, he thought, and relaxed: it was probably because of her friendship with Idan and Adi.

Their names filled the pages, especially the boy's: Idan said this and did that, proclaimed this, decided that . . . Assaf guessed that Idan was probably the guy she was looking for, the guitar player. She sounded completely in love with him. He continued reading, and the more he read, the more he saw between the lines: Idan wasn't devoted to her, he was toying with her – and maybe with the other one, Adi, too. If there was anyone he loved, it was himself. Assaf wondered how Tamar could miss it, why she didn't read what she herself had written! Tell me, Dinka, with all her brains and critical thinking skills, how is it that she can get this excited over Idan?

He looked at the date at the end of the last notebook – the diary ended a year ago, exactly. He ran through the dates of the other notebooks, put them in order, and saw that if there had been another notebook in the past year, one that could reveal to him why Tamar left on her journey, it wasn't here.

For a moment he sat disappointed and full of confusion. But he had no time to wallow in his disappointment. He had to keep running. Strange: nothing had sparked this new resolve, but since a minute or two ago, he felt some big hourglass running out, felt things rolling faster, coming closer to their brink.

He put everything back in the pack: clothes, sandals, note-books. He didn't know where to go now. Perhaps to Ben Yehuda Street, to look for that guitar player Sergei was talking about. He had no desire to meet him; he didn't even have the power to do a simple thing like just walk through a crowded street, or see strange people, or speak the words everyone uses. He had the feeling that in the short time he had been hiding in the bushes, something new had happened, something celebratory – not only for himself, but in general, for the world. It was impossible that such things would continue going as they had been until one hour ago. Suddenly it was vital that he meet her, in order to tell her that. Or maybe he wouldn't even have to tell her. Maybe she already understood, in this moment, wherever she was now, without even knowing who he was, without knowing anything about him. She was already feeling it.

IV

SHE DIDN'T KNOW WHEN she would see Shai again. He didn't show up for dinner the night after they first saw each other. Tamar didn't know whether he was in Jerusalem or if he had slept in a distant town – or whether he was intentionally avoiding her. She sat eating her daily serving of mashed potatoes, her eyes drawn helplessly to the door. The next night, Shai came. He sat with his head bowed until the end of the meal, answering none of her piercing looks, none of the shouts from her fingers. He finished his meal and left, and the next day he didn't come back.

But Pesach Bet Ha Levi came and ate with them, and was in a great mood. His thighs almost burst through his shorts. It occurred to Tamar that he probably never changed out of that net tank top – or washed it. He told jokes and for a long time waxed nostalgic over memories of his military service – he was the storage manager for some platoon band – and bragged about the wrestling meets he had competed in as a youth. Tamar thought if she kept waiting for Shai to decide to cooperate, if she couldn't do something immediately, she would simply lose her mind.

She sneaked a look at Pesach's rough face, a bit captivated by the brutal conflicts she found in it – the fleshy lips expressed corruption and bestiality; there was also an opaque tyranny in his heavy cheeks, in his dead eyes. Yet the face possessed a clumsy friendliness as well, a naked eagerness to be considered a 'good guy,' to be loved and worshipped by everyone. He got up, tapped on the pockets of his shorts, and said he had forgotten his pack in the car – and could he bum a smoke off anyone? Instantly cigarettes appeared from every side, tendered in his direction; Tamar despised their slavishness. But all at once – the motion of his hands in his pockets flashed in her mind a second time, and her heart pounded in her chest: his pockets. Empty. His net tank had no pockets. It was now or never.

She waited until someone, some lucky winner, lit his cigarette; he sucked in the pleasure of the first drag. She got up, told Sheli loudly that she was going to the bathroom for a minute and to leave her plate on the table. She left the dining room and ran with all her might.

The corridor was empty – one bulb, hanging by a cord, rocking its shadows against the walls. Tamar pushed on the knob – she was certain it would be locked; this was madness, she didn't have a chance – and the door swung open.

Pesach's office was dark, and she felt her way inside, circling around one chair and bumping into another. She found the table by what little early moonlight leaked into the room. She opened the top drawer – files and papers spilled out, it was a mess – but Tamar was looking for the red book, and it wasn't there. What were you thinking, he's probably stashed it in some money belt under his pants. She opened the second drawer – folders and old books and packs of parking passes for different cities.

She heard voices outside the door, in the corridor. Someone – possibly two people – was coming. They were walking fast. Tamar bent down and tried to hide under the open drawer. God, she thought, even though I don't believe in you, even though Theo would laugh at how I broke down and cried out to you in a moment of fear, please, keep them from coming here.

'You'll see – in the end he'll sell. I'll make him sell.' She recognized Shishko's voice. 'I *got* to get a motherfucking tape deck like that in my car.'

'Show him a grand and he'll sell,' said the other voice, which she didn't know. 'He'll give it up like a baby. What, he *won't* sell? Of course he'll sell!'

Their footfalls passed and faded down the corridor. She waited a little longer, exhausted by her terror. The bottom drawer had a lock. Of course! That's why he doesn't need to take the book with him, he's satisfied with a key. Tamar pulled on the drawer without a single hope. Then she gazed for a moment and couldn't believe what she saw: This is the first time in my life, she thought, that I've had more luck than brains.

The book was there, red and thick, its cover cracked, oily from Pesach's fingers.

At first she didn't understand any of it. The pages were full of lines and columns and initials and names and numbers. Everything was scrawled in tiny handwriting, surprising, considering the size of the hand that wrote it. She tilted the pages in front of the window, trying to get a bit more light. Her eyes scanned the lines, her lips parted in concentration: it looked like a code, and she knew she didn't have the time to crack it. She closed the book, closed her eyes, pulled herself together. When she opened her eyes, she realized the lines were names of cities, the columns were dates of performances. The lines and the columns crossed each other, creating little squares. A pulse was beating hard in her temples, her neck, even behind her eyes. She looked for the column with today's date. She found it. Then she crossed it with the line of Tel Aviv. In the box where they met, she found her name; she deciphered the initials: DS was Dizengoff Square, where she'd performed this morning, and SD was the Suzanne Dellal Center. The book shook in her hands. She tried to forget everything behind the door, anyone who could enter the room at any minute. Only now did she realize how brave Shai had been to make a phone call from here – or how desperate. It was ten at night, and their parents weren't at home, and she almost fainted when she heard him after so long. He spoke in a choked, hysterical voice, telling her about some accident he'd had. It was hard to understand what he was saying. He begged for them to come and take him, save him, only without getting the police involved; if they brought the police, it would be the end of him. She sat in the kitchen, the evening before the trig exam, and listened; it took a long time before she could understand what he was saying. His voice was different; its timbre and rhythm had changed completely. He was a stranger. He said it was a horrible place, it was a kind of a prison, and that all the others were half free, only he was a prisoner for life. And in the same breath he told her to ask Father to forgive him, and said that the beating was because of momentary insanity; the boss here, he said, is someone – for six months I couldn't decide whether he was Satan or an angel; it's completely mixed up, it's sick –

And while he was talking, she heard the squeak of a door under his words; she, in the kitchen, at home, heard it. Shai didn't. He continued to say a few more words, and then fell silent, and started to breathe deeply, trembling, mumbling, 'No, no . . . no . . .' Then she heard another voice – inhuman, like the roar of a predator attacking, a roar from deep in the gut, and one after another they came, the blows, like a sack full of dirt being slammed into a wall. Once, and again, and a scream, and a cry that, for a moment, she thought might be the cry of an animal.

From here, from this room.

Don't think about it. She flipped forward through the coming days. She searched for the lines where Jerusalem appeared, then she combed them for her name and his, and page after page she found nothing. From upstairs she heard the clanging of forks and spoons; they were starting to clear the tables. She had, perhaps, another minute, a minute and a half. Her finger ran over the days, stopping on next Sunday, and found only her name on the Jerusalem line. Shai would be in Tiberias. Her finger galloped along the lines, stopped on next Thursday. Her eyes widened: his name and hers, right next to each other. Shai would be performing in a place marked 'HP' and she'd be in 'ZS.' They would both be performing from ten to eleven in the morning. She closed the book and put it back in the drawer, and stood for a moment, shaking all over: in nine days, one week and two days, he would be in Hamashbir platform, she in Tziyyon Square. Only a few hundred meters away from each another. How could she make them meet? She would never succeed. She would get him out of here in nine days. All of her senses shouted, *Get out – now!* At least five minutes had passed since she'd left the dining room, and her plate remained on the table, and Pesach might send someone to find out where she had gone. But she still hadn't finished what she had to do there. She hurried to the door, opened it a crack, and peeked out. The corridor was empty. The naked lightbulb swung, scattering murky beams of yellow light. Tamar quietly shut the door and went back into the depths of the room, to the table, to the telephone. Her fingers shook so badly she pressed the wrong buttons. She dialed again; somewhere a phone was ringing. Please, let her be home, she prayed, with all of her heart. Please let her be home.

Leah picked up the phone. Her voice was alert, awake, as if she had been standing there waiting for this call.

'Leah . . .' Tamar whispered.

'Tami-mami! Where are you, girl? What's going on? Should I come to you?'

'Leah, not now. Listen: next Thursday, between ten and eleven, wait with the car –'

'One minute, not so fast, I have to write that down . . .'

'No, there's no time. Remember: next Thursday.'

'Between ten and eleven, but where do you want me to be?'

'Where? Wait –' Leah's yellow VW Bug flashed in front of her eyes. She tried to see the little streets of the city's center in her mind's eye. She didn't know which ones were open to drivers and which were one-way and which would be the closest to Shai, so he wouldn't have to run too far.

'Tamar? Are you there?'

'Just a minute. I'm thinking.'

'Can I tell you a little something while you think?'

'I'm so happy to hear your voice, Leah,' she choked.

'And I'm sitting here, biting my nails. It's been almost three weeks since I've seen or heard from you! And Noiku is giving me hell! Where is Mami, where is Mami? Just tell me, sweetie, have things turned out all right? Did you find it?'

'Leah, I have to hang up.' She heard steps in the corridor. She hung up the phone, and folded herself into a little frightened ball under the table. She waited a few heartbeats more. Complete silence. It was probably the fear making those sounds. At least she had managed to pass the message to Leah. Now she had to get out of here, quietly.

But when she reached the door on her tiptoes, she was overwhelmed by the urge to call someone else. It was crazy. It was the most unnecessary slalom between logic and madness. But the urge to talk to another person from her previous incarnation was burning in her. She was already at the door; she touched the knob and stood, for a long moment, torn. She had to get out of there – and who would she call? Her parents? She couldn't, not yet, she would fall apart if she spoke to them. Idan and Adi are in Torino right now; and even if they'd already returned, what would she talk to them about? Who was left? Halina and Theo. Halina or Theo? Like a sleepwalker, she turned back to the phone. Leah, Halina, and Theo. Her three girl friends. Her three mothers. *Theo is the mother of the brain,* she once wrote in her diary, *Leah, of the heart, and Halina, of the voice.* Without noticing, she picked up the receiver. Wild alarms rang in her ears, but she had no power to resist this desire. Talking to Leah had aroused in her everything she had suppressed and buried deep inside during the past weeks. And Tamar was awash in emotions, carried away by the memory of her other life, her everyday life, the freedom and simplicity of it, what it was like to do everything without checking seven times over that you're not being watched or followed; what it was like just to talk, to say whatever comes to mind. As if she were dreaming, like a drug addict craving warmth and love, she dialed another number.

There was a ring. Tamar imagined the black old-fashioned telephone with the round dial and the soft, quick, padding steps of the cloth sandals.

'Yes, hallo?' asked the sharp voice, with its deep, ancient accent. 'Hallo? Who's there? One moment . . . is it Tamar? My Tamar?'

✳   ✳   ✳

A hand. Red and heavy. With a square black stone in a gold setting. On the telephone, cutting the connection.

'I wouldn't have guessed,' Pesach said. He flicked on the lamp and flooded the room with light. 'From you, of all people. Making private calls from the home phone? Who'd you call? Anyone we know? Daddy? Mommy? Or someone else? Sit down!' he shouted, shoving her into his chair. He paced back and forth behind her. The nape of her neck turned to stone. She was fucked, just like Shai; she blew it in the same room.

'Now you have two choices. Either you tell me, of your own free will, who you spoke to, or we will make you. You decide.' He leaned his full weight on the table in front of her. Violence radiated off him like strong waves of heat; the muscles of his arms rippled under his skin like cubs in the womb. Tamar swallowed. 'I was talking to my grandmother,' she whispered.

'Grandma, huh? So now we have two more options,' he said slowly, and she was amazed to see how, in an instant, the folds of fat on his face were absorbed into him and his bones stood out, like the ghostly outline of a bare skull. 'Either I ask you for the number you dialed and you give it to me, of your own free will –'

Tamar was silent.

'Or we have the other option: I press redial.'

She looked at him, expressionless. Just don't show him you're scared, don't give him the satisfaction.

He pressed redial. Pesach held the receiver to his ear. There was silence, and one ring. Through his cheek, Tamar heard Theodora's sharp 'Hallo,' now sounding worried and afraid. Pesach held still and listened carefully. Theodora shouted again: 'Hallo? Hallo!! Who is this? Tamar? Tami? Are you there?' and then he hung up.

His mouth twitched a little, in hesitation.

'Well,' he said eventually, his face twisted in disgust. 'That just happened to sound like a grandmother.' Tamar's shoulders dropped a little in relief. How such a stupid mistake could turn into a life preserver – Damnit! she thought, I didn't tell Leah the street! Her fingernails dug into her palms: she had managed to name the day and hour, but not the street. What a horrible mistake – Pesach was walking around her, with menacing steps. Now he leaned over her, with all his size, his mass, his violence. 'Get up. You got lucky this time. It stinks to the sky, but you got lucky. Now open up your ears real good' – She sat, frozen, unable to stand, thinking of all the trouble she had fallen into from the first moment she came here, when she sang 'Don't Call Me Sweetie,' then when she called Miko a thief, and when she gave the money to that Russian woman. Again and again, she had acted according to her urges and against her own interests – 'one more time, if you so much as tickle the edge of my edge, you're finished. Even if you sing like Hava Alberstein and Yoram Gaon put together, when you leave here, you won't be able to sing anymore, for the rest of your life. Take my word for it. And listen good, *sweetie*' – of course he called her sweetie – 'I still don't know what you're doing here. Got me? This whole time, something smells fishy about you. I have a sixth sense, and I'm feeling it about you, and I'm never wrong about these things, never.' She felt it melting, moment by moment, the mysterious material that was supposed to stabilize and hold together all her organs and the features on her face. 'So let's be very clear. The man who can fool Pesach Bet Ha Levi hasn't been born yet. Do we understand each other?'

Tamar nodded.

'Now get the hell out of my sight.'

She did.


After she finished her last song, the audience applauded with shouts of 'Bravo!' and started to scatter. Some of them approached her, praising her and thanking her, asking about this song or that. She answered in detail, which she didn't usually do, talking at length – from the corner of her eye, she saw Miko approaching a nearby shwarma stand. She scanned those standing around her quickly; who would be the most appropriate? Whom could she trust? She saw two young women, tourists from some northern country, who spoke English to her with a rolling *r*. They wouldn't work. A tall, lean man with a goatee and a face that looked slightly Chinese moved toward her and spoke about the purity of her voice. 'This clarity,' he said. 'When you started singing, I was on the other end of the street – I thought I was hearing a flute.' Something about him rang false – or perhaps he put her off only because he made her feel false. Next to him was a slender woman with translucent skin, who rubbed her hands with restrained excitement and said she had something absolutely exquisite to tell Tamar but would patiently wait her turn. And then – an older, heavy man, who held a worn brown attaché case in his hand. He had the look of a humble, dedicated bookkeeper; he had good, big round eyes behind his glasses and a small drooping mustache; he wore a wide tie that had gone out of style years ago, and his shirt was falling out of his pants. She saw him hesitate, and there was no time for hesitation: she turned to him, flashed her most dazzling smile. He was instantly dazzled, shone back at her, and told her that even though he was 'a complete ignoramus in matters of singing,' yet when he'd heard her voice, he felt something he hadn't in many years. His eyes grew moist, and he grasped her hand in both of his. Then, quickly, before he had the chance to say anything else about her purity, she gave him her other hand as well, and her eyes suddenly gazed deeply into his, begging him. She saw him squinting in amazement, his eyebrows shrinking, when he felt the piece of paper shoved into his palm. Over his shoulder, ten meters away, Miko was lifting a pita above his mouth, obliquely licking the yellowish sauce that dripped out of it. He hadn't taken his eyes off her since the morning, and she knew that Pesach had given him special instructions after last night's incident. The short man finally grasped her despair and pulled himself together. He closed his hand over the paper, smiled a frozen smile. 'Goodbye,' she told him, firmly, and her hands almost pushed him away from her.

He probably had understood something. He walked away

quickly. Tamar's eyes followed him, worried. The slender, translucent lady, who had been waiting patiently, now stormed in: Tamar's singing reminded her of someone; 'You have to hear this, you'll understand me exactly: there used to be a great singer, her name was Rosa Raisa; she ran away from Bialystok, a Jewish girl, Rosa Bruchstein – now don't laugh, many thought her to be the greatest singer in the world after Caruso. Puccini and Toscanini both wanted her –' Tamar listened through her, looked through her, nodded to her like a puppet's head on a string; she saw the squat man marching off energetically. He had already passed by Miko, and neither of them had noticed each other. His round bald spot was flushed with effort, perhaps with excitement as well. She prayed she had chosen correctly, had bet on the right person. Someone laughed in front of her – the delicate lady was trembling from the pleasure of her own anecdote – 'so one day Rosa Raisa happened to be traveling through Mexico by train, and Pancho Villa, with his bandits, attacked her car and started shooting! She told them she was a singer, and they did not believe her; but when she opened her mouth and sang 'El Guitarrico' in the middle of the car, during the robbery, they not only released her, they gave her a little Mexican tequila, too . . .' Tamar smiled and thanked her. She picked up her money and tape player, called to Dinka, and went to Miko's prearranged meeting place. From the corner of her eye, she saw that the man with the brown attaché case had already reached the top of the street; she was glad that he didn't stop to read the note, that he didn't turn his head backward even once. She had prepared two more notes just like the first last night. She had thought to give them to three different people; but of all the people she sang in front of today, he was the only one she trusted. She had the strange intuition that he was the right person.

Moshe Honigman, formerly a court shorthand stenographer; today, retired, childless, and widowed for forty years. Aside from his somewhat routine career, he had developed a few modest hobbies: he was a collector of antique maps, travel guides to the Holy Land, and records by brass bands. He played chess by correspondence with amateurs from all over the world and had adopted the routine of learning a different language every year, to the level of simple street conversation. He was a lonely, passionate, and easily excitable man who had been overtaken by old age, apparently, in the middle of his childhood. On top of all his activities, he was also a devoted fan of detective novels, the kind you can find for five shekels in little secondhand stores, and in them, for two hours a day, he forgot his impossible yearnings.

Now he was pacing hurriedly through one of the streets that branch off from the Walking Street; his old heart was still beating wildly, but he did not allow himself to pause for a moment and relax. He could still see the girl's eyes, pleading, in front of him, and understood that she was in big trouble. The farther he walked, the more his thoughts expanded in front of him, becoming organized and methodical: he understood that someone was following her and that, probably, because of him, she had to hide her strange message to him. When he got excited, Honigman always went a little bit weak in the knees; he made himself slow down. Step by step, his mind grew clearer; fifty years of constantly rubbing shoulders with the criminal element – in addition to the books he swallowed, there were his years of shorthand in the courts – now informed his actions with supreme ease. Every once in a while, he stopped in front of a store window, batted at the sparse hair still sticking to his skull, and checked the reflection to make sure no suspicious characters were trailing him.

Excited and on alert thanks to the affair in which he was embroiled, Honigman walked through the streets, his thoughts in a whirl, weaving horrific plots that reached their climax the moment the girl turned to him. In between the story and his thoughts, he blessed the good fortune that made him look so normal, so average, so trustworthy. Consequently, he tried to look even more normal, mediocre, even, and in his effort to resemble a kindly, nearsighted grandfather, arranged his features into a horrible grimace.

After walking around like this for a whole hour, arousing the suspicion of most of the passers-by in the street, he entered Café Rimon, ordered himself a grilled cheese sandwich, and switched to his reading glasses. He removed a *Ma'Ariv* newspaper from his attaché case and opened it with a businesslike flourish. He hid his head (and most of himself) and then, and only then, finally opened the note.

'Dear Sir or Madam,' she had written,

*My name is Tamar and I need your help very badly. I know this must sound strange, but you must believe me, it's a matter of life and death. Please help me. Don't wait for a moment. Don't put it off for tomorrow. Now, right now, please call this number: 625–5978. If there is no answer, try again later.* Please don't lose this note!!! *Ask to speak with a woman named Leah. Please, for me: tell her how this note came to you, and most important, please,* please, *tell her the following: Tamar asked me to let you know: on the agreed hour, the agreed day, on* Shamai Street across from the taxi station. *After you do this, please, I beg you, destroy the note.*

His round, stunned face slowly rose from behind the *Ma'Ariv*. So he was right, damnit! The little one really was involved in some nasty business! He reread the note several times, trying to guess from where she had torn the sheet on which it was written. He held it up to the light to see whether there wasn't another clue still to be found.

'Your sandwich, sir,' said the waiter. Honigman looked at him, shocked. A sandwich? Now? At this time? He snatched up his attaché case, threw a bill onto the table, and made a hasty exit. On the street corner he found a public phone and dialed the number.

'Yes!' proclaimed a woman's strong, dry voice. Behind the voice he heard the noise of pots, water pouring, the sounds of working people.

'Mrs Leah?' said Honigman, trembling.

'Yes. Who is this?'

He breathed heavily, spoke quickly and quietly. 'Honigman speaking, Moshe Honigman. At the moment I'm afraid I do not have the chance to introduce myself properly. But I have a very special story to tell you, a story about' – he looked at the note again – 'about Tamar. Would you have a moment of time for me?'

Five minutes later, dizzy from the events of the recent moments, Honigman flew back into the café, forced the waiter to bring back his sandwich, which was still warm, and sank back into his chair with an expression of amazement and exhilaration. After no more than a minute, he started to become annoyed that Leah had not yet arrived. He stood up, looked out the door, returned to his seat, sighed loudly, and looked, again and again, at his watch (he had a watch that had been manufactured in the land of Israel during the British Mandate. Instead of numbers, the hours were marked by the names of the twelve tribes. It was twenty past Zebulun, and Honigman didn't know how he would manage to pass the time until ten to Naphtali). He constantly came back to the note, rereading it, his eyes stroking it as if it were a winning lottery ticket, and read the final words again and again:

*I thank you in advance for your great help. I wish I could return the favor, or at least pay for the phone call. I hope that, very soon, something good happens to reward your kindness.*

*With gratitude, and respectfully yours, Tamar.*

Only six days were left until the escape, and she had no clue how to make Shai meet her halfway between where the two of them would be performing. She was too frightened to think; not during the long drives, not in her bed. It was unreasonable, and irresponsible – but she simply couldn't break through the mask of fog that dropped over her the moment her thoughts reached the danger zone.

On Friday night, after supper, the boys and girls arranged their chairs along the walls of the dining room. Pesach and two of his helpers joined the group and sat down. Even Pesach's wife came, a small silent woman who gazed at Pesach adoringly and wore a tight-lipped smile. Shai came, too, dragging after Pesach, and sat where Pesach gestured him into a chair. A big comfortable circle was created; the conversation flowed easily. One girl, Ortal, a magician, said these wooden chairs were exactly like school chairs, the kind that break your back. Suddenly the conversation started to revolve around teachers, studies, field trips. For a few moments you could imagine this was some kind of summer camp or, as Sheli once called it, retreat for young artists.

Shai sat, retreating into himself, stubbornly avoiding her gaze. An eighteen-year-old old man. She sat facing him, and out of habit that seemed second nature she started absorbing his misery into herself. In a few moments, she wilted there in front of him, and her body bent into the same defeated position that he was sitting in. They were so alike at that moment, like two similar cards in a memory game, that if anyone had noticed, it would have aroused suspicions. Tamar thought about Friday nights at home, before they were struck by Shai's disaster. She remembered her mother's repeated efforts to manage a calm dinner, with no arguments or fights, at least once a week; to, once a week, be a *family*. Her mother even tried to light candles for a few weeks, to bless, and to establish some kind of family 'ritual,' during which each member of the family would talk about some 'exciting experience' from that week All at once, and for the first time since she had left home, Tamar missed her mother, the game goodwill that everyone else in the family constantly scorned, even with cruelty – Tamar thought of all her own cheap, sour jibes at poor Mother, who was so unfit for her abrasive family. Life with us has made her bitter, she complains about everything all the time, and perhaps this isn't at all in her character – truly, Tamar thought, newly enlightened – poor

Mom, she lived her entire life in hostile territory, afraid of being laughed at for the things she expresses so profoundly, so seriously, fighting her father's armor of sarcasm without a chance of cracking it – and fighting Shai's brilliance – and my own refusal to be her friend and sister and pet ... For a moment she forgot herself, forgot where she was. She was swept up in a wave of compassion, of sorrow, the sorrow of the irreparable, profound mistake that was her family: four lonely people, four people in the world, each saving his own soul. She felt a sudden need to talk to someone about these things without inhibition, someone from the outside, not from her family, with whom she could share some of the burden now tearing her heart apart.

Shai sighed. She heard it over the other noise in the room, and a sigh escaped her mouth, too. They sat, looking at each other. Who knew what their parents were doing right now, she thought, alone at home, facing each other from the two ends of the huge dining-room table. They would have returned from their vacation a few days before. 'We won't give it up, this year especially!' her father had announced decisively, with his cruel, tortured purposefulness. 'Life goes on. Period' – his voice cutting, that right eyebrow of his twitching like a lizard's tail, belying the guarded expression he wore on his face. The letters she had left with Leah had probably begun to arrive already. 'Don't look for me,' each one said, after a litany of the most normal and comforting stories she could make up. They always ended with: 'Everything is fine, I'm fine, really. Don't worry. Give me a month, no more than that. Thirty days. I'll explain everything to you when I get back. It will be all right, you'll see. Trust me, please. I promise.'

'Prepare yourself,' Sheli whispered to her, snapping her out of her thoughts. 'Whenever Adinush comes, he makes a commemorative speech – get your hanky ready.'

'My dear boys and girls,' Pesach opened, raising a glass of kiddush wine. 'Another week has passed, and we are all happy to be here, together, like one big happy family, and to welcome the holiness of the Shabbos.'

'A-*men*,' Sheli whispered, and Tamar nudged her, thigh to thigh, to get her to stop making her laugh.

'This week, each and every one of us made the effort, tried his hardest, did his work, and earned his Shabbos rest.' Tamar stared at Pesach; he seemed different again to her, full of Prize Day pomp, almost officially patriotic. 'The seniors here know the motto I always follow: Art is, at most, 20 percent talent, and 80 percent hard work.'

'And another 50 percent profit,' Sheli whispered, and someone on her right burst into laughter. Pesach flashed a black, scolding look in their direction.

'And I want to tell you again how proud and happy I am to be the one nurturing you. I know there are friends among us who go through some hard times here and there; it's well known that there is no prying into anyone's business. We respect privacy. In spite of this, let me say, as your guide and your collaborator, that each person here is a super-duper professional and is doing a great job, and never let us forget the noble principle that the show must go on. Even if a man gets up on the wrong side of the bed or is destroyed on the inside. The most important thing is that the audience never knows.'

'Here comes Rubinstein, and then we're done,' Sheli murmured out of the corner of her mouth.

'And as a great artist, Artur Rubinstein –'

'May his name be blessed,' Sheli continued, and a few voices whispered in response, 'A-*men*.'

'– once said: When you get right down to it, art is, indeed, the number one source of happiness for mankind!' Pesach quoted. 'And you all know, my dear boys and girls, that, in my opinion, each of you has the potential to be another Rubinstein. Adina, my wife, can testify if I don't tell her every evening, and every morning' – his wife, with her vacant face, nodded vigorously before she even heard another word – 'that perhaps, one bright day, it might turn out that one of those sitting here in our home right now will be the Rubinstein of the twenty-first century!' A few boys and girls applauded and cheered. Pesach silenced them with a wave of his hand.

'And I am also sure that even then, he or she will continue to remember the healthy, important lessons of how to give a performance, how to keep an audience, and how to maintain professionalism – at all costs, all costs! He or she will have covered all of those bases, here, with us, in our modest group, our family of artists. Good Shabbos, and *l'chaim*!'

'And for the glory of the state of Israel!' Sheli concluded, and took a deep breath of relief.

Pesach drank his cheap Conditon wine in one gulp, his Adam's apple bobbing up and down. A few boys burst into exaggerated applause and yelled, '*L'chaim!*'

'He's so pathetic,' Sheli whispered to Tamar. 'I can't even look at him. Last week I went to his house to bring over the Friday-night challahs – and he takes me, all swelled up with pride, and shows me his *personal room*. What can I tell you, Tami? It's the room of an adolescent from the 1970s: huge posters of Jimi Hendrix over half the walls. And then there's this skull, probably plastic, with, like, red lightbulbs in the eye sockets, and this long, dried, prickly plant in some bombshell, all, like, artistic and shit. And all his pictures, and his wrestling trophies, and this guitar from, I don't know, the days of yore, he probably stole it from the platoon band . . .'

'Now,' said Pesach, after wiping his sweaty face with an ironed handkerchief, 'let's have some fun! You, Tamar, the new one –'

She froze like a rabbit caught in the headlights. What did he want from her? Ever since he had surprised her in his office a few days ago, he seemed never to take his eyes off her.

'Sing something. These guys here haven't heard you yet.'

She shrunk, blushed, shrugged. It was clear to her that this was some kind of trap, some strategy to expose her hidden purpose here. A few boys started to cheer, '*Ta*-mar! *Ta*-mar!' clapping in time. One girl, the contortionist with the mean face, whispered resentfully, 'Leave her alone, she thinks it's beneath her to sing for us.' Tamar turned to stone. She couldn't answer that. She already knew people didn't like her all that much here – they thought she was arrogant, keeping herself separate from them; she was still shocked to see the hatred on the girl's face. Sheli immediately jumped in to defend her. 'Oh really? What do you want from her, rubber girl?' she yelled back, her voice thick and rough. 'What is it? Have you already forgotten what you were like when you first got here? Yeah, like you didn't sit here like an asshole for two months, afraid to open your stinking face!'

The rubber girl shut her mouth, frightened, and sat there blinking. Tamar gave Sheli a grateful look, but somehow, Sheli's rudeness depressed her even more.

Pesach raised a big hand and calmed everyone down with a smile. He spread his legs, hugged his wife to him, almost crushing her under the weight of his arms, and said, 'What's the matter? We're all family here! Sing us something so we'll get to know you a little better,' and his beady eyes scanned her patiently, cleverly, as if they already knew something about her.

'Okay,' she said, and stood up, careful not to look in his eyes.

'How about "The Flower in My Garden"!' yelled one voice, and everyone laughed. 'Sing something by Eyal Golan,' yelled another.

'I want to sing "Starry, Starry Night," Tamar said quietly. 'It's a song about Vincent van Gogh.'

'Why make us suffer?' whispered a lapsed yeshiva boy, and a few boys giggled.

'Shhhh!' said Pesach, overflowing with kindness. 'Let the girl sing.'


It was hard, almost unbearable. She didn't have her tape player, with the recorded accompaniment (Shai's). She felt completely naked in front of Pesach's gaze, and people were snorting and giggling all around her; Tamar saw a few people hiding their faces in their hands, shoulders shaking from laughter. (It had always happened that way, once she started singing, when she moved into her singing voice, which was very different from her speaking voice.) But as always, after a moment or two, she got over it: grew calm and became pure.

She sang to one single person there, who hadn't heard her sing for a long time, who remembered her singing like an amateur, hesitating, with a voice that still hadn't yet decided what it was.

She didn't look in his direction even once during the song, but she didn't need to see him to know he was there, listening to her with every cell of his tormented body. She sang about Van Gogh, how this world wasn't meant for someone like him. But at the same time, she was telling Shai, with the rich colors of her voice, with its gentle touch, all she had gone through during that time, during her coming of age, when he hadn't been paying attention; and everything she had learned since he had disappeared, about others and herself. Layer by layer, she peeled off the rough skin of her disappointments, the sobering realizations, until she reached the place where there was nothing left covering her, the bare kernel of herself. And from that place, she sang to him the final notes of the song.

He didn't look at her once the entire time. He just sat, his head resting on one hand, his eyes closed, his face twitching with a pain that looked impossible to bear.

Silence gripped the room when she finished. Her voice hung in the air for another moment, fluttering like a creature. Pesach looked around – he wanted to scold the gang for not applauding, but even he understood that something had happened and held his peace.

'Wow. Sing another song,' Sheli urged softly.

Voices murmured agreement.

Shai stood up. She was scared and disappointed. He was leaving – why was he leaving? Pesach flashed him a look and raised an eyebrow at Miko. Miko hurried to his feet behind Shai, who shuffled out, dragging his legs. He passed by her without a single glance.

She didn't feel like singing anymore, but if she stopped now, Pesach might make the connection between her refusal and Shai's exit. She thought he was watching her reaction with an especially piercing look. She stretched her tiny frame a little. What had he said before? Even if a man is destroyed on the inside, the show must go on.

So she sang, 'Somewhere in my heart, a flower blooms.' No one was giggling anymore. The boys and girls were sitting, more erect, watching her. Pesach was chewing the toothpick in the corner of his mouth, deep in thought; he, too, didn't take his eyes off her. 'Friends keep it safe,' she sang, 'its stem, its leaves'; her pain flew out, spreading into each word, because of the friends who didn't keep the flower safe enough, didn't even lend it a hand, just gave a guarded, friendly wave and flew off to Italy. 'Friends give it light,' she sang, 'and shade if it needs shade / so it doesn't wilt . . .' She mourned herself, her lost joy in life, and she focused so deeply on herself that she didn't notice when the room became *hers*: for a moment, the soil of everyday life fell away from everyone, and all of them shed the rudeness of the streets in which they stood, day after day, shed the indifference and misunderstanding, the humiliation involved in the mechanical routine of three songs, and off-you-go – of three-fire-torches-and-into-the-Subaru. Something in her concentration, her inward attention, reminded them of what they had almost forgotten: that beyond the temporal, miserable circumstances of their present lives, they were still artists. This knowledge returned, streaming into them now from the completeness of Tamar's being, giving them a new, comforting explanation for the harshness of their lives, assuaging the fear that nested in each one of them, that his life might have been a terrible mistake and could no longer be mended. Their running away from home became newly illuminated, along with their loneliness, their constant, present solitude; the inherent volatility and extremity of their natures, which had shaken each and every one of them all the way here. It was as if all those things came together at once when Tamar sang.

When she finished, she opened her eyes and saw that Shai had come back. He was leaning on the door frame, looking at her, and he had brought his guitar.

*       *       *

What would she do now? Sit back down, or keep singing and let him play? She felt a new excitement burning in the boys and girls around her. Sheli whispered to someone that Shai never played in those parties. 'He never wastes himself on us.' And Pesach said what she hoped, and feared, he would: 'Why don't you two do a song together?'

This was an opportunity she couldn't miss; it was also a moment in which everything could be exposed. She turned to Shai and prayed her voice wouldn't give her away. 'What . . . what do you want to sing?'

Here, she had spoken to him, in front of everybody.

He sat down, raised a tired head above his guitar. 'Whatever you like; I'll just join in.'

Will you join in on any song I sing? Will you join in on anything I do? Do you have the strength?

'Do you know John Lennon's "Imagine"?' she said, and saw how, deep down, his eyes smiled to her, a slight ripple in gray, forgotten lakes.

He strummed, tuned his strings, tilting his head with that light, sleepy smile at one corner of his mouth, as if he was hearing sounds in a way no one else could.

For a moment she forgot herself. He glanced at her quickly and started to play. Tamar cleared her throat – sorry, she wasn't ready yet, it was too overwhelming to be here with him, together. She simply stood and gazed at him: he was there in all his familiarity, the naked defenseless child, with a sweetness and brilliance and sense of humor that could drive you crazy – and with his feelings of being suffocated, everywhere, by every possible institution. Sometimes he felt the constraints overtaking his body, and he had to lash out, swinging away from the melting gentleness he showed her into a sudden, brutal attack on everyone, including her. This was the unbearable arrogance he had developed in recent years, like chain mail over his exposed body; he was always anxious, agitated, with such a trembling in the strings of his soul that she could sometimes feel the buzzing that emanated from him.

He raised questioning eyes to her. Where are you? What's going on? She was still dreaming: in full view of Pesach, with his suspicious eyes, she was dreaming. Shai escaped his weakness for a moment and hurried to save her, his little sister. He called to her over their secret frequency, his eyes flickered her nickname, which only they knew, and her heart leaped out to him through her overalls.

He played the opening bars again, opening a door for her, inviting her to join. She started quietly, almost voiceless, only a thin string of sound weaving herself into his tune, as if her voice were just another string on the guitar between his fingers. She had to be careful, so no one saw the changes on her face. But she didn't want to be careful; she couldn't be careful. He played and she sang to him, and inside her more and more blocks of ice began to melt, cracking and falling into the frozen sea between them. She sang of all the things that were happening to her and him, the world that collapsed over both of them, the things that might be in store, if only they dared to believe it was possible.

When the last notes evaporated, it was silent; no one in the room was breathing. Then everyone burst into loud applause. She closed her eyes for a moment. Shai raised his head, looked around wonderingly, as if he had forgotten there were other people there besides them. He smiled a brief, shy smile. A dimple deepened in his cheek. He and Tamar took care not to look at each other.

Pesach, a bit confused, with the wary feeling that he had missed something, yet still bewitched by what he had just seen, laughed: 'Now tell me the truth – how many years have you two been practicing this?'

And everybody laughed.

Sheli said, 'You two are in a different league – you're really pros. You should have played concerts together.'

In the awkward silence that spread from that comment, Pesach said, too loudly, as if ridding himself of the guilt of sending boys and girls to perform out on the streets, 'Go on, do another one!'

Tamar thought, Just not 'The Flute.'

Shai didn't look at her. He plucked one string and shook his head in that old motion to move a lock of hair off his right eye; his hair wasn't what it used to be, only the motion, full of charm and grace, remained. Then he asked into space, 'Do you know "The Flute"?'

Yes.

He lowered his head over the guitar and strummed, with his long fingers. Tamar always believed he had an extra knuckle in every finger. She took a deep breath. How do you sing it without crying?

*The flute,*
*It's simple and delicate;*
*Its voice is the voice of the heart,*
*The flute*

*Like the gurgle of streams . . .*
*Like a children's song . . .*
*Like the breeze blowing through a blooming orchard,*
*The flute.*

The boys and girls sat, quietly, serious, each one absorbed in himself and his thoughts. When she finished singing, one girl whispered, 'That was the best performance of that song that I ever heard.'

Sheli got up and hugged Tamar, and Tamar clung to her for a moment. It had been almost a month since someone had touched her like that – since Leah's hug in the alley. She cradled herself into Sheli with all her heart, hugging her the way she couldn't hug her brother, so close, and so unattainable.

Sheli wiped her eyes and said, 'I'm embarrassed, I'm actually crying!' and the girl with the red hat and pimples, the silent cellist, said, 'They should perform together like that – even in the street, Pesach.'

Tamar and Shai didn't look at each other.

'That might not be such a bad idea,' Pesach said. 'What do you think, Adina?' He turned to his wife, and the kids who had been there a while already knew, whenever he asked her a question, that she would shrug emptily, smile a frightened smile, and that Pesach had already made up his mind.

And he actually took the red book out of his pocket and started flipping through it. Oh, please, Tamar begged in her heart, oh, please, please, please!

'Next Thursday,' Pesach said, making some corrections in his book, 'you both happen to be in Jerusalem . . . let's give it a shot. Why not? You two will perform a duet in Tziyyon Square.'

Tamar's hands clutched her sides. She tried to penetrate Pesach's broad, teddy-bear smile. She was afraid he was laying a trap for her: that somewhere in her performance with Shai, Pesach hoped to somehow discern the truth about her. Shai didn't respond, it was as if he hadn't heard. Tamar could see how the playing had sucked the last drops of vitality from him.

'But I want you to give your souls out there!' Pesach's voice declared. 'Exactly like you just did, all right?'

A few boys and girls cheered. Shai got up, so thin he looked as if he were about to fall; he could barely pick up his guitar. Tamar didn't move. The others looked at her, waiting for her to follow; they actually expected her to leave with him. She stood, erect, tense. Shai walked out, and Miko hurried after him, with his silent tiger-steps. Someone turned the radio on, filling the room with jungle music. A boy with a red pirate's kerchief on his head started flicking the lights on and off. Pesach stood, held a hand out to his wife. 'Come on, honey – it's time for the young people now.' He gave instructions to two of the older boys, whispered something to Shisko, and left.

A few couples started dancing together. The girl with the red hat suddenly got up and danced, alone, hugging herself; she had never looked so free. Tamar watched her and thought that she would like to get to know her; she looked smart and gentle, and she certainly didn't belong on the streets, any more than Tamar did. Sheli was already dancing with one of her regular suitors, the long-limbed saw player with vaguely simian features. She extended a tanned hand to Tamar, calling her to come join them, so the three of them could dance together. Tamar looked at them, and for a moment got caught in a vision of *her* threesome. It was odd that she hadn't thought much about them for almost two weeks; she had taken a vacation from them until this evening. She shook her head to tell Sheli no, faking a bright smile. The three of them had never danced together, because Idan made fun of dancing – he probably couldn't dance. They never really touched each other at all, when they were still a threesome, or at least that's what she thought – they never even hugged, even in times of joy. Some silent agreement that neither of them would get more of Idan. But who knows – perhaps, for two weeks now, they'd been sleeping in the same rooms, watching marvelous landscapes. Again, here it came, rising up in her, alive, burning. She poured and drank down a whole glass of Sprite, trying to cool the burning that had suddenly erupted in her. It didn't help. She recalled all the recent weeks with the two of them: when it became clear that she would stay because of Shai, they were deep in preparations for the tour. That was when she started moving toward the strange new world, slowly getting swept up into it, walking around in places where there was some chance of finding him, making conversation with strange men in public parks, with backgammon and pool players and club bouncers; and they weren't with her, Idan and Adi. It was confusing: she continued to attend chorus rehearsals every afternoon, five times a week. The whole chorus was already feverish with the anticipation of traveling, and the threats of the conductor Sharona grew more and more hysterical, and everyone was repeating Italian phrases from the tourist conversation guides they were given – because the fact that they could sing Cherubino and Barbarina's arias wouldn't help them in restaurants and street markets over there. She herself worked incessantly on her beloved solo, got her passport, read tour books, and repeated, dedicatedly, *'Dove posso comprare un biglietto?'* But in reality, she had already moved way beyond all that. Sharona was the first to notice Tamar's lack of presence. 'Where is your head, and where the hell is your diaphragm? You're forgetting to support from below again! How do you expect them to hear you from the sixth balcony?' And after the rehearsals, when they passed through the Walking Street, she would try to tell them where she had been the night before, whom she had talked to – you wouldn't believe what kind of people there are, a hundred meters away from here, what miserable lowlifes, she would say, still using the voice and language of the threesome, meaning Idan's – but Tamar started to grasp how the waves of mockery previously reserved for anyone who was not them began slowly to change direction and were now directed toward her as well, as if she were now also infected with something, as if she brought some unpleasant smell into their shared space. Then the day came, the day after she saw those Russian boys in Lifta, and met Sergei, with his baby face and fragile body; she needed so badly to talk to someone close, to mourn with someone over what she saw – and Idan interrupted her in the middle of her story and said that it was a bit difficult for him to learn Italian and Wastoid at the same time. Adi giggled and said that it was quite true, 'you've been using a lot of new words lately, it's kind of hard to follow,' and lightly shook out her golden tresses. At that moment Tamar knew she was no longer one of them – that she was asking something of them that they could not, or perhaps would not, give her. She was silent, and walked by their side, quiet and beaten – and their conversation immediately renewed itself without her, as if a passing wind had blown by, a momentary disturbance. She continued to march along bravely, continued to smile at their jokes – and sharp, cold scissors snapped neatly around the contours of her body, cutting her out of their picture.

The dining room emptied, as the terrace outside in the yard filled with dancers. Music flowed through everyone. Clouds of marijuana smoke hovered gently. A boy whose long braid was woven with colorful stripes of cloth started playing the guitar, and the others joined in, singing from all the corners of the yard. '*A Star of David broke in two,*' he sang in a deep, hoarse voice, and they responded in a quiet murmur: '*Herzl's opinions died with the man,*' and him: '*Rotten in the grave,*' *with spikes of sabra fruit'*; they lifted their hands, moved them, and sang: *'But everything goes according to plan.'* Tamar stood at the window, in the half-empty dining room, and looked outside. They seemed like fragile stems to her, when they waved like that – children-stems.

> *My soul only wanted rest,*
> *No war games, no;*
> *But the army is my duty,*
> *I love the army so . . .*

(And here someone yelled with a terrible voice: 'I love it so much, *so much!*')

> *Like a man to hold a gun in my hand,*
> *Blow off heads, like a man,*
> *Like a man, march to my death, all alone,*
> *And everything goes according to plan –*

All of a sudden, from all corners of the yard, even from the dance floor, rose the roar:

> *'Fuck the Plan . . .'*

Once and again, dozens of times, for long minutes – it went like that for perhaps half an hour, like a prayer, a desperate, inside-out prayer. Even Tamar started humming along to it. She stood and hummed with everyone, *Fuck the Plan*, and while she did, the picture flipped around, and Tamar felt, with sudden conviction, that it was actually they who were right. They were being honest with themselves, they were daring to rebel, to kick and cry out, shout it with all their strength.

Because compared to them, Tamar thought, what am I? A good girl. Domesticated. Straddling the fence – while they – with what courage they refuse to participate in the cynical, hypocritical games of the world, of power-mad ambitions . . . For a moment, she actually envied them – their freedom, their nerve in breaking all the rules, their courage to despair, even to the edge of doom, to give up the security of a home and parents and family – who turned out to be another big illusion anyway, a different kind of tranquillizer, hallucinogen, fear killer . . .

When she turned to leave the dining room and go back to her room, a few boys and girls blocked her way – they danced in front of her, laughing, encircling her, bowing, asking her to stay. One of them, small and curly-headed, one of the three jugglers, begged: 'I swear on my mother's life, I never saw you until tonight – I didn't even know you existed!' He had a sweet face, and a high-pitched, adenoidal voice. 'But after the way you sang, you blew me *away*. Stay a while, waste a little of yourself on us, tell us who you are, come on – why not?'

Tamar laughed: No.

The street poet came over, knelt in front of her.

> 'Oh, Tamar Tamar,
> Do not go afar,
> Not to the cold room.
> Oh, Tamar Tamar,
> Cold indifferent heart,
> Hard hasty soul,
> Why won't you, Tamar,
> Make joy your goal?'

Tamar laughed: No.

Two girls popped up in front of her, beautiful, dark, mysterious – the twin mind readers: 'Do you mind standing between us for a moment? Give us your hands, just for a second – one to each of us – do you mind? – just for a second?'

She got scared. This was the last thing she needed. She tightened her lips into a shrunken half smile. The whole group gathered around her, calling out to her suggestively. Tamar's hands parted the crowd in two; she passed through them and walked out. She needed to be alone.

Sheli returned to the room two hours later, excited, smelling of smoke – perhaps she was drunk, too. She came in with much ado, tangled up in her dress; she woke Tamar and asked her to undo the hooks up the back. She apologized for her state. 'God,' she said, 'I'm so baked.' Tamar, half asleep, asked hesitatingly what that meant. Sheli burst out laughing. 'You've been almost for a month and you still haven't learned?'

Not Italian, and not Wastoid.

'Baked. On grass. Reefer. Cannabis. Hey, by the way, you and that guy – that Shai? –'

'What about him?' She regained her full senses in the blink of an eye.

'Calm down. I noticed that there was something going on between you two a long time ago.'

'Between us?'

'Come on – you guys are always giving each other these fiery looks – what do you think, I couldn't see it? Together, it's like you're high off each other . . . you touch your face, and he touches his face – what is it, a dance? And the way you sang with him tonight . . .'

'I don't know anything about him,' Tamar said, exaggeratedly firm.

'But perhaps you knew each other in a previous life? You should know, I believe in reincarnation.'

'Maybe in a previous life,' Tamar allowed.

'Did you see his dimple?' Sheli said excitedly. 'He's been here for maybe a year now, and it's the first time I've seen it!'

'Yes,' Tamar whispered. 'He's cute.'

'Just don't fall in love with him. Remember: he's already cracked out, totally burnt. He's barely alive.'

Tamar poured concrete and cement around her shaking vocal cords. 'So, why are they always watching over him? Someone is always walking with him – no one else here is being watched over like that, right?'

Sheli sat on her bed, wearing only her panties, completely indifferent to her own nakedness, as usual – she accepted her sturdy body with the same ease as she accepted any stranger. She laughed. 'You're something, you: just to look at you, anyone would think you're completely out of it, and what do we find out at the end? That you notice everything. The bulldogs? It's because he tried to run away.'

'Run away? But I thought whoever wants to leave can leave. No?'

Sheli was silent. She peeled some purple polish off her toenails.

'Sheli!'

Silence.

'Sheli, come on, help me out.'

'Look,' Sheli finally sighed. 'Pesach lets go of whoever is average, I mean as a performer. Easily. After they pay up all their debts to him, of course.'

'Debts?' Tamar became alert. She remembered Shai saying something on the phone about the money he owed here.

'He keeps these calculations, these accounts. That's what the black book is. How much we owe him for living here, for food – even electricity. So if you're a mediocre artist and you want to leave, you pay him – you beg your parents who you ran away from in the first place to give you money, you borrow from friends and steal from old ladies and little children in the streets – until you settle it down to the last dime. And then he lets you go.' She lit a cigarette and inhaled deeply. 'Now, if you're really good, you don't get out of here so quickly, because Pesach calculates it out in such a way that a lawyer couldn't get you out of here. He'll chase you to the ends of the earth. There are stories.'

The guy with the insane eyes, Tamar thought, the bumps of bones in his knuckles. 'And – that guy with the guitar, Shai – he's good, isn't he?'

'"That guy with the guitar," she says!' Sheli mimicked, and winked at her. She saw the look on Tamar's face and became serious immediately. 'He's the best. He's really something. Even in his condition, he's amazing. You heard him. But a while ago something happened – he tried to steal Pesach's car, his prize new Mitsubishi.'

'To run away?'

'I don't know. It's all rumors with him. They said he crashed into a wall, or some fence, totaled the Mitsubishi. And now he's got a life sentence until he pays it.' She exhaled a long stream of smoke. 'Probably after he's dead.'

Tamar lay on the bed and gazed at the ceiling. Who knew where she had been on the day of the accident; why, the same moment Shai crashed his car into a wall, she might have been sitting in the Aroma Café, with Idan and Adi, slurping up the last of an iced mocha from the bottom of a glass.

'Do you know what I thought when you sang?' Sheli asked tenderly. 'That everything about you comes from the deepest place inside you. No, really – I've been watching you for a long time, and I get you: everything you do or say, even the way you look at things, or talk, or don't talk – everything is 100 percent you, genuine. And me? Look at me, I'm all smoke and mirrors. No, don't say anything, just look at me – I do Rita, I do Whitney Houston, I do Zahava Ben – I always do what isn't me.' She was silent for a moment. 'Even being here. This shouldn't have been my life.' Her voice cracked. 'I wasn't meant to end up like this, in this hole, messed up, out of my head.' Suddenly the crack tore into a cry and she sobbed. Tamar, surprised by the quick transition from laughter to tears, rushed over to her, stroking her stiff dyed hair.

'Sheli,' Tamar whispered. But Sheli cut her off. 'Even this: even my name, right?' She sniffed noisily. 'A gift from my darling mother, who named me that to remind me, at every moment, that I'm *hers*, not my own self – hers, get it?'

Tamar patted her head, hugged her tightly, and tried to remind her how entirely her own she was, how generous and full of love, how she was the only one to help Tamar out when she had just come here. But Sheli wouldn't listen.

'Oh well. Look at what's come over us!' She cheered up all of a sudden, her voice taking off again through the tears and stuffed-up nose. 'Should we open a booth and collect sob stories for Yosi Siyas's radio show? So, we're agreed: you're not even thinking about falling in love with him. There are a few better candidates for that around here. Believe me, I've tried some of them out myself.'

'Don't worry,' Tamar said, 'I'm not falling in love with him, I'm only singing with him.'

'Yes.' Sheli laughed, her eyes still wet. 'They call it singing.'

'If I had a pillow here, I'd throw it at you.'

Tamar waited for her rolling peals of laughter, but there was only a short silence, followed by Sheli saying, with precision, '"Pillow" is a word just like mother's omelet. It's been erased from the dictionary.'

She lay down and fell asleep.


Tamar couldn't fall asleep. Not because of what she had heard about Shai, not even because of what she had learned about Pesach's accounting system. More than anything, it was that innocent sentence: 'I noticed that there was something going on between you two a long time ago.' It pierced her unexpectedly, reminding her of everything that had been taken from her, everything she had exiled herself from. Her heart shrunk in pain – her heart, the organ itself, actually hurt – and at that moment she so wanted there to be someone else in the world – a boy, perhaps, yes, a boy, not a sixty-two-year-old nun, not even Leah, someone around her age – someone about whom you could say about him and her: I noticed that there was something going on between you two a long time ago.

'Get rid of your Idan Schmidan,' Leah immediately said inside her head, as if she had been just waiting for the opportunity. 'Forget him already, enough! He's not worth the tip of your little finger!' Tamar covered herself with the prickly wool blanket and remembered, with pleasure, the last conversation about love she had had with Leah. 'No, don't stop me! Let me just say it for once!'

'You've already said it a thousand times.' Tamar smiled briefly and tucked her knees up to her stomach.

'Do you know what your problem is? You're looking for some guy who's also an artist, right?'

'I guess.'

'But why do you need to be with someone just like you, tell me that! What's with all this soul-mate bullshit? Do you really need another lunatic just like you? You need the opposite – no, listen to me. You need – you know what you need?'

'What do I need?' Tamar couldn't stop smiling now, and she covered her head with a blanket so that no one would see.

'You need a man with a big hand,' Leah pronounced. 'You know why?'

'Why?' She knew she would now be painted a picture.

'Someone who will stand with his hand up, open, strong, steady – like the Statue of Liberty, but without that ice-cream cone she's holding – only his hand, open, in the air. And then' – Leah raised her square, rough, nail-bitten hand and moved it gently from side to side, like a flying bird – 'even from far away, from any place in the world, you'd see that hand and know you had a place to land and rest. Am I right?'

'Oh, Leah.'


She didn't see Sheli the next day. Or the day after. It wasn't so unusual, they were both on a tight schedule. But now, for some reason, she missed her terribly. She asked a guy in the dining room if he had seen Sheli. He looked at her as if she'd fallen off the moon and said, 'Didn't you hear? She ran away with that guy, the saw player, yesterday morning. She still hasn't come back.'

Tamar was amazed, not only by what had happened, but by the fact that Sheli hadn't dropped even a hint of what she was about to do during their conversation, the night before she ran away.

Rumors started flying that day – she was seen with that guy in Rishon – she was seen in Kushi's Inn on the way to

Eilat. One of the bulldogs accompanying the three jugglers recognized her there, but she was hanging out with a few Eilati hoods and he was scared to mess with them. She even had the nerve to approach him and the jugglers, to joke around with them a little, and send greetings to Pesach and the gang. The guys said she looked totally stoned. During supper, Tamar managed to sit next to one of them; he then remembered that Sheli wanted to send special greetings to Tamar and Dinka. Tamar asked him to tell her everything he had seen or heard. What is there to say. He shrugged. She's on the binge of a lifetime. Tamar begged for him to remember what Sheli said – every detail was important to her. You want to know what she said now. The boy scratched his short hair. I don't know – she said she had eaten tons of tabs and went crazy, and where hadn't she been, bring on the mountains, bring on the Bedouins, the criminals, head trips, drugs, and fucking. Why didn't you tell her to stop? Tamar yelled, agonized that she herself hadn't interfered while she still could have. The boy looked at her contemptuously. What do you mean stop? What are you talking about? What's wrong with you? It's none of my business! Tamar thought she was losing her mind.

The next day, a police car arrived early in the morning, and two policemen with serious faces entered Pesach's office. They left almost immediately. Pesach came out of the room pale and frightened, the boys and girls had never seen him like that. He was completely confused as he sent them off to work. They talked, whispered, throwing more rumors into the air. Tamar tried not to listen to anything. It was her worst day of performances. They actually booed her at the end of Allenby Street by the Opera Tower, and rightly so. She stopped the show and ran away in tears. When she returned to the home at midnight, she was terrified to discover that all of Sheli's belongings had disappeared from the room: her books, her yellow shoes, her bag. Sheli's bed stood empty and bare. Tamar went out and ran through the corridors, but the home was dark and utterly silent, as if it had folded up into itself. She went into strange rooms, turning the lights on eyelids that were just closing in front of her. No one even yelled at her to get out – no one was speaking. Tamar sat on her bed all night long, hugging Dinka to herself and crying intermittently, frightened.

By six the next morning, she had heard. Later, as she was on the way from one performance in Ashdod to another, she saw Sheli smiling up from an old photo, published in the newspaper. A short article accompanied it: in Eilat, some drug dealer, an older guy, had enticed Sheli with an invitation to a special party for just the two of them, in his squat on the beach. It was hard to know what had happened there, exactly. A police officer was quoted as saying that they were both drunk, apparently, or wanted to take things to an extreme. One way or another – when the ambulance arrived, they couldn't save her.

She walked around, out of her mind, for the rest of the day. She thought she needed to cancel the plan because she couldn't stand it there another day. And she knew with complete certainty that she couldn't leave Shai there another minute – but where would she now find the strength to run away and take him with her? She didn't see him that day – supper was quieter than usual, and no one mentioned Sheli, not one word – and not on Thursday morning, either. It was the day of their performance together. The artists gathered in the corridor next to Pesach's office, waiting to find out their schedule for the day. Shai was the only one who didn't. She walked around, clearly agitated, certain that something would spoil her plans now. Shai would be afraid, and find an excuse not to go out today, or Pesach would change his mind at the last minute and not allow them to perform together, or things would change around at the home because of Sheli, or –

When she had almost become frantic, she saw his long legs coming, step by step, down the stairs. The thick belt wrapped around his waist almost twice, and his skinny body descended, joint by joint – and she knew, without a doubt, that when the moment came, he wouldn't be able to make it.

'You over there, the wonder couple,' Pesach called to them. He had recovered quite nicely since the cops had visited. 'You will be with Miko and Shishko. Hey, it rhymes! But you guys better knock them dead, you hear me?'

They nodded.

'Look at them.' Pesach bellowed with laughter. 'Blushing like a yeshiva guy and the woman he got for a *shidduch*. Look at each other a little – what's wrong? You can smile! Audiences like to see a young couple in love.'

Tamar dug a smile out of herself, but thought in terror: Two, he's putting two bulldogs on us, we'll never make it.

They sat next to each other in the Subaru, looking straight ahead. Miko and Shishko were talking loudly about some bar mitzvah they had been to the night before.

Shai bent and petted Dinka; she licked his hand constantly, looked at him with eyes full of love, and whimpered – she twisted herself around in the car, trying to put her head on his knees and Tamar's knees at the same time. Tamar hoped that the two in front wouldn't notice and wonder about Dinka's excitement. Shai's leg moved very lightly and touched her leg. Electricity coursed through her body.

She opened her palm carefully, hoping that the sweat of her fear hadn't blurred the letters. Shai didn't even notice the hand opening in front of him. Shishko said, 'I like buffet – that way you can just take whatever you want; it isn't some crappy waiter coming up and throwing some shit at you, here's some rice, here's some fries, pah!' Tamar opened and closed her fist a few more times. Shai noticed and understood that something was written there – she saw his eyes strain – she was scared – perhaps she had written letters that were too small? She raised her hand as far as she could in front of him, behind Miko's and Shishko's seats. Shai read: *Homeland Class, third verse, run after me.*

Tamar looked out her window. Jaffa Street was outside, neglected, covered in trash, heart-curdlingly miserable. She smeared spit on her finger, rubbing out the inked words. Shai stared out his window. She could see his fear – she could smell it, too. His Adam's apple was constantly moving up and down. He buttoned and unbuttoned the top of his shirt, over and over. And now she could actually hear the buzzing inside him. In their previous incarnation, she could track Shai down anywhere in the house by that buzz; it lasted for days sometimes, driving the entire family out of their minds, until it would eventually resolve itself into the shape of a new, marvelous tune he would play, or a new song he would write, or just a fit of rage, or an attack of fear. He would then throw his long, thin body down, bashing his head and body against the floor; only she, with her words, whispered in his ear, and her caresses, was able to calm him down.

They arrived at Tziyyon Square and went on a little farther, until they reached Queen Heleni Street. Miko showed them where he would park, and how to get back to the car. Shishko went down to check out the area. They saw him, here and there, walking with his skinny cat's saunter, smoothing out his thick Elvis pompadour. It's quiet, he reported to Miko over the cell phone, after a minute had passed. Except for the guarding soldiers and a couple of cops who are interested only in Arabs.

'All right, go to work.' Miko sent them off. 'Pesach is counting on you to give the show of your lives.'

Shai took his guitar out of the trunk. They walked off together, her shoulder at his chest. Dinka ran in front of them, indescribably happy. She ran on and came back and circled them; Tamar knew that from this moment forward, they would have three minutes to walk together as if they were free.

And yet – in the space their bodies were moving through, in the circle Dinka was sketching around them, they were truly free and together; for a moment, she could imagine that everything was normal, a brother and sister walking their dog through the center of the city.

Shai mumbled out of the corner of his mouth, 'It won't work. They'll catch us.'

Tamar muttered back, also without moving her lips, 'In about a quarter of an hour a friend of mine will be waiting for us in Shamai Street, with a car.'

Shai shook his head to say no. 'They'll track me down wherever I go. You have no idea.'

'I have a place where they won't find you.'

'For how many years? Do I have to keep hiding for the rest of my life?' His voice jumped a register. 'He'll find me eventually, he'll chase me to the ends of the earth.' She knew his complaining voice and despised it – this was how he used to sound when he couldn't find the kind of cereal he liked in the morning, or when he didn't have clean underwear. 'He'll kill me, I'm telling you – think about it.'

She had no answer for him. Another scary hole in her plan, and Shai continued drilling into her: 'What crazy idea did you come up with? Who are you, James Bond? You're just a sixteen-year-old girl, and this is life. Would you wake up! This is not *Entebbe: Operation Thunderbolt*! This isn't one of your novels. Leave me out of it.' He stopped and gasped for breath. He didn't have enough strength to walk and talk simultaneously. His voice suddenly softened tremendously. 'Can't you see the condition I'm in? Don't you understand what I am? I can't live without my fix. Give it up, Watson. I'm a lost cause.'

She swallowed. 'But I bought you enough for the first few days, so you'll be okay until we really start.'

'You – wha!'

He looked at her, shocked. His shoulders bent over as if someone had laid an unbearably heavy weight on them. They walked in silence for a few more steps. They were on Jaffa Street again, and walked very slowly, as if they were in a slow-motion movie. One minute of freedom left, no more.

'But the hiding place –' Shai said, more submissively. 'How long will I have to stay there?'

'Until you're clean.'

'Clean?' He stopped, amazed, and someone stumbled into him from behind. His guitar strings buzzed.

'But you said! You asked me yourself –' Tamar burst out

angrily, just like that, in the middle of the street, raging like a little girl and completely forgetting about Shishko, who could be watching them from anywhere. 'On the telephone! You said!'

'Yes, I *said*, sure I said . . .' He chuckled bitterly, and continued walking, pulling his legs along, starting to remember this sister of his who, at the age of eight, had been sent out by their father to bring bread from the grocery store when the news had forecast snow. There was no bread left by the time she got there, and snow had started falling, so Tamar went to another store, farther away, and the snow began to stick on the streets. There was no bread at that store, either, so Tamar decided to go to the Angel Bakery, and she walked like that for about three kilometers, in snow that already reached her knees, and then walked all the way back home, returning at seven in the evening. He remembered how she had suddenly appeared at the door, blue with cold, her boots soaked through, but with bread in her hand.

'You won't be able – you can't do such a thing alone. There are institutions for that' – his voice choked – 'and I'm not going to an institution! Forget it, they'd find me there in a minute, he has connections everywhere.' Waves of tears were reflected in his chin's trembling, up through his cheeks, and Tamar thought that, for as long as she could remember, she had actually been his older sister. 'It's no use, Watson,' he whimpered. 'Run away alone now, run while you can. He'll leave you alone, he's got no problems with you.'

Still talking to her as a man, the way he used to do.

'But why couldn't we succeed?' she whispered ferociously. 'I've prepared everything, I've read every book, I've been getting ready for months, I asked people, I really –'

She didn't know how to communicate to him everything she had done. 'Shaichuk, sweetie, Holmes, it's going to be terribly hard, it will be horrible, but you'll see – people have done it like this, on their own, or with friends and relatives, I know they have. And I can help you. You will get out of it. Don't give up because of him!'

They could now see the square in front of them. They had to

stop talking, but they were both too excited. Shai didn't look at her. He walked, bent, dragging his legs, shaking his head in disbelief. 'You're insane. You don't even understand what you're getting us into. This is not an exam in Bible Studies, that if you prepare, then you pass. You can't even imagine the withdrawal. I can kill for a fix.'

She stopped. She grabbed his shoulder and gently turned him toward her. 'Kill me?'

He looked at her for a long time, and all his facial features started to shake as he tried not to cry. 'It's like that, Tami,' he finally said in a broken voice, 'I can't control it anymore.'

In the square they found a shady place by the bank. Shai took his guitar out and put the open black case on the ground; then sat on the little stone bench and tuned his strings.

In spite of everything, his soul filled with joy as he started to play.

People stopped to listen; some of them recognized her from previous performances, and some recognized him, so that before she even started singing, a larger crowd than usual had already gathered. Tamar could see two tall policemen, standing far off by the railings, looking like twins under their hats; she was glad for them, she smiled to them with her eyes, and they both returned her smile – one of them nudged the other lightly, and they started moving closer. She decided she would sing 'Suzanne,' the song with which she had begun her short career as a street singer; and, as always, the moment people heard her voice, more and more of them stopped. There was already a circle surrounding them, four or five rows deep. She saw Miko's plaid shirt begin to move through the last two rows. She didn't see Shishko, and that worried her. She finished her song and bowed when they applauded. People approached and threw coins into the guitar case. A couple pushed their small child, in his three-quarter pants, to throw in a five-shekel coin. He waddled over, embarrassed, then ran back to his parents and was shoved forward again until he did it, to a round of applause from the crowd. Tamar forced herself to smile sweetly, but her whole being grew tense, readying itself for the coming moments. Shai didn't respond at all; he seemed to have detached himself from the situation, giving up any will of his own – as if he were depositing – or abandoning – his fate in her hands. When her eyes rested on him, she thought, despairingly, 'I have no partner – I'm alone in this.' Dinka got up, stretched her legs, sat back down again, then stood up again, unable to find a comfortable place; she felt Tamar's waves of nervousness.

'Homeland Cl –' Tamar said, and choked. 'Homeland Class.'

Shai strummed the opening chords. She felt her voice shrink in her throat, vanish in fear. She cleared her throat and Shai began again. This time, she entered the song on time. She sang about the farmer plowing the land in an old picture on the class wall, and the cypress trees, and white-hot sky in the background – and the farmer, why, he will make bread grow so we'll grow up.

She finished the first verse and listened to the guitar; she hadn't even noticed when Shai departed from the familiar tune and improvised for a moment or two, as if whispering something meant only for her, a tune quieter and sadder than the song itself, mourning privately, keening within the song of longing for that innocent, childish land that was already gone, that might never have been. She raised her head, moistened her lips. She saw Miko standing behind an older woman; Tamar, strangely relaxed, looked at her and thought she was very beautiful: an erect stance, silver hair pulled up into a bun on the crown of her head, her face burned by the sun, furrowed with the wrinkles of a strong character, her eyes blue and shining. She imagined Miko's fingers quickly opening her purse, invading it, feeling for what was inside. The newspaper he held covered his right hand, concealing his actions from the eyes of the people standing around him. She turned her head in despair, looking for Shishko – where was he hiding? Where was he preparing an ambush? –

> Oh, land of Shepherds –
> This is how we pictured it in our childhood
> That was beauti –

She stopped in the middle of the word, and as loudly as she could yelled, 'Thief! Pickpocket! With the plaid shirt! Police! Get him! There, over there!'

Miko's eyes looked at her, amazed, full of hatred, and a crooked, bitter mockery. No one touched him yet, they didn't dare, but he was trapped between the lines of people tightening around him – the cops jumped on him. People were yelling, running around, stepping on one another. Tamar held Shai's hand and pulled him after her. He got up heavily. Dinka leaped, confused, between the legs of the mob. Tamar yelled at Shai: 'Run!' He was walking, moving too slowly, as if he was trying to get caught. Dinka stood, barking loudly, and Tamar called to her, hoping she would run after her. The square was electric, people were storming all around them, running in every direction. Tamar heard police whistles, then a siren. They ran. That is, she ran, and Shai was trying; after ten steps, he began to gasp for breath. She took the guitar from him – she thought she heard steps following her. She ran, praying her message had reached Leah, that the kind man hadn't screwed everything up – but when she glanced at Shai, she thought that in his condition, he wouldn't even make it to the end of the street. His face had gone yellow, was bathed in sweat. 'Don't stop, don't stop, we're right there, another half a block, just a little farther . . .'

But he couldn't do it; he groaned, and spit up dark phlegm; he wasn't running any longer, walking instead, stumbling over his own legs. 'You run, I'm finished, run away.' 'Don't do this! Don't you dare!' she practically yelled. People watched the odd couple – a small girl with short hair with a much taller boy who looked terribly ill.

She lay the guitar against a café chair, let it go, put her hand around his waist, and, with all of her strength, lifted and pushed him. I have no choice, her heart pumped the words, no choice, I have no choice; she dragged him, she pinched him, she whispered to him to hold on; she cursed him through her bitten lips, her eyes fogged from the effort. She saw a little yellow spot in the distance and ran toward it. Leah's yellow Bug – she came, she got my message. Tears started flooding her eyes; vaguely, she could see Leah sitting, hands on the wheel, tall and serious and ready to move – the engine was going, loud, making those familiar rough sounds. In another minute, they would touch freedom.

'So, you thought you'd run away on us?'

Shishko. Leaning against the wall. Also panting heavily. Blocking the way. 'And to do that to Miko? Not nice. Friends don't do that.' His face tightened and became pointed with his hatred. 'All right, we're done playing. Get back into the Subaru. Quietly. Pesach will straighten this out. You'll be sorry you were born.'

Her legs nearly collapsed. What was left of her strength evaporated. It's not fair, she thought, not fair to lose to them like this, in the final moment. Shai was standing and crying ceaselessly, as if he were facing his end.

And then time stopped. Things were happening in another, unfathomable dimension: Shishko being shoved toward them – he almost fell on top of them, and when he whipped around, murderous, passionate for a fight, his eyes bulged with surprise.

'Hold it right there, buster,' an unfamiliar man said, a short, buttoned-up, good citizen. 'Think you're a tough guy, huh? Move aside, you two-bit crook, you hoodlum! The jig is up!'

Shishko moved aside, because although the man's voice was trembling and breaking with tension, he had in his hand a decisively long-barreled rifle, the likes of which Shishko had seen only in movies. He shrank against the wall, nervously arranging his pompadour, looking for a good moment to jump on the old guy and snatch the weapon – but the sheer absurdity of the man confused him – he was certain it was some kind of a trap, someone had put that dwarf there as bait, so that he would act hastily and somehow make the mistake of his life. So Shishko hesitated for a moment, exactly the time Tamar needed to push Shai into the back seat of the car and get in herself. Little Noa was sitting there, not recognizing her – and the chubby man, who somehow seemed very familiar to Tamar, she just couldn't remember from where, opened the front door, sat down, as slowly and courteously as if he had all the time in the world. His rifle was still aimed precisely at Shishko's heart.

'Listen, you should be careful with that,' Shishko said, chuckling a little. 'It's not a toy.'

'You will speak only when you are spoken to.' The little man swelled up in front of him, his bald spot blushing.

'Drive, Leah, my dear,' he said firmly, and the car sailed on its way, leaving behind a very angry and amazed Shishko, who was searching to the right and left for the devious partners of the armed, buttoned-down geezer – or the TV guy with a hidden camera.

'Mami!' Noa suddenly piped up, her arms shooting out from the car seat. 'Mami, I missed you. Where's your *hair*?'

'So did I, my love,' Tamar whispered, hiding her face in the girl's neck, inhaling her baby scent.

'The babysitter didn't show,' Leah explained. 'At the last moment. I had no choice, so I brought her along. Are you okay, Tami?' and she shifted gears in a way that threw everyone forward and backward.

'I'm alive,' Tamar murmured, hugging Noiku, her pure skin, taking in the girl's innocent look, full of laughter. Tamar thought of Sheli, who used to be a baby like this, once upon a time, and perhaps was even loved like this. Shai looked at Noa with no expression on his face – he had no strength left for even that. Tears still hung from his long lashes. Noa looked at him cautiously every once in a while; something in him looked suspicious – he could feel her discomfort and turned his face to the window. Leah saw Noa's reaction through the mirror – she believed in her little one's magic abilities as a judge of character – and frowned a little. Tamar kissed Noa's eyes and tiny nose devotedly, then she sank back into the seat, smelling her own sweat – she thought about taking a shower at Leah's, about sleeping on a soft bed, not having to be anywhere for a few hours. Everything had happened so quickly – it was hard for her to understand that it had already happened, but somehow she thought that it was a success, after all – her plan had succeeded – that is, the plan to infiltrate that place and break him out of there. That idea had worked out, hadn't it? She searched out Leah's eyes in the rearview mirror for a final confirmation – someone had to tell her it had really happened, happened in life, that her fantasies had touched reality . . . but Leah was completely focused on the road – and why did Tamar feel as if something still had not been completed? Why did she have some kind of itch in the depths of her memory? It was unclear where it was – as if someone was trying to tell her something, that there was still something urgent for her to do.

'Where are we going?' Leah asked.

'To your place,' Tamar instructed. 'We'll be at your place for two or three days, to rest a little, get our strength back, and then move on to a new place.'

'Where, exactly?' the little man with the rifle asked.

'Please, let me introduce you,' Leah said with her first smile. 'This is Honigman, Moshe Honigman. He brought me your note, then decided to stick around and offer his assistance until the end of all this.' Her hand tapped his knee affectionately. 'He's a bit of a nag, this Stallone you sent my way, but very nice,' and she winked at Tamar through the mirror.

Honigman wasn't listening to her, still refusing to relinquish his role as the bodyguard. His eyes scanned the streets alertly, his lips constantly mumbling into his fist as if he were holding a little walkie-talkie.

Tamar watched his strange motions, only gradually understanding who he was. She sent a piercing and excited look at Leah; Leah returned her glance with a shrug. 'Some commando team we are here, huh?'

'Where Dika?' Noa asked.

'Dinka!' Tamar jumped. 'We forgot Dinka!'

Dinka had been standing and barking in the tangle of

people's legs – she'd become confused in the excitement. She'd lost them.

We have to go back, Tamar thought feverishly. I can't abandon her, she wouldn't know how to get back home from here; turn around, now! But then she looked at Shai, his head dropping on his chest, as if he had no remaining life force in him. She knew she couldn't go back now – she would never go back. A heavy hand tightened around her throat, pushing down with all its strength. How could she have forgotten her dog? How could she have betrayed Dinka this way?

A heavy silence fell over the car; even Noiku felt it and stayed quiet. Leah saw Tamar's face. 'We'll find her, don't worry,' she whispered, without believing it.

'We'll never find her,' Tamar said; she leaned back and closed her eyes. She knew that a terrible, terrible thing had just happened, and she couldn't even begin to grasp its meaning. Dinka, who had been with her since the age of seven, her only true friend, her other half, was gone. Gone. A thought pierced her – it was as if something, or someone, needed to be sacrificed in order to rescue Shai. Dinka was the sacrifice.

A hand found hers. Shai, his eyes closed, breathing heavily, pulled her a little closer. She put her ear against his mouth, and he barely managed to whisper, 'I'm so sorry, Tamari, I really am so sorry.'

Honigman turned around. 'We need to take your friend to the doctor.'

'I'll take care of him,' Tamar answered shortly. Suddenly Shai, with the last of his strength, spoke. 'I am not her friend,' he muttered. 'She is my sister.' His head sank on Tamar's shoulder, where he whispered, 'She is the only person I have in the world.' And his fingers clutched her fingers, powerlessly.

V

FOUR DAYS AFTER TAMAR escaped with Shai and lost Dinka, Assaf marched quickly through Ben Yehuda Walking Street. He was almost running, trying, without much hope, to find that guitar player. Her backpack, on his back, was suddenly very heavy, full of life, whispering words and thoughts and crying for help; he passed through a circle of people watching a girl perform magic tricks; then stopped for a minute to listen to a very young violinist, almost a child, play. He saw another boy leaning against the wall of the bank, producing a nondescript sound from a sitarlike instrument with a bow that he held between his toes. Never before had he noticed the number of street performers there – he was even more surprised by how young they were, the artists – most of them were around his age, and he looked at them, trying to guess if they had any connection to that mafia Sergei had mentioned.

Another crowded circle had gathered down the street: people were surrounding a girl who sat on a chair, playing the cello. Assaf didn't understand anything about music and was still surprised that anyone had come up with the idea of playing that instrument in the streets. She was a tiny girl with glasses and wore a red hat, and Assaf felt that the people gathered around her not for the sad music, necessarily, but because she, the little girl with the big cello, was some kind of strange performance in herself.

Assaf and Dinka had already passed by the circle, but then the dog stopped, as if her body had just absorbed an unseen shock. She turned around, confused, feverishly sniffing at the air; she spun around and stubbornly shoved her way through the crowd. Assaf was dragged after her – he had no choice; he made his way through the audience and found himself standing in front of the girl playing in the center of the circle.

She was playing, her eyes closed, her face changing expression quickly, as if she were dreaming. Dinka barked loudly. The girl opened questioning eyes and looked at the dog; Assaf thought she went a little pale. She stiffened in her chair, flashed nervous looks to both sides, and continued to play, sawing at the strings without emotion. Dinka kept pushing forward, using all her strength; Assaf pulled her back. The people surrounding them started to scold him, telling him to move, take the dog away, stop interrupting. He got scared – he realized that now everyone was watching him, now he and Dinka had become the street performance . . .

The girl pulled herself together first; she stopped playing, leaned forward quickly, and whispered to Assaf in a choked, scared voice: 'Where is she? Tell her she's great, that we all think she's fantastic – terrific! Now run – *run!*'

She then straightened up and leaned back in her chair, closing her eyes tightly, as if erasing the event that had just occurred from her memory; she continued to play, spreading her strange melancholic charm over the audience.

Assaf didn't understand a thing she had told him; he especially didn't understand why he was supposed to run. Dinka realized it before he did – quick as lightning, she jumped up; his hand was still holding her collar – Assaf felt her practically rescuing him, pulling him forward and dragging him off with all her strength. He pulled himself together after a moment – they circled the girl, pushing their way through the audience, bursting out of the crowd. He thought he heard someone calling after him to stop; he didn't hesitate. If he had looked back, he would have been able to see a short, wide man looking at him, then quickly dialing his mobile phone. Assaf ran and thought. She knew Tamar, that's for sure – she recognized Dinka and wanted him to tell Tamar she was terrific. Now I need to think fast – they all think she's terrific? What did she do? Who are *they*? He ran, his mind exploding, collecting information, filtering, putting together pieces of the mosaic, testing all kinds of theories. He knew and did not know at the same time; his heart told him that he was going in the right direction, he was already in the best place he could be, deep in his 5,000-meter run; he sank into himself, listening to the story that started to snake through him. What's more, he found himself moving in astonishing unison with Dinka. Without looking at each other, they moved through the people, the crowded traffic, crossing streets the way they used to, when they were first friends. (Yesterday? Dear God, Assaf thought, could it have only been yesterday?) Only now, no rope linked them – only a quick glance every once in a while, confirmation, silent support – I'm here with you – I'm with you, too – nice turn – thanks – where are you now? – ten steps behind you, there are a few people between us, but don't worry, I'm following you, keep going – I hear someone running after us – I can't hear it, but turn down this alley – no, I'm not going down there, I smell something – where? – one more minute, just keep running, I'm getting close to something good, just don't stop running – don't make me laugh, stop talking, you're ruining my concentration; I hope you know where you're taking me – of course I know, and soon you'll know it, too. Hey, Dinka, this looks familiar, I think we've already gone down this alley by that high wall – open your eyes, Assaf, we were here just yesterday. You're right, this is the – you finally recognized it? – follow me, now we're here.

She jumped on the green gate, standing on her hind legs and pushing the knob with both her paws; they both galloped inside. Assaf peeked over his shoulder and saw there was nobody there. His pursuers hadn't reached him yet. He entered the yard, ran over the stones, passed the well; between the trees, their branches heavy with fruit. He found himself wrapped up in the deep, familiar silence.

But before he could hurry behind the house to the window facing west, for the basket that would descend with the key, a little airborne, bulrush basket, he noticed something strange. He felt the air around his ears cool suddenly

– the door to the house was open, swinging slightly on its hinges.

He leaped inside and Dinka followed. They halted together, shocked, and stared.

The entrance hall looked as if a hurricane had hit – disaster everywhere. The floor was covered with hundreds of books, flung open, torn, disgraced. The tall cupboards had been pulled down and broken, as if they had been smashed with an ax. Even the altar had been shoved from its place, exposing a lighter rectangular patch of floor; it looked as if it had been moved to check for someone hiding underneath.

He thought, Theodora. For a moment, he didn't dare run upstairs, because in order to get there, he had to step on books. Then he started running, stepping on books – he knew instantly that what had happened here had something to do with him, with his visit to her. He galloped up the round stairs, miserable, his mind full of horrifying pictures awaiting him at the end of the corridor, everything he knew from horror movies and his most gruesome computer games. A frightened child began weeping in his mind – Don't surrender to it, Assaf thought, don't surrender. Theodora is so small, he thought, like a little chick; how could she survive such cruelty? He took a fleeting look into the pilgrims' hall; the beds had been turned upside down, the mattresses torn, slashed by knives. You could still feel the hatred of those who had done it in the air. He bounded up the last six stairs in one and a half steps, opened the blue door, and forced himself not to shut his eyes in fear.

In the first moment, he couldn't see her at all in the mess of the room. Then he discovered her – on her rocking chair, her eyes wide. She looked like a rag doll someone had forgotten on a chair. No spark of life filled her eyes; an eternity passed, and finally her mouth opened slightly, her eyes moving over to him.

'Assaf,' she murmured voicelessly. 'Is that you, *agori mou*? Run away from here quickly.'

'What happened, Theodora? What did they do to you?'

'Run before they come back; go, find her, keep her safe.'
Her eyes closed.

He hurried to her, knelt by her side, took her hand. Then he saw the open wound stretching from the edge of her temple to the corner of her mouth.

'Who did this to you?'

She breathed slowly and held up three tiny straight fingers. 'Three,' she signed to him. Suddenly her hand clenched his arm. 'Beasts, and more than that – the big one was the devil.' She was so weak she could hardly speak. But her hand tightened on his arm as if her entire personality were concentrated there. 'Remember, he is balding – oh, Satanas! – and he has a braid down his back, may he be hanged by it, amen!' Her eyes closed again, as if she had fainted, but she continued to rage, even with her eyes closed, and Assaf was relieved to notice that she had very little difficulty speaking. 'He asked about Tamar, the bat, the butting ox, the evil spell – and when I said nothing, then smack! He hit my cheek! But don't worry, my dear.' A faded hint of a familiar smile, the rebellious child she had been, shone from deep inside her. 'I bit him so that he shall never forget the strength of my mouth.'

'But what did they want?'

She opened her eyes and smiled tiredly. 'Her.'

'And how did they know to come here?'

'Perhaps you can tell me.'

His long lashes fluttered and closed for a moment in pain – he was the one who had brought them here. But how? Someone must have seen him when he came here before – someone had recognized Dinka and was sure that Tamar had been hiding in the house.

Theodora moaned and signaled to him that she wanted to get up; Asaf couldn't believe she would have the strength to stand. She did, holding on to him, swaying like a tiny flame of sheer will. They stood still for a moment, until the color returned to her face.

'Better now. It was very bad at night. I thought I would not live through it.'

'From the beatings?'

'No, he only slapped me once, but from the despair.' Assaf understood.

One of her fingers traced along his wrist. 'Did they see you again, on your way here?'

'They saw me,' he admitted. 'They chased me. I ran away, but they still might be around.' As soon as he said it, he knew what he hadn't dared to think until that moment: whoever was chasing Tamar believed they were partners.

'Then,' Theodora reasoned, 'in a moment or two they will start to wonder whether you came here again, and now they will be searching for you, not for me. They shall not be gentle with you. My dear, you must leave.'

'If I leave now, they'll catch me.'

'If you remain, they will catch you much faster.'

They were silent, scared, both imagining the beating of their hearts as the sound of steps running in the corridor. Dinka looked up at them, her eyes shining, her body trembling with nerves.

'Unless,' Theodora said.

'Unless what?'

'Unless something distracts them.'

Assaf didn't understand. 'What on earth could dis –'

'Quiet! Don't disturb me.'

She started walking around the room, clearing space between the piles of books, between the broken shelves, stepping on fragments of plates, on heaps of letters bound by thick yellow rubber bands. Assaf had no idea where she found the strength to move, to think, to worry for him, when her entire life had been poured out and trampled.

A little wooden cupboard was thrown on its side, blocking the entrance to the small kitchen. She opened the cupboard and took out a white cloth parasol with thin wooden ribs.

'In Lyxos,' she explained gravely, 'the sun is very strong.' Assaf tensed up and his lips grew pale. She's gone crazy, he thought. The shock has thrown her completely off balance.

Theodora looked at him and divined his thoughts. 'Please, my dear, don't worry. I am not losing my mind.'

She tried to open the parasol. The wooden ribs moved quickly and silently, but the gentle white fabric disintegrated once the parasol opened and fell on her head like snowflakes.

'It seems I shall have to relinquish my shade, but where have I put my shoes?'

She spoke with a strange matter-of-factness, as if reducing her entire being into the little actions before her. She removed a tiny pair of black shoes, wrapped in yellow newspaper, small as a girl's, from a hidden drawer. She blew on them, scattering a cloud of dust. She wiped them off, shining them with the sleeve of her gown, then sat on the edge of her bed and tried to put them on. He could see her fingers getting tangled in the laces.

'What a foolish old woman your new friend is.' She gave him an embarrassed look. 'She has not tied her shoelaces in fifty years and has already forgotten how!'

He knelt before her and, with the utmost reverence, like Prince Charming with Cinderella, tied her shoelaces.

'Look, my feet have hardly changed since then!' she crowed with evident pride, stretching her leg out in front of him, forgetting the terror of the situation for a moment.

His face was level with her wounded face, the clotted blood pooled over her entire cheek. She saw the shock in his eyes. 'The ways of the world are wondrous.' She sighed. 'No man has touched my face for fifty years, and the first one – was a slap.' A spasm of sobs passed between her eyes and stopped at the edge of her nose. She said, 'Enough. Enough! Now tell me please, quickly, what is it like there?'

'It doesn't look too good,' he said. 'You have to have it bandaged.'

'No, not there! There!' and she pointed over her shoulder, toward the outside.

'There . . . ?' He hesitated. What could he tell her? How can you describe the outside world in half a minute? 'You have to see it to understand,' he whispered.

Her worried eyes delved deeply into his in silence. Assaf

knew it would be a long time before he could ever digest the things he was witnessing here.

'I will walk out through the gate, then turn in the direction of this hand.' Theodora took a deep breath, and he realized she didn't even know which was left and which was right. 'And you will wait another few minutes inside the house. If they are waiting out there, why, they will most certainly hurry after me, to discover what the old woman is up to . . .'

'What if they catch you?'

'That's it, exactly. I want them to catch me, not you.'

'And if they hit you?'

'What will they do to me that they haven't already done?'

He looked at her, thrilled by her bravery. 'Aren't you scared?'

'Scared? Of course I am. But not of them. It is only the unknown that is frightening.' She lowered her head and spoke to some stubborn thread on the sleeve of her gown. 'Please tell me, when I go out, when I pass through the outer gates, what will be the first thing I see? What is the first thing there, on the outside?'

Assaf tried to recall it: her street was a side alley and pretty quiet. Cars parked along it and drove slowly through; on the corner was a bank branch and an electronics store with a television set playing in the window. 'Nothing special,' he mumbled, then stopped, understanding the stupidity of his words.

'And the noise, yes? I am most afraid of the noise. And the light. Perhaps you have sunglasses for me?'

He didn't. 'It might be a little difficult at the beginning,' he said, feeling a great urge to protect her, to swaddle her in cotton. 'Just be careful on the street. Always look to your left and your right and your left again, and you mustn't cross when there is a red light . . .' The more he spoke, the more scared he got, as he understood just how much she needed to learn in order to survive a full five minutes in the city's center.

They went down the stairs. It was still hard for her to walk, and she leaned on his shoulder. Slowly they walked down the round corridor, and Assaf felt that, for her, it was also a journey of mourning, of separation from something to which she could never return. Amazed, she said, as if to herself, 'When the walls of the Old City fell, I did not go out. And I did not go out when there were the explosions in the streets and in the market, although I wanted to give blood so terribly. And I did not go out when Yitzhak Rabin, may his memory be blessed, was murdered, and I knew that the whole country was passing by his coffin. And now, suddenly . . . *Khristos kai Apostolos!*' she mumbled when her eyes discerned the ruins of the entrance hall, and she fell silent. Assaf thought she would faint now, but she actually let go of his supporting arm, stretched her tiny frame tall, and when he saw the deep crease lengthen from her nose to her chin, he knew that no one would ever defeat her. He tried to clear a path for her through the books, but she said there was no time for that, and gracefully she tread upon the covers, touching and not touching them, as if she were floating.

Just before she reached the door facing the yard, she stopped. She clasped her hands together nervously.

'Listen,' Assaf blurted, 'maybe we don't have to do this. I'll manage. I run quickly, they won't catch me.'

'Quiet!' she ordered. 'Now listen: go to Leah. She may be able to help you. Have you yet heard of Leah?'

Assaf hesitated. He had encountered her name in the diary several times; he remembered some mysterious debate that had continued for a few months, and a few more conversations about that matter with Tamar – something about a baby, and panic, and hesitation. Something that resulted – if he remembered correctly – in a trip to Vietnam. But of course he couldn't tell Theodora that he had looked through Tamar's diary.

He asked where he could find Leah. Theodora stretched out her arms in irritation. 'Why, this is the trouble, that Tamar does not speak! She once told me, 'There is a Leah.' Very nice, I say, and perhaps half a year later she says, 'Leah has a restaurant.' *Bon appétit*, I say! But where? What? Who is she to you? And what have you to do with her? Then she is silent, and what now? Whom have we left?' She looked at him sorrowfully, then bent to Dinka, stroked her ears, unfolded one of them, and whispered – Assaf heard fragments of her words – 'To Leah . . . the restaurant . . . understand . . . quick like an arrow, hurry!' Dinka watched her, ears pricked. Assaf thought Theodora had truly gone a bit mad if she believed Dinka could understand that.

Suddenly Theodora grasped his hand with both of hers. 'And you will, of course, tell Tamar that I went outside, will you not? She'll never believe it!' She giggled in girlish joy. 'She'll be frightened, my Tamar! But do listen, do not tell her that I went outside for her or she will torment herself – she has enough torments without my adding to them. *Pou pou!* Even that word, "outside" – it tastes quite different in my mouth: I am going outside. Soon, I shall go outside. Here, outside I go.'

She opened the door and looked at the wide yard. 'I know this side a little; sometimes, when Nasrian brings the laundry from the washerwoman or the groceries from the market, I stand here and peek out through the open door. But when you stand here' – and she took one grand step over the threshold and was breathless – 'what beauty! Everything is so wide!'

'Look, look,' she murmured, and in fluent Greek she spoke rapidly to herself. The words rolled over one another, her hands grabbed her head as if it were about to explode – then her legs began to carry her on their own. Assaf thought he should run after her, but he was afraid to leave – perhaps someone was waiting to ambush him by the big gate. He remembered Muki's first steps, how he had worried for her, and how wonderful it was when she traveled from the bed to the table on her own.

Theodora was already walking away from him, moving like a little tugboat carried over a rushing river. She opened the gate that gave onto the street, and she looked right and left. It seemed that no one was there, because when she turned her face to Assaf, there was a big, slightly dreamy smile on it. Actually, Assaf thought, if there is no one there, she doesn't have to go out! One minute! Wait! You can come back!

But no force in the world could have stopped her now, and the gate swung shut behind her. Assaf was left alone in the empty yard. He imagined her pacing up the street, her eyes opening wider and wider. He was afraid for her. He thought he would see her running back in a minute, escaping the outside world and fearfully closing herself up in her room for another fifty years. In his wildest imagination he could not have guessed the joy that flooded through her as she faced the tsunami of the everyday. All her pain and her weakness vanished; her legs took her to Jaffa Street. On a hot night fifty years ago, she had arrived here by an old bus, then by the horse-driven wagon of a Bukharani peddler who dropped her off in front of her prison gate. Now she was standing, all her senses wide open in the face of the wonder of the street. Her face trembled with a thousand expressions, a thousand hearts beat in her chest, all the smells, the colors, all the voices and noises – she had no names for the things she saw; there were no names for her new feelings. Every word she knew failed her, one after the other, and if you could die from life, this was the moment.

She ignored the dozens of cars, the crowds of people; she didn't notice two of Pesach's men, who spotted her the moment she came to the main street (Look, Shishko, there's your crazy nun – call Pesach – follow her wherever she goes). She marched straight into the road, blind with joy, completely indifferent to the honks roaring around her, to the screeching of brakes. She knelt in the middle of Jaffa Street, clasped her little hands together, and for the first time in fifty years, she prayed to God with a heart bursting in gratitude.


Five minutes later, he was running at top speed, scared to death; his hands beat the air wildly, and his eyes could hardly see a thing. For the first time since he had started this journey, he couldn't control his breath at all. Dinka felt the change in him at once, and now and then she would look back at him in concern. He couldn't have imagined how horrible the experience would be – every pair of eyes that rested on him made him tremble; he felt that people were scattered all over the city, lying in wait only for him. He was right: for four days now, all of Pesach's people had been busy chasing Tamar down and, since yesterday, him as well. All performances outside Jerusalem were canceled; the artists were ordered to keep an eye out and report – the rumor in the home said something about a 2,000-shekel prize, no less, for whoever could supply useful information; and the bulldogs were given clear instructions to cease all regular trade immediately and scout the streets, looking for Tamar or that new boy, the tall guy who popped up out of nowhere and was moving through the city with Tamar's dog, shoving his nose into everyone's business and always keeping one step ahead of Pesach and his people.

So it happened that Assaf, who had slipped out of Theodora's house and was trying to stick to side streets, unknowingly, and from the start, drew a train of attention behind him. He ran after Dinka, placing his fate in her hands, in her feet – he didn't care where she was running, as long as she was taking them both away from the dangerous area of the violated house. He was trying so badly to disappear that everything he saw also became invisible; so he missed the sight of a short man standing at the junction of King George and Agrippas Streets by the falafel booth, trying to fix – as he had been since yesterday, it seemed – a Subaru with its hood up. An amputee sitting in the lottery booth informed the man that he had just now seen a boy and a dog fitting his description and told him where they went. The short man received the information without a word and dialed. Someone answered before the phone had rung even once. The short man delivered the message; the man listened and hung up. In the same moment, to his amazement, the boy and dog passed in front of him. Assaf, on his wild marathon, paid no attention to that man, either, the skinny one with thick sideburns who followed after him half-running, while he dialed and spoke very quietly into his phone: there they are, now they're by the rubber girl, she – the dog stopped – what happened? Just a minute (he was speaking very fast and was no doubt feeling like a sports announcer). Now they're going into the crowd, I can't see them from here, tell everybody to get over here now, send a car, too – I have them, okay, I heard you, stop yelling, wait, one minute – what is it? What's happening?

It so happened that the rubber girl noticed the dog, one moment before she managed to twist her whole flexible body into the big glass aquarium so you could close the lid on it. Suddenly her eyes, glassy with inward concentration, focused sharply. Her bitter face twisted and twitched; she untangled herself, untying knot after knot with popping sounds. She unstitched a leg from under her armpit and an arm from around her ankle, stood up and shouted, 'Shishko! The dog! That girl's dog!'

The street burst into activity. People were taken aback and started running in every direction, stumbling into one another, bumping into four murky-eyed men emerging from four different alleys and trying to break into the circle of bystanders. Assaf and Dinka snuck out of the explosion. They flew, split up, reunited again three streets later, finding each other by the sense, the deep internal terrified knowledge, that the whole world was after them. The city was a hunting field and every man around them was a hunter in disguise. Now everything was up to Dinka alone, because Assaf was almost paralyzed by fear; he had no chance on his own. She dragged him after her, called to him, and pushed forward with Super-Dog powers – she was a sled dog and a St Bernard, a seeing-eye dog and a wolf. In a narrow, dead-end alley, she dove with him into a little yard, and they both waited, huddled together in terror – they saw the skinny man, who reminded Assaf of a dried-up Elvis Presley, pass them and disappear. Dinka growled; Assaf placed a hand over her mouth. One minute later, they went back into the alley and ran in the opposite direction. Another minute of crazed running – there was no chance, Assaf thought. They're going to catch me in the next alley. And then, a short bark of joy, and in front of his eyes was a gate with a sign: LEAH'S. He cried out in amazement. Dinka rose on her hind legs and opened the gate.

He ventured a last glance behind him and almost fell with a sigh of relief into the yard.

A young palm tree stood in the center of the little yard, with a few tables and chairs scattered around it, set for dinner. An old couple sat at one of them, chatting quietly, and didn't even raise their eyes to look at him as he entered. Assaf and Dinka crossed the yard and climbed three steps into a large room. Tables were set there as well, and diners occupied almost every table. Assaf trembled, and didn't know what to do. Whom should he approach? People looked at him . . . he felt so dirty and drenched in sweat, a real appetite spoiler – but Dinka was already galloping past the tables, pushing him through the swinging door, and suddenly Assaf was in a kitchen.

His senses were overwhelmed by a million mixed-up impressions – a cook, a big bubbling pot, the scents of unfamiliar dishes, a frying pan whispering, someone calling 'Arugula with Roquefort!' from the outer room through a little opening. A young boy, slicing mountains of tomatoes; a little round man standing in the corner who looked as if he absolutely didn't belong; and a tall, angry woman who snapped around and faced him. Her face was scarred by long gashes, badly healed. She stood in front of him, crossed her arms over her chest, and hissed: What the hell was he doing in her kitchen?

Then she saw the dog and her eyes lit up. 'Dinka! Dinkush!' she yelled, and knelt in front of her and scratched her ears and hugged her. This is exactly how Theodora had hugged the dog, Assaf thought, and tried to catch his breath. 'Dinka, Mamush, sweetie, where've you been? I've been looking all over the city four days for you! Tziyyon, quickly, give her some water, look how thirsty she is!' Assaf took advantage of the opportunity to peek through the swinging door for a moment to make sure they hadn't broken into the restaurant yet.

The woman slowly rose and stood in front of him. 'And who are you?'

Her gaze was so sharp he couldn't speak for a moment; he had no idea how to explain to her the wild rush into her restaurant's kitchen. All her workers – the two waiters, the boy cutting vegetables, the cook, his hand raised to point out to the sous-chef the shelf on which he could find the arugula – they were all standing, frozen, mid-motion. He looked around him in distress. Then he put on his professional armor. 'Perhaps you know the dog's owner?' he asked, in the most formal voice he could summon from inside him, the Form 76 voice.

'I asked, Who are *you*?' Her voice was biting; it was a voice that said, Don't get smart with *me*. She looked at him with such obvious suspicion that Assaf was practically insulted, and almost burst into the angry detailed speech that had been slowly formulating inside him for two days now ('What the hell do you mean, Who am I? I am the one who's been running all over the city with that dog in order to return her to the legal owner, and the one who's been attacked by everyone I meet, the one who's been chased after so they can tear me apart,' etc.).

Instead, he said, 'I work at City Hall, and I am looking for the owner.'

'Then you can leave her here,' she said decisively. 'Good-bye. We're working here.'

She was already at the door, holding it open and putting a big strong hand on his shoulder. The little kitchen returned to life – the boy returned to slicing tomatoes, and the cook affectionately patted his assistant's cheek.

'No,' Assaf said. 'I can't.'

The woman paused, and the room stopped again. 'Why not? What's the problem?'

'Because . . . because . . . you're not the owner.'

'Oh really?' Her 'really' spiraled around him, binding him like chicken wire. 'And how, exactly, do you know that I am not the owner?'

Dinka, who was noisily lapping up water, stopped and barked. She left off, stood before Leah, and barked at her with an unusual ferocity. Water shook off her whiskers, but she didn't stop to lick the droplets. She stood between the two of them, stared at Leah with hard eyes, and for a moment it seemed she was about to stomp her feet impatiently.

'Stop it, Dinka,' Assaf said, embarrassed. 'It's Leah – what's the matter with you?'

But she didn't calm down. She circled Assaf as if drawing a line around him, then sat down, erect, her back to him, facing Leah, and barked another bark, its meaning very clear.

'Would you look at this,' Leah said quietly.

Something was poking his back, under Tamar's backpack. He wanted to turn around, but then it pushed harder; it was as if an iron pipe were shoving into him.

'Please answer the lady's question,' an old man's voice said behind him. 'Unless you want me to spray you with dumdum bullets that will tear you apart and splatter you on the wall.'

'Moshe!' the woman said angrily. 'You don't have to give such a detailed description; people are eating here!'

I'm going crazy, Assaf thought. A rifle? They're threatening me with a rifle? What's the matter with them? What does Tamar do that everyone loses their mind over her?

'I am counting to three,' said the man. 'And after that, my finger will squeeze the trigger very slowly.'

'You will do nothing of the kind, and stop talking nonsense!' Leah spat. 'And put up that cannon of yours, right now. Samir, go set a table for two in the private room, and give Dinka something to eat here. You, what's your name?'

'Assaf.'

'Come with me.'

She took him to a little room where there were only two tables, both of them empty. She sat in front of him: 'Now explain, from the beginning and all the way to the end. And I'll only tell you once' – she touched her nose slightly – 'this nose can smell a lie.'

Assaf showed her the form and explained to her Danokh's method for locating the owners of lost dogs. But Leah scarcely looked at the form; she examined Assaf closely, focusing on his face, as if attempting to absorb his being. 'By the way,' she remembered in the middle of his explanation, 'I'm Leah.'

She extended a large manly hand to him and was surprised to feel his crushing handshake.

'Now, where did you get that?' She pointed at his swollen nose.

He told her.

'I don't understand, what were you doing there? How did you get there?'

He told her about Sergei as well.

'And where'd you get that from?'

She pointed to the long scratch on his forehead; he'd almost forgotten about that one.

'This one? Where did it come from – oh, that's from yesterday, from a police detective.'

And he told her.

And Leah listened.

All the way through how they were chasing him across the city.

'This is hers,' he said, finally taking the bag off his back, and told Leah how he had taken it out of the baggage check.

She didn't say a word. She only sat, staring at him, two vertical creases in her forehead deepening tremendously. She shook herself awake. 'But with all this running, you probably haven't eaten a thing today! Now eat. We'll talk more later.'

When she said that, he felt a strong bite, deep in his gut. 'But what about Tamar?' he muttered, and swallowed. 'I don't think there's much time. We have to hurry.' Leah saw his Adam's apple bobbing up and down, and heard his answer, and something shifted inside her. She had run this restaurant for over twelve years, and until this moment, she had never met a person who rejected an invitation for a meal. 'Tamar is in a safe place,' she said, breaking all of her rules of caution. 'First, you eat.'

'But I don't have any money,' he remembered desperately. 'I was robbed.'

'This is on the house. What do you like?'

'Everything.' Assaf smiled, and stretched his legs, feeling as if he'd finally drawn a lucky number.

'You'll get everything,' she pronounced, standing up to her

full height. 'I'm going back to the kitchen, but don't worry – I'm not leaving you.'

He sat and devoured with pleasure the pageant of dishes Leah began sending in to him. The food was delicate and well spiced, with one flavor after another dazzling and bewitching his senses each in turn; they were clearly saying one thing: somebody here wants to make Assaf happy.

From the passageway to the kitchen, Leah peeked in at him every once in a while, taking a good, deep, thoughtful look at him, enjoying his rude healthy appetite tremendously. She froze at one point, and tilted as if she had just experienced a back spasm or been stabbed by an idea. She called Samir over, exchanged a few words with him in the corner – she told him to go to the house, send the babysitter home, and bring Noiku over here. At once. Samir looked at her, surprised. 'Over here? In the middle of dinner? Are you sure?'

Yes, yes, she was sure. Quickly; she needed to find out something important.


'Look, I know that she disappeared,' Assaf said. He felt it was time to talk business. Leah sat in front of him, stirring black coffee. 'And I also know she's in some kind of trouble. I want to find her. Will you help me?'

'I would love to,' she said plainly. 'But I can't.'

'Oh,' Assaf said with disappointment. 'Theodora wouldn't either.' A long silence passed; there was some tension. Leah thought, with wonder, What, you talked to Theodora as well? Something in him moved her very much. She didn't even know what it was. Assaf was silent. He thought it wasn't fair – someone had to help him now, because he couldn't do it on his own anymore. Leah didn't feel comfortable refusing him, either. She tried to liven up the conversation. 'You know, I've never met Theodora.' She shrugged. 'Sometimes I think she's just one of Tamar's inventions, I swear. Well?' she said, carefully probing, expectant, 'you know that she sometimes invents all kinds of crazy ideas by now, don't you?'

Assaf thought about Victorious. He saw the girl standing on the barrel and smiled.

'Also' – Leah felt she was walking on a very thin rope, talking about Tamar to a total stranger; and yet her gut was telling her she was doing this *for* Tamar – 'it's very important to her that her friends don't meet each other. She has to be alone with each of them, as if they're off in their own world.' She stopped, noting the effect of her words on him. On top of everything else, he had a gorgeous smile. 'When I ask her why, what does she tell me? "Divide and conquer"! What do you think about that?'

'What do *I* think?' It was a pleasure to be promoted to the rank of Commentator on Tamar's Affairs, as if, on his travels toward her, he had gathered enough experience and knowledge that he could use them to explain her. He said, 'Maybe . . . maybe this way she has more freedom. I mean, she has' – suddenly Reli's word jumped into his mouth – '*space*.'

'Exactly what I was thinking!' Leah replied, excited. 'If you ask me, her "divide and conquer" lets her be a completely different person with each one of her friends. Don't you think?'

'That's exactly what I was thinking,' Assaf concluded. 'Her freedom is the most important thing to her.' He sat, troubled, for a moment. Something completely different was confusing him – something about Reli and Rhino, as if, for one second, it occurred to him that perhaps there was something in what Reli had said.

Leah rested her head against her big palm and looked at him, and also through him a little bit; she was carried away by a distant idea, played around with it a little, and returned to him. 'Tell me, you –' How to ask this? 'Do you do anything, outside of school? Like art or something?'

'No . . .' He laughed. 'Why do you ask?'

'Oh, nothing. I was just thinking.' A slight, satisfied smile passed over her lips. Assaf wondered if his photography could be considered art. Perhaps, yes. The teacher of his photography course thought so; at the exhibit they put together at the end of last year, five of his photos were shown. But he never thought of himself as an 'artist.' There was something almost distasteful when he thought about it; perhaps because Reli insisted on introducing herself as an 'artist' and it had always seemed fake to him. Real artists were Cartier-Bresson, or Diane Arbus, and all the others whose works he adored and studied; but who was he compared to them?

A screaming bundle was shoved in front of his eyes. Samir returned, with a sigh of relief, passed off to Leah one angry little girl, and explained that she had been napping when he got there and screamed all the way here.

Assaf guessed that she was two or three years old. She was tiny, with ivory skin and very black, straight hair, and black slanted eyes that were now screwed up angrily and almost hidden. He shifted his eyes from her to Leah and back, trying to connect the big dark woman with the scarred face and the little girl with the slanted eyes, and suddenly understood – it was all so simple.

'Leah,' a voice called from the kitchen, 'what about the marinade?'

Leah stood up, the screaming girl in her arms. She hesitated for a moment in front of the kitchen door, turned, and thrust her onto Assaf's lap. Now he had a little girl on his hands. She was surprisingly light; she seemed to weigh about half of what Muki did. Muki was, as his mother said, 'a girl with two thighs on the ground.' And this little one was like a feather, and she smelled good and was so beautiful – from the little you could see through the tantrum she was having, screaming and beating her tiny fists in all directions. He smiled at her, and she screamed. He licked his lips like Dinka's, and she kicked. He barked, and she went silent. She looked at him, surprised, expectant. He barked again and wiggled his ears. She glanced slyly from him to Dinka. Something started popping up from between the tears; he held his finger in the air, she sent out a finger and touched his. She still had a few hiccuping sobs in her smile; he nodded yes, and so did she. He shook his head no, and so did she. This way, without words, with nothing more than looks and winks and making faces, they said hello; and all his yearnings for Muki unfolded and swelled up, aching. Noa sent her little hands out to touch his face. She ran a hand over his eyes, his swollen nose. She touched the blue bruises, and Assaf sat, his eyes half-closed, and allowed it, and rejoiced inside. When he opened his eyes, he saw Leah was back, and he wanted to give her child back to her, but Noa wouldn't let go of him.

'I see Noa is fond of you,' Leah said gravely. 'Now –'

But Noa wouldn't share him with anybody, either. She held his face with her two hands and aimed it toward her, and began telling him excitedly about a hamster they had in nursery school that got caught in broken glass and bled . . . Assaf repeated her half-words, and decoded them one by one. When Muki was that age when children say only one syllable of each word, Assaf had prepared a special dictionary so that her nanny could understand her. Leah sat to the side, listening to their conversation, and her big face shone. 'Now listen' – she said, when Noa finally agreed to let go of him for a moment and started playing on the floor with Dinka – 'I want to tell you something.'

He dropped his smile, instantly sat at full attention. She crossed her hands, creating a little finger-tent in front of her mouth; above the finger-tent, her eyes stared at him, narrow and sparkling. 'You should know that if you ever, I mean, ever, do anything bad to that girl, I will chase you to the ends of the earth and strangle you with these ten fingers – did you hear what I just said?'

He choked out some answer. He remembered Theodora telling him something similar, but sitting here with Leah, he could easily imagine that she had actually done such things before.

'I may not be the smartest person in the world,' she began, with the strange festivity of the opening of a speech. 'And God only knows how many stupid things I've done in my life –' She unconsciously touched the long scars – three bastards

315

from a rival gang had slashed her with a razor stuck in a potato. 'And I don't exactly have a college degree. I only finished ninth grade. But I understand a little about human beings, and I've seen you for an hour now, and I know what I need to know.'

Assaf didn't understand what all this was leading to, but he didn't want to interrupt.

'This is the situation,' she said, and spread her hands on the table. 'Tamar got mixed up in something.'

Drugs, Assaf thought.

'Something very bad, involving all kinds of shady characters, even criminals.'

He listened. Until now, nothing she had said surprised him. (One thing did surprise him: that he was able to sit here, with all his tension and fear, and speak this easily and naturally with a person he had only just met; Assaf felt like someone who, without paying any attention, had mastered the steps of an extremely complex dance.)

'It'll be just like how they chased you when you came here,' Leah continued. 'And so let's say, let's just say that I tell you where she is now – and *suppose* you go there. They'll be on you again before you know what hit you, and as smart as you'd be about it, you can't run away from them. They're better than you are at these things. Now do you understand what I'm worried about?'

He didn't say anything.

'That's why I think you'd better leave the dog here.'

'Why?'

'This is what I'm thinking: They're looking for a boy with a dog, right? If you leave here without the dog, I bet you no one will even look twice at you – I know how their minds work.'

Assaf was thinking.

'What do you say?'

'I'm taking Dinka and will keep looking for Tamar.'

She sighed, looked at his bruised face. 'Tell me' – she asked what people used to ask her a million times, fifteen years ago – 'aren't you afraid of anything?'

'Sure I'm afraid.' He laughed and thought, You should have seen how I shook in front of those guys at the swimming hole, and how I shook on the way here. 'But I'll find her.' He didn't know where he had gotten this confidence from. He felt that he, too – like that old man with the rifle – was now talking as if he were a hero in a movie. 'No, I'm sure of it,' he muttered, sailing off into his thoughts, forgetting himself for a moment. 'I'll find her sooner or later . . .'

She watched him with a strange pleasure: the way he leaned forward in his chair, putting his knees together without putting his feet together; his hands so awkwardly clasped, each finger turning in a slightly different direction knitted with the others in a dreamy, childish gesture, as if he were making a wish; his shy internal smile that hovered on the outside, leaving two spots of light in the corners of his mouth. Leah was overcome.

'Yes . . .' she whispered, oddly weak, as if answering his thoughts.

'I've walked after her so far, I feel as if I already know her,' he muttered, to his own surprise – the words simply fell out of him.

'That's exactly what I've been thinking from the moment we started talking,' she said quietly.

'What?' He pulled himself together, surprised by their dreamy conversation.

'Come on,' she said, and stood up. 'We're going on a little trip.'

'Where?'

'You'll see in a minute,' and as she stood, said another thing, this time to herself: 'Us girls have to help each other out.'


She gave a few instructions to the cook, prepared a bottle of water for Noa, and wrote something on a piece of paper and put it in an envelope. Assaf didn't ask a single question. When they walked out the front of the restaurant, he looked carefully right and left. The alley was empty. He noticed

Leah looking to both sides as well; even Dinka inspected the terrain. In the parking lot, Leah introduced him to her old yellow VW Bug and strapped Noa into a high-tech safety car seat that seemed at least as expensive as the car itself. They drove through the little streets for some time. Occasionally, Leah would pull over to the side and wait for several minutes, and only then drive on. At one point she braked suddenly in a street that seemed completely empty, turned sharply into a little parking lot, and waited. After a moment, two men passed them, running; Assaf recognized one of them, the skinny one who had chased him before. He looked at Leah, impressed, and couldn't understand how she had guessed where they were before she saw them. 'A dog knows another dog.' She chuckled, and drove off in the other direction. And against traffic. They drove this way a long time, her senses dictating how they drove. Assaf noticed she was looking in the rearview mirror more than through the windshield and didn't ask a thing.

'Listen,' she said after a while, 'don't be offended, but I want you to close your eyes. It's better if you don't see where we're going.'

He understood immediately and closed his eyes. He heard her say, 'So that even if, God forbid, they ever caught you, you wouldn't be able to tell them where you went.'

'Do you want me to blindfold myself?'

'No.' She laughed. 'I believe you.'

It was pleasant for him to be riding in the car like this, to relax a little after a day of running, and before what was waiting for him. Noa had fallen asleep in the back, and Assaf thought he wouldn't mind taking a quick nap either.

'Do you want to listen to music?'

'No.'

'Do you want to hear a story? Don't open your eyes!'

'Yes.'

So Leah told him about the restaurant, and about the hard years of her apprenticeship in France; along the way, she had to say something, only a hint, of course, about her previous incarnation, and glanced at him to make sure he wasn't horrified. He wasn't. She took a deep breath and straightened both her hands on the wheel, continuing to speak quietly, in the same manner she sometimes used with Tamar. She didn't even try to struggle against the strange urge that had come over her, to open herself up to this boy – on the contrary, she abandoned herself to this pleasurable, addictive element that was in the air around Assaf. For a moment, she hesitated over whether to tell him about Shai, but she decided she had already said too much, and even for what she'd said, she would probably get a piece of Tamar's mind. Anyway, it was better for him to discover the rest on his own. Every now and then, she looked over at him and thought that she could see exactly what he would look like, in ten years, and in twenty, and in thirty. There were moments when she thought he had fallen asleep, and she would stop talking – he would then emit a light 'Hm?' and she would continue. She told him about Noiku, that she was the greatest gift life had ever given her, and that it was thanks to Tamar, in more ways than one, that she had been able to take that step. Suddenly she laughed. 'I don't know why I'm telling you all this. You probably think that I tell my life's story to everyone I meet?'

'Sure. Tell me more.'

The road continued. Noa sighed a little in her sleep. Leah spoke. Then she was silent. Even without opening his eyes, he could feel her growing tense. They drove down a bumpy hill; the orange light of the late-afternoon sun rested on his eyelids. Leah was now driving very slowly. 'If you'd've asked me,' she abruptly said in a different voice, 'I probably would have told you.'

'What?' Assaf asked.

'That this is where I dropped Tamar off two days ago.'

He opened his eyes. He saw they were standing by an empty bus stop. A cardboard sign swayed on a near electric pole: TO SIGI AND MOTI'S WEDDING. Leah raised her sunglasses, scanned the place, looking carefully in the rearview mirror. Noa woke up and started to cry. She saw Assaf and smiled at him. He traced his finger along her delicate cheek. She held his finger and said his name.

He got out of the car, and Dinka, who had slept all the way there, jumped out after him and shook herself. Leah took out an envelope and gave it to him. 'Give this to Tamar, from me. It's a letter to explain everything so she won't hate me. Take good care of yourself.' She blew him a kiss. 'Good luck, Assaf. And take good care of her.'

She turned around and drove off.

He immediately stepped off the road, into the valley, and curled up behind a rock. He waited to make sure that no other car was stopping. Complete silence. No engine and no footsteps. He was all alone, and no one had followed him. But he felt uncomfortable not knowing where he was.

A path curved between the rocks. Assaf began walking down the path; Dinka grew alert again, sharp. Again and again, Assaf had to call her to him. By a bent oak tree he stopped her, went down on his knees, and whispered in her ear, 'We have to be very quiet. Don't bark now, okay? Not a sound, until we see what's going on. Promise?'

They descended farther. The valley was much deeper than it had seemed at first. They passed over a narrow creek, treading slowly and quietly. When they were between two small hills, they heard the voices.

He didn't know where they were coming from. There were the sounds of struggle, and shouts and moans. A very young man, maybe even a boy, was screaming hysterically: It won't help you, you can't keep me here, I'm not your prisoner. And a girl was crying, or begging for something.

Dinka broke away from his hand, and only before the peak of the little hill did he manage to grab her and lie on her. They both gasped. Assaf whispered to her, pleaded for her to be quiet: Dinka, quiet, not yet. He didn't know what to do now, confused and scared as he was. Perhaps because of this, he removed his belt and tied Dinka to the thin trunk of a tree by her collar. She looked at him, so terribly insulted that he could hardly do it. Then he crept to the peak of the hill. Below, behind a thick tree, he saw something dark that looked to him like a big mouth. It turned out to be the mouth of a cave. A very young guy was standing there, sweating and panting, his hands shaking at his sides. He was tall, very skinny, and swaying on his legs. After a moment Assaf noticed someone else there, lying on the ground, motionless at the guy's feet. Assaf thought it was a boy with very short hair – now he was completely confused: Who were they? Where was Tamar? But the guy noticed him over the edge of the hill; his eyes lit with fear and he started to run off in the other direction. Assaf ran after him, confused. The chase took only a few seconds; the boy ran slowly, weakly, but every time Assaf almost touched him, the boy's fear pushed him a few steps farther up the valley. Assaf knocked him down and lay over him near a clump of bushes, and immediately twisted his arm back, the way they had done to him so many times over the past few days. The guy lay under him and cried, and begged Assaf not to kill him. Assaf thought vaguely that this was strange and irrational: it was impossible for someone this frightened and frail to be one of the people threatening Tamar. The guy tried to get up – his body twisted and curled. Assaf pushed him back down and yelled at him not to move. At that moment he heard quick steps in the bushes behind him. He turned, too slowly, saw something coming down on him from above, and the sky cracked in two and fell apart. After a moment, he started to feel the blow to the side of his head, a hard blow. Then he felt nothing.

VI

'DON'T MOVE! DON'T GET up! If you move one inch –!'

Assaf heard it, but he had to move; he was afraid that if he continued to lie down, his brains would leak out of one of his ears. The pain now pulsing through his skull, joined with the pain from the beatings he had gotten in the morning, now powerfully reawakened by the most recent blow; the agonies danced all over his skull, as if cheering the new pain on and welcoming it.

'Who are you?' Tamar screamed. 'What do you want?'

Assaf looked at her, trying to put together the picture in front of him; but the short hair he saw refused to go with the voice he heard. A thought filtered in through the fog in his head: It's a girl . . . no, a boy . . . who is that?

And suddenly another sharp pain passed through him – it's her. But where is her hair? Where is the black mane?

Barks rang out over the hill; Tamar – perhaps because she was so intent on Assaf – didn't hear them. Assaf wanted to tell her, 'It's Dinka,' but before that, he would have to sit up, to lighten the pain in his head. He rose a little, and Tamar leaped up, stood above him, and swung a big piece of two-by-four. The next time he looked up, his eyeballs hurt, too. A row of rusty nails was sticking out of the wood, and Assaf hoped they hadn't cut him. He touched his head above the ear – he couldn't feel any blood. Just another big warm bump to add to the collection. The skinny guy was sitting on the ground, not far from him, leaning against a rock, his eyes closed.

'Why did you come here?' her voice choked out, shrill with tension and fear. 'What do you want?'

Assaf started to understand: she thought he was one of the

men chasing her. She needed an explanation. Heavily, he tried to stand.

'If you even dare try to get up –!'

He didn't know what to do. She was flickering in front of him, coming nearer, then moving farther away, seeming wild and scared and dangerous. He looked at her and thought that even like that, twitching in anger, with her short hair, a piece of wood in her hand, and wearing filthy overalls, even like that, she was a lot prettier than what he had imagined. Or at least, than what she had written about herself in the diary. He simply sat and looked at her, trying to match up how she looked with everything he knew about her; and to everything he had imagined and hoped for, secretly, in his heart. She was still very different from all that; her eyes, for example. Theodora had mentioned them, something about her bold, teasing look – but she hadn't said a word about their unique color, that mixture of blue and gray (he had once photographed a similar color – autumn clouds in the skies above Hatsofim Mountain at dawn). Also the way they were placed so far apart from each other, her eyes, as if there was room between them, quiet; *space*.

He had so many things to tell her, and didn't open his mouth. Not because he was afraid of her, but because this is how he always was with girls, with every girl, almost. And when he was with a girl who really excited him, he could feel himself starting to descend, step after step, submissive, accepting, down the ladder of evolution.

He sat, clasped his hands over his knees, and waited. The skinny guy rocked back and forth, his eyes closed, as if both of them were her prisoners. The longer the silence stretched, the more Assaf's anger at himself grew: after this entire arduous journey he had taken, traveling so far to find her, he had hoped he would be a little different with her. He had felt himself starting to change a little, even with Leah – and what had come out of all of it? He was still the same miserable soul, afraid to open his mouth.

Suddenly the guy said, without opening his eyes, 'Isn't that Dinka?'

'Dinka?' Tamar shivered, and looked in the direction of the barking.

Assaf said, 'I brought her to you.'

'*You* brought her? But how . . . from where . . . ?'

'Doesn't matter. I had to bring her to you, so I did.' He sent his hand to his shirt pocket and touched the paper there, the barely legible printed-up letters of Form 76. 'Never mind,' he muttered, crumpling it into a little paper ball and shoving it into his pocket. Subtract another 150 shekels toward a telescopic lens he would not be buying this year.

Tamar stepped backward quickly, not taking her eyes off Assaf. She climbed the little hill, and when she yelled 'Dinka!' the dog simply tore the belt off the bush and flew to her. A cloud of dust rose where they met, and cries of amazement, and barks. Assaf watched it and, even with all the pain, had to smile. He scrambled up, trying to recover. He knew that now he would simply leave here, return home, and for the rest of his life hate himself for being such a loser – and still was unable to change anything. If Roi had come here instead of him, he would have already started talking, charming her with exaggerated tales of adventure; mainly, he would make her laugh. Make her laugh? Just that? Hah. He would have her rolling on the ground in laughter.

As soon as he moved, she raised the two-by-four in front of her. Assaf took two steps forward, shrugged, showed her his hands were empty – if she just let him pass he would go home. His mission here was over, and tomorrow was another workday at City Hall. Tamar looked at him in doubt, because his entire internal debate was sketched on his face, which now seemed full of sorrow and strife. She didn't understand who he was, and for a moment she wasn't so sure that he really was dangerous – but she was still scared. When he took another step in her direction, she spat, 'Dinka, go!' Assaf looked at her, stunned (he couldn't, of course, have known that Tamar's father had agreed to buy her a dog, only under the condition that it undergo special training to protect Tamar, if necessary. Now, nine years later, Tamar suddenly remembered that strange condition). Dinka's ears pricked up and she didn't move. 'Go, Dinka, go!' Tamar yelled, frightened, unwittingly imitating the South African accent of the trainer. Dinka took a few steps, went over to Assaf, rubbed her head against his knee, and put her nose into his palm. Tamar stood, amazed. She had never seen Dinka make this gesture to anyone but her. Assaf said, 'Someone found her walking through the city and brought her to City Hall. I'm working there over summer break –'

'In City Hall?'

'Yeah, my father knows someone there – never mind. So I walked around with her a little. We were looking for you.'

Tamar looked at Dinka, as if asking her to confirm his words. Dinka looked right, looked left, passed her tongue over her muzzle, then rose on her hind legs and placed her paws on Assaf's chest. Tamar let the wood fall from her hand. 'I can see you also got beaten up on the way,' she said. He passed a hand over his collection of injuries.

'I don't usually look like this,' he said, embarrassed.

'I don't usually hit like this.'

Assaf didn't say anything. Shifted his weight from one foot to the other, scratched his ankle with his shoe. 'Oh, you have a few messages,' he suddenly remembered. 'From Theodora, and from the pizza man, also from Victorious, and Leah, and Noa. And from a guy named Honigman who was at Leah's place.' With every name, her eyes grew larger. 'And from someone in Lifta, Sergei, and also from a detective who once almost caught you, and a girl who plays the cello in the Walking Street with a red hat.'

Tamar took one step toward him. He thought she had eyes like a wolf, sober, sad. 'Did you meet *all* of them?'

He scratched Dinka with embarrassment. 'She took me to meet them.'

Shai was off to one side, swaying and mumbling by the rock. Neither of them took any notice. For each of them the world was only a pair of eyes. Tamar came closer to Assaf. She studied him with total absorption, forgetting herself, as if she were draining something out of his eyes, his face, his big, clumsy body. Assaf didn't move. Usually such a look would be torture, make him bubble and stumble. Now he felt only a slight weakness in his legs.

'I am Tamar.'

'Yes, I know.' After a second he remembered. 'I am Assaf.'

A moment of embarrassment. Should we shake hands? Too formal. They had already gone to a deeper place than that sometime before.

Tamar escaped first. She pointed: 'And this is my brother, Shai.'

'Your brother?'

'My brother. Why, didn't you know?'

'All this time I thought he was – I mean, that you and he – but I didn't know at all!'

She understood immediately. 'You thought he was my boyfriend?'

Assaf laughed nervously, blushed, shrugged. A tiny wheel in his brain started turning, more quickly than the others, making a noise that went somewhere along the lines of 'So, if that's the case, then maybe – maybe –' Things started moving inside Assaf in a new and confusing rhythm; in his soul, in his body, he felt the wild notion that some new tenant was now breaking into him, immediately starting to *furnish* him inside at a wild tempo, moving heavy tables and tossing out moldy armoires, bringing in something light, airy, flexible, bamboo-like. All of a sudden Assaf felt that he had to settle a very important matter between them, now. He took off her backpack and handed it to her. She snatched it up, hugged it to her chest, and stared at Assaf, suspicious. 'Even this –?'

He straightened his shoulders, preparing for the blow he was about to deliver. 'Listen, uh – I read through the notebooks a little. I mean – I had no choice.'

'You read my *diary*?' she screamed, utterly taken aback. It hurt him when she distanced herself by even one step. 'You read my diary?' Her eyes went black with rage; in a blink the war flag of her privacy flew over them, and Assaf knew he had lost her the moment he had found her.

With the same suddenness, she took the flag down and just

looked at him, her eyes pained, disappointed – but waiting for an explanation.

'I only read a little,' he mumbled. 'Just a few pages here and there. I thought that maybe, through the diary, I'd be able to find you, you understand –'

She didn't respond; curving her lips a little, pensively, as she always did when she was thinking. Even in the midst of her rage, she was amazed that he had told her so soon after he had met her, because he could have hidden it and she would never have known. Strange, she thought, how he seemed to need to get it off his chest at once, as if he didn't want there to be any lies or concealment between them.

'So you read it,' she repeated slowly, trying to grasp that thing that was not yet completely clear: he had read her private diary. It was the worst thing anyone could have done to her. Now he knew about her, he knew her and the way things stood between her and herself. She looked at him cautiously – he didn't seem particularly appalled or disgusted. She blinked a little, nonplussed. Something new was happening here – she needed time to understand it.

Assaf mistook her silence: 'Look, don't worry, I've forgotten all of it by now, anyway.'

She felt a strange pinch of sorrow. 'No, no, don't forget anything,' she said quickly, surprising him, but herself even more. 'Everything you read there is me; it's who I am. Now you know.'

He said, 'Not really.' He actually wanted to say, I would actually like to know more, but it was almost impossible for him to speak in long sentences without having to swallow in the middle of them.

'So what now?' she asked, a little embarrassed by his size and how close they were still standing, face-to-face. 'I mean, what do we do now?'

Suddenly she missed her long, thick hair. At least she could have hidden behind it a little, and wouldn't feel so bare, almost naked. And why was she saying such nonsense? What was this mutual 'do'? What did they have to do together? Did she have anything to do with him? She tried to step backward and couldn't; fissures opened within her.

'Whatever you decide.'

'What, what did you say?' She didn't understand. The warmth flowing from his body was a lot clearer to her than his rough, awkward words. He was silent. Why was he so quiet? She hugged herself with her arms, as if it had grown cold. She lowered her head and smiled to herself a smile she hadn't used in a long time – but then again, nothing made her laugh, right? She glanced at his left ear, his right sneaker, licked her lower lip, which was dry, shrugged for no reason, moving her shoulders and rubbing her arms, feeling as if she had no control over any of it. Her body was starting to move as if it were playing out some role in an ancient ritual, or in a dance whose rules had been prearranged, millions of years in advance, and were out of her control.

'Anything I decide?' She smiled. Her heart made a quick slalom. Assaf smiled back, shrugged, and stretched his arms above his head. Suddenly his whole body contracted; he kicked the earth a little to loosen his legs, ran his hand through his messy hair. His back was itching terribly – his upper back, between the shoulders, in that place you can't reach on your own.

Her smile widened a little. 'But you said that you came here to bring Dinka to me, so you did, didn't you? What now?'

He gazed profoundly at the tips of his sneakers; he had never noticed their remarkable design, the fascinating combination between the body of the shoe, which was black, and the soles, which were white. After a moment they seemed silly and ugly, and, most of all, terribly large. How could he have been walking around in these monsters for a whole year now? No wonder everyone had been laughing at him, no wonder Dafi was so embarrassed by him; the only remaining, fatal question was: Had Tamar noticed them already? Or could he, perhaps, still save something? He quickly moved one of them behind the other, and almost lost his balance. Oh great. This was the last thing he needed right now – to fall down, right here, in front of her. What do you do, damnit? His face felt hot; who knew how many pimples were popping out on his face, right this minute, and the itch in his back was driving him crazy. What was wrong with him?

Again, he stretched his shoulders, and the full length of his arms, then crossed them over his chest as if to pull strength from himself. He said what he didn't believe he would dare. 'If you want me to . . . I mean, maybe you want me to stay?'

'Yes, yes.' She went silent, and panicked. Where had those two yeses come from? Was that what she wanted? When had such a will evolved in her? What did she have to do with him – she didn't know him at all. Why would she ever make him participate in this, her most fatal and private affair? 'Wait a second.' She forced herself to laugh, suddenly many years more mature than he. 'Do you even know what you're getting into?'

Assaf hesitated. He understood that she was running away from somebody, he said, and he could see that Shai was not in the best –

'He's been on heroin for almost a year.' Tamar cut him off, examining his reaction. She was relieved by what she saw in his face. 'I've been here with him for two days. He's having a good moment right now, but just before you showed up, we were in the middle of –'

'Yes,' Assaf said. 'I heard. But why is he like that?'

'He's in withdrawal. Do you know what that is?'

Assaf nodded; another new possibility, no less exciting than the others, took form in his mind – perhaps the drugs she'd bought weren't for her?

'So tonight and tomorrow and tomorrow night will be the peak' – she reported in a stiff voice, carefully checking the effect of her words on him – 'the peak of the withdrawal. At least this is what some . . . experts told me.'

'Leah?'

'*What?*' She was so shocked that the cover of formality was torn from her voice, leaving it exposed, naked of all estrangements. 'Yes. Leah's been through it, too.' Silence. She peered at him, vaguely aware that he would surprise her again and again in all kinds of ways. She also knew she didn't have the time to digest this now and had better return at once to the solid ground of fact. 'Usually, in his condition, it takes up to four or five days, withdrawal. We've already been through two and a half; so think about whether you really want to stay, because it's not going to be easy.' She lingered, adding with tired seriousness, 'Because what do you need this for?'

'What? No, that's fine, just tell me something.'

'Yes?'

She had turned to help Shai, who had thrown out his hands for help like a weak baby; she had also turned around to give Assaf the chance to leave now that he knew, before he felt any obligation.

He already stood beside her. 'So why . . . why is he actually in such bad shape? Doesn't he have the drug here?'

'He's trying to get over it here. We . . .' She didn't know how to say it. 'We're here, working together, so he'll get over it.'

Shai screamed; sharp pain racked his body. Within a second, he went from half-asleep to curled up in pain and howling. Tamar looked at Assaf; their intimate moment was over. Her eyes said, 'Are you staying?' His eyes said yes. 'Then let's take him back to the cave,' she said. Assaf had more questions; he also had things to tell her, about Theodora going outside – but now he had to act, to be nothing more than a decisive action. He caught Shai under the arms and helped him stand up; he was surprised by the lightness of the body he was holding; it was as if Shai were completely hollow. Shai grabbed Assaf's shoulders with the fingers of a drowning man. Assaf thought how strange it was – they hadn't even spoken one word to each other, he and Shai, and they were already entangled like this.

This thought came back to him a few dozen times that evening and night, until it melted away. Shai was screaming and crying and vomiting all around him. Sometimes he lay, staring, scratching his arms and legs until he bled. About once a minute he would yawn a noisy, big yawn, until his jaws nearly popped out. One moment he would fall asleep, exhausted – then the next, his body would twitch and jerk almost into the air with the force of the pain. Assaf and Tamar tended him continuously, cleaning and washing and wiping, changing his clothes, giving him things to drink. Assaf didn't even notice the sun sinking, the night deepening. Time was composed not of moments but of actions; in every moment, something else needed to be done. Only Shai's voice could be heard in the cave; Tamar and Assaf hardly spoke to each other. They quickly developed a language of eye signals and hand gestures instead, like an operating-room team, or two deep-sea divers. Assaf erased from his mind any thoughts of the world outside the cave. There was no world. There were no people dear to him. There was no Rhino who might call the police to search for him, and there were no people chasing after both him and Tamar. When he thought about the two days Tamar had been here alone with Shai, he didn't understand how she could have borne it. Later, he realized that she probably hadn't closed her eyes once since she'd arrived here; but she uttered not a single word of complaint. She leaned over Shai, in front of him. He passed a towel to her. She gave him the empty water bottle and signaled him, with her eyes, to bring a full one over. Her lips curved into the words 'toilet paper' and Assaf thought she had lips as beautiful as a picture. He went to the corner of the cave and brought two rolls. She had already removed Shai's pants. Assaf took the filthy toilet paper from her hand. At the same time, they both noticed Shai was wearing Snoopy-print boxer shorts; they both stared at them, and then at each other, to confirm that it was really true. Snoopy, in the middle of all this.

An hour, and another hour. Three hours, five hours, eight. In the few moments Shai slept, they hardly spoke, because they were tired, but also because it seemed strange to strike up a polite, first-date conversation, like two people who have just met. They lay on the ground, across the second mattress, beside Shai's sleeping form, their legs resting on the ground. They breathed deeply, gazed at the ceiling, at the walls of the cave, tried, and failed, to sleep a little. They were careful not to touch, and each felt, in the other's presence, charged with new and exciting powers; but those powers also agitated them too much to permit sleep. Sometimes Tamar would flash a slightly miserable smile at him, a smile sympathetic to his troubles – you never asked for any of this, her smile apologized, and Assaf would respond with his best smile, his most trusting smile. But she saw that he was slowly being worn down, that he was losing out to it – not the physical effort, he seemed completely solid, made of strong stuff – but because of Shai's torments, because of this reality he was suddenly plunged into, with no preparation.

At two in the morning, Shai woke up out of his mind and started looking for a fix. He was certain Tamar was hiding another one there. He interrogated her over and over. How much, exactly, had she bought from the dealer in Tziyyon Square? Half a bundle, right? That's five fixes. So where is the fifth? I've taken four already, so where is the fifth?

The explanations didn't help; she had already told him a thousand times, he used up the entire stash while they were still at Leah's. He ran around the cave like an animal, tore through the groceries she had stacked up, searched in the guitar she had brought from home, in his shoes, made her and Assaf take their shoes off and looked in there as well. In his insanity, he managed to uncover the hollow where Tamar had hidden the cattle prod and the handcuffs. He sat and stared at them for a long moment. Tamar thought that once he had discovered what she had prepared for him, those things that, in her stupidity, she thought she would have the courage to use, he would murder her. But his mind was working in a completely different way; his world was divided into only two things: his fix and everything that was not his fix. The hand-cuffs didn't interest him. His brain didn't interpret the cattle prod as something that could help him now. Assaf saw them, however, guessed at their use, and looked in shock at Tamar. She shrugged: What choice did I have? Assaf began to see the dim outlines of everything Tamar had planned and done.

Later, Shai collapsed in despair, and started to ransack his mattress. He made holes in the foam along its length and width; every once in a while, he would produce a moan of hope, a cry of joy, then thump the mattress in disappointment. Assaf and Tamar watched him, motionless. Assaf thought, He doesn't care at all that I'm here – he's completely indifferent to the fact that someone else has joined Tamar, he's interested in just one thing. Tamar thought it was interesting – how long would Assaf be able to handle this insanity? When would he say goodbye and break away, or just disappear without saying a word? At one point, when she was busy with Shai, she could feel through her back that Assaf was at the mouth of the cave. She took a quick glance backward and saw him standing up straight for a moment, stretching to his full height, inhaling the cool night air. She willed herself not to look, to give him one more chance to take another step outside, and another, and disappear. What does he need any of this for, she thought. Why would any normal human being get involved in this? People who were closer to her disappeared in situations that were a lot easier to deal with than this. Afterward, when she heard his quiet humming behind her as he took a water bottle from her, or the dirty clothes, or whatever was burdening her at that moment, her body coursed with gentle streams of warmth.

Shai pulled himself up with difficulty and crawled on all fours to one corner of the cave. He tried to claw through the hard earth; for a few minutes, only the sounds of his digging and his quick gasps could be heard. They couldn't take their eyes off him; it was like watching a nightmare while awake. He dug quickly; grains of dirt flew behind him; strange growls escaped his mouth. But suddenly he cocked his head. His eyes sparkled at them along with a mischievous, but totally sane, smile. 'Will you at least tell me if I'm hot or cold?'

And the three of them burst into rolling, surprised laughter, like three kids at summer camp. Shai laughed, too; for a blink of an eye, he could see himself as he looked from the outside. He waggled his behind at them, and Tamar fell down, lay on her back, exhausted by the tension of the past scene, stretched her arms, and laughed until tears came to her eyes; through her tears, she peeked at Assaf. He had a sweet, masculine laugh.

Later, the pain returned; Shai claimed that all the bones in his body were falling apart from the pain, he could feel them crushed and crackling, his muscles tearing – this is what he said – dividing, shrinking, and curling up inside his body. He didn't know he had muscles in so many places – behind his ears, for example, in his gums; Tamar, who could still recall how, at home, he was able to describe every passing stomachache in whiny detail, had to overcome the repulsion that the description itself – not the pain – aroused in her. She tried to take his mind off it, to cheer him up a little. She spoke about the diaphragm, which is a kind of a muscle there is no way to actually feel, and still, you can't sing without it. She impersonated Halina for him, ordering Tamar to 'support! Support from the diaphragm!' She performed a whole routine of Halina, and how she would react when she heard about Tamar singing in the streets. 'Oh really? And they liked it? Very interesting . . . but tell me, how could you sing so high after Kurt Weill? You could never do that for me; after you sing Kurt Weill for me, you always take a break . . .' Shai didn't laugh. Assaf laughed a lot. In spite of how serious he looked, Tamar saw it was easy to make him laugh. She enjoyed doing it. She thought that Idan had never laughed at her jokes; perhaps he didn't even have a sense of humor. And Assaf discovered the dimple Theodora had told him about and started to piece together what Tamar had been doing on the streets over the last month. He wondered if he would ever hear her sing; he decided to start following concert advertisements in the newspapers, and if he found her name, he would – then the bubble of his illusions burst: he was only dreaming. He didn't even know her full name! But he didn't have time to lose heart, because Shai started hallucinating about some maggot, he called it the 'craving,' and it was crawling through him, sucking him up from the inside; he felt it crawling, devouring his flesh with every turn. He thought he was falling apart completely, into organs, muscle fibers, cells, in its mouth. His legs ran away from himself, he started convulsing severely; then his hands flew off. Assaf saw it and couldn't believe it; the long, skinny body looked as if it were tearing itself apart in shuddering spasms. Tamar lay on him and held him down forcibly; Assaf saw the small, almondlike muscles in her arms, and just as Theodora promised, his heart simply flapped its wings and flew to her. She didn't stop talking to Shai, telling him she loved him, and that she would help him, that in a day or two it would be over and a new life would begin. In the tangle of arms and legs, Shai suddenly went limp and fell asleep.

She rolled off him. Not a drop of energy was left in her. There were sweat stains under her armpits, and stains of Shai's vomit and urine on her overalls. Assaf could smell her, and knew that she could smell him, too. She lay down, watching Assaf with those wide-open eyes of hers, eyes that saw too much. She had the feeling that she was completely naked to him here, and she didn't care; and she didn't have the strength to understand what was happening to her. At first, for instance, it bothered her that Assaf could see Shai naked, because of the damage to Shai's own privacy; but also because she herself was exposed along with her brother's flesh: it was the material from which she, too, was made. After a few hours she had gotten used to it. Now she tried to sleep. She heard Assaf getting up quietly, going to the mouth of the cave. She examined herself and couldn't find, anywhere, the tremor of anxiety over whether he would run away; they'd probably crossed some border together, she thought. He went out, his body swallowed by the darkness. Dinka sat up and looked, too. One minute passed, and another. Tamar thought, bravely, that it was very good for him to get some fresh air, even go for a little walk; perhaps he even went to take a piss. Another minute passed. She heard no footsteps from the outside. Tamar told herself that she would always be grateful for what he had done, even if he didn't come back. Then she thought, with wonder, that she didn't know his full name. Dinka's tail started thumping, raising dust from the ground. The form of Assaf's body reappeared from the darkness. Dinka lay back down, and Tamar began breathing again. He came and lay alongside her, across the mattress, not touching her. She felt what pleasure there is even in good breathing; she heard his quiet breath by her side, and for some reason, it made her happy to hear him. She thought it was a strange way to get to know someone, to make friends with someone, because this is what is happening between us, she thought cautiously, we're somehow becoming friends, getting closer to each other. It wasn't very clear how it was happening – almost without words, without any concrete knowledge – without anything *happening*. Now that he was lying so close to her, she was even amused by how little she knew about him. Where did he live? Where did he go to school? Did he have friends or a girlfriend? All these facts were unknown to her, and still, she felt that there was something about him which she already knew – something clear, solid, which, for the time being, was also enough for her.

There were also moments when it hurt – it was all mixed up. Something, perhaps something new, was happening here – at a time when she had to be completely devoted to Shai, with no distractions. She was too tired to clarify for herself what the precise problem was – at any other time, she would rush to sharpen such a conclusion, sharp as a knife, but at the moment, she didn't have the power or the desire to do so. She only felt a certain disjunction within her: as if Shai was becoming, for a time, only the reason for this new connection. There – she had managed to figure it out, after all. She got scared, sat up for a moment, looked around the cave. She saw the fluorescent camp light blink and fade. She checked that Shai was sleeping, that Dinka was sleeping, that Assaf was looking at her. She lay back down. More than anything, it was disturbing to think that Shai couldn't even understand what was floating through the air around him – or perhaps it was all just in her imagination? Perhaps it was another romantic fantasy and Assaf wasn't interested at all? Perhaps he was just a good guy who decided to help her out? In her terrible fatigue, she rolled over – her hand hit Assaf's chest. Oh sorry. Never mind. For a moment I forgot you were here. Where else would I be? I'm falling asleep a little, is that okay?

Sleep. You haven't slept at all in the last two days, have you? I don't really remember. I don't think so. Sleep. I'll be awake.

When he told her to sleep, told her he would stay awake, when he so gently, delicately, took on the burden of standing guard – no, it was better not to think about that now. For a moment, she was almost tempted to expose the terrible weight that had her by the throat, to tell him everything that had happened to her since she had begun her journey, and what she had endured here in the cave with Shai during the first two days, because if there is a hell, she thought, it was here during those two days alone with him, before Assaf came. But she felt that if she even opened her mouth a peep, allowed another tiny scratch in her armor, a stream would burst from her that could take her apart in a minute. She shouldn't do it yet, she shouldn't. Besides, she told herself, panicking slightly, she hardly knew him, really.

She turned on her side, facing him, smelling his sweat, and thought how much fun it would be to take a shower after all this was over. Perhaps they would meet again, after all this had passed, when it was all over, in the outside world. In a coffeehouse, perhaps; they could show up, all washed and clean and perfumed, and tell each other who they really were. Perhaps she would buy him some expensive deodorant as a funny thank-you gift. Here, again, she wasn't thinking about Shai, she was letting herself daydream, as if someone always had to be a sacrifice, she thought, so that others would be able to start something new. What are you talking about? she scolded herself. What do you mean, something new? He's not even thinking about anything involving you. She fell asleep, as she was, muddled by those confusing thoughts, lying on the ground.

Assaf sat up and watched her sleep, his heart overflowing. He wanted to cover her, wipe the dust from her face, do something good for her. The best thing he could do was not to wake her, so he didn't move, only watched her, endlessly thinking how beautiful she was. She moaned and curled up on her side, her head resting on her folded hands. She had long, delicate fingers; a thin silver chain, almost invisible, encircled her dirty ankle. He looked at her and couldn't be satisfied. He talked to her in his head, conducting a lively conversation: You know, I've never seen eyes like yours; *Yes, I've been told that here and there. By the by, do you know how I got them to be like this?* From looking at the world with wonder? *Oh, it's impossible to be with you! You read absolutely everything, didn't you?* No, just a few pages here and there. *It's not fair that you know all those things about me and I don't know a thing about you! Would you, for example, be willing to let me read your diary?* I don't have a diary. *But if you did?* If I did? *Yes, if you did, would you, would you be willing?* What do you need my diary for when for you I'd recite the whole thing?

She opened her eye a crack and saw him smiling to himself, his fingers clasped together like a child making a wish, and she fell peacefully back to sleep. Assaf stood up, stretched. At some point, he thought, no later than tomorrow, he would have to call Rhino and his parents in America before Rhino alerted the entire Israeli police force. The thought annoyed him – the outside world was sending a cold hand in, tapping him on the shoulder, again raising the question of how to tell Rhino about Reli. It seemed even more complicated now, and he didn't know why: perhaps because until now, he realized, he couldn't even begin to grasp what Rhino felt toward his sister. Perhaps. But perhaps it was hard for Reli to deal with Rhino as well. He stood up in the fluorescent light, which was dwindling away. He searched through the cave, found the bag with batteries that Tamar had prepared – he could tell at once that she had bought the wrong batteries. He remembered how he always, in his heart, had blamed Reli for not loving Rhino enough; it was always so clear to him, to everyone, actually, that Rhino loved her so much *more* than she loved him – you couldn't even compete with all his love and care and generosity toward her. He searched between the groceries and canned food, found a few packages of cookies closed with wire twist ties, and started to peel the plastic wrap off them. He was uncomfortable with his thoughts. For example, Rhino repeated and talked about missing Reli so much, it had become a ritual, some unavoidable part of their conversations; Assaf could repeat, by heart, word for word, Rhino's moanings over Reli: how he had lost her, what a fatal mistake it was not to press her into marrying him right after the army, what an idiot he was to agree to her decision to go to America. He pulled the wires from the plastic wrap and twisted them together into two long strands. He pulled out a roll of black tape from his jeans ('Electrician's tape is also like a handkerchief,' his father would say); then he placed the six little batteries side by side, minus to plus and plus to minus, taped the wires to the batteries, and taped the ends of the wires to the lamp. And to tell the truth, it was okay to do that now – they never, in all their conversations, actually spoke about Reli herself, about how she felt, Assaf thought. His heart ached and he didn't know why, or because of whom, and he felt nervous, felt that he might be betraying Rhino with these thoughts. Instead, he considered what would happen now to Rhino, and how he would stand the news from America, how he would go on living when he discovered that the woman he loved wouldn't stay with him.

When he opened his eyes (he must have fallen asleep without noticing it), Shai wasn't in the cave. In a blink, Assaf jumped up, wondering whether he should wake Tamar; not yet, he decided. He whistled quietly to Dinka and went outside. It was almost light; a pink stripe stretched through the skies from the east. Assaf ran, Dinka by his side; he tried one direction and found nothing; tried another direction, nothing there, either. He stayed as calm as he could, knowing that Shai, in his condition, couldn't go far. Only this knowledge let him postpone the court-martial he had brought against himself. Dinka ran before him, searching, sniffing. Assaf trusted her more than he trusted himself. He ran after her. Only now did he notice how, since coming here, Dinka had stepped aside, as if she felt her job had ended the moment she introduced him to Tamar. In the middle of their desperate running, he called her to him, bent over her, stroked her fur, and pressed her head against his, their scents mingling together, and she stood still, absorbing him again – and again they turned to run.

A truck passed in the road above them; Assaf got scared: Shai mustn't get to the road; he'd get run over, and if he didn't get run over, he'd hitchhike to the city, and once there, he'd manage to find a fix, and the first full three days of withdrawal, all that effort, would have been for nothing. There was also a worse scenario: the moment Shai got to the city, whoever was searching for him would discover him. Assaf started sweating all of a sudden; he wanted to kill himself for falling asleep and letting Tamar down.

Shai was standing on the slope, by a bold pine tree, hunched over, green splashes dribbling from his mouth. Assaf ran to him and caught him just before he fell. Shai's eyes were already rolling back in his head, and still he muttered to Assaf not to stop him now, that he had to get to the road. He even offered Assaf money, a bribe, if he told him where Tamar had hidden the fix. Assaf put his arm between Shai's legs and hoisted him over his shoulders, the way you carry an injured man, walked back with him to the bottom of the valley, found the little hill, and slid back into the cave. A moment before they went in, Shai pressed forcefully on Assaf's neck, making him stop. 'Do me a favor, please – if she is asleep, don't tell her I left. Please, don't tell her, don't tell her,' he begged. Assaf thought about it for a moment: his loyalty to Tamar versus Shai's passionate desire not to disappoint her. 'Okay. But this is the last time you try to run away.' Shai moved his long fingers – it was probably a yes. Assaf laid him back down on the mattress, arranging his thin limbs as if he were arranging a rag doll. Tamar heard their movement by her and woke up. She opened her eyes, stretched with pleasure, momentarily forgetful. 'Mmmm ... I slept so much ... Hey, you, why are you up?' Assaf was silent. Shai looked at him pleadingly. Assaf shrugged. 'Nothing. I just wanted to stretch a little.' Tamar smiled at him, a sweet morning smile. Shai, from his mattress, fluttered his eyelids at him as a thank you. A spark of pure, living emotion passed through his murky eyes, and Assaf smiled back at him. Tamar saw the exchange of looks; she closed her eyes and thought maybe everything would work out after all.

The new day that shone was a little easier than the previous one. Shai suffered less, but was still moved to spend hours searching for his fix in the mattress and the corners of the cave. He was certain that he had seen the missing fix yesterday, had actually seen it, only now it was hard for him to remember where. Assaf and Tamar had stopped answering his repeated questions. They massaged his legs regularly to alleviate the pain and get the blood circulating. Every hour they made him take a few sips of water, and sometimes Assaf had to hold him down so that Tamar would be able to pour a few drops into his mouth with a baby dropper. When she did that, he looked like a sick, overgrown chick. When her eyes met Assaf's, she knew he was now seeing the same picture, in exactly the same way, perhaps even in the same words, and felt a slight tingling, as if, for the blink of an eye, she had peeked into Assaf's innermost being. It struck her what she used to think, that she was missing the Lego part in her soul that could connect her to another person. Perhaps this matter, too, now requires some reexamination, she thought.

Below, deep in the valley, there was a little brook, thin as a string. She went to it, carrying the dirty sheets and their clothes. While she crouched there, rubbing the clothes through the water, she thought that since she had first entered Pesach's home, she had hardly had any time alone; it had been one of the hardest things for her there, because since childhood, she had always needed to be alone with herself, for at least an hour or two each day. She needed it the way she needed air. Now she was a bit confused, because from the moment Assaf had arrived, she could actually allow herself these short 'vacations,' to walk around the valley a little, breathe by herself. And somehow – it was as if that deep need disappeared. She washed herself in the spring water and rose from her bathing as happy as a girl: '*Friends give it water / like a spring on a hot day . . .*' she sang cheerfully, hanging the clothes to dry on the branches of a bush in a hidden place by the cave. '. . . *Like a spring on a hot day / this is why it is in love . . .*' and stopped herself in time, laughing at her foolishness. She gave herself a sharp talking-to, and soon returned to her senses, reminding herself what was what – but as she did she actually stood and gazed at her blue overalls blowing lightly in the breeze next to Assaf's T-shirt.

She had prepared clothes to change into, but Assaf didn't have anything else, so he wore some of the clothes she had brought for Shai – the few that fit him. Later, when those got dirty, too, he wore one of her big T-shirts, one of those she'd brought especially to serve as work clothes here. It was from her fat period, she told him, and he said it was hard for him to believe she ever could be fat. She laughed – Wait until you see the pictures, I was like an elephant! And his heart expanded in joy, because there was a hint of a future in that 'wait until you see.'

Oops, Assaf thought when she took out her toothbrush, 'I don't have one.'

'Use mine,' she said, after she finished. And Assaf – yes, yes, if his mother saw this with her own eyes, it would be the most unbelievable part of this entire epic adventure – brushed his teeth with her toothbrush, without missing a beat.

The vomiting stopped. The huge yawns, too. Diarrhea started, and that was also a test that had to be passed, and they passed it together, both of them; actually, the three of them, because Shai was starting to be himself again. Shame returned as well, and he started asking questions about Assaf, who he was and what he was doing there, and Tamar said, simply, He's a friend.

But when Assaf told her he had to go back to the city for an hour or two, her face grew so sad that Assaf almost gave up going. 'It's okay, go,' she said, as if she had decided instantly, without the possibility of appeal, that he would never be back. She sat down with sudden exhaustion, her back to him, and seemed angry with herself for wanting to believe in him. He explained to her exactly the things he had to do. He tried to speak in the most reasonable, calm way he knew how, but he felt that she had already built a wall between them, and he didn't know what to do to calm her. Besides, how could she even dare to doubt him after their night? He looked at her angrily, despairingly, feeling how that complicated, twisted part of her was rising and taking control over her – how she gave herself away to the rat's attack with a strange pleasure; and he felt he would never be able to convince her with words alone.

When he left the cave, she got up and thanked him for everything he had done – her politeness was almost insulting. He said goodbye to Shai as well and, mainly, to Dinka, who also seemed worried when he walked out: she ran after him, and then to Tamar, stitching up, again and again, what was being pulled apart between them. When he had already gone far from the cave, he turned around, because he heard – or thought he heard – Tamar calling him silently, as if checking to see whether he could hear her that way. He ran to her, almost flying on a wave of painful excitement. Tamar herself was shocked by the wave that washed over her at the sight of him returning. Yes, what did you want? he asked, panting. Why did you come back, she wondered. Because you called me, and also because I forgot to give you a letter from Leah. A letter from Leah? Yes, she gave this to me for you, but when I got here there was the matter with the plank and the head and we started with Shai and I forgot. He gave her the letter. They stood in front of each other, formal, torn apart. She folded the letter in her hand and crumpled it. He saw a blue vein beating rapidly in her throat and almost sent a finger out to soothe it. Only then did he remember to ask why she had called him. 'Why?' Tamar wondered. 'Oh, wait a minute, yes, listen.'

She asked him whether he would be willing to do her one huge last favor. Assaf spread his arms out in despair, even stomped his foot. Why the *last* favor? Why? But he didn't say anything. He wrote down the telephone number she gave him and listened to her instructions, the many detailed warnings she gave him, and the question she asked him to ask them. In fact, the mission seemed a little too big, and entirely unsuitable for him, and she knew it. 'Clearly, I'm the one who needs to talk to them. I know. But how can I from here?' He said he would do it. 'Then tell me one more time what you're going to say to them,' and she made him repeat the question exactly the way she wanted it asked, and he repeated it, a little amused by his first look at her tough side, but also unnerved by the strange entanglement of her family affairs, now exposed to him in all their ugliness. She felt it, too, of course, and after he had successfully passed the test and repeated after her precisely, her hands dropped and all the toughness evaporated. 'Look at me; I'm telling you things I've never even told my best friends.' 'Listen, I'll be back at three.' 'Yes, yes, I need to go back to Shai.' And she turned back to the cave, being realistic to the point of pain, knowing how hard it would be for him to return to this hell after he tasted, for a moment, his normal life.

He climbed to the road, caught a bus, and took his bearings, noting landmarks and street names, until he could locate exactly where Leah had brought him when his eyes were closed. Back home, he listened to the messages on the machine. (Roi called again, and with a cautious voice suggested that perhaps he and Assaf should meet for a man-to-man talk. It seemed to him that Assaf was stressed out, going through some kind of tough time, and they'd better clear it up, yes? No, Assaf said, and skipped over to the next message.) His parents said that they were going for a three-day trip through the desert and he shouldn't worry about them. Assaf smiled: three days . . . they always gave him exactly what he needed, even in their disappearances from his life. He listened again to their cheerful voices: they were already fully recovered from their jet lag; they had visited Jeremy's high-tech company that morning, and even Father, who'd been an electrician for thirty years, said he had never seen anything like it.

Then there were seven messages in a row, all from Rhino; the last one said that if Assaf didn't call him by twelve, then he, Rhino, was calling the police.

He had ten minutes left. He drank three glasses of mango juice, one after the other, and called the workshop. Rhino's roar silenced the noise of the machines behind him for a moment, and Assaf remembered instantly exactly why he loved Rhino so much, as if he even had a need to remember that. Assaf told him everything, not hiding anything except for the news from the United States and what was happening to him when he was with Tamar (meaning – the most important things). Rhino listened without interrupting – that was another thing Assaf liked about him: you could tell him an entire story, from beginning to end, and he wouldn't interrupt you with lots of dumb questions. When he'd finished, Rhino quietly said, 'So you did it, huh? You turned Jerusalem upside down and inside out, but eventually you found her ... You want to know the truth, Assaf? I never thought you'd pull it off.' It was only then, for the first time, that Assaf actually grasped that he had managed to do it, to find Tamar. Odd that the thought had never occurred to him before – maybe it was because, from the moment he'd found her, he had been plunged into the new mission of caring for Shai, and once that happened, who even had time to breathe? Rhino then asked quickly, with military precision, a few matter-of-fact questions: Did Assaf know the people who were chasing Tamar and Shai? Were Tamar and Shai, in Assaf's opinion, in danger from these people? Where exactly was Leah's restaurant, and was it possible for him to describe a few landmarks to locate the cave, in case of emergency? Three times he warned Assaf to make sure he wasn't being followed now, because as long as he was hidden in the valley he was protected, but walking around he was an easy target, and there was probably someone looking for him. Then he casually asked what was new in the Diaspora.

Assaf said he hadn't actually managed to talk to them, they'd only left him a message, a pretty dry one saying they were going on a trip for three days, but it sounded like everything was pretty much all right. He felt he was talking too fast, and hoped Rhino didn't hear it against the noise of the sharpeners and metal saws in the background.

Then he dialed the number he'd written down on a chocolate wrapper. That conversation lasted for just three minutes, but was even harder. He set a meeting time and place – at a coffeehouse in a mall, midway between their homes; he described himself so they could recognize him, remembering to include the recent developments in his looks.

He showered for a half-hour, put on clean clothes, and went to the mall. He felt disoriented as he walked through the bubble of air-conditioned air, between the polished stores. He seemed artificial to himself there, as if he were only a double of the real Assaf, who was off where he should be right now. With the emergency money his mother had left him in her sewing box, he bought four hamburgers (one for Dinka) and a few packs of chocolate bars, because Shai couldn't stop gorging on chocolate and had almost exhausted the supplies Tamar had prepared. When he walked among these lighthearted people, he remembered the feeling he sometimes had when he entered Muki's room while she slept: she used to sleep the way little children sleep – on her back, her arms and legs flopped out, abandoning herself to the world – and Assaf would sense, then, how innocent she was, unaware of anything – and feel a terrible need to protect her. He felt it again there, too, in the mall – that all those people walking around didn't really know what was going on so close to them, how dangerous, dark, and fragile life was.

When their meeting was over, he was sweating and exhausted; he almost considered going back home to take another shower. There was no physical cause for this feeling – he had met a couple of very clean, well-dressed, reserved people, slightly younger than his own parents, and a lot more educated than they; very rational, who hardly let him open his mouth. They were prepared with a better answer for everything he said, and despite the fact that *he* had come to talk to *them*, they behaved as if they were the ones doing him a favor. They also argued with him – especially the man – as if he were guilty of something, and they were struggling to make him understand, admit even, how right and hurt they were. Assaf simply did not know how to behave around them. He didn't even try to argue with them. He passed the information on that he was asked to pass, refused to give any further details, and asked only one question of them, the question Tamar wanted him to ask, and was amazed to see how hard it was for the man in front of him to give up, to bend, to agree to anything.

But the moment it happened, the man's face started to shake. First, the right eyebrow, which trembled like a creature with a life of its own – then it was as if his whole face was coming unstitched, and then the grown man began to cry bitterly into the palms of his hands. The woman also burst into tears, while people turned and stared; they didn't touch each other, or try to stroke, comfort, or calm each other down. They sat, separate, distinguished, and both wept their own terrible tears; Assaf knew, from the little Tamar had told him, that he was now witnessing the most impossible from these two: a complete collapse of their façades. He didn't know how to calm them down, so he talked about Tamar. They wept, and he spoke. He said she would help them, that they could trust her 1,000 percent, that everything would be fine, and other such nonsense. They couldn't stop sobbing; the tears had probably been gathering inside them for too long. After they had calmed down a little, they sat, speechless, miserable, even pitiful. Then the conversation started again from the beginning, as if they hadn't heard a single word he had said before that moment. They asked him hesitating, submissive questions he had no answer for, because he didn't know a lot about Shai and Tamar, or what they had gone through before he met them. They kept asking, even when he didn't know the answers; he had the feeling that these were questions they hadn't dared ask anyone this entire time, not even themselves. He sat silent, responding sometimes with a word or two. Eventually he had to stop them, because the hamburgers were getting cold, but mainly because he knew that Tamar was in the cave, certain he was never returning; that was an unbearable thought.

When he left, he thought how right his mother was, who was sometimes shocked by the thought that in order to perform the hardest, most important profession – that of parenting – you don't have to get the approval of any entrance committee, or even pass a minimal exam for certification.

The three of them sat outside the cave, devouring the food he'd brought. That is, Assaf devoured it, and Dinka with him; Shai was starting to taste here and there; only Tamar couldn't swallow a thing. Her eyes never left Assaf, and they were shining and happy, as if Assaf were a huge surprise gift. After they ate, they napped a little in the sun, lying out in a kind of triangle – Shai's head on Tamar's leg, whose head was on Assaf's leg, whose head was on her backpack – and Shai, for the first time, was talking about some of the things that had happened to him over the past year. Through his jeans, Assaf could feel Tamar shrinking as she heard about the places, the humiliations, the miseries Shai had endured. From time to time, Tamar also spoke, mentioning some amusing performance she had given in Ashdod, or in Nazareth, describing the endless driving and singing in the street in front of strangers. Assaf listened, spellbound, and thought that he would never be capable of doing what she did. Just to think about how she had planned this so far in advance without ever giving up or breaking down – truly, someone like her should have been a marathon runner.

Shai and Tamar started to swap stories of street performing, but they also spoke of Pesach; when they mentioned his braid, Assaf knew he was the man who had hit Theodora. But Tamar seemed so happy and lighthearted just then, he didn't want to tell her what they had done to Theodora. She spoke about the bulldogs and their pickpocketing, about the poor Russian woman, and the father and child in Zikhron Ya'Akov, and all the others she had seen robbed. Later, she and Shai demonstrated for Assaf the many ways people put coins in the hat. Shai directed, and Tamar executed the different characters gracefully: those who tried to hide how little they gave, those who threw money at you as if they had just bought you; those so delicate at heart they ultimately don't give you anything; those who send their kids to put money in; those who listened to the entire performance and, the moment you finished the last song, on the very last note, would evaporate . . .

She played and laughed and moved lightly and gracefully – you could see her body returning to life, see her sprouting through the armor that had been covering her. She felt it, too; she felt a little like the name of that book by Yehuda Amichai, only the other way around – The Fist *Becoming Again* an Open Palm with Fingers – when she finished, she sank into a royal curtsey. Assaf applauded, wishing she would let him take her photograph, that he might capture all her facial expressions at once.

Shai asked Assaf where, exactly, he was from. It was the first time Shai had asked him a personal question. He also asked where he studied; he mentioned two guys from Assaf's school he knew. Assaf (who, as everybody knew, never forgot a face) said he thought he once saw Shai at a Ha'Poel match – could that be? Shai laughed – it certainly could be. Assaf asked whether he was still going to games. Shai said, 'I used to. For me, everything is in the past tense.' Assaf asked, 'So what's up with Manchester United? Their poster is hanging in the cave.' Shai laughed. 'She brought that – she got confused and thought I was a fan. A dire miscalculation, Watson!' and he tossed a few thin twigs at Tamar. Tamar smiled. 'What's the difference between Manchester and Liverpool – isn't it all the same?' The two boys protested, explaining to her that no sane Ha'Poel fan would ever support a team like Manchester. But why? she demanded to know, savoring the conversation. 'Explain why to the kid,' Shai sighed, 'because I don't have the strength.' So Assaf explained that a true Ha'Poel fan could never support a winning team like Manchester. 'We can only identify with losing teams, only teams that *almost* take the championship, like Liverpool (that was Shai's team) or Houston . . .' 'So now, imagine, I have Manchester over my head.' Shai moaned. 'How will I ever recover with Beckham and York watching over me!' Tamar laughed joyously, her heart full; she remembered some urgent question that had bothered her, not so long ago, something along the lines of – if, during the execution of a certain mission, a person decided to seal up his soul, and then the mission ended, could he go back to being himself? Assaf told them about a friend of his, Roi, another fan of Ha'Poel, an ex-friend, actually – who didn't have a single yellow thing in his entire room – not a cup, not a piece of clothing, not a vase, not a rug – not a single bit of evidence of Beytar's yellow. They jabbered on, and Tamar listened, with double pleasure. She swallowed their words like a medicine curing two different pains. Every once in a while, she threw out a question – for instance, about that 'ex-friend' of Assaf's, and he told her about it, without hiding anything. Tamar listened attentively, thinking with relief that Assaf was the complete opposite of her – in what interested (and bored) him, in his rhythms, in the kind of family he came from, in his absolute inability to pretend. She liked, for example, the fact that he spoke slowly, weighing his every answer, analyzing each one carefully, as if taking full responsibility for every word he uttered. She'd never thought she would have the patience for someone as unhurried as he was, or that she would like such a pace. He's the kind of person, she thought, who would remain exactly what he is, even if you turned your back on him for a while. He has a clean voice, she told herself, and it wasn't something you could learn from a voice teacher. Through his jeans, she felt his blood slowly pumping through the vein along his thigh and thought he would probably live for a hundred years, and grow and change that entire time, but slowly, and he would learn a lot of things, in his methodical, profound way, and never forget one of them.

They had to go back into the cave, because two hikers were descending from the far side of the valley, along one of the trails. They should have watched those two men, who didn't seem dressed for a hike through the fields, but the three of them were so relaxed and content, they didn't pay attention. They had lost their instinct for suspicion by the time they gathered up their things, covered the mouth of the cave with bushes, and disappeared inside.

Just then the pains returned, as if a short vacation had just ended, and Assaf and Tamar went back to taking care of Shai. The muscle pains again, weaker already, still racked his body; the cave was filled with the stink of the lotion that Tamar used for them. At first Shai whined that the lotion was giving him hot and cold waves of pain – then he was in agony again, and he lost control. He attacked Tamar: she was torturing him, she was cruel, and who needed all this? How bad had it been for him before, anyway? And now he would never be able to play again the way he did when he was using, only God and Jim Morrison felt that way, and he'd had it, and now it was gone. After a moment, he thought he was going to get his fix after all, a miracle had happened, and he was now in a taxi, on the way to Lod. He was lying down, describing the entire journey to them with amazing vividness, even mentioning the dusty Judas tree at the entrance of that fucked-up neighborhood over there. They didn't know what he was talking about, but they listened, hypnotized. Here, he was telling the taxi driver to stop and wait at the curb; here, he was approaching the house with the tall wall, knocking on the gate – the landlord wouldn't open the door, but removed one brick from the wall . . . I can't see him but I hear him, and I know what he has in his hand, and I put money through the hole in the wall, and he, oh God, passes me the bundle, I have it, and I'm already in the taxi, go on, go, go. I cut the edge of it with a razor blade, God, where are the wicks, Tamar, where are my wicks?!

This is what he shouted out, rubbing his hand on his thigh, as if he were rolling paper on it. Suddenly he trembled and cried, 'These trips – I can't take them anymore!' He fell asleep for a moment, woke up wildly, stood up, perched himself on top of his mattress, full of energy, and started preaching at them. What are people? he asked. People are nothing, secondhand merchandise, all of them. They are scared to death by ingenuity – why, every human society has only one purpose: to castrate its people, to domesticate them. It is true for countries and nations and families, especially for families! He would never have a family, never! What did he need this bulk of hypocrisy for! To create more children, and make another generation miserable? Why, people will devour their own offspring sooner than destroy their polished public image or lose face in front of their friends. He hardly breathed – his eyes nearly popped out of their sockets; his entire face looked as if it were covered by a layer of dust. Tamar knew it was no longer the withdrawal but his rage and terror erupting now, without the protection of the drugs. When she tried to sit him down, he shoved her with all his strength – she fell on her back and cried out in pain. Assaf jumped up to stop Shai, but Shai had already laid off, with his hands at least: he yelled that she was like them, too, trying to strangle his genius, tame and domesticate him; as his rage grew, his words grew crueler and rougher. Assaf thought he had to end this torture, but when he looked at Tamar, he saw, or felt, that she would forbid him to interrupt; it was between her and Shai. He wondered whether she wasn't torturing herself, punishing herself, using Shai's words, the way she used to lacerate herself in her diary.

Then Shai relaxed for no evident reason, folded up, lay on the mattress, clung to Tamar's hand and kissed it, begged her to forgive him for hitting her before, and for everything else. He cried from the depths of his heart: she was so good to him, she was like a mother to him, she'd always been like this, even though she was two years younger, he would never let her go; only she, in the entire world, understood him, and hadn't it always been like this? Wasn't it like this at home? It was worth living, if only for her. Suddenly he sat up and, as if in a nightmare, stood up again and roared out that she actually wanted to kill him, that she always envied him for being more talented, more of an artist, more *complete* and *absolute*, and she knew that he'd be nothing without the drug, he would be castrated like her, because it was quite clear that she would compromise her art eventually, sell it for nothing, go and study law or medicine and marry some geek who worked in a law office like Father, or worse, in computers, someone like this lump of meat here.

When he finally fell asleep, they both left the cave and dropped, exhausted, by the trunk of the terebinth tree. Dinka sat in front of them; she looked as depressed as they were. Tamar thought she would have exploded in a moment: if he had continued to lay it on for one more second, the dam would have burst and everything that had been mounting in her would have poured all over him. It was on the tip of her tongue: that the only reason she was here was because of him, because of him she missed the trip to Italy, and the chorus, and maybe her entire career. Her guts twisted inside her with hate for him, for those ideas of his she knew so well, because every time he was in one of his 'moods' or fighting with their parents, he would burst into her room, without asking if she had the time or energy for him, or if she even felt like listening. He would lock the door and start to lecture her in some kind of cold rage, a strange fire that could burn as long as an hour. He would speak and swing his arms and bubble over, quoting all kinds of philosophers she didn't know, talk about 'noble egoism' and describe how, ultimately, every person acts only according to his absolute selfishness. It was like that, even in relationships between parents and children, even in love, and he wouldn't leave until he forced her to admit he was right, that she was afraid to accept his ideas of justice, because if she did, her entire petit bourgeois point of view would collapse. Sometimes, especially over the past year, she had had the feeling that these thoughts had succeeded in leaking into her like poison.

Now she told Assaf about those things, things she kept in her stomach and didn't even tell Leah about, so as to not shame Shai.

'I also think about humanity and egoism like that sometimes,' Assaf said, to her surprise. 'It's pretty depressing to think that, in some ways, he might be right.'

'Depressing, yes,' Tamar said bitterly. 'It's also pretty hard to say he's completely, totally wrong, because how can you respond to him?'

'There are three answers,' Assaf said, after thinking. 'First, I – well, every time I manage to overcome my egoism a little, I somehow feel better.'

'But Shai and his philosopher friends will call you self-righteous about exactly that!' Tamar pounced on him. 'You're afraid to act differently from everyone else, and you prefer to feel good because you are simply afraid to be "bad."' Yes, she thought in her heart, that's the problem: he really is afraid to be evil. He's just a professional 'good guy.' That's why he's here with me. He will never understand me.

'On the contrary,' Assaf said seriously. 'If egoism is something common to everyone, then only when I overcome it do I suddenly feel like I'm *different* from everyone, right?'

'Really?' Tamar smiled, a bit surprised. 'Wait, that was the first one – what's the second?'

'Second is something that Theodora told me when we were talking about something else: it's clear that there are people in the world like the kind Shai tries to be, but there are others, too. For example, the kind who pulled Shai out of the swamp so he wouldn't drown – right?' He gave her a deep, piercing look, and her heart turned a somersault. 'And by the way,' Assaf continued, 'she said, Theodora, that it is especially for the other kind that life's worth living.'

At that moment, an unpleasant, quarrelsome thought passed through her – I wonder what Idan would say about Assaf. But before giving herself up to that thought and all the havoc it might have wreaked in her, she wondered, with more interest, what Assaf would say about Idan, if she ever decided to talk about him.

'The third?' she asked.

'The third happens when I don't have such a good answer for philosophical questions; there's a little field by my house, and once in a while I really have to go there. There's a little junkyard next to it, old, full of garbage and thousands of glass bottles. I put a bottle on a rock and snipe stones at it. An hour or two like that, twenty, thirty bottles, and it helps me, it cleans me out.' He laughed. 'And get this – I name every bottle. Not only people's names, but names of thoughts as well, of' – here he hesitated for a moment – 'of what you call "the rats" . . .' Tamar glanced at him with a wounded look, stung by his invasion into her privacy – then was flooded by a delicious wonder (we have a secret, she thought, we're starting to share a mutual secret, like what Leah said about real couples . . .) 'So I simply smash them up, one after the other, and feel better, until the next time.' He chuckled apologetically. 'I'm a geek, I know.'

'You're not a geek,' she said immediately, perhaps a little too quickly. 'Will you take me there with you sometime? I could gladly smash a few bottles now.'


They returned to the cave. Shai had passed out, and every once in a while would shout in his sleep, his body twitching as if someone were beating him up in his dreams. Tamar and Assaf decided to sleep in shifts, but neither of them succeeded in falling asleep. During Assaf's turn, Tamar lay on the mattress, covered by a thin blanket; her eyes were open, and she looked at him; she didn't speak, but she had to watch him all the time, as if the sight of him, his big clumsy motions, the smiles he gave her from time to time, were some kind of rare medicine she had to take on doctor's orders.

Shai slept three hours (but claimed that he hadn't slept a wink). He got up, devoured four chocolate bars, and went back to sleep. He was grumpy, maybe regretting his outburst of rage, but unable to apologize. At about one in the morning, he woke up, took the guitar, and went outside to play. Assaf and Tamar sat inside and listened. It sounded wonderful to Assaf, but Tamar heard easily how he was struggling with the strings, losing the rhythm, desperately chasing down something that used to be hidden in his playing, even a week ago. She thought his sound had become imprecise and flat. Silence fell. Tamar signaled to Assaf that they had to go out now, but before they managed to stand up, they heard a smash, wood thumping and snapping, and the twang of strings. Shai returned on his own and looked accusingly, scarily, at Tamar. 'I don't have it. I told you, I've lost it for good. What am I worth without it?' He collapsed on the mattress, curled up, whined to himself in a monotone. Tamar lay by him. She hugged him with all of her body and hummed a tune like a lullaby; and he, in the blink of an eye, probably out of his terror and despair, fell asleep.

'Don't you want to know what Leah wrote in the letter?' she asked later, during her shift, as they sat, hunched together by Shai's sleeping body, covered by one blanket, trying to warm each other.

'What did she write?' Assaf was embarrassed.

Tamar smiled. 'No, I want you to say that you're curious.'

'I'm curious, I'm curious, of course I'm curious. What did she write?'

She gave him the crumpled paper. *Tami Mami*, he read. *Don't be mad at me, but I'd have to be crazy not to. Bruce Willis & Harvey Kytel rapped up in one!! Plus isn't that hand just like the Statue of Liberty's? P.S. Noiku also aproved.*

Assaf didn't understand it. Tamar nudged his shoulder with hers and wanted to hear what his impression of Leah was. He described what had happened when he showed up at the restaurant, and only then did he remember that he hadn't yet told her about Theodora.

Tamar listened, and choked back a cry of astonishment. When he finished, she asked him to tell her the entire story again, in more detail this time, to explain his first meeting with her, and what they did to her, and her first steps out of the house, and how she looked at the street, and what the expression on her face was at that moment. Tamar stood and paced the entire length of the cave. She said it drove her crazy that she couldn't be with Theodora now, for her first steps outside the jail of her home. In her heart she thought, If Theo finally got out, perhaps there was a chance that Shai could succeed in escaping his jail as well.

'But how on earth could it be that she told you how the

two of us met? How did you get Leah to tell you everything? And everyone else? What did you do to them?'

He shrugged. The truth was, it surprised him, too, every time he thought of it.

'You're a magician. Look how you can make people talk to you. What a gift.'

In his head, a tune was playing: warrior, thief, knight, magician. I have been three of them already; only the knight was missing (and for a moment it troubled him: he had no idea how he would ever be a knight). Suddenly Dinka gave a nervous bark. Assaf went to check the cave outside and didn't see anything. After that, they let the subject drop.



At two in the morning, it was his turn to stand guard, and this time it was Tamar who said she couldn't fall asleep anyway. They went to the opening of the cave and tried to sit this way, or that way – or perhaps this way? Eventually, they sat back to back, and were both surprised at how many feelings and caresses and conversations they had in their backs – in their backs! In that indifferent part! – it confused them both so much that they forgot about everything that was happening there and spoke of more immediate concerns. Assaf described, for the third time, the meeting he had had that afternoon with her parents in the coffeehouse. He didn't hide anything from her, except what might hurt her too much. She told him about the events of the past year and tried to explain how a couple of civilized, intelligent people like them could behave that way, give up on their son, almost without a fight, cut him off – and cut off the sorrow for him, too, it seemed. She told him everything: about Shai's quarrels with them, about the feeling he always had that he and they actually lived on two different planets, and how, about two years ago, he began to disappear for days at a time, wouldn't come home at nights, and, when he finally did come home, refuse to tell them anything. He was seen in all kinds of places, and their parents refused to believe it. Then came his thefts, small and large, because he needed money, and more and more money for his drugs, leading up to that last horrible scene, when Father had tried to keep him from leaving the house, and their fistfight.

'So I understood, during the first week, say, that my father was angry and hurt and humiliated – fine, that's all true. But after that? And my mother? How? In all this time, and it's been over a year, they only went to the police two times. Can you believe it? Twice! If their car had been stolen, they wouldn't have stopped nagging, they would have used their connections shamelessly, but their son! And when the police told them that he was over eighteen and they couldn't interfere if he left the house of his own volition, they stopped even trying!' She smacked her open palm against her forehead. 'Can you comprehend that? Would your parents let something like that happen?'

'No,' Assaf said, and adjusted his back against hers, thinking about how much he wished she could meet his parents, just once; immediately, his whole body was flooded with the knowledge of how good she would feel with them, the way Rhino did, and he saw with perfect clarity how she would come to his house – she would play with Muki and talk to his mother in the kitchen, and after that, she would come into his room and he would close the door after them – and he decided that he had to remove a few embarrassing things from the room – relics from his previous life, like his horrendous collection of Boglins figurines in all colors, especially the monstrous Doink, a photocollage of him and Rabbi Kaduri, and the faded Power Rangers poster that had been there since he was ten.


She went in to see Shai. He was awake and asked her for water. When he finished drinking, he lay and looked at her, and asked her to forgive him for everything he had done and said. Then he said, very quietly, with glacial soberness, that there was no point to his life if he couldn't play. Tamar explained that there was no chance that he would be able to play right now the way he used to do, but in about a month or two, this, too, would come back to him, with all the rest. He nodded as she spoke, and then said she was deluding herself, but he had no illusions. 'Why don't you leave me here to die?' and she tried very hard not to let him see what went through her at the sound of those words. 'You still don't get it, do you, Sherlock?' She made the effort to smile at him. 'I will never let that happen. Whatever you do, as much as you try, I will follow you and hold on to you. You still don't understand that you have no choice?' For one long moment, their eyes hung on each other in a silence. Only the two of them could understand what was said there, without words, the way they had always spoken, since childhood, as if they were identical twins, two keys to the same safe.

'Really, you will protect me?'

'What do you think?'

'That . . . yes.' He took a very deep breath, and his wasted chest expanded with it, and she knew he had just given her a big present, the biggest he could give. 'Go on,' he nudged her, his voice mock-scolding her. 'Turn off the violins in the background. And bring me some fruit or something – I'm dying of hunger here. And go to your boyfriend, go on – I can see you're desperate to get back to him. I'll manage here.'


She went back to Assaf and reported dryly that Shai was a little better now. They sat in silence for a few more minutes. The better Shai got, Tamar felt, the more room she had for Assaf, and also for herself, for all the things she couldn't even let herself think about before.

She told Assaf about Sheli, about her joy in living, her grace and humor and self-destructiveness. She spoke for almost an hour without stopping, and Assaf listened. She described how Sheli had helped her carry the mattress and opened her room for her, how fearless she was. Only then, when Tamar talked about her, did the horror start to sink in. 'There is no Sheli,' she said, shocked, as if she had found out about it only now.

'She's gone, she'll never be around again. In the whole world there will never be another person like the person she was. Do you understand? I'm saying the words and can't really grasp it. Why can't I grasp it? Tell me. Is there something wrong with me? Am I missing something?'

She couldn't see his face because they were sitting back to back, but she thought she had never before met a boy who knew how to listen the way he did, as devotedly, as warmly. Then – she didn't even know how it happened – he got her to talk about singing. She told him about how completely her life had changed three years ago when she made her parents give her singing lessons, and how she had flourished and felt for the first time that she was worth something. She also told him about Halina, who had believed in her from the very beginning, and wasn't put off by her prickly nerves. Assaf said he knew nothing about music; the hardest thing for him to understand was how she could sing in front of an audience. She laughed, and said that each time it seemed unreal to her, but she was curious to know what about it seemed hardest to him. He thought for a while, and she waited patiently. 'To give something from inside yourself,' he finally said. 'Something that really comes from within you, to give that to people you don't know, when you don't even know how they'll react ...' 'You're exactly right,' she said, 'but that's what's fun about it, you see? To stand in front of strangers, every time, and each time you have to try and conquer them ...' 'I understand, I guess, but I'm different. I could never do that.' He chuckled silently to himself, because he imagined himself singing in front of people – and she pressed her back into his even harder, to absorb the shaking of his laughter, so not one tremor would be lost. 'Because I'd probably stop after every line and think, Did it come out all right? Was it bad? Was that the way it was supposed to be?' He shrugged. 'Doesn't that ever happen to you?' 'But this is exactly what I've been trying to learn all these years!' she gasped, astounded by how he had put his finger on exactly the most complicated problem she had been struggling with for years; even Halina had never put it so well. 'Because I have to learn how to give *up*, do you understand? I have to give up the self-examination, all the crappy second-guessing. I still don't really know how, and every time I stop to think about the last note, it's over; that's it, I clench up and freeze and I'm lost.' He was willing to let her keep talking all night; he didn't understand how he was capable of sitting quietly, and with such restraint, when his back was on fire, when what he wanted to do now, more than anything, was run through all the mountains, roaring out with all his might that it was happening – that all his life until this moment was only an introduction, a warm-up – that he was finally *starting to be*. She spoke, and he didn't know whether he was healthy or sick – his entire body ached with trying to compress itself into her; even his teeth hurt him, even his fingernails. 'But when you sing well,' he asked, clinging with all his might to some pretense of a calm, stable voice, 'what's it like then – how does it feel?' 'Oh, it's the best.' Tamar laughed. 'For me, it's almost a mystical experience, it feels like everything in the universe is in the right place . . .' Like the way I'm feeling now, she thought. 'Tell me, do you think you'd ever want to come hear me perform?' 'Sure, yeah, but you'd have to explain it all to me beforehand.' 'Don't worry, you'll come prepared.' He wanted her to sing for him now and cursed himself for being too shy to ask.

Every now and then, one of them would get up and check on Shai; and the other, left alone for that brief time, would crave the other's touch. Dinka barked and sniffed the air. There were strange noises crackling in the bushes, but Assaf and Tamar were wrapped up in their moment. Afterward, after everything had ended, they never stopped wondering how they could have been so deaf and blind to everything happening around them, or how they could have let down their guard with such criminal negligence.

Almost unconsciously, they leaned head to head. Tamar asked if her spikes bothered him, and Assaf said that, no, they were actually very soft. Then he told her how surprised he was when he saw her like that, because everyone had prepared him for a huge mane of hair. She asked whether he liked it the way it was now; he said yes. 'Only "yes?"' she asked, and Assaf said that he liked it very much, and that it didn't even matter to him what kind of hair she had, because either way, he was sure she'd be beautiful; he thought she was very, very beautiful. And he fell silent, amazed and dazzled by himself.

Dinka barked, more loudly this time. Tamar felt his heavy head against her head, the pleasure was almost unbearable. She almost got up and walked away – because what would happen when everything was over here, or if the magic didn't work when they left the cave? She didn't move from him, until the warmth of his body melted all those sharp icicles, until the pleasure spread throughout her body. This is reality, she thought in a haze; here, my imagination is touching reality right now, and the balloon is not exploding in my face. Assaf asked her if anything was wrong, why she had sighed, and she said it was nothing – but a strange sentence flashed inside her: 'Congratulations, we are pleased to announce your acceptance into Humanity.'

'I wanted to ask you to do something before but, I mean, I didn't have the courage,' Assaf said (and couldn't believe he was talking like this, as if he knew what he was doing).

'What? Just say it.' Her voice behind him was soft and generous.

'I want you to sing for me.'

'Oh, that.'

She didn't even straighten up; she didn't want to distance her body from his. She sang to him naturally, effortlessly, in no way attempting to impress him. She sang 'How does one lonely star dare?' Her voice sounded different to her, and she couldn't understand why. *'One star, alone, I wouldn't dare . . .'* Back to back, they closed their eyes. *'Yet I am not alone . . .'* She sang quietly, knowing that something in her voice had changed, even since the last time she had sung in the square – a very slight change, as if the childish purity in it had disappeared entirely and been replaced by something new and strange, even to her.

In the middle of the song, Dinka got up and began to pace. She barked a few times in all directions.

'There must be some animal in the bushes,' Assaf said after she finished singing. It was nice to feel her quiet breathing through her back. He still hadn't told her about his love of photography, but he didn't feel like talking about himself.

'Should we take a flashlight and look?'

'No, stay like that.'

She remembered something: 'Tonight, a few hours ago, in Milan, my chorus gave their last concert of the tour.' And added: 'And Adi sang my solo.'

'Would you sing it for me here?'

'Really? Would you like me to?'

'Yes. If you don't mind doing it for such a small audience.'

She stood, pulled herself up tall, so he could see her putting on her black concert dress with the deep opening in the back, and her high heels that made her look at least three years older; walking gracefully, smoothing her stylish knot of curls. She bowed graciously to the stalls, curtsied to the balconies and the golden boxes. Then she cleared her throat a little and waved once to the pianist.

'Hold on a second,' Assaf said, and jumped up. 'Someone's there.'

And then it happened – so fast, it was like a car accident. Until it was too late, Assaf refused to understand exactly what was happening, because they had been so close to the happy ending, and suddenly everything collapsed on top of them. A silly thought flashed through his head: the feeling you get when you play Snakes and Ladders and you finally reach 99, only to fall down a snake, then, down, down, down to 13.

And what a 13.

\*    \*    \*

'Like a military operation,' Assaf thought a second later; 'like a nightmare,' Tamar thought. They came from all sides, beyond the hill, behind the rock; at first it seemed like dozens, but then it was clear there were only seven: six bulldogs and Pesach. At first, from inside the storm of fear, Tamar was tormented mainly by the thought that they had been there all the time, listening in, desecrating these precious moments with their presence.

Someone hit Assaf on the back, someone else knocked Tamar down. They heard beating and yelling from within the cave; then Shishko appeared at its opening, dragging Shai, who was bewildered and scared; blood poured out of his mouth.

'The Temple Mount is ours!' Shishko said, and looked at Tamar, hate in his eyes. 'Now let's take care of Abraham's Tomb.'

Assaf saw her face crumple, and whoever was holding him from behind shoved his head into the ground again. He thought he might get used to the taste at some point, the way things were going.

Pesach had a plan.

'Look at that, Shai, my boy,' he said, standing in front of him. 'Look what I'm holding in my right hand, and what I'm holding in my left hand.'

Shai tried to focus his eyes. Assaf raised his head from the ground. This time it wasn't shoved back down. When he saw the braid, he knew all was lost.

'Something you'll really like,' Pesach said smoothly, 'something that will make you feel all right.'

Tamar sighed deeply, her face flat on the ground.

'What is it?' Shai asked weakly, his legs stepping forward of their own will. 'Show me, show me.'

'In my right hand I have a gram. Heat-sealed, straight from central.' Shai moaned in distrust, and desire. His hand moved forward with a life of its own. Within a blink of an eye, he had been completely bewitched.

'Don't touch the merchandise!' Pesach scolded him. 'Now look here, at what's in my left hand. Surprise! A nice little tab. A motherfucking tab! It'll make you fly to the sky! So what do you say, where do we start?'

Shai breathed heavily, his long, delicate neck arched forward. Like a swan's neck, Tamar thought. About to be chopped off, Assaf thought.

'Because I heard,' Pesach drawled. 'I was informed, by reliable sources, that your nice sister here is doing a little withdrawal for you on her own here. Is that true?'

Shai nodded. In the moonlight Assaf saw that the ash-green pallor had returned to his face.

'So maybe you're not even interested in what we have to offer?' Pesach asked in a soft voice that sent a chill down Assaf's spine. Like a magician, Pesach closed his fist on the two doses. Shai, as if he were under a spell, shook his head to say no, and choked in bitter disappointment when he saw the drugs disappear.

'Shai!' Tamar screamed with all her power. 'Shai!'

The one holding her shoved her head back to the ground, but her scream had had its effect: Shai trembled, took a step back, opened his eyes wide. It seemed to Assaf that now, suddenly, new eyes were revealed.

'No,' Shai said.

Pesach brought his hand to his ear in an exaggerated gesture. 'Come again?'

'I said no,' Shai moaned weakly. 'I'm done with it, I think.'

'You think you're through?' Pesach asked, creeping toward him like a cat. 'But you know you're not done with it, and you never will be done, because there is no force in the world that can keep you from it. And do you know why?' He bent to Shai and placed a heavy hand on the frail shoulder. Even at a distance Tamar felt the waves of repressed violence that rippled around his body. Assaf looked at the other men who stood there, observed the spectacle they made, each seeming to mirror the powerful gestures of the huge man with his own body. 'Do you really want to hear why you will never be done with it? Because you are *nothing*, you are less than *nothing* without your fix. You can't go through half a day without it. You wouldn't dare go into the street and speak to people without it, you can't go to a coffeehouse or have a conversation with a friend or hit on a girl – and getting laid without it? With your complications? Don't make me laugh. In your dreams at night, maybe you can get it up without your fix. So I, Pesach, your father and mother and friend and girlfriend, your professional agent and your future, I suggest that you take it, take it for your own good.'

While Pesach spoke, Shai's head was bowed; with every sentence he shrank, as if he were being hammered into the ground. When Pesach finished, Shai straightened up, shook his hair off his eyes, and said no.

'It's a shame about you,' Pesach said. 'You had Jimi Hendrix fingers. But have it your way.' He took one step back and signaled Shishko. Shishko approached, skinny and gloomy, and took Shai's right hand, palm up, his strumming hand. Shai groaned in terror and tried to pull his hand away.

'The truth is, I'm still deciding' – Pesach scratched his head – 'if the first finger will be for the Mitsubishi you totaled, or for our friend Miko, who's now eating meatloaf in a Migrash haRusim holding cell. What do you think?' he addressed the men standing, hypnotized, around him. 'Perhaps we better break it first and decide later?'


'You'd better not,' said a new voice, slow and heavy, from right above the cave. Assaf thought he was going crazy. Shishko froze, and with a cry Shai yanked his hand away and held it behind his back. The bulldogs stared in all directions, afraid, while Dinka barked crazily at the sky. Pesach retreated a little, standing in the shadows, his eyes darting around him wildly.

'I got a little mixed up,' said Rhino, coming down from the top of the hill, almost above their heads. 'What's this place you've found for yourselves? My legs fell asleep for a minute. Hey, Assaf.'

Emphasis on the A, of course.

✻   ✻   ✻

In the days following, when Assaf replayed the events in his head, he had the feeling that the ending should have been a little different – more dramatic or something, with fire and smoke and a superhuman struggle over life and death that would have lasted for hours –

In reality, the ending was almost anticlimactic. It became clear that policemen were also there, nine plainclothes cops who had been hiding around the valley, in the bushes and weeds, since the early hours of the evening, now rumpled and out of sorts. There was also an officer from the narcotics division, a quiet, phlegmatic man in glasses, who had been in the same tank platoon as Rhino in Lebanon, and later told Assaf that he – how should he say it? – owed Rhino his life. He'd recorded Pesach trying to convince Shai to take the drugs. 'Yes, yes, we certainly have enough evidence,' he droned coolly, for all the world like a detective at Scotland Yard.

It lasted no more than ten minutes. The world turned over and then turned back. Pesach tried to run; for all his immense weight, he was quick and nimble, and it took four policemen to catch him. Even then he didn't give up – there was a scuffle with fists and some bruising; Tamar remembered that Pesach had been a professional wrestler in his youth. But eventually they forced him to the ground, facedown, and tied his wrists. When they picked him up, he looked miserable, empty, and scared. The policemen handcuffed the rest of the gang as well, sat them back to back, and forbade them to speak. (One pair of handcuffs got lost during the struggle with Pesach, and when it turned out there was nothing to use on his wrists, Tamar went into the cave and emerged with a new pair. She handed them to the cops with utter nonchalance, prompting one to ask whether she could replace his faulty night-vision goggles, too.)

The policemen looked around the cave. They tried to understand what had gone on there. The narcotics officer asked Tamar a few questions and took notes. To judge by the slight fog on his glasses, you could imagine that he was almost excited.

'And what if you hadn't succeeded?' he asked eventually in his even voice. 'You must have understood that all the odds were against you. What would you have done then?'

'I would have succeeded,' Tamar said. 'I simply had no choice.'

Shai sat to the side, leaning on a rock, dazed, awash in sweat. Tamar went to him, sat by his side, and hugged his shoulders. They whispered. Assaf heard her say, 'Tonight. Right now. We'll simply take you there, and you'll knock on the door and go inside.'

He said, 'They will never agree to that. You saw it – they didn't even look for me.'

Tamar said that they would have to talk about it, all of them, together, about this whole horrible time, but she knew they were waiting for him. Shai laughed – he wanted to know how she could be so confident. She signaled to Assaf; he crouched beside them and told Shai quietly about the meeting that afternoon in the coffeehouse, what he had asked them, and what they had told him, and how they had cried at the end of it.

'I don't believe it,' Shai said. 'He cried? In front of people? You actually saw tears?'

The cops left, herding a small, angry, defeated procession before them. Rhino stayed with the three others. He offered them a lift home and said that tomorrow they could come back here when it was light and pick everything up. Assaf felt his heart sink. What, was this how everything ended? Because there had been a kind of magic here, living with them, with her, with the entire painful routine and rare moments of happiness.

They climbed up the valley, Dinka first, Rhino supporting Shai. Later, Rhino passed Shai back to Tamar and walked with Assaf. Assaf asked him how he had organized all this; how had Pesach discovered where they were, anyway? Rhino told him that for a few days now, since some girl who'd run away from the home had died in Eilat, the guys from the narcotics division had been sitting hard on Pesach, tapping his phones and putting together a nice little file on him. All they needed was the cherry on top. When Rhino called his friend, the unflappable fellow reacted with near-excitement. 'And then it was easy. Today, in the afternoon, someone called Pesach – perhaps it was even me – and explained exactly where he might find his two runaway birds. After that, it was in the bag.'

The moon disappeared. It was hard to see anything in the dark. A few times Assaf tried to tell Rhino about Reli and couldn't find the words. They went through the thick bushes. The only sounds that could be heard were the breathing of his companions and Shai's wheezing gasps. Assaf glanced to the side; Rhino seemed a bit more pensive than usual. Assaf thought that talking to him might be unnecessary now.

They crowded into Rhino's little truck. Everyone was silent. Only once, Shai said, 'Now, for instance, I wouldn't say no to a joint.' Tamar knew how scary it was to stand in front of whatever might happen, totally naked, without the shield of drugs. Assaf sat and looked over the dark landscape, thinking to himself, That's it – in ten minutes, this will be over. In five. In one.

Only one light illuminated the yard in front of the house. Tamar peeked out of the truck window and remembered how she had left a month ago. Dinka smelled her place and started wriggling through the car, and Assaf – Assaf saw the beautiful house, the well-manicured garden, the two silver cars in the driveway, and his heart sank a little.

Shai stepped out and stood in front of the gate. Dinka leaped out and rolled in the grass. Shai turned to Tamar: 'Well, are you coming?'

Tamar looked at the house. 'You go,' she said. 'You meet

them first. You need to talk. I'll come home tomorrow morning.'

Assaf gazed at her in amazement – Rhino sat with his back to them, tapping on the wheel. He suddenly had a lot of back.

'I thought,' Tamar said hesitantly, 'I think I need another night there. I haven't said my goodbyes to it properly.'

'Alone?' Rhino asked in a low voice. 'How can you stay there alone?'

There was a silence.

'Dinka will come with me,' Tamar whispered.

'Eh . . . I . . . me too,' Assaf said, with a strange weakness.

Rhino shrugged, leaned his head on his hands, his two elbows on the wheel. In front, through the windshield, they saw Shai pass through the gate, walking the paved path alone. They knew that he was only beginning to find his way back to life; they weren't at all sure he would succeed. When he reached the door, he turned to face them. He looked like a hunted animal. Assaf and Rhino together gave him a thumbs-up. Tamar nodded at him. He knocked on the door. It didn't open. He waited exactly one second and turned, angry and insulted, to march back to the truck. But then a light came on in the house, and another one after that. Shai stood, ready to run. Then they saw the door open. Shai peered in, with a long, joyless look. Slowly, he stepped inside, and the door closed behind him. Assaf heard a choked voice beside him and saw that Tamar's face was wet. Until this moment, he thought, he hadn't seen her cry.

'I'm not crying,' she whispered in his ear, frightened at the feeling bearing down and crushing her. With his finger Assaf touched the stream of tears that coursed down her cheek.

'No, no.' She smiled through her tears, still refusing to surrender. 'I'm just a little, I don't know, allergic to sadness.'

Assaf tasted his finger. 'It's tears,' he determined, and all the way back she sobbed bitterly on his shoulder, shaking hard, letting go of all that she had been through in the past few months.

∗    ∗    ∗

Rhino brought them to the bus stop above the valley. He left them and went on his way. It was still dark, but a little brighter already. Dinka ran around them, her tail up; they walked along the side of the road, then down the valley, helping each other at the rough places, finding excuses to touch, to hold each other. They hardly spoke. Tamar noticed that she had never met a person she felt so comfortable being silent with.

## A Note on the Author

DAVID GROSSMAN IS THE author of six novels and three works of journalism. His most recent novel was *Be My Knife*. He lives in Jerusalem.

## A Note on the Type

The text of this book is set in Linotype Stempel Garamond, a version of Garamond adapted and first used by the Stempel foundry in 1924. It's one of several versions of Garamond based on the designs of Claude Garamond. It is thought that Garamond based his font on Bembo, cut in 1495 by Francesco Griffo in collaboration with the Italian printer Aldus Manutius. Garamond types were first used in books printed in Paris around 1532. Many of the present-day versions of this type are based on the *Typi Academiae* of Jean Jannon cut in Sedan in 1615.

Claude Garamond was born in Paris in 1480. He learned how to cut type from his father and by the age of fifteen he was able to fashion steel punches the size of a pica with great precision. At the age of sixty he was commissioned by King Francis I to design a Greek alphabet, for this he was given the honourable title of royal type founder. He died in 1561.

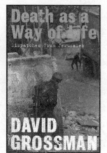